THE QUEST OF YOUTH

BY THE SAME AUTHOR

The Broad Highway
The Amateur Gentleman
The Money Moon
The Hon. Mr. Tawnish
The Chronicles of the Imp
Beltane the Smith
The Definite Object
The Geste of Duke Jocelyn
Our Admirable Betty
Black Bartlemy's Treasure
Martin Conisby's Vengeance
Peregrine's Progress
Sir John Dering
The Loring Mystery
The High Adventure

Sampson Low, Marston & Co., Ltd.

THE
QUEST OF YOUTH

BY
JEFFERY FARNOL

LONDON
SAMPSON LOW, MARSTON & CO., LTD.

PRINTED IN GREAT BRITAIN BY PURNELL AND SONS
PAULTON (SOMERSET) AND LONDON

TO

"PHIL"

IN GRATEFUL AFFECTION

I DEDICATE THIS BOOK

CONTENTS

THE QUEST OF YOUTH

CHAPTER I

IN WHICH DOCTOR WOTHERSPOON PRESCRIBES

A STATELY chamber, high, spacious and luxuriously furnished, from priceless rugs on polished floor to richly carved ceiling; an elegant chamber of an exquisite, almost feminine, refinement; yet nothing was there so stately, so elegant, so altogether exquisite and supremely refined as the gentleman who sat reading in the deep elbow chair beside the open lattice; a tall, handsome gentleman whose garments, each a miracle of sartorial achievement, clung to his shapely figure as if they loved him, and whose pale, delicately-featured face, adorned with glossy whisker *à la mode,* bore the proud stamp of birth and high-breeding, and might have been commanding by reason of its clean-cut line of nose and chin but for the droop of over-sensitive lips, lacklustre eyes, and general air of weariness and languor; indeed Sir Marmaduke, Anthony, Ashley, John, de la Pole, Vane-Temperly looked precisely what he was, to wit—the last and very finest of a long line of fine gentlemen, bored to extinction with everything in general and himself in particular.

A soft rapping at the door, and a discreet, gentleman-like person entered softly, coughed delicately behind a finger, and stood bowing until the student condescended to become aware of him.

"Yes, Paxton?"

The gentleman's gentleman bowed a little lower and murmured:

"Doctor Robert Wotherspoon, sir. Are you in, sir?"

Sir Marmaduke sighed, closed book on slim finger, and inclined his head languidly, whereat Paxton bowed himself out and presently returned to announce:

"Doctor Wotherspoon!"

Hardly was the name uttered than in upon the chaste seclusion of that stately apartment strode a shortish, thick-set man with a stamp of heavy boots, a jingle of rusty spurs, and swirl of spattered coat-tails, a heavy-breathing man who tossed whip and weather-beaten hat at a chair (which they missed) and, stumping up to Sir Marmaduke, halted to stare down at him, legs wide apart and square chin in hairy fist.

"Tongue!" he snorted.

"My dear Bob!" exclaimed Sir Marmaduke, recoiling.

"Show it!" vociferated the doctor.

"My good Robert!"

"Pulse!" Sir Marmaduke's arm was seized, and masterful fingers forced themselves beneath delicate, frilled wrist-band, all in a moment. "Now, tongue!" barked Dr. Wotherspoon.

"Gad so, Bob—you mistake, I——"

"Not a bit, Tony—y'r bilious! 'Sliver! Eating too much! Doing too little! 'Sbile!"

"Horrible!" ejaculated Sir Marmaduke, and, gently but resolutely freeing his wrist, he shook his visitor's hand. "In heaven's name sit down, Bob, and pray allow me a word——"

"'Sbile!" growled the doctor, thudding into the nearest chair. "Prescribe skipping-rope! Nothing like jumpin' t'shake liver . . . frees ducts!"

"I wished to consult you about young Bellamy, your god-son——"

"'N' your nevvy, Marmaduke!"

"True—confound him! I hear the young fool is in trouble again."

"No—out! Boy's bolted."

"You mean he has positively absconded?"

"'S'it, Marmy! Hopped the twig—cut his stick—'tleast, so Thombury writes."

"Ay, Thombury—a most excellent man of business."

"'N' lively as a dried herring!"

"My dear Robert!" murmured Sir Marmaduke, lifting white hand with sublime gesture of reprobation. "Really!"

"Es really!" nodded the doctor, "Thombury's a creeter b'got 'twixt 'n' ink-pot 'n' a roll o' parchment! A mummy, that's what! Rupert Bellamy (dev'lish name) is young 'n' wild as a colt! Now how may mummy manage colt? Can't! An' that's what again!" Saying which, Doctor Bob wrenched snuff-box from pocket, opened it, dug thence a large pinch, some of which he inhaled with three loud snorts, the rest he scattered over himself and immediate neighbourhood to Sir Marmaduke's manifest horror and discomfort. Said he:

"Pray remember, Bob, that after your godson's——"

"'N' your nevvy! Y'r own sister's only child, Marmy!"

"She is dead!" said Sir Marmaduke gently.

"An' his father, too!" nodded the doctor.

"Which is perhaps as well, Bob," quoth Sir Marmaduke, frowning slightly. "However, after Rupert's lamentable failure at your own noble profession, the worthy Thombury agreed to admit him into his office, purely out of regard to myself, and now—you say the youth has——"

"Bolted!" quoth the doctor. "But what——"

"Also he is in debt again."

"Six hundred odd pounds!" nodded the doctor.

"So I understand. He wrote me a highly charac-
teristic letter——"

"Which y' ignored o' course!"

"Of course!" nodded Sir Marmaduke.

"Having paid 's debts once a'ready."

"Twice!' sighed Sir Marmaduke. "What has become
of him, Bob?"

"Dooce knows! Why trouble? Boy's nothin' t'
you—never was! Y' never trouble t' see him."

"Happily not since his infancy."

"S' if he wants t' go t' the dooce, dooce take him—
eh, Tony?"

"By no means, Bob, for though he is an infliction
he is also a relation and I must act accordingly——"

"Pay 's debts?"

"Certainly."

"Because o' y'r name—eh?"

"Precisely!"

"An' what o' the boy?"

"He is a problem does not interest me."

"Umph!" exclaimed the doctor. "Ha!"

"However, I shall re-establish his credit, of course."

"Because o' y'r name—eh?"

"Yes, and——"

"Y'r name 's got a lot t' answer for, Marmaduke
Anthony!"

"What may you mean?"

"Bile 't present—y'r liver, Tony, Y'r yellow as a
guinea!"

"Pooh—nonsense, man!" exclaimed Sir Marmaduke,
glancing uneasily towards an adjacent mirror. "To be
sure I am aware of my forty-five years——"

"Umph!" quoth the doctor.

"Life has long since lost its zest and savour——'

"Ha!" quoth the doctor.

"Existence," sighed Sir Marmaduke, warming to his
theme, "is become a growing weariness, a dawning

calamity, a nauseating prospect of monotonous to-
morrows stretching drearily away to the inevitable,
and distressing end——"

"'Sbile!" snarled Doctor Bob. "Bile! Spleen
Liver!—that's what!"

"Nay, my dear Robert, do but reflect," sighed Sir
Marmaduke, viewing the doctor with his sad, lacklustre eyes, "forty-five is a tragic age! Youth's pinions
are clipped, and where we were wont to soar, high above
consequences, scornful of difficulties and dangers, our
eyes upon the zenith, poor Middle-age must trudge it
in the dust, his gaze bent earthwards, Common-sense
and Respectability his companions to point out the
ever growing difficulties of his way—And I was forty-
five—yesterday, Bob!"

"Ho!" barked the doctor, "And what o' that? Look
t me—I'm fifty an' full o' life 'n' vigour, sound wind
'n' limb—eat well, sleep well, drink well—'n' why?
Because I don't trouble 'bout m' own confounded
carcass, too infernal busy wi' other people's. Th' only
trouble wi' you, Tony, is Marmaduke, Anthony, Ashley,
John de la Pole—'n' all the rest on 'em! Y'self an'
y'r name's too much for ye—an' that's what!"

"And this morning," sighed Sir Marmaduke, glancing
at his companion with twinkling eyes, "this morning
my fellow discovered a grey hair above my right ear!"

"Grey fiddlestick!" snarled the doctor. "Look 't
me! Damme, I'm grey all over, an't I? Yet full o'
vigour 'n' energy!"

"You were distressingly energetic as a school-boy,
I remember——"

"So were you!" retorted the doctor. "A very imp
o' mischief! D'ye mind scaling the church-tower?
D'ye mind settin' Farmer Barton's rick afire? Ha' ye
forgot y'r fight wi' the big butcher-boy?"

Sir Marmaduke's gloomy brow cleared somewhat.

"I had him quite groggy in the fourth round!" he
murmured.

"'N' licked him in th seventh!" cried the doctor. "Begad, ye were spry 'nough then——"

"But to-day I'm forty-five, Bob! A weary soul disillusioned with everything, finding joy in nothing, not even—himself!"

"Try falling in love."

"Never again, Bob!"

"B'cause a brainless little fool jilted ye—years ago!"

"Never again!" repeated Sir Marmaduke, mournfully.

"Then marry without and get children——"

"Heaven forbid!" exclaimed Sir Marmaduke, shuddering. "To see myself repeated in miniature would be most abhorrent!"

"Then travel."

"Five years I wandered, Bob, and found teeming cities as desolate as the wilderness.'

"Then why not shoot somebody? Y've had no duels lately—eh?"

"No, Bob! I regard duelling, now-a-days, as a wearisome social function and, moreover, being an accurate shot, the outcome is ever distressingly certain. Hence, even this polite pastime fails me." Here Sir Marmaduke shook his head again and, though his eyes twinkled, sighed more dismally than ever. "Forty-five!" he murmured. "Grey-haired! Life a desolate waste! A sorry world and myself the sorriest creature in it——"

"Spleen!" barked the doctor. "All cursed spleen! Your disease is ease, Tony! Too much luxury, leisure an' lucre! You've become such a personage y'are scarce human, so rich 'n' influential you've no need for effort . . . 'n' effort's life! Could a b'nef'cent fate pauperise ye, strip ye o' rank 'n' wealth, rig ye in homespun 'n' send ye into an unfriendly world t' make a living—ye'd starve— perish, an' that's what!"

Sir Marmaduke smoothed arched eyebrow with slim finger and pondered the question:

"Perish?" he murmured, at last, "I venture to think not, Bob!"

"Y'd perish!" snarled Doctor Robert, diving for his hat and whip.

"I should suffer," mused Sir Marmaduke, "I should endure a thousand discomforts, beyond a doubt, but— perish?"

"In six months—less!" snarled the doctor.

"Perish——?" repeated Sir Marmaduke. "No——"

"Yes!" snapped the doctor, rising. "In less'n six months or—come back younger than y' went!"

"Younger? How so, Bob?"

"Lookee, Tony! T' learn the virtues o' Poverty and Adversity, t' front Misery undismayed, t' learn the greatness o' true humility is beyond the powers of any splenetic fine gentleman; to comfort another's sorrows, t' share 'nother's hardships needs just an ordinary man who has n' time t' bother 'bout his bile-ducts or grey hair, and is never older than he feels. And here's the secret of youth, Tony man—work—f'others, if possible, but work! F'get y'self in other folks' worries, work wi' 'em, suffer wi' 'em, an' you'll be young again 'fore ye're old. Goo'-bye t' ye!" And, with a pounce, Doctor Robert Wotherspoon seized Sir Marmaduke's hand, shook it heartily and, jingling across the room, went forth like a tornado, the door slamming behind him.

Sir Marmaduke drew a deep breath, and leaning in the open window, heard his old school-fellow roar for his horse, watched him stump down the steps and mount that unlovely, hard-worked animal, and jog ungracefully upon his busy way.

Such a rat-tailed, four-legged monstrosity! And eight or nine sleek horses stamping impatient hoofs in his own stables!

Sir Marmaduke frowned at the smug trimness of carefully tended gardens and wide spreading park and away to the western horizon all glorious with sunset, his sombre eyes more wistful than ever.

At last he turned and, seated at his writing cabinet, indited certain letters, wafered, sealed and directed them; then, taking hat and cane, he stepped out into the fragrant evening.

CHAPTER II

It was as he leaned against the stile leading into his pet preserve that Sir Marmaduke first heard it—a wild, sweet strain of music which seemed to voice all the heart-break of a sorrowing world.

Ineffably sad the music rose from the green depths before him, now swelling to a golden chord, now dying to the hushed sobbing of a single string. And staring into the leafy gloom shot, here and there, by the glory of sunset, Sir Marmaduke held his breath to listen, and thought of his own ardent youth and all the disillusion the years had brought, the sorrow of dreams unrealised, of lofty aspirations unfulfilled, the tragedy of boyish ideals shattered and broken, of youthful faith and trust betrayed, mocked at——

The music ended abruptly, voices shouted, there was the sound of flight and pursuit and out from the wood a man came running, a small, rough-clad man who carried a fiddle and bow; then his pursuers were upon him, two men in velveteens, who seized him roughly by arm and collar and began to drag him away, unheeding his whimpered pleading.

"Stop!"

The gamekeepers halted instantly and turned to stare.

"Bring him here!" said Sir Marmaduke.

"If y' please, sir," said the elder keeper, knuckling bristly eye-brow, "us caught this here cove, your honour, a-poaching, sir."

B   9

"With a fiddle, Martin?"

"Why, sir, us did foind a couple o' snares, your honour, and——"

"You may leave the man here and go."

Forthwith the keepers touched their hats and hurried away, whereupon the fiddler shook small fist after them.

"Ya-ha!" quoth he; then turning to his deliverer, swept off his battered hat, bowing low, and Sir Marmaduke saw his hair was silvery white.

"Sir, pray accept my thanks," said the Fiddler, "and my hospitality also if you will. Go with me and you shall fare worthily, I promise."

"You play very wonderfully!" said Sir Marmaduke, alling into step beside him.

"So say they all, sir," answered the Fiddler, with a quick, bright nod, "though to be sure they mostly call for jigs and such, poor creatures! But I can do other things equally well—see here, friend!" and glancing shyly at Sir. Marmaduke and furtively round about, he drew from deep pocket of his wide coat-skirts a newly-killed pheasant. "Bonny work and a bonny bird, I think ye'll allow?'

Sir Marmaduke nodded, and smiled a little ruefully.

"I should like to hear you play again if you will?" said he.

The Fiddler thrust the poached bird back beneath his coat, tucked instrument beneath pointed chin and with sweep of bow, broke out into a heartening quick-step.

Thus, side by side, went they through the sunset glow, the little Fiddler playing, with tireless zest of the true artist up-lift above fatigue, merry lilting catches, stately measures quaintly harmonious, tunes of ancient days, plaintive and wistful, songs old yet ever new like the recurrent wonder of life itself; melodies that seemed to voice the hopes and aspirations, the joys and sorrows, the gloomy doubts and courageous beliefs of generations long since passed away and out of mind. And sometimes as his magic fiddle sang and laughed, wailed and sobbed, this elfish player would dance a few fantastic steps, would chuckle gleefully or groan for very sympathy, while Sir Marmaduke listened enthralled by the musician's genius, yet viewed his strange, bright eyes, and silver hair, his elfish look and queer, wild antics in growing perplexity.

"Aha!" cried the little Fiddler suddenly, "I've played ye music of our fore-fathers, songs o' the forgotten folk and—you have understood, so do I ken ye love the thing divine and salute you, sir, as a true amateur."

"And I," answered Sir Marmaduke, bowing also, "hail you, sir, as a true master."

"'Master' d'ye say? Why true, sir—I am—so they used to name me once—in the golden days—in Italy was it? Ay, surely—Italy the home o' the fiddle."

"Pray, sir, who are you?—Your name——"

"A wild body," answered the Fiddler, "ay, a queer, wild body wi' half a soul—'tother half was buried wi' one who died—and my name? Faith, I've forgot it years since! But 'tis no matter, call me Jack as do they all—Fiddling Jackie—I play at country fairs and wakes, at weddings and christenings—all folk love my Ginevra and so do I," here he kissed his fiddle, "for 'tis Ginevra lifts me above sorrow up to the very feet o' God. 'Tis Ginevra calls back to me the soul of her—my beautiful one that is dead, for only those that die are truly alive— Ginevra knows. And hearkee friend, because ye love music and, loving, understand, you shall hear me play to them, if you will—all those happy, happy ones who throng to the call o' my fiddle when I play among the hush o' trees at evening-time."

"Whom do you mean?" questioned Sir Marmaduke, gently.

"The dead, sir—the souls of the blessed dead who truly live and do love all great, good things—those happy dead who are alive in God for evermore—especially one—the one, she—she that goes beside me now. Ah no!" he laughed, "No, no—you cannot see her for she died years ago, but her soul is ever with me—smiling on me from the sunbeams, whispering to me in the falling rain at night, looking at me from the flowers— she is in all beautiful things, sir—my Beautiful! 'Tis for her I play when I'm alone at such an hour as this, when weary day sinks into the kindly arms of night, and the world is hushed—music that lifts my soul to God and her—my Beautiful—my Rose—withered—blasted— trampled and mired—Ah God!" The little Fiddler shivered violently and raised shaking hand to wipe his brow that gleamed suddenly moist. "Sir," sighed he, "great waters are deep, but deeper is Love! Knives are sharp, but sharper is Grief—and prayer is good—but music? Ah 'tis the language o' God, and thus do I hold converse with her still, so is my grief tempered to my endurance, for, sir, God is merciful."

Thus as they trudged the leafy ways, this strange little Fiddler talked, and sometimes his bright eyes gleamed brighter for their tears, and sometimes his lips curved to a tender smile; and Sir Marmaduke's perplexity was changed to ineffable pity.

So they came at last to a tall hedge in whose wild tangle was a small wicket-gate broken and weather-worn; opening this, the Fiddler passed through, beckoning, and Sir Marmaduke found himself in what had once been a carefully tended garden, but was now a very wilderness of sprawling bramble and dank weeds, beyond which desolation rose the jagged, blackened ruin of a house.

"Yonder," said the Fiddler, pointing with his bow, "yonder we lived, she and I, for her sweet mother was dead, here she played as a child, and hither come I when I may. Sit ye down, friend, here upon this tree-stump—she hath sat here, many's the time—we used to call it her 'throne'."

"Sir," said Sir Marmaduke, glancing about him, "I perceive I am upon holy ground!" And removing his hat he stood bare-headed, whereat the little Fiddler smiled with shining eyes and touched Sir Marmaduke with his bow, a touch that was a caress.

"Oh, sir," said he, "such ready understanding, such reverent sympathy is divine, I am grateful! But hush— they wait! They are all about us—she is here—between us! Pray be seated and I will begin."

Then tossing off his own hat, shaking back his long, white hair, the Fiddler lifted his face, a pale oval in the dusk, and setting bow to string with reverent gesture, began to play.

. . . A golden, singing note that swelled to die away upon a minor trill, a solemn, poignant summons thrice repeated—then, up soared a noble melody whose stately measure grew louder, swifter, wildly joyous, that seemed to voice the Spirit of eager Youth untouched as yet by care; of dewy dawns and cloudless skies, a young world unstained by sin; and life was a sweet thing, a gift of the God who taught the sun to shine, the birds to carol and children to laugh and sing; life was indeed a thing of joy—and yet—it was also a sacred trust to be lived and used to noble purpose——

And Sir Marmaduke, spell-bound by the ever-changing beauty of these strains, forgot his years and was young again with belief in the Ideal, faith in Man-kind, the World, the Future, and Himself, eager with life and bold for achievement——

But now the changing music took on a deeper, sterner note and seemed like the Voice of Judgment:

"Oh man behold thy youth, the young and eager soul of thee fresh from the hands of God! Bethink thee what thou wert, what thou art, and what thou mightest have been. Grieve, grieve for all thy noble dreams unrealised, for these many years spent to no man's profit but thine own! Alas, selfish man, living but to thine own desires, what hast thou achieved but

weariness and solitude? And whither—whither tends
thy lonely way?"

Again the music changed, and now the voice was
kinder, the voice of a familiar friend:

"Oh lonely man weary of soul, take comfort since
in this world are many that need thee, thy strength, thy
service. So, while life and strength be thine use them,
forgetful of thyself, and in the service of these, thy
brethren, find again the glory of thy youth. For he
that serves his fellow, serves his God."

Thus, rapt and inspired by these noble strains, Sir
Marmaduke felt his heart swell responsive, and sighing,
bowed his head in a new humility. And in this moment
the angel within him, that better self so long shackled
by cynical convention, by slothful ease and selfish
indifference, this deathless angel, bursting his fetters,
arose while the music swelled to an ecstasy of triumph,
a very pæan of praise—that ended in a sudden, harsh
discord, and starting round, Sir Marmaduke looked up
to see the Fiddler pointing with his bow.

"The moon!" he whispered, "'Tis at the full to-night
—and the moon is evil to me—'tis like a dead face—so
pale—so pale—like hers—my Beautiful. Dead!" he
moaned. "Dead! I saw them—I watched them lift
her from the water, her long hair—all a-drip with green
slime, her dead face so pale and still—Oh, my Beautiful!
Her sweet voice for ever silenced—my loved one! And
now—now the pallid moon doth mock me—a dead
thing peering and mocking me from God's heaven—an
evil—evil thing!"

Sir Marmaduke rose, words of comfort on his lips,
hands out-stretched, but the little Fiddler shrank away.

"Off!" he cried. "Touch me not for I am a thing
accursed—her murderer lives and laughs yet—the moon
knows and mocks me! Ah God, that he should eat and
drink and she cold in her grave!" And now, letting
fall his violin, the Fiddler covered haggard face in
clutching fingers while great sobs shook him, and when

Sir Marmaduke would have comforted him, he screamed and beat him off, weeping and sobbing the while. "Leave me!" he panted, "Leave me, 'tis my black hour —leave me to the moon and torment." And, with a wild cry inexpressibly desolate, the little Fiddler threw himself face down before that tree-stump which had once been a child's throne, and clasping his arms about it, set tear-wet cheek against its rugged bark, weeping still and moaning passionate endearments and broken lamentations.

So at last Sir Marmaduke turned slowly away and left him lying there, his silver head against the rotting tree-stump.

CHAPTER III

GIVETH SOME DESCRIPTION OF EVE-ANN ASH—A QUAKERESS

SIR MARMADUKE leaned upon his cane and stared at the hay-rick. To be sure he had seen many a one ere this, but never before had examined one with such interest and singular attention. For Sir Marmaduke was travel-worn, and spent with unaccustomed fatigue; he had walked far, by long and dusty ways, and his elegant and be-tasselled boots, ill-suited to such hard, rough travel, had pinched him for miles, and thus, foot-sore, weary and aching with such unusual exercise, he viewed this particular hay-rick earnestly and with the eye of appraisement.

It was a lofty stack, unthatched as yet, and would be soft—a luxurious couch for aching, weary limbs, and it filled the air with a drowsy fragrance, a soporific and most alluring sweetness; also a ladder was reared against it invitingly.

Sir Marmaduke limped forward and, climbing this ladder, a little stiffly, was presently lying outstretched half-buried upon this scented couch, staring dreamily up at a star that winked rakishly down at him.

"Forty-five!" he murmured. "Ridiculous! I am a preposterous fool, of course—and yet——" Here he sighed, stretched himself more comfortably and fell blissfully asleep——

He awoke suddenly to the touch of a hand upon his mouth and the whisper of a voice in his ear:

"Hush!"

The whispering voice, like the hand, was unmistake-ably a woman's, and this hand, though warm and soft, was strong and vital.

"Really, madam——" began Sir Marmaduke, remov-ing the hand that he might articulate.

"Oh—wilt hush!" hissed the voice, and back came the hand heavier than ever. Sir Marmaduke "hushed" perforce.

A shapely arm, the curve of a shoulder, a mane of glossy hair, these he saw, for the moon, high-risen, was very bright.

And then upon the stillness was a mutter and growl of voices drawing slowly nearer. At this, the girl sank prone in the hay, peeping cautiously down, and Sir Marmaduke doing the like, saw three men approaching, one of whom bore a lantern by whose yellow beam, and the moon's clear refulgence, he beheld:

One: A man in a smock-frock.

Two: A shortish, stoutish, sober-clad man in a wide-brimmed hat.

Three: A tallish, thinnish man, also in a sombre garb and wide-brimmed hat.

"Oh, brother!" sighed the stoutish man, "Oh, the poor, foolish lamb!"

"The little fool!" growled the thin man.

"Nay, but think of her wandering—desolate——"

"She should be whipped!"

"Nay, Ebenezer!"

"Trounced, Jeremiah, drubbed, thrashed!"

"Thou'rt over-hard, brother!"

"And thou'rt too soft, Jeremiah! This cometh o' thy doating affection, thy constant petting and pam-pering."

"Nay, Ebenezer, rather hath thy harshness drave her from us."

"Lookee, measters," said the man with the lantern, "'twunt do no good to argle—bargle about it. If Miss

Eve be run away it be for we to run arter 'er, I rackon, or else go back t'bed."

"True, Jacob, true!" sighed the stoutish man. "She can't ha' gone far—let us go on!"

"This hay-rick!" exclaimed the thinnish Ebenezer. "Get thee up the ladder, Jacob, and look a-top."

"Beant no ladder nowheers 'bout as I can see, Master Ebenezer, sir."

"There should be."

"Ay, so theer should, sir, seeing 'twas me as left it ere 's evening—but theer beant no ladder nowheers now."

"And she'll be 'pon the road, brother, I tell thee! Come, let us haste—come!"

"But this rick, Jeremiah!"

"Nay, the road, brother. 'Tis London she'll make for—and so dangerous for a maid and—— Oh, brother, if she be gone indeed, if we ha' lost her—home will be an ill place—life very dark——"

"Peace, man! Hold thy tongue, Jeremiah, it don't bear thinking 'pon. Come, if she be for London 'tis by reason o' that debauched scoundrel Denton, heaven smite him!"

"Hush, brother!"

"Come then—the London road, and haste ye!"

And away they trudged, all three, the lantern bobbing like a will-o'-the-wisp.

Sir Marmaduke sat up and beheld the girl face down amid the hay, and there came to his startled senses an unmistakable sob. Sir Marmaduke shrank and stared a little wildly from earth to heaven and round about; and after the fourth sob, he spoke:

"Pray why do you weep?"

"Because," she answered, in a voice deep and soft with tenderness, "I love every hair o' their grey heads, and it do break my heart to leave them—the dears!"

"Then I suggest you return to them."

"No—no, I can't—not yet."

"May I inquire your reason?"

"Because I be running away to get married," she answered in matter of fact tone. "And yet"—here her voice sank to its deep tender note—"'tis hard to leave my two dears. You see, I am the only child they ever had—or will have."

"Your—uncles?'

"Yes."

"And are you indeed running away to London?'

"Yes.'

"With—a man?'

"My lover, sir."

"A man your uncles think a scoundrel?"

"Because they don't know him as I do."

"And do you know him well—very well?"

At this she turned to view her questioner in surprise:

"Why, yes, sir," she answered, "he is—my lover."

Here Sir Marmaduke leaned swiftly to peer into her face, a rarely beautiful face, lighted by eyes that met his searching scrutiny wholly unabashed and virginally frank.

"And do you love him, child?"

"Yes—I—think so. He is such a grand gentleman, so brave and handsome and loveth me with all his soul. He tells me so—often!"

"And so you are meeting him to-night?"

"Yes—we're to be married in London. But indeed, sir, thou'rt full o' questions."

"Then pray forgive me."

"Nay, verily I be glad to talk o' my love to thee, 'tis a thing I durst not mention except to old Nannie, and she be deaf—But oh, sir," and here the girl raised her head to stare up at the rising, full-orbed moon, "verily love is—very different from—what I dreamed."

"Why so, child?" he questioned, studying the serene beauty of her face as well as he might.

"'Tis this troubles me, sir—when I am away from my love I wish to be with him, yet when I am with him I—long to be away—almost."

"Why?"

"I think perhaps 'tis something in his eyes—or his voice——"

Here she knit her brows and frowned up at the moon in troubled perplexity. For some while she sat, shapely arms clasping rounded limbs, seemingly forgetful of her companion.

"Have you known your—lover, very long?"

"Almost a fortnight, sir. And now I'd better go!" sighed she, donning a deep-brimmed straw bonnet. "I'm to meet him at ten o'clock."

"But the ladder?" question Sir Marmaduke.

"'Tis here. I pulled it up after me."

"You must be a remarkably powerful young woman."

"I am, sir," she nodded.

"And you were not afraid when you found me here?"

"'Deed, but thou didst startle me at first, but I had none other place to hide—and when I'd viewed thee well I saw thou wert none dangerous."

"Ha, because of my sober middle-age, child?"

"Nay, sir, I'd no time to mark thine age or sobriety, 'twas thy snoring vexed me."

"Snore?" exclaimed Sir Marmaduke, blenching a little. "Did I, in fact, snore—surely not?"

"Indeed, sir, so loudly I had to wake thee lest my two dears heard thee."

"Accept my humblest apologies, pray!" said Sir Marmaduke, smiling somewhat ruefully, "Egad, in common with everybody else, I thought only—other people did such a thing! To snore upon a haystack, especially having regard to the circumstances, was in the extremest of bad taste. Still, I rejoice that I didn't frighten you away."

"Because I saw thee for a gentleman!" She nodded.

"Ay, my clothes, child—so confoundedly out of place on a rick."

"Thy face!" she answered, tying her own into the shadow of her bonnet. "And now, good-bye, for I must be going."

"Then," answered Sir Marmaduke, reaching for his hat, "if you will permit I will walk with you."

"Oh, pray do, and thank thee kindly, I should like thee to meet my lover."

"Thank you," said Sir Marmaduke, a little grimly. "I surely will. I gather from your uncle's remarks concerning him that his name is Denton?"

"Yes, sir, Robert Denton. Come thy ways then!" and before he could aid her, she had swung the heavy ladder into position and was descending; and all with such unstudied grace and natural ease as he found altogether admirable. And now Sir Marmaduke descended in turn, as dexterously as stiff joints and tight boots would allow, and they began to walk on together.

"You go too fast for a middle-aged man," said he, after they had gone some distance.

"Art thou indeed so old?"

"Distressingly so!" he sighed.

"'Tis hard to believe," said she, turning to view him with her frank gaze.

"And my hair is turning grey.'

"Nay, by this light it looks very dark and glossy."

At this he felt an unwonted glow of pleasure, which, he told himself, was ridiculous.

"You are of the Quakers, I think?" he inquired.

"Yes, and my name is Eve-Ann Ash."

"A strange pretty name and suits you."

"And what is thine?"

"Oh—faith—Hobbs, John Hobbs."

"And doth not suit thee!" she said, turning to view him again. "Thou hast an air so grand and stately." And her voice was frank as her eye, whereupon Sir Marmaduke felt again that unwonted glow of pleasure, and hid it in a laugh as near embarrassment as he had ever known.

"Dost know London, Mr. Hobbs? Hast ever stayed there?"

"Frequently in the season."

"Dost know—Vauxhall?"

"I have seen it."

"My lover hath promised to take me there. Oh, Mr. Hobbs, 'twill be wonderful! I have only seen London once, all my life hath passed here in the country at Monks Warren."

"And consequently," nodded Sir Marmaduke, "you are as sweet, as fresh and unspoiled as Nature herself. Ah, child, there is no place may compare with this gentle Down Country."

"But my lover tells me there is no place like London—and indeed I do yearn to go there."

Sir Marmaduke sighed, his delicate, high-bred features lost awhile their habitual serenity, and he glanced up at the moon beneath slender brows knit in something very like a scowl; and then her hand was upon his arm and he wondered to feel it trembling.

"He will be waiting me at the edge of the coppice yonder!" she whispered. "Pray—pray wait here!" Then, quick and light, she hurried on, and presently he followed slowly after; thus he presently heard a full, mellow voice:

"My goddess! My angel! By Venus, but you're more beautiful than ever to-night. Come, I've a chaise waiting——"

"Nay—wait, Robert!"

"Not an instant! In a few hours we shall be in London and then—hey for the parson, and then——"

"Indeed—no!" said Sir Marmaduke, gently, stepping forward the better to see this impetuous swain. A tall, youngish, handsome gentleman of a particularly dashing air, and dressed in the extreme of fashion, yet with a little two much glitter in eyes, rings and buttons; a very

determined gentleman who, recovering from his surprise, turned upon the speaker with a certain joyous
ferocity:

"Ha, sir—and what the devil——" His speech
ended abruptly as his fierce eyes met the supercilious
gaze of two other eyes serenely contemptuous.

"A mutual surprise, Mr. Denton, I think—and mutu-
ally unpleasant!" and Sir Marmaduke's tone was as
contemptuous as his look.

"Damnably!" retorted Mr. Denton, fierce and
hectoring.

"This being so," continued Sir Marmaduke, "pray
let us part, sir; make your bow to the lady and go."

"Eh—eh, go?" stammered Mr. Denton. "Go, is it?
Begad, sir, d'ye dare——'

"This instant!"

Mr. Denton swore, took a threatening step forward
and raised his whip; Sir Marmaduke crossed his hands
upon the knob of his cane and bowed:

"Your whip, sir? Take care!" His voice was soft
and he smiled, but in the curl of those mocking lips, in
the keen eyes and serene immobility of his stately figure
was a deadly menace, an unshakeable calm and self-
confidence more daunting than any speech.

Mr. Denton's arm was slowly lowered, his fierce eyes
wavered, and he muttered a savage oath; then turning
to the girl with arms outflung in compelling gesture:

"Eve——" he began, but Sir Marmaduke's icy tones
cut him short:

"Mr. Denton, there are creatures, shaped like men,
who are (I think) wholesomer dead—pray begone, sir,
and remove temptation from me."

For a moment it seemed Mr. Denton meant to leap,
his eyes glared, his nostrils palpitated—then uttering
a hoarse, inarticulate exclamation, he turned and plunged
headlong into the shadows of the little wood; and when
all sound of his going had died away, Sir Marmaduke
reached out his hand to the wide-eyed trembling girl.

"Come, child," said he, "let us go."

"But what—what does it mean?" she questioned breathlessly.

"That I am going to take you back home."

"Home?" she repeated, in slow, dazed fashion. "Yes—I suppose so—he has gone—left me, and I——" Here, all at once, she sank down at the foot of a tree, her head bowed upon her hands, while Sir Marmaduke stared helplessly at her and the tree and the moon and back at her again; finally he ventured to touch her bowed shoulder.

"My poor child!" said he gently, "and yet it is better you weep now than break your heart later on. So weep, my child, weep!"

"But I'm not weeping," said she, glancing up at him clear-eyed, "I'm wondering—wondering why he went—why he left me."

"Well," answered Sir Marmaduke, glancing up at the moon again, "perhaps because I asked him. And now—will you go home?"

"Yes," she sighed, rising. "Oh yes, there be naught else I can do."

"Nothing!" answered Sir Marmaduke, and they turned back side by side. And after they had gone some distance she questioned him suddenly.

"So thou art acquainted with Robert Denton?"

"Not so," answered Sir Marmaduke gently. "I merely—know of him!"

CHAPTER IV

IN WHICH THEY TALK BY THE WAY

"JOHN HOBBS," said she, turning to regard him with wondering look, "do all folks always obey thee?"

Sir Marmaduke, having pondered the question, nodded gravely:

"Usually," he answered.

"But he ran away! He left me—and at thy bidding!"

"Does this grieve you?"

"No! I be only wondering. He was afraid o' thee, I saw it in his face!"

"Yet I'm none so frightful, am I, child?"

"Nay. Yet when didst order him off, thine eyes were turble fierce, Mr. Hobbs."

"Then pray forget it. Tell me of yourself."

"And he—obeyed thee! And he be a stronger man than thou."

"Undoubtedly. But——"

"Then, Mr. Hobbs, why did he leave me—at thy bidding? Him I thought so brave and strong!"

"Perhaps because he is indeed what your uncles name him."

"I wonder?" sighed she, wistfully.

"Did you—love him—truly?"

"Yes—I"—here she glanced up at the moon with the same look of troubled perplexity—"I think so."

Sir Marmaduke smiled.

"*DO* you love him?"

"I despise cowardice!"

c   25

"But do you truly love him?"

"Besides," she continued in her smooth, soft tones, "he is not a godly young man—he cursed and swore, and when he raised whip to thee his look was wickedly evil."

"So then—you don't love him?"

"I shall never love any man again—never!'

Sir Marmaduke laughed so joyously that he wondered at himself.

"Why, child, you know nothing of love, you have never loved any man yet."

"Oh, indeed, sir, and how dost know this?" she demanded, turning to look at him with her frank, level gaze.

"By your eyes, child. Your love is asleep like your womanhood, waiting for the one man to wake it, and then—you will love him, not for his looks or ways, but merely because he is—himself."

"Which seemeth foolish and unreasonable, Mr. Hobbs."

"Love is always unreasonable," quoth Sir Marmaduke.

"Oh! Then pray hast been much in love, Mr. Hobbs?"

"Never," he answered, frowning suddenly, "though I have fancied so, once—and do not call me Mr. 'Hobbs' I beg."

"Why not?'

"Because your lips should utter only lovely sounds.'

"But if thy name is Hobbs——"

Sir Marmaduke wrinkled delicate nose at the unwelcome name, wishing he had chosen another.

"Call me—well, pray call me 'John'."

"Nay but," said she shaking head at him, "to name thee John on so short acquaintance would be vastly familiar, wouldn't it?"

"So please call me John," he smiled, "and tell me of yourself."

"Verily, sir, 'twere waste o' breath. I'm but a simple, homely maid to oversee the dairy wenches and take care of the still-room, and go to chapel o' Sundays—my life is very simple indeed, sir."

"But sweet and good, I'll vow."

"Nay then, thou'rt wrong, for I be full o' sin—stubbornness and pride, and very prone to anger, alas! 'Twas but yesterday I slapped Penelope for spilling a pan o' cream, and then she cried, poor wench—and so did I and went and prayed God's forgiveness on me."

"And surely your prayers are answered."

"I wonder!" Here Eve sighed and shook her comely head. "Only to-day I pulled Joan's hair for spoiling the butter! 'Deed, but I'm a woeful backslider, a very weak vessel with no grace in me. I know 'twas selfish and wicked in me to run off to-night and leave my two poor dears to grieve—but oh, I do long to see Vauxhall—the lights in the trees—the fountains! Oh, Mr. Hobbs, if thou couldst only know!"

"But you love the country, also?"

"With all my heart! The scent of a hay-field of an evening, the song o' birds at daybreak, a wood at sunset, the ripple of a brook—I love them all! And yet—London, its wonderful streets, its palaces and—Vauxhall Gardens—Oh, Mr. Hobbs!"

"Can you not call me ' John '? "

"Surely, sir—but I've known thee such a little while. And thou'rt such a grand-seeming gentleman!"

"My clothes, child?"

"But mostly thy face—so proud—thy manner—so grand!"

"Have you any sisters, brothers?'

"A sister, sir—my poor, poor Tabitha!'

"Ah—is she dead? Forgive me, pray!"

"Not dead, sir—oh no, thank God! And yet—worse, so my uncles say. See'st thou, she married a——" here the rich voice sank to an awful hushed whisper, "a play-actor! We never see her now, of course."

"Yet her husband may be a very good fellow?' ventured Sir Marmaduke, smiling.

"Nay, 'tis impossible, sir! All play-actors be children of Satan! But I do miss Tabitha sorely, and pray for her often—oh, very often!"

"Then all must be very well with her."

"Art thou a godly man, John Hobbs?"

"I hope so."

"Dost pray—constantly?'

"I—I fear not," he answered gravely, "not since I was a little child."

"Alas!" she sighed, shaking lovely head at him in reproach, "I feared so. Thou hast a worldly seeming. And yet——"

"And yet?" he questioned, turning to meet her grave and gentle scrutiny.

"Thou'rt not altogether evil and unregenerate, I think."

"I—trust not," he answered, gravely.

"Verily, thou'rt luxurious in thy habit—and this is a sin. Thou'rt very prideful and arrogant—and these be sins. And yet thou hast a good face, John Hobbs, and thine eyes are kindly-gentle when thou dost smile."

Sir Marmaduke smiled forthwith. And, at this moment came the mellow chime of a distant church clock striking the hour. They had reached a stile, and here Eve-Ann paused to count these silvery strokes with a nod for each.

"Eleven!" she exclaimed in awed tones. "Eleven o'clock—oh gracious me! I ha' never been abroad so late in all my life. I be usually abed and asleep at nine— oh, 'tis shameful! Come, let us haste!" And with swift, lithe movement she was up and over the stile before he could so much as lift hand to aid her; so he clambered over in turn as gracefully as stiff limbs and tight boots would permit.

"Is your home far?" he inquired as they went on again.

"About two miles."

"Then, Eve-Ann, pray do not hurry."

"Wherefore not, John Hobbs?"

"Because I would not bid you 'Good-bye' too soon."

"'Good-bye'!" she repeated. "'Tis a sad word."

"It will be!" he answered. "So please do not hurry, Eve-Ann."

The road stretched before them white beneath the moon, but chequered, here and there, by the inky shadows of hedge and tree; the summer night was fragrant with the languorous scent of honeysuckle, and over all the country-side reigned a solemn hush; Sir Marmaduke sighed:

"Shall you regret saying 'Good-bye'?" he questioned.

"Yes," she answered softly, "I have so few friends, sir."

"You will think of me as your friend, Eve-Ann?"

"Yes, Mr. Hobbs."

"Then call me 'John'."

"Very well, John, to please thee, I will—oh, but verily 'tis a wonderful night, John."

"Yes," he answered, and then halting suddenly: "Eve-Ann," said he, "since I am and would be truly your friend, you must promise most faithfully that should the man Denton seek you again you will not believe his promises—never trust yourself to him again, child! You will never—never go away with him!"

"Nay, friend John, I might," she answered thoughtfully.

"In heaven's name—why?"

"He is so rich, John."

"Rich?" exclaimed Sir Marmaduke fiercely, halting again to peer into her face.

"Indeed, John—he told me so."

"But you don't love the fellow."

"Nay, I begin to think—to be sure that I don't!" she answered plaintively. "But then I need the money, John, woefully!"

"Money!" quoth Sir Marmaduke, bitterly. "You, too!"

"Yes, John, I need it more than anything in the world."

"And would—sell yourself to get it—you?" And leaning near he surveyed her beneath frowning brows; but meeting the steadfast serenity of her look, beholding her clear, unabashed gaze, his brow cleared somewhat: "Oh, child," said he, gently, "what would you with money?"

"I be no child, John," she answered, shaking her head, "and I need the money to save Monk's Warren for my two dears.'

"Monk's Warren?"

"The farm, John. 'Tis all my uncles have left and—hush!" Hoof-strokes muffled in the thick dust, and presently a horseman loomed upon them against the white road, a big, heavily built man astride a powerful steed.

"Quick!" whispered Eve, and drew Sir Marmaduke into the denser shadow of the hedge. But the horseman had espied them for, checking his pace, he called out in loud, imperious tone that broke unpleasantly upon the solemn night silence and grated harshly upon Sir Marmaduke's over-sensitive ear:

"Who's sweet-hearting, eh? Kissy-cuddling in the shadows, eh? Which o' ye is it this time? Is it pretty Nan? Is it Bess, or Prue? Tush I can see the gleam o' your petticoat! Come out, little rogue, and show your pretty face. What, must I fetch ye?" So saying, the man urged his horse towards them, head and body stooped forward from the saddle, peering.

"So—ho, there y'are, my pretty trollop! Is it Nell or——" The words ended in a gasp of sheer amazement, and when next he spoke the man's voice was hoarse with sudden rage:

"Why, damme it's Eve—it's Eve-Ann Ash, by God—and with a man—midnight'"

"Yes, Squire Brandish," said Eve-Ann in her smooth, serene voice, "'tis I, for sure. Now go thy ways in peace."

"So Mistress I catch ye, do I? Will ye be coy with me and kiss your lad on the sly, like the rest on 'em? You and your cursed modest airs and be damned —cuddling your lover at midnight ye jade, ye sly vixen——"

The ferrule of Sir Marmaduke's cane obtruding itself violently into the speaker's waistcoat silenced him for the moment; then, gasping in pain and amazement, Squire Brandish was looking down into an oval face adorned with black whiskers, a pale, high-nosed, contemptuous face with eyes that seemed to look through and beyond him, lips which, parting upon white teeth, spoke in accents carefully modulated:

"Fellow—be off!"

Squire Brandish leaned down, heavy chin viciously out-thrust:

"Fellow—hey?" he demanded fiercely. "D'ye know what I am—d'ye know who——"

"Perfectly!" answered Sir Marmaduke. "You are a disease we would be free from, a plague, a loathly pest and contaminate the air."

Squire Brandish's answer was a passionate blow with his riding-crop, but Sir Marmaduke, expectant, parried the stroke, and answered with a lightning riposte, driving his cane full into the folds of the squire's cravat, and rocking him in the saddle so violently that the horse reared; but recovering with desperate effort, the Squire spurred the snorting animal upon Sir Marmaduke who, leaping nimbly aside, struck twice with whizzing cane, and the Squire's horse, smitten across the nose, whinnied, swerved and galloped off down the road, his frantic rider shouting and wrenching at the bridle all in vain.

"And now, Eve-Ann," said Sir Marmaduke, smoothing his ruffles, yet panting a little, "let us go on."

"Oh, John—oh, John Hobbs, thou'rt not hurt?"

"On the contrary, I feel surprisingly—young!"

And then she was beside him, so close that her garments brushed him, her breath fanned his cheek, and he thought of violets in dewy woods, had a sense of cows in byre, sunny rick-yards, and all else that was sweet and wholesome and cleanly fragrant.

"He meant thy death, John! I thought to see thee —crushed under those murderous hoofs—there was murder in his look! Oh, friend John—if he had killed thee!"

"Why, Eve-Ann—child, do not tremble."

And then his arm was about her and, as she clung to him all warm, soft loveliness, there rushed upon him the sense of vivid youth, of health and abounding vigour from the mere contact of her slender, shapely body.

"Oh, John Hobbs," she murmured, cheek pillowed against him. "Oh, friend John, I shall feel shame and blush for this to-morrow—but death came so nigh thee—in such hateful guise. And thou'rt so strong— so sure! And to-night——"

"To-night," sighed Sir Marmaduke, bending above the beautiful face so near his lips, "to-night——" here, stooping lower, he paused to view the dark curls that clustered in silky tendrils about her little ear, "to-night, child, you have indeed found a friend—old enough to—father you." And, lifting resolute head, he looked from her glowing loveliness to the pale serenity of the orbed moon.

"Nay, verily, John, I had rather have thee for my friend."

"Trust me, child."

"I do, friend John, most strangely, seeing we ha' known each other so short a while."

"Two hours!" said he. "And so soon shall say farewell."

"Art travelling far, John?"

"To London."

"But thou'lt perchance return and—hark!" she cried, starting from him in sudden alarm for, upon the pervading quiet was a throb of galloping hoofs drawing rapidly nearer and louder. "Oh, 'tis Squire Brandish coming back! Come away, he means thee harm——"

"Would you have me run from the fellow?"

"No, only—come with me, John."

"Where?"

"To my temple—come—quick, I tell thee!'

So saying, she caught his hand in her warm, vita clasp, and led him up the grassy bank, through a gap in the hedge, and so into a corn-field beyond which, dark and mysterious, loomed the woods.

"Where is your temple, child?"

"Come, and I will show thee. Besides, 'tis a nearer way to Monk's Warren."

So, hand in hand thus, they presently came among the shadow of the trees.

CHAPTER V

THROUGH leafy glooms shot athwart by the moon's level beams, she led him unfaltering; beneath tangled boughs, amid mazy thickets, flitting on before him through light and shadow until she seemed to him some creature of faerie, half dryad, half goddess, and this wood a place of mystery and magic whereby the sober dignity, the sedate gravity of forty-five years was forgotten quite; old Father Time cut a caper backwards, the weary yesterdays were engulfed in to-day, and to-day merged into the deep and pregnant silence of this magical summer night; the world and Sir Marmaduke were young again as he followed Eve-Ann through this moon-lit wood.

"John," she whispered suddenly, "if there be truly elves and faeries I do think they must come to dance hereabourt! I love every tree, every leaf and twig. See, yonder is my 'temple', I often come here to think, and sometimes say my prayers—there, by the altar!"

They had reached a little glade shut in on all sides, a narrow grassy aisle pillared by the rugged boles of ancient trees and roofed by their myriad leaves; and as he gazed, the moon's level beam fell upon an oblong, weather-worn stone, deep buried in the age-old turf.

Instinctively Sir Marmaduke bowed his head.

"And surely," said he, softly, "no place so fit for a maid's prayers, for here, indeed, is a true Temple of God."

"Oh, John," she sighed, "now dost speak like a truly godly soul and one of the elect. So when next I pray here it shall be for thee—thy future happiness."

"Happiness, child?" he repeated a little sadly. "Only the young are happy, and youth is quick to go."

"But surely age, John, bringeth wisdom, and with it kindliness and sympathy?"

"Not always, alas! Age may bring heart-ache, disappointment and—bitter disillusionment as certainly as wrinkles and—grey hairs!"

"Not if we be true children o' God, friend John, for with Him in our hearts we must be ever young, since He is age-less."

"Eve-Ann," said Sir Marmaduke, bowing his head, "when I grow solitary and the way is dark, I shall think of your sweet faith, and thank Fortune for you and this solemn hour."

"Nay, rather give thanks to God, John."

"But is not Fortune, Chance, Destiny—are not these all names for God?"

"Ah no, indeed! God is our Father, our Almighty yet merciful Judge Who liveth high in heaven yet marketh the fall of a sparrow. So give all thanks to the God who loveth thee, John."

Then she went on again through the magic twilight, and so they came presently out of the wood into a meadow that trended downwards to a little brook, beyond which were many barns and ricks with, beyond these again, the tall gables of an ancient and goodly house.

"There is Monk's Warren, my home."

"So soon?"

"John Hobbs," said she gently, "though thy discourse is at times a little worldly, yet do I know, I am sure thou art a very good man—an honourable gentleman— nay do not interrupt me for, if we be truly friends there is that I needs must tell thee lest thou think me better than I am——"

"'Twere impossible, child!"

"Ah, John, pray hush, for what I would tell thee is very hard, very shameful for any maid to confess——"

"Then don't—don't!" said he, catching his breath sharply. "Let me think of you as I will!" And remembering the man Denton, his unclean and evil reputation, Sir Marmaduke shivered.

"But indeed, John, I must, for our friendship's sake, my heart bids me, and so—do not look at me, John!—To-night —nay do not turn from me—yet, John!—to-night I——I would have had thee—kiss me, and thou didst not, and thine arms about me! So didst thou save me from wickedness, and so am I now a little less shameful than I should ha' been, and—oh, friend John, so do I thank thee from my heart, and honour thee most truly! But I told thee I was a weak vessel, prone to sin, and now thou dost know it."

"Oh, child!" said he, drawing deep breath, "Eve-Ann, now indeed I know you for a very child of God!" And taking her hand, he had bowed reverent head and kissed it almost before she was aware.

"Why—John Hobbs!" she exclaimed, a little breathlessly, "no one ever—kissed my hand ere now——"

Sir Marmaduke instantly kissed it again.

"Good-night!" she whispered, "Oh good-bye, friend John!'

"Good-night, Eve-Ann."

"Thou 'lt come again—somewhen?"

"Most surely! God keep you, child!'

"And you, John.'

"And you will—pray for me, Eve?"

"Daily, John—Good-bye!"

Then she went from him down the slope, crossing the brook by the little bridge where she turned to wave a last adieu and was gone.

Sir Marmaduke stood awhile gazing thoughtfully towards that ancient house, then sighing, he went his solitary way, limping more than ever now, and with every step his age seemed to grow upon him until he felt more time-worn and patriarchal than Methuselah.

CHAPTER VI

IN WHICH SIR MARMADUKE EATS BREAKFAST

" Now that be-feathered, crook-billed harbinger,
  That rosy-wattled herald of the dawn,
  Red comb a-flaunt, bold-eyed and spurred for strife
  Brave Chant-i-cleer his strident summons raised."

> (By which fine phase I'd have you know
> The cock had just begun to crow.")
>> Vide : The "Geste of Duke Jocelyn."

AWAKING then to which shrill summons, Sir Marmaduke, roused from that deep and pleasing mystery hight sleep, opened his eyes and sat up to behold Chanticleer in the very act of crowing again, which performance achieved, the bird looked at him coldly, first with one bright eye, then the other, and arching disdainful neck, strutted haughtily out into the brilliant sunshine.

A truly glorious morning. From without the barn, which had been Sir Marmaduke's bed-chamber, came the pleasant, homely cluck of busy hens, while from near and far rose the joyous chorus of newly wakened birds, such a piping and whistling as might have gladdened the heart of any man.

Thus Sir Marmaduke, little dreaming what the next four-and-twenty hours were to bring forth, stretched luxuriously upon fragrant hay-pile and, breathing deep of the sweet morning air, took joy to be alive, blinked

37

drowsily at the sunshine flooding in at the open door, and had composed himself anew to slumber when upon his consciousness stole a thought, a most persistent thought that banished sleep, that grew to a desire, to a vehement yearning, to a dire necessity: ham and eggs, bread and butter, fragrant coffee. Sir Marmaduke sat up broad awake, for hunger was a new and exquisite experience, and therefore sufficiently remarkable, his mouth was actually watering! Sir Marmaduke, drawing on his boots, very nearly chuckled. Rising, he donned coat and hat, took up his cane, and sallied forth in quest of breakfast.

The new-risen sun made a glory all about him, from wood and copse, from every tree and hedgerow birds carrolled in blithe chorus; but Sir Marmaduke, rejoicing in his hunger, strode along the road, his gaze scanning the adjacent prospect for the welcome sight of inn or wayside tavern, his mind wholly devoted to the consideration of ham and eggs and coffee.

Some half mile's tramp brought him to a village bowery with trees, a cosy, sequestered hamlet whose thatched cottages fronted upon a pleasant green. And here, sure enough, was an inn, a comfortable place, of aspect most inviting, with its latticed casements bright in the sun, its wide, hospitable doorway flanked by roomy oaken settles; but just now these settles were deserted, like the village itself, the door fast shut; and Sir Marmaduke, consulting his watch found, to his surprise, that it was scarcely half-past four.

Thus it befell that a certain sturdy son of the soil on his way so early, beheld a very grand gentleman seated in solitary state before the inn, slim legs outstretched, head bowed, lost in gloomy contemplation of the stocks that stood adjacent, a truly Olympian person, clad in such attire as was seldom seen so far from London; though, to be sure, the lustre of these elegant, betasselled boots was somewhat dimmed, and the perfect-fitting blue coat, with its crested gold buttons, showed somewhat dusty, and with strands of hay adhering to it here and there.

The countryman halted to stare, whereupon the gentleman raised his head, and showed a face that matched his clothes; for his curling hair, which he wore rather long, was slightly disordered, while in one glossy whisker a small hay-stalk had contrived to insinuate itself; nevertheless in his lean, aquiline face was a look of command and serene assurance, it was in the high, imperious carriage of his head, in the smiling condescension of his nod, in the motion of the slim yet compelling hand with which he beckoned the countryman nearer, who obeyed, perforce, knuckling forehead as he came.

"Good morning!" said Sir Marmaduke.

"Which the same to ee, sir, I'm sure," sighed the man. "A rare fine marning, sure-ly!"

"Then why do you look so troubled?'

The countryman glanced keenly at his questioner, shuffled his feet, rasped new-shaven chin, and sighed again heavily:

"Reason enough I rackon, sir."

"Are you also waiting for breakfast?"

"Breakfus' sir?" repeated the man, staring, "Lord no—I've 'ad it, leastways arl as I could swaller—an' that not s' much as would choke a titmus! Y'see this here trouble's been an' ketched me in the appetite, sir.'

"Pray what is your trouble?"

"A thing as don't bear talkin' 'pon, sir—nobbut I doant think 'pon it marning, noon an' night. But thinkin' be one thing an' talkin' be another, so I'll bid ye good-day, sir."

"Are you in any particular hurry?"

"Sir, I be never in no 'urry about nothin'.'

"When does this inn open?"

"'Alf-past six, sir, five o clock o market days.'

"And to-day is not market-day—of course?" sighed Sir Marmaduke.

"Why no, sir, it beant.'

"Then you may sit and talk to me."

The man stood hesitant, but, meeting Sir Marmaduke's eye, he obeyed the slight, though imperious, gesture of Sir Marmaduke's slim finger and, seating himself bolt upright on the extreme edge of the settle, he touched his hat and, shutting his mouth tight, stared hard at nothing in particular.

"Well?" inquired Sir Marmaduke.

"Same t'ee, sir."

"You are very silent."

"I be sir—'tis natur! I beant much of a talker to nobody no'ow, nowhen an' nowhere, an' to strangers never an' no time."

"Admirable Jacob!" murmured Sir Marmaduke.

"Eh?" exclaimed his hearer, starting.

"You live hereabout, Jacob?"

"Ay, sir, I do, but——"

"And work at Monk's Warren?"

"Why so I do, sure-ly," answered Jacob, edging a little further off and eyeing his questioner very much askance. "But Lord, sir—Lord love me, 'ow might ye know as I do be Jacob Jarraway an' works at Monk's Warren an' arl——"

"Pray what is the name of this village?"

"Harting, sir."

"The stocks, now," murmured Sir Marmaduke, nodding lazily at that new-painted, gaudy erection, "I've never seen a handsomer pair——"

"Stocks!" growled Jacob, frowning at them fiercely.

"You keep them in such excellent repair, Jacob."

'Not me, sir, not me—that be squire's doin'—ay an' 'e 'ad furriners over from Petworth to do it, too! An' wot be more, squire be allus findin' someun or other to fill 'em—man, ooman or child, it doant matter to he—dang 'im!"

"The Squire?" murmured Sir Marmaduke.

"Ah, Squire Brandish, sir. 'Tis ill for the likes o' we since 'e come back again from furrin parts."

"A hard man, is he?"

"As a flint! Ah, a reglar bad un be Squire—there was Nancy Warrender, poor young lass, went 'eart-broke arl along of 'e an' drownded 'erself years ago, but I ain't forgot! An' there be others as didn't kill theirselves but——"

"Is he the cause of your trouble, Jacob, my good fellow?"

Now hearing the sympathy in Sir Marmaduke's voice, reading it in his look, Jacob leaned nearer and spoke in hoarse whisper:

"Sir, I tell ee theer be many as would j'y to see 'is bleedin' corpse—ah, many! And I be one! And because why? Because now 'e be arter Eve Ash— ah, an' means t' get 'er, fair ways or foul!"

"Are you sure?"

"Ay—sartin sure! An' she so innocent as a babe! But her two uncles know—an' I know!"

"How?" Sir Marmaduke had turned to stare at the stocks again, but Jacob saw his slim hands tight-clenched upon the gold knob of his cane. "How d'you know? What makes you so sure?"

"Because I heered un say so las' time 'e were drunk— an, and in this very inn too! ''Ere's to Eve-Ann,' says 'e, 'olding up 'is glass. 'Eve-Ann as is agoing to be mine, one way or t'other!' says 'e. Whereupon I took an' throwed my liquor over 'e, thereby losin' my good ale, an' 'e 'as me clapped into they stocks into the bargain—an' the paint on 'em still wet, dang 'im!"

"And what then, Jacob?"

"Then along comes Master Ebenezer and gets me out—ah, and there on the green, afore arl the village, —'Brandish,' says 'e, moighty fierce-like, 'come you anigh my land again, lay s'much as finger on my niece, ay, or any servant o' mine,' says 'e, 'an' I'll shoot thee for the wild beast th' art.' 'Tidn't your land, 'tis moine!' says Squire moighty fierce tu, 'or 'twill be in a week or so,' says 'e. 'A week—ay,' says Master

D

Ebenezer, quiet-loike, 'toime enough for the Lord to strike thee dead first!' says 'e, and away 'e goes an' me arter 'im."

"The excellent Ebenezer!" murmured Sir Marmaduke. "And he—a Quaker!"

"True, sir, but then 'e be a man tu!" nodded Jacob.

"And they are to lose their farm—in a week?"

"Ay, sir—an' that be my trouble! 'Twill be a bad day for the folk 'ere-about. Why Monk's Warren do ha' belonged to they Bywoods sence ever 'twere a farm—ah, ages long, I rackon! But Lord, 'ere I be a-maggin' o' my troubles and, wot be worse, my masters' troubles, and to a stranger as I aint never clapped eyes on afore!"

"But a very sympathetic stranger, Jacob, and one who would like to help."

"Thankee, sir!" sighed Jacob, rising heavily, "thankee kindly, sir, but theer ain't nobody as can help we—unless 'e makes a corpus-carkiss o' Squire Brandish, dang 'im!"

"Do you mean murder, Jacob?"

"'Twouldn't be no murder, sir—it couldn't! It beant no murder to tread on a adder, be it? No, says you—and no, says I. For, lookee sir, in this 'ere world there be good men and bad uns, but even the good uns has some bad and the bad uns some good—generally, but Squire be arl bad, from 'ead to fut, through an' through, ide an' 'air—so the sooner 'e be dead, the better!"

At this moment, from somewhere behind the inn, rose a loud, clear whistle or call, and thereafter a booming voice in jovial bellow:

"Ahoy—aloft there! Show a leg, ye lubbers—tumble, up and lively, me lads! You, Tom, pass the word for Jarge!"

"There be Ben Barter, sir," said Jacob, "used to be a sailor once, one o' Lord Nelson's men, an' 'e can't nowise forget it. He'll sarve ye breakfast now if you ax 'im—ready an' willing is Ben."

"Why then, Jacob, if you'll come with me, you shall drink ale, and plenty of it."

"Why, sir, I beant no-wise in no drinkin' moind, that I beant, never more so—no! Nobbut, as seein' you're so kind and me so low in sperrits, an' Ben's 'ome-brew the best in arl Sussex, I doant moind if I du—and thankee koindly!"

Following the despondent Jacob into the spacious inn-yard spicy with stables, Sir Marmaduke beheld a short, thick-set, hairy fellow, a broad man in every sense, for his broad, cheery visage seemed the broader by reason of a pair of wiry whiskers that stood out from his cheeks like the studding sails of a ship; also his shoulders were broad, his striped trousers, extremely wide and roomy, were supported by a wide belt and flapped above a pair of broad-toed shoes offset by wide steel buckles, moreover, as he made a leg to Sir Marmaduke his new-shaven mouth expanded in a broad smile, quoth he:

"Good morning to your honour! Will it be break-fast?"

"It will," answered Sir Marmaduke, smiling also.

"Why then, we've beef, cold, your honour, roast or b'iled, sir, 'am-rashers, an' eggs warm from the 'en, your honour, tea, sir, or coffee. If these will serve——"

"They will!" answered Sir Marmaduke, heartily. "But first, ale for my friend, Jacob, and then soap and water, and if you could fine me a razor I should esteem it a favour."

"Ay, ay, your honour!"

Very soon Sir Marmaduke found himself in a fragrant, sunny chamber where stood a great four-post bed, its snowy sheets redolent of lavender, a most inviting bed, whose broad, voluptuous swell obtruded upon his consciousness, as it were, so much so indeed that more than once he must needs pause in the delicate operation of shaving to regard it with the eye of desire. Indeed a most seductive bed!

In due season, his ablutions satisfactorily accomplished, he descended to find breakfast awaiting him, a generous dish of ham and eggs flanked by joints of beef, the roast and the boiled, such a breakfast as would have appalled him yesterday—to-day he sighed in huge content, and, sitting down, ate and drank with such appetite and gusto as amazed him.

After some while, his hunger gloriously appeased, he leaned back to survey this pleasant room, massive rafters above, red tiles below, and a great, open fireplace, where logs crackled cheerily, beside which stood a pair of riding-boots, newly polished, their toes and heels sedately together.

Sir Marmaduke yawned, and instantly bethinking him of the four-poster bed, was about to rise, when in through the open lattice came the landlord's broad, good-humoured face.

"The 'am and eggs, sir?" he inquired.

"A delectable memory!" sighed Sir Marmaduke.

"And the beef, your honour, roast and b'iled?"

"That also."

"Hunger be a fine sauce, sir."

"And divine experience!" nodded Sir Marmaduke. "He who has never known hunger is a poor, miserable wretch!"

"Why, as to which, sir," answered the landlord a little dubiously, "I dunno. But my 'eart goes out to a man as can tackle his vittles free an' hearty of a morning."

"Jacob had his ale, I hope?"

"Ay, ay, sir, and afore 'e went bid me thank your honour."

"He tells me you were one of Nelson's men."

"True enough, sir—Ben Barter, gunner's mate aboard the old *Bully-Sawyer*, seventy-four, Cap'n John Chumley."

"Honoured to know you, Ben Barter."

"You do me proud, sir," answered Ben, touching finger to eyebrow.

"You have a guest staying here, I see," and Sir Marmaduke gestured languidly towards the boots on the hearth.

"Why yes, sir," answered Ben, eyeing the articles in question beneath lowering brow. "A London gen'leman, as comes down off and on like—but sir, there's gen'lemen as can take their liquor like gen'lemen, and there's them as can't, d'ye see? And sich like, being drunk, is owdacious."

"*In vino veritas!*" murmured Sir Marmaduke.

"Mebbe so, sir, but not knowing I can't swear to that. But last night this here gen'leman drinks brandy 'till he forgets hisself and frights my daughter and the maids, whereupon I run him aboard, d'ye see—whereupon he begins heaving bottles and glasses, whereupon again I was obleeged to let fly one as took him amidship—twixt wind an' water, as you might say, whereupon Jarge and Tom hauled said gen'leman aloft to bed."

"And this person's name?" inquired Sir Marmaduke sleepily.

"Denton, sir, Mr. Denton, a friend o' Squire Brandish."

Sir Marmaduke blinked in the sunshine, and yawned behind his hand.

"Then 'tis possible Squire Brandish may visit him, here?"

"Ay, sir, him and Squire is supping here together this evening, more's the pity! When him and Squire drinks together, well—they drinks!"

"Which," yawned Sir Marmaduke, "is good for trade, at least. Bye the bye, I noticed a particularly attractive bed upstairs."

"All swans-down, your honour, and 'eartily at your service."

"Thank you. I'll to it."

"Wot—now sir?"

"At once."

"And what time shall I wake your honour?"

"You won't!"

"Ay, ay, sir.'

"I walked a long way yesterday—trudged, tramped until I limped and ached with fatigue, so pray see my rest be undisturbed, Ben Barter."

"Surely, your honour."

Then, having condescended to bestow a smiling nod upon the round-eyed landlord, who instantly touched eye-brow and made a leg, Sir Marmaduke took his leisurely way upstairs; locking chamber door, he undressed, got into bed and, ensconsed between fragrant sheets, sighed blissfully, stretched luxuriously and, closing his eyes, fell into a deep and dreamless slumber.

CHAPTER VII

WHICH DESCRIBES HOW SIR MARMADUKE MADE HIS WILL

A BEAM of sun awakened him and, turning his face from this glory, he reached sleepily for the bell-rope to summon Paxton, his valet, then, remembering his whereabouts, sat up immensely glad to find no bell-rope, and to know that the soft-treading Paxton was miles away, together with all other luxuries that had been his life hitherto.

Thus sat Sir Marmaduke, looking about him glad-eyed and tingling with a strange, new zest of living, an eager expectancy of joys to be, on tip-toe for adventure, his old-time weariness forgotten quite. Before the eye of his mind was a fair prospect of rural things—shady woods, fragrant meads and sunny, winding lanes leading on and on, he cared not whither: and, with all this in his mind, he thought, of course, about her—she who had seemed the very embodiment of all that was young, and fresh, and sweet.

Forth he sprang and began to dress, humming softly to himself the while, as he had not done for many a long day. But suddenly he fell silent as, borne to his sharp ears, came a mutter of voices.

" . . . Eve Ash, I tell ye!"

In the act of pulling on a boot Sir Marmaduke paused to glance towards the open casement.

" . . . Last night in the lane . . . with a man! A shameless drab, I tell ye, Bob!"

Having achieved his boots, Sir Marmaduke rose, for these words were spoken by a voice he recognized.

"And with a man, eh?" questioned a second voice, also familiar. "Tall, dark fellow—eh? Fashionable clothes, pallid face, and whiskers?"

"Ay, by the Lord! D'ye know him? I'd ha' thrashed him where he stood."

"Would you, begad?"

"Ay, would I—but he ran off, damn him!"

"Did he, begad?"

"Ay! D'ye know the fellow, Bob?"

"I know him for a middle-aged buck, and therefore dangerous to coy virginity. Egad, our handsome Eve's reputation is sadly blown upon, I fancy. But,oh demme, what a gorgeous armful o' ripe loveliness she is!"

"Ay, damn the prudish slut, the sly jade's no better than t'others for all her demure airs . . . an artful trollop a——" Sir Marmaduke's hand had grasped the water-jug, thrust it out of the window and inverted it, all in a moment; then, leaning forth he beheld Squire Brandish and Mr. Denton seated immediately below, very wet, and staring up at him in gasping, wild-eyed amazement.

"Scum!" quoth Sir Marmaduke, and let fall the water-jug to crash in flying splinters on the ground between them.

"Da—damn you, sir!" gasped the Squire, but, drawing in his head, Sir Marmaduke took his hat and strolled downstairs, swinging his cane airily before him, to find a protesting landlord and two very damp but raging gentlemen, who raved and cursed, roaring threats, of blood and vengence.

At Sir Marmaduke's sudden entrance Mr. Denton fell back a pace, scowling, but Squire Brandish leapt forward, hairy fists clenched, but recoiling as suddenly before the lightning thrust of a gold-mounted malacca cane.

"Hold off—animal!" said Sir Marmaduke. "Attempt no brutal pawing lest you blind yourself on my stick."

Here his smooth tones were drowned in the Squire's frenzied roar, a farrago of oaths, threats and coarse vituperation whereto Sir Marmaduke listened, swinging his cane gently to and fro much as if he had been beating time, until the Squire failed for breath; then:

"Fellow," said he, shaking head a little wearily, "I find your manners intolerable as your looks."

"Ha, you . . . you——" gasped the Squire, whirling fists aloft in a very ecstasy of fury. "You shall pay for this—you shall answer to me . . . with your blood . . . your life, damn ye! Oh, you shall answer ——"

"With joy!" nodded Sir Marmaduke, "I intend to kill you just as soon as you will, because, as I informed you at our first meeting, you are a disease to be eradicated——"

"Ha, by God!" roared Squire Brandish. "If I only had my pistols here——"

"Not 'ere, sir!" said Ben Barter, scowling and shaking his head. "There's plenty o' places where gen'lemen can murder theirselves nice an' quiet, but not in my gardin!"

Trembling and inarticulate with rage, Squire Brandish turned upon the speaker, who instantly set himself in a posture of defence.

"Avast, Squire!" growled he. "I ain't a quarrelsome cove, but being a free-born Englishman I aint to be struck, gentry or no! So belay it is, Squire! 'Ands off or t'will be 'ands on—and fists at that, d'ye see?"

But now, as the squire scowled at Ben and Ben at the Squire, Mr. Denton interposed, and drew his ferocious companion out into the garden, whereupon Ben shook his head, and becoming aware of round-eyed maids and staring men who peered in at the half-open doors, he scattered them with a gesture, and shook his head until his wiry whiskers quivered:

"Lord, sir," he exclaimed, his eyes twinkling, "you nigh drownded of 'em!"

"I did my best!" nodded Sir Marmaduke. "Which reminds me that I owe you for one large china ewer, pray note it in your bill."

"Sir," answered Ben, "under these here circumstances—no—but if you could ha' managed to shiver it on Squire's figure-'ead——"

But at this moment in strode the Squire himself, as fierce and threatening as ever.

"See here—you!" he exclaimed, stabbing hairy forefinger at Sir Marmaduke. "Who y'are I neither know nor care, but I demand satisfaction and I'll have it—if you're man enough, ay, damn ye. I'll dabble my boots in your blood yet, d'ye hear? I'll be waiting for ye—ay, I'll give you your quietus in Down-along Spinney this evening at half-past eight—if you don't run away again."

Sir Marmaduke merely bowed.

"As to a surgeon?" suggested Mr. Denton, leaning in at the lattice. "Must have a surgeon, y'know——"

"Bah!" cried the Squire. "He'll be beyond a surgeon when I'm done with him!"

"Seconds, then?"

"Seconds be damned! You'll be there to witness and give the count."

"A little irregular, Brandish!" demurred Mr. Denton. "Yes, a leetle irregular, my dear fellow. What does—er, the gentleman say?"

Sir Marmaduke glanced at the speaker and shrugged disdainful shoulders.

"At half after eight!" said he and turned his back upon them, whereat Squire Brandish cursed him fluently and strode away with a stamp and jingle of spurred heels.

"A dool—eh, sir?" inquired Ben with lugubrious shake of the head.

"A duel, yes," murmured Sir Marmaduke, staring out at the sunny garden.

"'Tis said as 'ow Squire's shot his man in a dool already, sir."

"The better reason to shoot him, Ben."

"And at 'alf-past eight, sir?"

"Which leaves me ample time for supper."

"Ay, ay, sir—but 'twill be a bit darkish for shooting."

"We can stand the closer."

"Lord!" exclaimed Ben, his good-humoured face growing unwontedly troubled. "Sounds uncommon blood-thirsty, sir."

Then, as if prompted by sudden thought, he hurried from the room, and was presently back again bearing pens, ink and a very large sheet of paper.

"What now?" inquired Sir Marmaduke.

"Considering the circumstances, sir—your will."

"Gad so! You're vastly obliging."

"Why d'ye see, sir, his honour, Cap'n Chumley, fout a dool once and made a will—in case o' accidents. I were a witness."

"Which gives me an idea!" nodded Sir Marmaduke, and sitting to the table, he took pen and paper and wrote as follows:

> In the event of my sudden demise, I do will and bequeath all monies so ever that I die possessed of to Eve-Ann Ash of Monk's Warren, Sussex.
>
> Marmaduke, Anthony Vane-Temperley.

"Two witnesses needful, eh, your honour?"

Sir Marmaduke nodded, whereupon Ben drew a boat-swain's pipe from his pocket and, leaning from the casement, sounded a shrill call, in response to which summons presently appeared a ruddy-faced, shock-headed fellow.

"Jarge can write his name as good as any print, sir."

"Excellent!" said Sir Marmaduke, handing the blushing George paper and pen, together with half-a-crown, and showing him where his name must go.

"Steady it is, Jarge," quoth Ben a little anxiously, "take a deep breath, lad, and—easy does it!"

Thus encouraged, George squared his elbows and fell to work with infinite care and many twirls of spluttering pen and sympathetic tongue; which task accomplished he sighed, rose, knuckled an eye-brow and departed, beaming. And now Ben seized the quill, much as if it had been a hand-spike, plunged it into the ink, shook it and, bending over the paper, opened his eyes very wide but shut his mouth very tight and duly affixed his signature; which done, Sir Marmaduke sanded and, folding this document, handed it to the surprised land-lord.

"Ben Barter," said he, "I desire you to take charge of this for me until such time as I come and ask for it—agreed?"

"Heartily, sir."

"And—not a word to anyone! Agreed?"

"Ay, ay, your honour, nary a word, sir! 'Twill be safe stowed along o' me, and you can lay to that, sir."

"Thank you, Ben."

"And now, talking o' supper, sir, 'ow might b'iled mutton and caper sauce—wi' trimmings, soot your honour?"

"Excellent well, Ben."

"Very good, sir, and—say in an hour's time." And away he rolled, forthwith, leaving Sir Marmaduke to saunter forth into the garden; and walking here, he came upon a small arbour bowered in honeysuckle, breathing which languorous fragrance he sighed, remembering when and where he had scented it last . . . then, even as he sighed, heard the sound of quick, light feet and, glancing round, beheld her of whom he was thinking. Now seeing her thus unexpectedly he stood motionless, full of a sudden, great content because of all the unstudied grace and artless beauty of her; the glossy auburn hair which, despite prim, restraining cap, curled rebellious against her glowing cheek, the deep, grave eyes set wide beneath low-arched brows, the full-lipped, vivid mouth and resolute chin; and then the demure grey gown that, veiling her from rounded throat to slim feet and ankles, yet could not quite conceal the noble, vigorous shape below. Thus, seeing her hasting towards him, so unconscious of her own loveliness, Sir Marmaduke forgot all else.

And then—she had caught his hands in her warm, smooth clasp and, viewing him with eager, troubled eyes, began to question him, panting a little with her haste:

"Oh, John! . . . John Hobbs, what . . . what is this they tell o' thee? That thou'rt to fight Squire . . . that wicked man, and . . . because o' me?"

"No," he answered, smiling reassuringly. "No!"

"But . . . thou'rt to fight?"

"Not because of you, Eve-Ann."

"Then why—why?"

"Because I have a strong antipathy to his person."

"Nay, George saw and heard, so did Betty . . . and Betty told me 'tis to-night at half-past eight in Down-along Spinney . . . and oh, John—John, 'tis dreadful sin to fight."

"But extremely human," he answered lightly, "and I am grown astonishingly human since I met . . . that is to say—of late."

"Ah, dost mean since meeting me! Oh, John, so I make thee so very human?"

"I do confess it."

"And so thou must pour water on Squire and that hateful Denton——" here her red lips quivered mirthfully, "and oh—run the hazard o' thy life!" Here she sighed and her clasp upon his hand tightened. "Oh, friend John, now do I beg thee, beseech thee—forego this evil. Indeed he is a very evil man, yet if he hath offended or wrought thee harm forgive him in God's name."

"Nay, child."

"Then for his sake . . . thine own sake!'

"Ann, it is impossible."

"Then . . . oh, John . . . for my sake."

Here she looked at him with such passionate entreaty that he stooped and kissed her hands because he knew her pleading vain.

"John," she whispered, "oh, friend. . . if thou rt killed!"

"It would resolve many difficulties, child."

"And rend my heart . . . for verily I am a lonely one . . . and thou art my friend."

"Always that!" he answered fervently.

"Yet wilt thou fight?"

"Yes."

"In Down-along Spinney . . . at half-past eight! If thou shouldst die there in such sinful fashion . . . if he kill thee!"

"But indeed I do not mean to be killed."

"Ah, John, mock not thy poor friend, for verily she is very heart-sick because o' thy stubborn pride . . . And even if thou kill this evil man his blood would be upon thy soul for ever! So wherefore peril thy body, John, thy soul?"

"For my poor humanity's sake, perhaps," he answered gently.

"Will nothing move thee?"

"Nothing."

At this, reproaching him, she wept; and now again she pleaded, but finding him still unmoved, grew the more impassioned; finally she turned from him with a wild and hopeless gesture:

"God pity and forgive thee, John . . . God shield thee from harm——" And with this desolate cry she turned and sped away, leaving him staring mutely after her.

And presently being come into the little arbour, he sat there, head bowed in sombre reverie for, experienced duellist though he might be, the thought of death obtruded itself, the possibility of his sudden translation into that great unknown which lies beyond the

grave, awed him. Yet life he had ever held lightly—
until now; and, to be sure, his death would benefit
others. Nevertheless he watched the sun sink lower
and lower, and looked round upon this quiet garden
with eyes a little wistful.

At last, hearing the landlord's cheery hail, he rose
and sauntered back to the inn, there to be saluted
by a right savoury odour, and to find the boiled leg
of mutton (with trimmings) awaiting him in steaming
succulence; to the which he did ample justice.

CHAPTER VIII

WHICH TELLS HOW AND WHY SIR MARMADUKE THREW AWAY HIS CANE

THE western sky was aflame with sunset as Sir Marmaduke reached that strip of woodland that went by the name of Down-along Spinney; a place where rabbits scuttled with a flash of white tails; a place where thrush and blackbird piped their plaintive even-song; a place remote, far removed from all human habitation, and divided by a strip of green sward from the denser woods, and hence a place where, with small chance of interruption, two gentlemen might slaughter each other to their hearts' content.

Coming out upon this grassy level, Sir Marmaduke paused to glance about, but seeing no signs of his antagonist, leaned against an adjacent tree and, folding his arms, stood lost in thought. And lolling thus, hearkening to the myriad stealthy noises of this remote solitude, he knew himself in danger; remembering the man Brandish, his murderous rage, and the irregularity of this coming encounter, with none to witness the event but the discredited Denton, he knew this danger very grave, yet was content it should be so since life, hitherto, had fallen so far short, so much below his soaring, youthful dreams—also, his will was safe in honest Ben Barter's keeping.

A distant church clock struck the half-hour, and Sir Marmaduke glanced up and around, listening for a sound of voices, the rustle of leaves that should tell of his

antagonist's approach, but heard only the vague wood-
land sounds and the mournful piping of the blackbird.

And now, as the slow minutes dragged by, he began
to grow impatient, glancing often at his watch and pacing
restlessly to and fro. The sun had set, the woods
to the west were a deepening mystery, backed by a
crimson glory. Frowning upon this, Sir Marmaduke
continued his slow pacing up and down until the clock
rang out again, telling the three-quarters. Shadows
were creeping all about him, in a little it would be dark;
the blackbird's mournful song was ended, over all things
was a brooding silence, a quiet that somehow seemed
to grow ever the more ominous, and Sir Marmaduke,
with his gaze upon that lessening glory in the west,
hearkened, vaguely expectant; at last, uttering an impatient exclamation, he turned to be gone—took three
strides and halted—to stare back over his shoulder, back
towards the denser gloom of the woods behind, whence
—sudden and sharp—came the report of a gun.

For a long moment he stood staring in the one direction, then, moved by a sudden impulse, he turned and
hurried towards those leafy mysteries and, coming upon
a narrow path, followed it beneath tangled boughs,
pushing his way amid briar and bramble until, all at
once, he left the leafy glooms behind to find himself in
a small, grassy glade where the last effulgence of day
seemed to linger, a rosy glow whereby he recognised the
place for that which Eve-Ann had named her "temple".
Here was the avenue of trees whose mighty boles rose
like the columns of a cathedral, and yonder the age-
worn stone she had called her "altar", and yet—
strangely changed, surely—its shape different. Sir
Marmaduke, perplexed, turned thither, peering—then
hurried forward to halt suddenly and stare down in
wide-eyed horror; for there, huddled in awful fashion, his
mangled face upturned, his blood fouling this ancient
stone, lay the dead body of Squire Brandish.

E

Killed by a shot-gun, and at very close quarters, this was horribly evident. A stealthy rustle amid the leaves, and glancing up he saw a hand, brown and shapely, that grasped a gun, then the bushes parted and he was staring into a pale, set face, wherein eyes, brimfull of horror, stared back into his.

"Eve!" said he in whispering voice. "Eve-Ann— Oh, my God!"

"Go away!" she whispered back. "Go away!"

In one moment he was beside her, and had grasped the gun to find its barrel yet warm with the recent discharge. Mutely she suffered him to take it, and mutely watched him thrust little finger into the muzzle to bring it forth grimed with burnt powder.

"Oh, child!" he groaned; and beholding the look in his eyes, she bowed head suddenly upon her hands, shrinking from him, and with face thus hidden, questioned him, breathless and eager:

"Dost not—hate me?—Oh John——"

"No, no—never that, child. Am I not your friend?"

"Even though I—though thou dost think——"

"Nothing!" he answered fiercely. "Nothing! But you must not stay here."

"No—no, I be going."

"Ay, but where?"

"Anywhere away from—this!" And averting her head she made a shuddering gesture towards the still and dreadful thing at her feet.

"Then I will go with you."

"No—ah, no!" she whispered.

"Come!" said he. "No, first we must hide this!" And he scowled at the weapon in his hand, a handsome piece with a silver plate inset upon the stock whereon, in deep-graven characters he made out the name: EBENEEZER BYWOOD.

"'Twas hanging in the kitchen——" said she, breathlessly. "Oh hide it—hide it! Come and I'll show thee where!"

So she brought him to a tree gnarled and warped with years, and pointed him a narrow fissure in its writhen bole, into which he thrust the gun, butt first, and heard it thud down into some cavernous depth where he prayed it might rust and rot away unseen again by any human eye; then, turning towards Eve-Ann, he reached out his hand, to find her regarding him with a strange and eager intensity.

"He . . . was a very wicked . . . a very evil man!" she whispered.

"So, God forgive him!" answered Sir Marmaduke.

"And was . . . on his way to . . . kill thee."

"Eve . . . Eve-Ann. . . . Oh, child, do you mean . . . this was your reason?"

"Come!" she whispered, shivering violently. "Oh, let us go!" And forthwith she led the way into the wood. But as she hasted before him along the narrow path, he heard her gasp suddenly, and turning aside she shrank against a tree and leaned there.

"Eve—what is it?" he questioned anxiously, for he saw her body shaken by violent tremors.

"Oh, John," she gasped, "if they catch me—will they . . . hang me in irons . . . like that awful thing on the gibbet at the cross roads?"

Sir Marmaduke recoiled, his very soul sick with horror.

"Don't!" he cried. "Never think of it! None would ever suspect you, child—they could not!"

"Denton will!" she gasped.

"Denton?"

"He saw me struggling in Squire's wicked arms— he saw me strike him!"

Sir Marmaduke stood appalled. That Denton, of all people, should have seen! Denton, this mean-souled hanger-on! Very gently Sir Marmaduke turned the trembling girl until he could look into her pale face.

"My poor child," said he, softly, "tell me what chanced."

"He and Squire met me . . . in the wood . . . they spake evil—shame of thee and me . . . and Squire caught me in his arms . . . and Mr. Denton laughed . . . bade Squire good luck and . . . left me struggling."

"And then?" questioned Sir Marmaduke, softly.

"I broke Squire's hold and ran away."

"And then?"

Eve shook her head and was silent.

"And—the gun?"

At this she stared at him wildly:

"I cannot tell thee more . . . Oh John, I cannot—must not!"

"Where was the gun?" he demanded hoarsely. "Had you got it? Where was it—tell me?"

"No, John— I cannot!" she whispered. "Not even if they . . . hang me like—that awful thing." Here the shuddering fit seized her anew and sinking down at the root of the tree she crouched there, while Sir Marmaduke stared down at her helplessly. In his agitation he had grasped his cane in both hands, bending it in nervous grasp until, all at once, it snapped and he stood a moment looking at it in vague surprise. When next he spoke his voice was as calm, his look as serenely assured as ever.

"Eve-Ann," said he, smiling at his broken cane, "be comforted, have no fear, no one can ever suspect you—they shall not—no, not even Denton! Wait you here, you must not go alone—so wait, child, promise me."

Speechlessly she nodded, whereupon he turned and hurried back along that winding path, heedless of clutching briar and bramble, until he beheld again that sprawling thing whose glazing eyes stared up at the darkening sky. Sir Marmaduke looked once, made a sudden, swift gesture of one hand, then hasted back to find Eve crouching where he had left her, dimpled chin upon rounded knees and wide eyes staring on vacancy.

"Come, child!" said he and reached her both his hands. So she rose, and they went on side by side, she still clasping his right hand, clinging to it like a frightened child.

"Oh friend, good friend John," she whispered suddenly, "but for thee—ah, but for thee now should I be lost indeed! Surely 'twas the kind Lord God sent thee to me, John."

"Yes," answered Sir Marmaduke, solemnly, "indeed I think He did."

"Where do we go, John? Where may I hide?"

"Nowhere," he answered lightly, "there is no need.'

"No . . .no need?" she stammered.

"None, my child. So I shall take you back home to Monk's Warren."

"No! no!" she cried, in sudden panic. "Not there . . . never there, I cannot, dare not—must not!"

"Eve," he answered, gently, "Eve-Ann rest assured —no one can possibly suspect you—now."

"Ah, but they will, John, they will—indeed they—must!"

"Must?" he repeated sharply. "Why 'must'?"

But, instead of answering, she loosed his hand to hurry on before, like one possessed.

"I will go to London!" said she, "Yes to London for sure—Tabitha will hide me . . . I'll go to London!"

At last, being come out of those dismal woods, they turned, of one accord, to glance back at that place of Gloom within whose grim depths, out-sprawled amid the deepening shadows, lay all that was mortal of Squire Brandish, beside whose ghastly form now lay a broken, gold-mounted walking-cane.

CHAPTER IX

THE moon was rising to stare down at them from a cloudless heaven, a full-orbed moon whose very radiance was of itself a menace to all poor fugitives and whose ghostly, pallid beam turned every shadow to dens of horror whence eyes might be watching and avenging hands reach out to grasp; a cruel, prying moon, whose pitiless, searching light showed Sir Marmaduke the deadly pallor of his companion's cheek and the wide terror of her eyes when she turned, ever and anon, despite frantic haste, to cast fearful looks behind, to start and peer and listen, breath stilled between parted lips, ere she hurried on again like the hunted creature she knew herself to be.

Thus, Sir Marmaduke, limping on beside her, almost forgot cramping boots in his vain attempts to soothe her panic.

"I tell you, child," said he in his most placid tones, "I assure you these fears are utterly groundless——"

"Hurry . . . Oh . . . hurry!" she panted in breathless whisper. "There! What was that rustle . . . in the shadows, yonder? 'Tis there again! Oh God . . . they're coming!"

"No, no child—it is nothing to fear. The hedges are full of strange sounds at night, as you should know surely."

"Behind that tree—look, they are watching us——"

"'Tis only your fancy—see, 'tis but leaves——And,

62

Eve-Ann, even if we are pursued they will not take you."

"Ah, but they will, they will . . . they must! Twas why I fled, and now . . . now I'm afraid."

"My poor child you're all distraught, and small wonder! Calm yourself, pray!"

"Yes, yes, John . . . yes, I will! Oh, but I'm a coward. Forgive, John . . . forgive me!"

"Reach me your hand, Eve-Ann."

"Oh, but thou'rt wondrous kind, John, and gentle! And there's comfort and strength in thy touch. But, oh, John, I believed myself so brave—once, but now . . . when I think of . . . them hurrying after me . . . the roads and inns all watched . . . waiting . . . waiting to take me."

"Not you, Eve-Ann," he answered gently. "Hush now, be calm, child, let us go more slowly and I will tell you about London." And, forthwith, he began describing to her the undreamed-of marvels of the 'wonderful city'; he told her of its pride and cruelty, its riches and glory, tales of ancient days and stories of his own experience; he told her something of the World of Fashion and its great ones, of fête and ball and courtly pageant until, for very wonder, she forgot her terrors awhile and plied him with eager questions.

But, all at once, they stopped of one accord as from somewhere adjacent rose the notes of a fiddle, rich and sonorous, like some golden voice upraised in passionate triumph.

"Why, 'tis Fiddling Jackie!" exclaimed Eve. "So late and so far from home!"

"Home?" questioned Sir Marmaduke.

"Monks' Warren, he always stays there when he wanders our way, my uncles knew him before his trouble, and love him yet. Come, I must speak to him."

The Fiddler was sitting under a tree, white head bowed above his beloved instrument, nor did he pause in his playing until Eve's gentle hand touched his silvery hair.

"Ah, is it you, my angel?" said he, taking and kissing her slim fingers. "And you too, my tall friend!" here he smiled up at Sir Marmaduke. "I have been playing to God. I glorify His blessed name for all His mercies —ay, especially—one! Oh, a marvellous, great blessing my 'Angel o' light'!"

"Is—is all well at . . . at home?" she inquired anxiously.

"Passing well!" answered the Fiddler with smiling nod.

"And my uncles—Uncle Jeremiah?"

"Shall glorify the Lord henceforth since He hath wrought marvellously in their behalf and delivered them from evil."

"How?" demanded Sir Marmaduke, bending closer to study the speaker's face. "How has He delivered them? And from what evil—speak, friend?"

"Nay, sir," answered the Fiddler, shaking his head, "Who am I to speak forth the workings of Almighty God—Genevra shall—heark ye!" And setting fiddle beneath chin, he raised his bow, but Eve's hand stayed him.

"Not now, dear Jackie," she murmured in her caressing tones, "'tis late, so get thee home and . . . oh, Jackie, tell my two dears I am safe and well . . . oh, bid them for God's sake . . . say to them as God loveth me and knoweth all, to speak nothing . . . no matter what befall—bid them be silent! Thou wilt, Jackie, thou wilt tell them this?"

"To be silent for God's sake and thine, my Angel, ay, I will—I will!" cried the little Fiddler, leaping nimbly to his feet. "I will bid 'em laugh and sing and clap their hands praising the Lord, for His mercy endureth for ever! I go—I go!" So saying he cut a caper, laughed, bowed and hurried away on dancing feet, his white hair gleaming beneath the moon.

"I wonder," said Sir Marmaduke, looking after him with eyes of perplexity, "I wonder what he meant?"

"Poor Jackie!" she sighed. "He is one o' the afflicted!"

"Do you know his story, Eve?"

"I know he had an only daughter who died, John, and upon the day she was buried they say he set fire to his cottage and wandered away a madman. And yet he is very good and gentle, and I have loved him since I was a child. Come, let us go!"

Now as they tramped on again, she questioned him suddenly.

"Thy cane, John, where is thy fine cane?"

"It broke and I threw it away," he answered.

"'Tis pity, for now dost need it, I think—art weary, John?"

"No."

"Yet dost limp."

"Occasioned by my boots, child."

"Then take them off."

Sir Marmaduke started.

"My dear Eve-Ann!" he expostulated.

"I love to go bare-footed," she nodded. "Oh, 'tis delicious in the dewy grass of a morning. And the grass is dewy now, John."

"Naturally!" he answered.

"And would be deliciously cool! . . . And my feet are burning."

"Oh—really!" said Sir Marmaduke. "Why then . . . I suppose——"

"Yes!" she nodded, "I'm going to!" And down she sank with her back to him and, when she rose, he was aware of the white gleam of shapely feet and ankles.

"Now you, John!" she commanded, levelling imperious finger at his boots, those elegant discomforts.

"I?" he exclaimed. "Impossible, child!"

"But they hurt thee?"

"Yet can I endure them."

"Nay, 'tis foolish! Take them off, John, and go in comfort."

"Eve-Ann," he demurred, "I have never walked abroad bare-footed in my life, and I'm too old to begin now."

"Nay, thou'rt childish, John! Try now and learn how joyous it is. Oh, I'll turn my back, be sure."

"Why then if I must——" he laughed and, stooping, tugged at his boot, but finding it vain sat down to it, strove and struggled until he was breathless and his swollen foot as fast imprisoned as ever, "I require . . . a . . . boot-jack!" he panted.

"Nay, let me, John!" and, dropping her own foot-gear, she turned, sank before him on rounded knee and, seizing the refractory boot in strong hands, pulled, lifted, and off it came; "Now the other!" she commanded, and mutely he obeyed.

"Thank you!" said he, sighing in grateful relief.

"And—silk stockings, too!" she exclaimed in awe-struck tones. "Take them off, John."

"My dear soul," he began, but she rose to stamp white foot at him in sudden petulance.

"Oh, John, such mock-modesty shames thee!"

Sir Marmaduke laughed and stripped off his stockings with a flourish.

"There now!" she exclaimed as they walked on again. "Is it not verily delicious?"

"Beyond expression!" he answered. "And now, pray where are we going?"

"To London town."

"Yes, but where to-night—where can I procure a chaise?"

"Oh, please, no chaise, John."

"The mail then."

"Nor the mail coach . . . the roads will be watched so we must go by field-paths and by-ways, friend John we must walk."

"Walk?" he repeated, somewhat aghast. "Walk to London, Eve-Ann!"

"Verily, John."

"'Tis a long way, child, a weary way."

"But I am very strong!" she hastened to assure him, "and if . . . if thou go with me?"

"Assuredly!" he answered.

"Then, oh, what matter the distance, for indeed and verily, thou art a great comfort to me."

Here, being awed by her artless fervour and finding nothing to say, Sir Marmaduke walked on in silence until, espying the dim and scattered lights of a village, he instinctively turned thitherwards, but his companion's touch arrested him.

"Not that way, John."

"But surely there is an inn yonder?"

'Yea. The Ring o' Bells, come, let us go on."

"But you must have shelter for the night."

"Not at an inn, John."

"Where then?"

"Why, I'm none tired or sleepy, John—pray let us go on."

"But you cannot walk all night!"

"I could, John, but if thou'rt weary let us rest awhile—yonder in the dark of the hedge."

"No, no," he answered. "I'll walk as far as you desire, Eve-Ann."

So she hurried on again, careful to avoid the village, nor did she abate her speed until these homely lights had vanished behind them.

"Though to be sure you must have some sleep!" he remonstrated.

"Yes, I suppose so," she sighed, "but not yet and—not in an inn! When we must sleep let us find some barn or rick."

"Rick?" he exclaimed.

"Thou has slept on one ere now, John.'

"True!" he nodded. "Though indeed what is well enough for me is hardly suitable for——"

"And 'tis a glorious night, John, so warm and still and the world so beautiful! And we are together, with God all about us—Oh surely nothing evil may come nigh us?" She had lifted her face to the splendour of the moon, and thus, beholding her pure and reverent look, her gentle eyes, and tender mouth, Sir Marmaduke felt a sudden gladness; for:

"Here is no man-slayer!" he thought. But, and even as he watched, these gentle eyes grew fierce and bright neath quick-knit brows—these tender lips and rounded chin, grim-set and resolute, her slim hands clenched themselves in sudden fury, insomuch that guessing the dreadful reason, he bowed his head that he might not see, and questioned her, whilst dreading her answer:

"Eve-Ann, what is it? Why do you look so?"

"Ah, John—John Hobbs," she cried with passionate stamp of white foot, "how I do hate—abhor—despise myself . . . oh vile and foolish me!"

"Why?"

"That I should ever have dreamed myself—in love with Robert Denton! Oh, the very thought is shame! And to-night—to-night, but for thee, I should have trusted myself to him—I should be with him—now! He saw me in Squire Brandish's wicked arms . . . and laughed . . . and left me—struggling!"

"And then, Eve-Ann?"

"Well . . . Squire Brandish is dead, John!"

"But you are not with Robert Denton!"

"Thank God!" she murmured. "Thank God—and thee, John, and thee!" Here she turned to look at him, her eyes brim full of tenderness, her hands outstretched to him. And gazing deep within those gentle eyes that met his, so purely frank and unafraid, he clasped those hands, and when he spoke his stately calm and proud serenity were forgotten quite:

"Eve-Ann," said he, in shaken voice, "these hands
. . . these hands are pure . . . innocent and stain-
less—confess, confess!"

"I cannot!" she whispered.

"Confess, Eve, confess you are shielding someone."
Now at this she freed her hands and shrank away
from him averting her head:

"No!" she whispered.   "No—no!'

"Child, I do not ask who it is you would protect,
only——"

He saw her eyes grow wide in sudden horror as, uttering a gasp, she sank at his feet, one arm wildly out-flung;
and looking whither she pointed he saw two men watching them from the shadow of a tree.

"They're come . . . to take me!" she moaned.

"No—no!" said Sir Marmaduke, stooping to touch
her bowed head with gentle hand. "Not you, Eve-
Ann. Be comforted, child!" Then turning, he began
to approach these watchers and, drawing nearer, espied
the dull gleam of a gun-barrel.

"Now then," cried a gruff voice, "what be your
game?" Sir Marmaduke lengthened his stride and halted
within a yard of the men, each of whom carried a gun.

"Who are you?" he demanded.   "What do you want?"

The foremost of the twain, a middle-aged man in
a fur cap, goggled at Sir Marmaduke's bare feet, then as
his eye roved up over slim, shapely legs and elegant
person, his mouth opened and he gaped into the haughty
face that frowned back at him.

"Well, what do you want?" repeated Sir Marmaduke.

"No offence, sir," said the man, touching fur cap.
"Y'see, here's me an' Joe taking a bit of a walk-like,
an' spyin' you an' the lady—not knowin' oo you might
be, we just stepped into the shadder o' this 'ere tree
to wait till you'd gone by, d'ye see?"

"I understand!" answered Sir Marmaduke, with
gesture of white finger towards the gun.   "Good luck to
you!"

"Thankee, sir—and good-night to ee!' answered the twain in cheery chorus, and off they strode shoulder to shoulder. Then Sir Marmaduke turned, and seeing Eve prone upon the grass, hurried forward in a panic, thinking she had swooned; but as he paused beside her she stirred and spoke in weeping tones:

"Oh, John, I thought they had come to drag me away to prison and . . . the gibbet!"

"Hush, child, hush!" said he, and sinking upon his knees, took her within the comfort of his arms and began to stroke her bowed head, sun-bonnet and all. "You are overwrought, I suppose—yes, yes of course! And should you fall sick and no woman to tend you—oh, damnation, you should be safe in bed and asleep!"

"Don't—don't swear, John!" said she in voice between laughter and tears, whereat Sir Marmaduke, dreading hysteria, glanced wildly about in quest of water and, seeing none, seized her nearest hand and began to beat its open palm; whereupon she laughed and, seeing the horror in his look, laughed the louder and, sitting crossed-legged upon the sward, laughing still, she bowed her face upon her hands, rocking to and fro.

"Good God!" ejaculated Sir Marmaduke, and stood watching her in horrified perplexity. Then all at once her laughter ceased and she looked up at him wet-eyed.

"My poor John!" said she gently. "And did I fright thee?"

"I . . . I thought," he stammered. "I feared——"

"Hysterics, John? Nay, 'tis over, and I am brave again, thanks to thee. But thou—why thou'rt all of a tremble!"

"An hysterical woman is—is a terrible experience!" said he. "Especially in a field at midnight!"

"Midnight?" she exclaimed. "Then we had better don our shoes and stockings, for we must find a place to sleep."

"Ay, but where, child?" inquired Sir Marmaduke, pulling on his boot.

"Come and I will show thee."

"Do you know where we are, Eve?"

"Yes, yonder is Willowdene Wood, and there is a great, old tree shall be our shelter. Come!"

So he followed whither she led, until before them, within a grassy hollow, rose a tree, huge and of immemorial years, whose wide-spreading boughs and leafy branches made a thick canopy, and whose gnarled roots formed mossy niches.

"I love this old tree!" said Eve, laying her hand upon its rugged bole.

"Yes," he nodded, "and this was old when the great Cæsar was writing his Commentaries."

"So here will we lie and rest, John."

"I wish I had a cloak for you, child."

"Nay, bracken will be better! Help me pull some, John."

And so, having strewed bracken for their beds, they presently lay down beneath the kindly shelter of this ancient tree; but presently, hearing a rustle, Sir Marmaduke glanced round to behold Eve upon her knees, head reverently bowed and hands crossed, absorbed in silent prayer.

And after some while, being yet upon her knees, she ventured to question him:

"Dost never pray, John?"

"I'm afraid not—except in times of stress."

"Which is . . . a little cowardly, John."

"Very!" he answered.

"So will I pray for thee. Though indeed I would Uncle Ebenezer were here!" she sighed.

"Why, Eve-Ann?"

"Because he is so powerful in prayer, and hath the Lord's ear, John. However, I will do my best," and folding her hands, she prayed aloud, thus:

"Dear Lord, I beseech thee to bless this John that is thy son and my good friend; as he hath comforted and protected me, do Thou so by him—bless him, oh

Father, sleeping and awake, defend him from all enemies, especially himself, and bring him at last to thy everlasting glory, Amen!"

"Amen!" said Sir Marmaduke reverently.

And now lying outstretched in the gathering darkness, for the moon was failing, they began to talk, thus:

EVE: Art cosy, John?

SIR M.: (Stealthily tucking a handful of bracken between himself and a too-intrusive tree-root) Extremely!

EVE: And sleepy?

SIR M.: (Stifling a yawn) Never more wide awake.

EVE: Then may I talk?

SIR M.: Pray do.

EVE: Well, John, why art thou so unlike all other men?

SIR M.: Have you known so many other men?

EVE: (Sighing) Very few—but none like thee. Who art thou, John, and—what?

SIR M.: A discontented, melancholy, middle-aged person.

EVE: Oh? And what beside?

SIR M.: A misanthropic creature unhappily aware of his years and growing more elderly with every breath.

EVE: Poor John! And yet despite thy burden of years, thy back is straight, thy hair black and thine eyes very quick and bright. And where is thy home, John?

SIR M.: I have lived here and there and found content nowhere.

EVE: But why is this?

SIR M.: Perhaps because I have expected too much of life . . . Perhaps because I am my own disappointment.

EVE: I think thou didst yawn, John!

SIR M.: Then pray forgive me, for I find myself ;most wearisome topic.

EVE: (Reproachfully) I would thou wert not so light

and flippant, for verily, John, life is a very serious
thing, especially for thee, because thou'rt a man and,
I think, moreover, a great gentleman and rich, and
therefore with great powers for good.

SIR M.: Or evil, Ann!

EVE: Or evil, John. Yet do I know thou art
brave and generous and good despite thy worldliness.

SIR M.: I am very sensible of your good opinion
. . . but worldly—am I?

EVE: Oh, verily, John! And I fear a backslider,
but thou'rt a gentleman, to be sure, and this makes
me to wonder why thou shouldst be asleep upon our
newest hay rick.

SIR M.: Because I was desperately weary.

EVE: And why shouldst tramp the country and
trouble thy self with such as I?

SIR M.: Because I could not do a better thing.

EVE: (Kicking petulant foot) Oh, John Hobbs,
but waste my breath!

SIR M.: How so, child?

EVE: Thou dost answer all my questions telling me
nothing.

SIR M.: What shall I tell you, my child?

EVE: No more, I thank thee. And I am not a
child! And when I found thee on the rick thou didst
—snore!

SIR M.: (A little shocked and perturbed) A highly
objectionable habit. I trust I may not repeat the
offence. Good night, Eve-Ann!

A silence.

SIR M.: Have I offended you?

EVE: 'Tis only my evil temper . . . I told thee I
was passionate, pray forgive me, John . . . And thou
mayest call me thy child an' thou wilt—though I be
twenty-two turned . . . Good night, John.

SIR M.· (Gently) Good night, dear woman.

And here fell another silence wherein he hearkened to
her soft breathing and stared away to the sinking moon.

F

But, all at once, he must needs think of that blood-soaked, sprawling thing whose unwinking eyes were, even now, glaring up at this self-same moon—unless the hateful, stiffening thing had been found and already upon people's lips was the awful word—murder . . . Perhaps the hue and cry was up . . . the Avenger of Blood upon their track! Instinctively he strained his ears for some sound of pursuit; and was profoundly glad that Eve had so wisely checked his desire for the comforts of an inn . . . for assuredly the main roads would all be watched as a matter of course. So must they go by devious, seldom-frequented ways (even as she had said) until they might lose themselves in the teeming myriads of London . . . And their descriptions would be circulated broadcast! Therefore to-morrow he must effect a radical change in their appearance. . . . To-morrow! And, even now, Vengeance might be striding close upon their heels!

Sir Marmaduke sighed and stirred restlessly, and in that moment came a slim, cool hand to touch his hair, his hot brow, and steal thence to clasp his hand; then, in the gathering darkness, a whisper:

"Oh, John, friend John—how I do thank God for thee!"

"Then God make me worthy, Eve."

"Good night—the Lord bless thee, John!"

"And you, Eve-Ann! Good night."

And thus, hand in hand amid the dark, this simple country maid and excessively fine, fine gentleman presently fell asleep.

CHAPTER X

GIVETH SOME DESCRIPTION OF BREAD AND
BUTTER

OPENING his eyes Sir Marmaduke sat up to behold the wood pierced by radiant beams of early sunshine and gemmed with sparkling dew-drops that spangled the mossy ling, while birds, near and far, filled the leafy aisles with the fervour of their glad singing, but nowhere was sight or sound of Eve Ash. Thus, being at some loss, Sir Marmaduke took himself by the chin and was instantly discomforted by its bristly feel and yearned amain for the luxury of hot water, soap and razor.

And presently was a rustle amid the leaves, and rising to his feet, he espied Eve coming towards him through the sunny green, in one hand a comfortable sized jug, in the other a bundle wrapped in snowy cloth.

"Good-morrow, John!" said she, and to his wonder he saw her all fresh and neatly trim from slender ankle to new-combed ringlets apeep beneath her bonnet. "Verily, thou hast slept well, John!"

"Indeed yes!" he answered, hatefully aware of stubbled chin and rumpled garments. "Which at once raises the embarrassing question: Did I snore?"

"Only—now and then, John!" she answered gravely but with dimpling cheek. "And here is our breakfast, milk and bread and butter—a new loaf!"

"But where in the world——"

"There is a farm-house just beyond this wood. Canst be content with only bread and butter and milk, John?"

75

"'Twill be nectar and ambrosia, child! But you look amazing neat, Eve-Ann," he sighed a little reproachfully. "While I——"

"There is a brook over yonder, and I've a comb in my pocket if——"

"Blessed woman! Now if you happen to have a razor also?"

At this she laughed, a low gurgle of sound that he thought delightful to hear, so that he laughed also, while it seemed to him the birds sang more blithely than ever.

"'Tis good to wake in such a world on such a morning and hear you laugh, Eve-Ann," said he; and so away to the brook, there to kneel and wash, finding it an awkward business, to be sure, but very refreshing; then having dabbed himself somewhat dry with his handkerchief, and smoothed his damp locks with Eve-Ann's pocket comb, back he went, gloriously hungry, to find breakfast ready, to wit: two mugs, of remarkable solidity, brimming with new milk, and a pile of bread and butter all set out upon the snowy napkin.

"Dost like bread and butter?" inquired Eve, surveying the tower of slices a little anxiously.

"I don't know."

"They are rather thick, John, I fear!"

"But with plenty of butter, Ann."

"Art hungry?"

"Astoundingly."

"Then I had better cut more for so am I."

And presently, sitting side by side beneath this ancient tree, they ate and drank; and Sir Marmaduke learned that bread and butter, fresh and properly cut, amid such surroundings, on such a morning and with such a companion, can be as appetizing, as delicious and far less cloying than any highly-spiced or cunningly seasoned dishes soever.

O ye Experienced Eaters, ye Gastronomical Experts

whose over-educated and pampered palates must be subtly titillated and wooed from course to course—all ye to whom bread and butter be nursery memories to shudder at, could ye have been happily blessed with such mouth-watering hunger as was this our middle-aged, over-bred, fine-gentleman, could you but have sat where he did, have watched Eve-Ann smoothe on the yellow butter (slightly salt) with one deft sweep of the knife and delicate turn of the wrist, have noted the supple movements of that slender yet capable hand as it sliced evenly through crust and crumb, had she glanced up at you, bright-eyed, beneath the brim of her sun-bonnet to inquire:

"Another slice, sir?"

Then you would surely have answered like Sir Marmaduke:

"Thank you—I will!"

"Though there is only the crust left, John!"

"Amazing!" he exclaimed. "A whole loaf between us—prodigious!"

Breakfast over at last, Eve folded the napkin tidily, viewing the very solid crockery with dubious eyes.

"They will be awkward to carry along!" said she. "The woman made me buy them, and now——"

"For how much, child?"

"She asked a shilling, but accepted eightpence—and that was too much!"

"Indeed?" smiled Sir Marmaduke. "Henceforth, Eve-Ann, I will do the paying. As for these things, leave them——"

"But—oh, John—eightpence! And to leave them behind!"

"'Tis better than carrying them——"

"'Tis woeful waste!" she sighed: but with a last glance at this so aged and most hospitable tree, they turned and went their way.

"You are very silent, Eve-Ann!" said he after they had gone some distance.

"I be thinking what a to-do will be making back home at Harting, John, for surely they will ha' found—him by now."

"Why think about it, child?"

"Ah, John, 'tis in my mind and will be for ever, I think. And yet, come what may, I am ready. For in the night the Lord answered my prayer and hath given me strength to endure all things . . . unfearing . . to the end—ay, even the gallows if needs must be. And now thy poor feet John, are they well?"

"My—feet?" he exclaimed, turning to look into the gentle serenity of her eyes.

"Do thy boots irk thee?"

"No, no, Eve—and heavens, child, what if they do!"

"You must buy others, John, so soon as you may."

"You are a strange child—and very womanly, Eve."

"Yea, verily, I am twenty-two, John."

"And do you ever wear any colour beside grey?"

"Of a Sunday I go in black, sir."

"Then at the first opportunity I will get you a gown of blue or pink or——"

"Nay, John, I thank thee, this is very well——"

"Blue would suit you admirably!"

"Nay not blue—not blue, John, pray!"

"Then pink——"

"Nor pink—oh never! I couldn't indeed. Colours are so—so very worldly, John, and vain-glorious. I should feel as though the very trees had eyes to stare at me. Oh I could never go in colours."

"Why then, perhaps something white with sprigs on it?"

"Sprigs, John?"

"Of flowers. Though I should prefer plain blue. However, I think we should be wise to alter our appearance, to effect a radical change."

"A change?" she repeated, catching her breath. "You mean—they will be after us—looking for me! Very well, John, do as thou wilt—I will wear anything!"

"Even a blue gown with tucks and frills?"

"No, no, 'twould never do for walking, John—'twould tear!"

"But would suit you! Also a bonnet—no, a cloak with a hood, and a few pairs of stockings——"

"And a basket, John, with a lid!"

"And a pair of light walking shoes——"

"And a looking-glass, John, please."

"To be sure, a folding mirror, also cups and saucers—no, mugs and platters, knives and forks, a cooking-pot, brushes and combs and a knapsack——"

"'Deed, John, we shall need a waggon!" she smiled.

"A waggon?" he repeated, musingly. "A cart? A horse? A pony! Excellent suggestion!" After which Sir Marmaduke walked awhile lost in thought; and the sun being so glorious, the birds carolling so blithely and his boots so much easier, he actually began to whistle, softly, a sprightly air until, catching himself in the act, he turned to Eve to voice his wonder:

"Astounding!" she exclaimed.

"Oh—what now, John?" he questioned starting.

"I . . . whistled!"

"Well, John, and what then?"

"A person of my sober age! Eve-Ann I have not done such a thing since I was an irresponsible urchin!"

"Wert ever an urchin, John?"

"To be sure I was."

"Nay, 'twere hard to believe."

"Why, pray?"

"Because no urchin could ha' grown into anything so stately and dignified as thou, John."

"Ha, child, tell me now, can any man be dignified with a chin like a porcupine and whistling like a plough-boy?"

"Only thyself, John. Thou'rt dignified even asleep and thy hair all touzled!"

"Even when I snore, Eve-Ann?"

At this she laughed aloud, and he thought the sound particularly sweet and good to hear.

"Oh, John, thou wouldst be stately anywhere or when since thou art—thyself."

"Then must I seem an extremely trying kind of person."

"Not to me, John. Oh, never to me!" she exclaimed so fervently that he must needs turn to glance at her.

"Child, I wonder why?" he questioned.

"Because thou'rt a man never dismayed, John, and so gentle. And because, despite what thou art and hast been, canst eat bread and butter and enjoy it . . . and sharing the perils of a poor, hunted creature, canst tramp cross-country in tight boots and whistle——"

Sir Marmaduke laughed again, but hearing the sincerity in her soft tones, reading it in her clear, direct gaze, his bristly cheek took on an unwonted flush and his dark eyes glowed beneath their long lashes.

So they walked and talked until the sun rose high, and the day so hot that Sir Marmaduke was for sitting down to rest, but Eve shook her head.

"See yonder, John."

Looking whither she directed, he beheld a tall, slender spire soaring high above the green.

"Petworth!" said she.

A vague, small town upon a hill bowery with trees; Sir Marmaduke lengthened his stride.

"There," sighed he, "will we eat and drink and rest awhile."

"Pray, John," she inquired suddenly, "how didst break thy cane?"

"Eve-Ann, it snapped."

"And didst throw it away?"

"Which minds me I must have another, stronger and——"

"But to throw it away! Oh fie, John, and the knob all gold!"

"And I am plaguily thirsty!" he sighed. "As you must be."

"Nay, John. But go thy ways into the town, I'll wait here."

"Wait?"

"Indeed, 'twere wiser—folk might know me. So I'll wait thee in the little coppice yonder."

"But your gown, Eve-Ann—a bonnet or cloak and —what not? How in the world am I to buy such things?"

"A hooded cloak will be best, John."

"But it is a long, rough tramp to London, Eve, and you will require other shoes and a change of stock-ings, also a different shaped gown, something bright with ribbands and flounces—most essential!"

"Ribbands and flounces be idle vanities, John, and ill to tramp rough ways——"

"Tush, child! And you could buy 'em all in a moment."

"Nay indeed, John, no woman could ever buy such things in such wicked haste——"

"But under the circumstances, Eve?"

"I might be recognised, John. So rather will I be as I am than run such risk."

"Then if you won't buy them I must!" sighed Sir Marmaduke.

"Poor John!" said she, sighing also, but with smooth cheek dimpling. "And thou'rt thirsty, moreover! So get thee gone, buy what thou wilt and hurry not, shalt find me waiting in the green yonder . . . And here is my purse, John."

"Then keep it in your pocket, child."

"And . . . John . . . if it must be coloured, please let it be blue. . . . And there is a milliner's shop opposite the Angel Inn."

"A milliner's!" exclaimed Sir Marmaduke. "Now heaven aid me!"

CHAPTER XI

TELLETH HOW SIR MARMADUKE WENT SHOPPING

He found Petworth, this small and peaceful town, drowsing in the mid-day heat, its narrow streets and cobbled ways echoing sleepily to leisured footfalls, lumbering waggon-wheels, and the occasional murmur of voices droning from shady corners and dim interiors; a place seemingly void of all bustle and fretful haste, where Time stole on unhurried feet; indeed a small, pleasant town, ages old, and very neat and clean from its ancient roofs and chimneys to its worn and narrow footpaths.

But Sir Marmaduke, being parched with thirst, heeded little of all this for, as he traversed this sunny street, before his imagination rose a vision not of sparkling water, nor of wine red or white, still or bubbling, but of ale creaming in foam above cool tankard-brim, so that his thirst increased and he quickened his pace until at last, towards the end of the little town, upon the left hand side of the street, he espied the Inn of the Angel, an ancient, cosy-looking house with two or three steps before the open portal.

Entering a cool and shady tap-room Sir Marmaduke saw the place apparently deserted, but from somewhere adjacent came a murmur of voices, above which hoarse muttering rose one high-pitched and excited:

". . . bloody murder and arl, I tell ye!"

"An' a woman in it tu, I'll warrant me!"

"Well, beant theer generally—allus a woman in it?"

"Ay, sure-ly. There's women mixed up in ever-think, so there be!"

"Ah—and especially wi' Squoire Brandish! A rare un for the petticuts were Squoire!"

"And him a dead corpse—why, I seed un ere in Petworth las' week, I did!"

"Ay, that 'e wur—drawed un a pint wi' my very own 'ands, I did."

Here Sir Marmaduke rapping loudly, there presently appeared a rotund, heavy man in apron and shirt-sleeves who, having duly drawn and set forth the ale required, shook heavy head and blinked round eyes, solemn and owl-like:

"Sir," quoth he, "I dunno wot this here country o' ourn's a-coming to!"

"Indeed?" said Sir Marmaduke, turning to blow the froth from his ale.

"No, sir—that I don't. You ain't heered the noos, p'raps—if you ain't, you will."

"Shall I?"

"Ah—that ye will!" answered the man with portentous nod. Sir Marmaduke raised the tankard and drank thirstily, yet watching the speaker's heavy visage the which seemed to bloat with the import of those horrors he was eager to describe. "I only heered it myself ten minutes ago, and sir—my pore innards is all of a quake—that they be!"

"Ah!" exclaimed Sir Marmaduke, sighing ecstatic as he set down his half-emptied pewter. "And why should you quake, pray?"

"Because I got bowels, sir."

"So I perceive," nodded Sir Marmaduke, "but why should they trouble you?"

"Because this here noos be enough to make any man shiver, ah, and freeze his blood and marrer into the bargain—that it be!"

"Dear me!" exclaimed Sir Marmaduke. "What is your news?"

The man closed his eyes, opened them wide, rolled his head, cleared his throat and said:

"Bloody murder! . . . And not fifteen mile from here! A pore gen'leman well beknown to me."

"Tell me of it."

"Why, sir, 'tis Squire Brandish, a sporting gent with 'is throat cut from ear to ear, his 'ead shot clean off and stone dead into the bargain, pore soul! And him in here only las' week—ah, and a-standing on that very i-dentical spot where you're a-standing—and now a murdered corpse by the 'and of nobody knows oo!"

"Shocking!" said Sir Marmaduke, staring down into his tankard. "And have they no clue, no suspicion as to who did it?"

"Why there be some talk of a woman as has vanished—but 'tis the man they're after."

"A man?"

"Ah, a young buck by all accounts, a London gen'leman as quarrelled wi' deceased, and has likewise vanished—but——"

"But?" inquired Sir Marmaduke, lifting the tankard to his lips.

"But, sir, this here gen'leman 'as vanished, leaves his jooled riding-whip beside the corpse, and they're pretty sure to trace him by that."

"And a young buck is he?"

"Ah, so they say, sir. One o' they bang-up, heavy-toddling bloods, a reg'lar Corinthian, sir."

"And left his whip, did he?"

"Ah—that 'e did, sir, alongside the mootilated corpse."

"Then, depend upon it, he's the man."

"Why so everyone do seem to think, sir, and they're arter him a'ready, seekin' an' a searching for 'im—'igh and low. Likewise the roads is all watched and expresses a-posting for London at this minute, sir."

"Then they ought to take him."

"Why so they ought, sir—ah, an' so they will, I'll wager, and 'ang 'im dead, and then clap him on a jibbet—properly tarred, I 'opes."

"Properly tarred!" nodded Sir Marmaduke. Then, having finished his ale he paid for it and bidding the heavy man "Good morning," went forth into the sunny street.

And now, though he walked slowly, his keen gaze roved constantly, and once, hearing quick steps behind him, he paused to glance into a shop window until this hurrying pedestrian had passed; then he became aware that this window bore the legend:

ARTHUR MOAPS

HAIRDRESSER TO THE QUALITY

EASY-SHAVING

Now in the middle of this window, surrounded as it were by a halo of toupets, wigs, and false hair of various shades, was the waxen head of an ænemic gentleman whose eyes goggled glassily but whose too regular features were off-set by a splendour of glossy, raven locks and curling whisker. Stepping into this emporium Sir Marmaduke beheld its presiding genius, a somewhat superior person and rather like the waxen image in the window, since he also possessed goggling eyes, sleek hair and magnificent whiskers whose glossy splendour bore eloquent testimony to their possessor's unremitting care and delicate art.

Receiving Sir Marmaduke's order he appeared shocked and a little aghast, for his whiskers quivered in an agitated manner and his eyes goggled more than ever.

"Eh, sir—remove 'em, sir? Oh, sir!" he exclaimed caressing his own facial adornments. "Can you reely part with such truly beautiful——"

"And pray cut my hair close—crop it!"

"Yessir! Very good, sir! But, sir, as regards these whiskers, sir, whiskers are all the mode, sir. I've

tended the whiskers of the Quality from an earl down
to a right-honourable, and never seen a handsomer pair!
And then, sir—oh, sir, think o' the ladies. There's
nothing can captivate the Sex, sir, like a pair o'——"

Here meeting the lightning of Sir Marmaduke's
eye, the barber became dolefully mute, sighing dejectedly as he plied in turn comb and scissors, lather-
brush and razor.

Thus, after some while, Sir Marmaduke, his erst
while curly locks close shorn, passed tentative hand
over smooth-shaven cheeks and surveyed his so altered
appearance in the glass, what time the barber (this
dejected wight) sighed mournfully and shook reproachful head.

"They was whiskers, sir, to aloor the female eye,
sir, to warm the female 'eart, and now—they aint! A
pity sir, a pity!"

"I shall need a razor," said Sir Marmaduke, studying his reflection with critical eyes.

The barber's gloomy brow lightened somewhat.

"To-be sure, sir, a razor—or shall it be a pair?"

Sir Marmaduke nodded. "Also a small mirror."

"Then, sir, a pair it is! And . . . a mirror! And
I won't say, sir, as a smooth face don't become you, sir.
Soap now, you'll require soap perhaps—and a brush?"

Sir Marmaduke nodded.

"And seeing, sir, as the best o' razors—even mine,
sir, is apt to grow dull, now and then—may we 'umbly
suggest a strop?"

Sir Marmaduke nodded.

"A strop it is, sir!—And, looking at you again,
sir, I won't say as a smooth face don't make you look
younger! Razors, mirror, soap, brush, strop—and
shall we agree to a small bag to put 'em in, sir?"

"Yes," answered Sir Marmaduke, "also I will take
a hair-brush and comb."

"Cer—tainly, sir! An 'air-brush and comb—to be
sure! And now, sir, when the sun ketches you, so, I

won't say as you don't look young enough to be your
own son, sir! Ree-markable! A brush and comb—
so! Now shall we add thereto a small pot o' bear's
grease?"

"Thank you—no!" said Sir Marmaduke.

"No!" repeated the barber. "No bear's grease!
—Though to be sure, sir, whiskers is all the fashion,
quite the mode and very genteel! A gent without
whiskers is like a flower without smell, sir—and your
departed a-dornments might ha' graced the noble visage
of any o' the bong-tong—dook, earl, marquis or baronet!
Razors, mirror, brush, soap, strop, brush and comb,
bag to keep 'em in and—no bear's grease! Will that
be all, sir?"

"Quite!" answered Sir Marmaduke, drawing forth
his purse.

"Then much obliged I'm sure, sir, and good-day!"

Out in the quiet street he became more than ever
conscious of his altered appearance, so that, as he went
he stole surreptitious glances at his reflection in the
shop windows until, all at once, his glance was attracted
by a neat board above one of these windows, whereon
was painted in chaste characters:

THE MISSES BLYTE.

It was a cosy little shop tucked shyly into shady
corner, a demure little shop in whose trim window the
fascinated gaze might behold an alluring assortment
of fripperies feminine, delicately intimate and daintily
belaced and frilled (the which Sir Marmaduke regarded
somewhat askance) together with a bewildering array of
caps, hats and bonnets with deep brims, narrow brims
and no brims at all, backed by gowns and frocks of
varied colour and shape, with necks cut low and waists
tucked high.

Sir Marmaduke glanced up the street and down,
a little desperately, bent resolute head and stepped

into the dim little shop to be confronted by a tall, angular lady who bridled at him, and a short, plump lady who dimpled.

"Your pleasure, sir?" demanded the bony lady.

Sir Marmaduke removed his hat and bowed:

"Madam," said he gently, but with keen gaze unwavering, "I desire a gown."

The plump lady tittered, while her bony sister seemed to develop more angles, especially as regards nose, chin and elbows.

"A—what, sir?" she exclaimed, viewing him from head to foot with the dispassionate eye of a strong-minded woman. "A—what, sir, if you please?"

"A gown, madam. Also a hat, cap or bonnet——"

"Pantaloons or breeches you mean, I think, sir?"

"Oh . . . sis—sister!" tittered the plump lady.

"Rosamond, pray command yourself! You, sir, will find a tailor's shop adjacent. We bid you good-day, sir!" Here the bony sister curtseyed profoundly.

Again Sir Marmaduke bared his head and bowed lower than before; then drawing a ribbanded quizzing glass from his bosom, and holding it to his eye, began to study the various garments exposed for sale—dresses, frills and furbelows—with the profoundest interest.

"A gown, madam," he repeated, "blue or pink, sprigged or otherwise, with a bonnet suitable for a young lady. Also a warm, hooded cloak."

The bony lady folded mittened hands, cocked high-bridged nose and emitted a loud and disdainful sniff.

Sir Marmaduke instantly bowed:

"This, I think, will suit," said he, indicating a blue sprigged muslin, "I particularly admire the frills and ruffles."

The bony lady snorted, while her plump sister, hiding behind a flowered bed-gown, gurgled and choked.

"That gown, sir," quoth the bony lady tonelessly, "is a confection at four guineas!"

"Pray be good enough to wrap it up for me, madam."

"Rosamond!" said the bony lady, "service if you please!"

"As to a hat now, or bonnet?" mused Sir Marmaduke, glass at eye. "Something with a sweep of brim, yet not too large——"

"This, sir," said the plump sister, dimpling, "is young and pretty and the flowers match the frock."

"Admirable!" said Sir Marmaduke, "I will——"

"A new model, sir!" quoth the bony lady. "Value thirty-seven shillings and sixpence."

"Have the goodness to wrap it up——"

"Impossible, sir! It must be boxed!"

"Boxes, madam, are awkward to——"

"Boxed, sir! Rosamond—service if you please!"

His purchases completed, Sir Marmaduke bowed and departed, his usual stateliness of deportment somewhat marred by reason of his impedimenta, more especially the bonnet-box, which proved particularly elusive and difficult to manage. He had just recaptured it from the middle of the roadway when his eye was arrested by a long, rough frieze overcoat, which unseasonable garment hung at the open door of a dingy shop wherein, perched crossed-legged upon a counter littered with male garments of every description, squatted a little, fierce-eyed old man busied with needle and thimble.

"That great-coat——" began Sir Marmaduke.

"Two-pun, ten!" quoth the little man, scowling over horn-rimmed spectacles.

"I'll buy it——"

"Show's yer money!"

Sir Marmaduke did so; then, having selected a pair of second-hand boots (villainous of aspect yet withal roomy) together with certain other articles of

G

attire, he ordered them to be wrapped up and got himself into the great-coat.

"Goin' to wear it—hey?" enquired the little, old man, busied with string and paper.

"It will be easier to carry."

"So 'twill. But it makes me sweat to look at ye! And arl them packages, too!"

"I can manage," said Sir Marmaduke, clutching fiercely at the elusive bonnet-box.

"Pretty load ye've got. Better lemme send 'em."

"Thank you, no."

"Then tek my advice and get a waggin.'

"Good morning!" said Sir Marmaduke and edged himself and parcels out into the quiet street.

He next bought a knapsack into which he crammed such other necessaries as he chanced to remember, and with this strapped to his shoulders and parcels clutched beneath each arm he set out along the dusty road.

CHAPTER XII

CONCERNETH ITSELF CHIEFLY WITH CLOTHES AND—A BONNET

Thus heavily laden, Sir Marmaduke trudged out of sleepy Petworth and, turning aside from the high-road down a grassy track, made for that strip of wood-land where Eve had appointed to meet.

The sun felt hotter than ever, the parcels unwieldy, and Sir Marmaduke, unused to any burden more cumbersome than a walking-cane, made an awkward business of his porterage; nevertheless, and despite heat and rough going, he tramped devotedly on. But his progress was slow, for, hugging his many pack-ages to himself beneath each arm, it resulted that so often as one fell he was obliged to set down the many to recover this errant one, hence between himself and his many rebellious burdens was strife and struggle unremitting. . . . And the sun blazed! And his frieze overcoat hampered him! And his face itched with crawling perspiration and no free hand to wipe it away! Small wonder then if his habitual serenity became a little ruffled? . . . And then his way was barred by an uncommonly high stile.

Sir Marmaduke swore pettishly and, casting down his burdens all of a heap, dashed the trickling sweat from his brow with petulant fingers and glanced at his watch. Two hours! She had been alone and waiting him for two mortal hours! An eternity!

Catching up the parcels he hurled them over the stile and, having clambered over in turn, collected them and trudged resolutely on again.

The path he now followed trended down hill past a ruined cow-shed, a path which zig-zagged in an undecided manner until eventually it lost itself in a little wood, a shady coppice. He had reached the grateful shade of this cow-shed when the bonnet-box (this most wayward and wilful of his burdens) sprang from his clutch and careered gambolling down the slope; he was pursuing this when the bulbous parcel containing his new-bought garments wrenched itself free and began a sluggish chase of the bonnet-box which had bounded lightly into the dim interior of the cow-shed. Sir Marmaduke let fall the rest of his parcels and mopped his face, cursing fiercely; then stooping for his package of clothes, stepped into the byre.

A desolate place long since out of use, deserted alike of man and beast. In one corner a mouldering heap of stable refuse whereon lay an old pitchfork with broken tines; beholding this, Sir Marmaduke took off his overcoat. Around and above him crumbling walls and broken roof, an age-worn ruin to rot and rot unheeded. . . . What place better suited? Sir Marmaduke opened the parcel.

And presently out of this tumble-down cowshed strode John Hobbs in very truth, clad as yeoman should be, from soft-brimmed hat and belcher necker-chief to worsted stockings and rough, thick-soled shoes; while hid deep beneath that heap of stable-sweepings lay the broad-cloth, silk and fine linen which had erstwhile clad the stately form of that haughty patrician Sir Marmaduke, Anthony, Ashley, John, de la Pole, Vane-Temperly.

"So far so good!" quoth John Hobbs, glancing down at his rough apparel, and wholly unaware that, despite homespun and frayed velveteen, his lean, aquiline features seemed more high-bred, more refined and delicate by very contrast.

Then, having recaptured his remaining parcels, he trudged on again, slouching his shoulders and plodding heavily in keeping with his clothes.

Reaching the wood at last, he pushed in among the leaves, looking about him as he went, but with never a glimpse of the shapely figure he sought.

A small wind was abroad filling the green with vague, soft rustlings which seemed to follow him as he quested vainly to and fro until, hot and weary, he paused at a loss and there rushed upon him the dreadful realisation that Eve-Ann was gone. Instantly fear seized him, and tossing aside his burdens he began a systematic search, ranging the wood from end to end, but still without success. And now anxiety grew to alarm for her safety, and alarm to panic, so that in sheer desperation he began to call her name. Then came the wind again, soft and fragrant and cool, that touched his hot brow like a caress, a wind which stirred the leaves behind him and, turning, he saw Eve watching him from an adjacent thicket.

"Oh, Eve—Eve-Ann, where have you been?" he demanded sternly.

"Following thee, John . . . peeping at thee from behind bushes that rustled!"

"And I thought 'twas the wind!" said Sir Marmaduke, and sinking upon a log that chanced near, he drew out his handkerchief, a vivid bandana of unearthly hues, shuddered at it, but therewith mopped perspiring brow, while Eve viewed him in ever-increasing wonder.

"To hide!" he exclaimed, "and I so anxious for you! I feared——"

"So did I, John, 'twas why I hid. . . . Thou'rt so—oh, indeed, so dreadfully changed!"

"Dreadfully?" he repeated.

"Thy rough clothes!" she sighed. "Verily thou mightest be a ploughman—but for thy face."

"Indeed?" said he, stroking his shaven cheek. "I trust my altered features may at least meet with your kind approval?"

"Yea, verily, John, thou'rt so much younger and better looking I did not know thee!"

"Oh, indeed?" quoth he, a little ruefully.

"I mean," she explained, "'tis as if a much younger man looked at me with the grave, wise eyes of John Hobbs. Thy nose and mouth seem different, thy chin bigger. I see now why folks are apt to do thy bidding. Yea, John, I like thee so—despite thy rough clothes."

"Which reminds me," said he, rising. "I have bought you a bonnet and things."

"A bonnet! Oh, John!"

"Also a gown and—er—stockings. I got them safely as far as this wood, I remember, but I must have dropped them somewhere——"

"Thou didst throw them down, John—over yonder by the brambles."

"Then you were watching me—all the time?" he questioned reproachfully.

"Of course, John! And the gown—is it blue?"

"And sprigged!" he nodded.

"Show me, John—show me."

Sure enough beyond the brambles they found the divers parcels and packages, each and every somewhat the worse for wear.

"This," said Sir Marmaduke, dragging a dinted object from the thorny tangles, "this contains your bonnet, I think."

"It—it looks very battered, John."

"It does!" he nodded. "And well it might, for 'tis certainly the most high-spirited and restive bonnet that ever man had to cope with."

Down sank Eve upon the turf to take the travelworn object in her lap, and as she loosed string and wrapping he saw her slim fingers were trembling; then:

"Oh!" she sighed in awe-struck whisper. "Oh . . . 'tis wonderful!"

"And happily seems to have escaped serious damage, which truly is wonderful. In this box is——"

"But I—I can never, never wear it, John!"

"Not wear it, Eve-Ann?"

"Ah, never—'tis too beautiful! 'Tis for only a great lady to wear——"

"Yes!" he nodded, "'twas why I chose it. I hope 'twill fit. Now in this box——"

"But, John, I'm only Eve Ash and——"

"Exactly! And in this box you will find——"

"But I cannot tramp the country in such a beautiful——"

"Then you can cover it with your hood."

"Hood, John?"

"Precisely! I have a hooded cloak here for you somewhere. But first open this box and let us look at your gown."

Quick-breathing, she obeyed; and beholding her shining eyes, flushing cheeks and rosy parted lips, he thought her more beautiful than ever as, clasping her hands, she sat gazing down at this dainty garment, with its innumerable tucks and flounces, in a rapt and speechless ecstasy.

"Oh!" she breathed, at last; and then again: "Oh John, 'tis like a dream!"

"The milliner called it a 'confection' I remember."

"I have sometimes dreamed of such a gown, John, for I am often very worldly and vain in my dreaming, but——"

"And now, child, go and put it on while I sit here and set forth our dinner——"

"Oh, but I couldn't—eat!" she cried.

"Ham and beef, child, sliced thin, bread, butter and a bottle of light wine."

"But, John——"

"Eve-Ann, go and change your dress."

"Very well, John—but didst buy a looking-glass?"

"Being a man of my word, I did!" he answered, and doffing his knap-sack he loosed the straps and emptied its various contents before her on the grass . . . an agglomerate mass, a greasily, glutinous mess, from which he recoiled in shocked dismay, while Eve stared aghast.

"Oh, John!" she exclaimed, shaking reproachful head, "the butter is melted."

"Evidently!" he answered ruefully, watching her extricate two spoons, one fork, a cork-screw and the looking-glass from a shapeless-something that had once been a pound of butter.

"'Tis no way to carry butter, John."

"So I perceive!" he answered. "The grocer fellow couldn't have packed it securely—throw the confounded stuff away!"

"Nay indeed, that would be wicked waste."

"But we cannot eat it——"

"Indeed, but we shall, 'twill be butter again when it cools. . . . But 'twas kind in thee to remember the looking-glass. . . . And all these—these wonderful clothes, they must ha' cost thee a vast deal o' money, John! And they be much—oh, much too fine and grand for country wear."

"Then don't wear them, child."

"And yet—if 'twould please thee——"

"Eve-Ann, go and put them on—this moment!"

"Very well, John!" said she, suddenly meek, and rising, vanished into the green.

Left alone, Sir Marmaduke fell to considering the present state of his affairs and the future possibilities of pursuit, capture and prison. . . . And what then? he asked himself. The mute evidence of his broken cane would be damning, and how prove his innocence? What voice could bear testimony on his behalf? Not one! On the other hand, he was known to have quarrelled with the murdered man, to have gone forth with the avowed purpose of exchanging shots with him . . . thus, by his impulsive act, he had placed himself in a position of danger very real and grim.

And yet, far from regretting this so quixotic act, Sir Marmaduke felt pleasantly thrilled, and happily assured that, foolish or no, life had become full of a new and vivid interest, and that under the like circumstances he should commit such folly again.

Now, sitting in this pleasant shade, his back to a tree, he began to whistle softly, the while with pencil and memorandum he jotted down the following:

Estimated distance to London . . . 60 miles or thereabouts.

Time required to go afoot . . . 4 days or 40 according to weather, circumstances, and Eve-Ann.

Further items to our comfort:

A cooking-pot.

Herbs (various) with pepper, salt, etc.

An extra pair of stout shoes (for Eve).

The same (for self).

A strong stick, iron-shod, but light (for self).

A bed, mattress, etc. (for Eve).

The same (for self).

A light, portable tent (for Eve). N.B. Waterproof.

A folding stool (for Eve).

A bucket.

A kettle.

An axe.

A strong horse or pony for transport. N.B. No vehicle.

He was racking his brain for additions to this list when, hearing a rustle, he glanced up, and the whistle died upon his lips.

"Eve!" said he, softly. "Oh . . . Eve-Ann!"

Shyly, wistfully she looked down upon him beneath her bonnet's shady brim, all shrinking loveliness from that same coquettish bonnet to gown's ruffled hem; for this artful garment, cut and fashioned by expert fingers, served but to mould the splendid beauty of her form in all its vigorous young womanhood. Then, all at once, as she met his look, she turned away, hiding her face from him in her two hands.

"Oh, John," she whispered, "wherefore dost eye me—so?"

"Forgive me, pray," he answered, viewing her still, "but the change is . . . wonderful!"

"These clothes, John?"

"Of course."

"Indeed," she sighed, "I feel so—worldly! And I cannot lose sight o' myself, but these things be so beautiful . . . that I do love the sight o' them. I love the feel o' them and—alas, John, this is wicked vanity! Dost think such fine raiment may change the heart and mind as well as the body, John?"

"Sometimes maybe, Eve, but not yours."

"Then tell me, John, pray tell me . . . do I look —am I well, clad thus?"

"Yes," he answered softly, "you are . . . very well!"

Hereupon she bowed her head to peep down through parted fingers at the glories which arrayed her, while Sir Marmaduke gazed in rapt delight so bewitchingly did the artful coquetry of bonnet and gown offset her own natural shy demureness.

"I feel like someone else, John," said she at last in hushed tones, "someone very grandly genteel who never, never milked a cow or touched a churn in all her lady-like days. The whole world seems different, and, oh John—even thou!"

"Because I am staring again? Forgive me."

"Nay, 'tis the look in thine eyes, John."

Sir Marmaduke laughed a little oddly, and turned away.

"I trust your ladyship is hungry?" said he. "Come, sit down——"

"Not on the grass, John, 'twould stain me."

"Then upon my great-coat . . . there! Now if you will cut the bread I—confound my memory—I forgot salt and pepper!"

"But didst not forget my looking-glass, John! And what matter for salt if thou'rt truly hungry?"

Thus saltless they dined and made a hearty meal of it notwithstanding. And while they ate they conversed thus:

EVE: I wonder when we shall reach London?

SIR M.: So do I . . . Will you have more beef?

EVE: Nay, I thank thee . . . London is a long way off, John.

SIR M.: It is a fairly good walk.

EVE: (wistfully) Art anxious to be there, John?

SIR M.: (With the utmost decision) Certainly not!

EVE: Prithee why?

SIR M.: Because I much prefer the country. However, by hard walking we ought to reach our journey's end in four or five days.

EVE: (Softly) Oh! . . . so soon?

SIR M.: As I say, by dint of good, hard walking. . . . May I trouble you for another piece of crusty bread.

EVE: (bowing head over loaf as she cuts) I . . . cannot walk very hard in my beautiful raiment, John.

SIR M.: But, child, are you not longing for the joys and wonders of London?

EVE: Nay, John, not—not very much.

SIR M.: Then—of Vauxhall Gardens?

EVE: Nay, John, not now.

SIR M.: Why this change?

EVE: Because I think . . . nay, because I know now that I prefer the country, also.

SIR M.: So you are content to wander awhile among these rustic solitudes . . . just you and I, child?

EVE: (viewing him bright eyed) Yes, John.

SIR M.: Then we must procure a pack-horse immediately.

EVE: (amazed) A horse? But why, John, what for?

SIR M.: To carry your tent, child.

EVE: But we have no tent.

SIR M.: That is why I must acquire one—at once. Also an iron pot to cook in and a host of other necessary things—so we must have a horse.

Now at this she laughed suddenly, but grew as suddenly grave again.

"Ah, John," she sighed, "friend John, thou'rt wondrous kind and thoughtful."

"Eve-Ann," he answered lightly, "the truth is I detest carrying bundles—this knapsack, for instance."

"Then will I bear it for thee, friend, and I can do without a tent."

"True," he nodded, "but you will do better with one."

"Verily thou'rt my friend, John, so would I be thine."

"To carry my knapsack?"

"To know more about thy real self, John; to share thy troubles and sorrows if I may, for often have I seen a sadness in thy looks and wondered. What is thy grief, friend John?"

"Myself."

"Ah, do not mock me."

"Heaven forbid! I am my own trouble, child, though I generally blame Circumstance or my fellows, anyone and anything but myself—as is the human custom!"

"Is it that thou dost . . . love hopelessly, one that lovest not thee?"

"No, no! this, at least, has been spared me."

"Hast ever loved, John, deeply—truly loved?"

Sir Marmaduke started, scowling down at the knife he chanced to be cleaning upon a tuft of grass, and for a moment his strong, slim fingers tightened convulsively about the haft, then, lifting his head, he glanced into his companion's face and, reading all the wistful tenderness and womanly sympathy of her regard, his usual cold restraint was forgotten awhile.

"Yes—once!" he answered. "It was years ago, and I was young then."

"Well?" she questioned, breathlessly.

Sir Marmaduke frowned and shook his head:

"Ill!" he answered, "so let us talk of better things."

"And hast.. . . never loved again, John?"

"And never shall; my heart died twenty years ago.'

"Art sure, John—quite sure?"

"Certain!"

"Can hearts die, indeed? I wonder!'

"As surely, Eve-Ann, as certainly as last years' flowers. . . . And now, since I have eaten the last crust, let us pack and be gone."

CHAPTER XIII

TELLETH OF A BARN AND TERRORS BY NIGHT

NIGHT found them in a country wild and desolate, an interminable grassy slope, void of sheltering bush or tree, where a riotous wind buffeted them, and a driving rain lashed them, out of a blusterous dark, in gusts so fierce that they paused of one accord and turned from this vicious blast to get their breath.

"Oh," gasped Eve, shrinking before the rush of wind and rain, "oh, this is . . . most dreadful, John!"

"Highly unpleasant!" he agreed.

"This rain will quite ruin my poor clothes!"

"This rain, child, means an inn!"

"Ah, no, no! pray no, John."

"As you will, Eve-Ann, but the grass will prove uncomfortably damp to sleep upon, and is growing more so."

"Let us find the barn I told thee of."

"A happy thought!" answered Sir Marmaduke, peering hopelessly into the rain-filled gloom.

"But 'tis so dark, so very dark and . . . oh, John . . . I have lost the way!"

"Indeed, child, I was beginning to suspect as much. Now had we taken the lane, as I ventured to suggest, an hour ago——"

"But we didn't !" she retorted.

"We might, Eve-Ann, by now have been basking at the fire-side of some inn or cottage——"

"But we are not!" she exclaimed sharply.

"So I perceive, child. Confound this wind!"

"The rain is worse, John! Alas, my beautiful gown!"

"And you must be sick with fatigue, Ann."

"No—indeed no!"

"I can hear it in your voice, child. And I'm weary myself, heaven knows!"

"And 'tis I led thee astray," she exclaimed in bitter self-reproach. "'Tis I lost the way and——"

"So did I, child—egad, I've never found it yet, nor wish to, so what matter? Now if we chanced to have a tent——"

"But we haven't, John!"

"Exactly true, alas! Come, let us go on. Take my arm and throw away your bundle."

"Throw away—John, how canst bid me do such thing! Here are spoons, forks, half-a-pound o' butter——"

"Away with them, child, we'll buy more."

"Never, John, 'twould be sinful!"

"However, take my arm, Eve-Ann."

"Your coat feels very damp, John."

"And your feet are wet through, of course, Eve."

"Of course, John, so are thine. But 'tis my sad, beautiful stockings I grieve for, they will be quite spoiled, I doubt."

"You shall have others."

"Thou'rt a very prodigal, John, I fear. But I have never worn—silk ones before, and oh, John, the joy of them! The smooth glide of them when I walk! But these be merest vanities and vain things, alas! And yet do I take such joy in them and grieve they should be spoiled. How it rains!"

"An infernal night!" said Sir Marmaduke cowering as the blast smote him, "A night to drown Romance, child, to chill even the hot vigour of youth and render a middle-aged person miserably deject, for who—

who can preserve faith in his destiny with rain trickling down his neck and oozing into his boots? No one, especially a forlorn bachelor person of forty-five."

"Yet I am with thee, John!" Here the hand tightened upon his arm, "and thou'rt glad o' this, John? Please say thou'rt glad!"

"Yes, Eve—and no."

"Why verily I do know I have been sore trouble and expense to thee," she sighed. "I ha' made thee share my fears and troubles."

"This is why I am glad of you, child. In trying to serve you I forget awhile the weariness of my own futility. But——"

"And there is a light!" she cried, "See—over yonder!"

Looking whither she directed Sir Marmaduke descried a small ray, a yellow shaft that pierced the windy dark, and hastening towards this most welcome beam, presently made out the loom of a large barn.

"Is that you, Tom—eh, who is it?" demanded a high-pitched voice in answer to Sir Marmaduke's knock.

"Two travellers who have lost their way."

"Then I might tell 'em to find it again, but not me, I've too much heart! Specially if you can pay your footing. I couldn't turn a dog away—hey, don't shake the door down!"

"Then open it."

"Well, so I will if you'll ha' patience, friend."

Ensued a sound of fumbling, and the door swung open upon a wide and lofty interior lit by a bright fire whose crackling flame showed a rough-clad fellow who peered at them from an aquiline face with eyes remarkably close set.

"A woman, hey!" he exclaimed, staring at Eve's cloaked form.

"A lady, yes," nodded Sir Marmaduke.

"Very welcome, I'm sure! Step in!" said the man nodding and rubbing his hands together. "This is

Liberty Hall, sir and mam, and aint such a bad barn
as barns go. I've known worse, 'tis fairly weather-tight,
and also it aint my barn, so make y'selves at 'ome,
sir and mam."

"Thank you!" said Sir Marmaduke perfunctorily.

"Don't thank me, sir, I'm only Jimmy Vamper—
never trouble to thank Jimmy. Lord, Jimmy wouldn't
turn ye away if you was two dogs—leastways, in sporting parlance, one dog and a b——"

"The door," said Sir Marmaduke, hastily, "you
have forgotten to bar it."

"Ay, ay!" nodded the man. "Make yourselves quite
at 'ome friends, don't mind Jimmy. There's plenty
o' fine noo hay in the corner yonder for you and your
lady to kip on, ye see it aint my hay, so no thanks
to Jimmy Vamper.'

"But the fire is yours, Mr. Vamper, I presume, and the
black pot upon it gives forth a most appetizing aroma."

"All true enough, sir," nodded Mr. Vamper, rubbing
his hands, "and to said fire Jimmy makes ye welcome,
but a supper meant for two can't be expected to do
for four, now can it, it aint reasonable—now is it?"

"However it is hot," said Sir Marmaduke, "and
smells nourishing."

"And friend, well it might, prime beef, sir, with
onions, turnips and——"

"So, Mr. Vampire, I will purchase it of you——"

"Oho!" exclaimed the man, lifting pot-lid to snuff
the fragrant contents. "It'll come dear, friend, ah—
that it will."

"How much?"

"Well, say—three bob and a tanner!"

"Take five shillings," said Sir Marmaduke drawing
forth well-filled purse.

"Nay, John," murmured Eve from where she sat
warming feet and ankles at the cheerful blaze, "he
named but three and sixpence, and that was too
much——"

H

"To be sure," nodded Sir Marmaduke. "I was forgetting this most welcome fire, take six shillings, Mr. Vamper."

"But . . . John——"

"Are you very hungry, Eve?'

"Yes, John, but——"

"Then let us say seven shillings, Mr. Vamper.".

At this, Eve glanced from Sir Marmaduke to the black pot and frowned darkly.

"Very noble indeed, sir!" said Mr. Vamper, bowing and rubbing his hands harder than ever, "but under the circumstances, and having regard to your lady wife, Jimmy absolutely refuses to take a penny more than five bob!"

"And here," said Sir Marmaduke, counting out the coins, "are your seven shillings, and he dropped the money into Mr. Vamper's ready palm.

"Sir, Jimmy bows submission to your wilful generosity. And I reckon you'll find enough in the pot for you and your lady."

"But what wilt thou do, friend?" questioned Eve.

"Heaven bless your eyes and soul, man, Jimmy shall do well enough on bread and cheese and an onion, never trouble your lovely head about poor Jimmy! Though to be sure, there's Tom, a toughish problem is Tom—occasionally, especially when hungry—poor Tom!"

"Tom?" enquired Sir Marmaduke, glancing about keen eyed.

"My pal, sir, my mate and comrade. Half that supper was his, been expecting him hours—am expecting him. But then 'tis bad travelling, and maybe Tom's found some other ken and will doss other where, d'ye see."

And thus, seated beside this most comforting fire they supped, while the great barn about them rumbled to the sound of buffeting wind and driving rain; a huge, dim place spanned by mighty beams and rough-

hewn timbering, where monstrous shadows danced in
the flickering firelight, and whence came strange
stirrings and rustlings, vague, mysterious sounds from
roof and walls so that Eve, glancing about, edged a
little nearer to Sir Marmaduke.

But the fire was comforting, the stew savoury, and
what with this and their bodily fatigue Eve presently
began to nod drowsily and Sir Marmaduke stifled a
yawn, while Mr. Vamper, on the far side of the fire,
paused in his voracious mastication to smack his lips
over something he imbibed wetly and often from the
neck of a squat, black bottle.

"Shrub!" he exclaimed suddenly, his voice, grown
unpleasantly strident, shocking Sir Marmaduke's over-
sensitive ear, "Shrub!" he repeated, "Will you or
your lady try a suck?"

Sir Marmaduke shuddered:

"Thank you—no!" he answered, politely grim.

"Ah well, there aint much left for Tom as 'tis,"
sighed Mr. Vamper. "D'ye know, friend, I never
taste Shrub but I think o' murders—executions—
the nubbing-cheat. Y'see the first time I tasted
Shrub was at an execution, I saw three of 'em kick—
and me, little Jimmy, a reglar toddling infant—
Lord!"

Eve's breath had caught suddenly, and Sir Marmaduke, leaning near, took her hands that had clasped
each other so fiercely:

"Child," said he, gently, "I think it is time you
went to sleep."

"Sleep?" she repeated in choking whisper, and
he saw horror look at him from her wide eyes.

"Come let us make you a bed."

"Where, John?"

"Over yonder, mem!" said Mr. Vamper, pointing
with the evil-looking knife he held. "The hay yonder,
nice and sweet, mam, you can have any of it—all
of it, ye see it aint my hay, and if 'twas you'd be

welcome to it with all my heart, Jimmy's oath, mam!"

In corner remote from the fire they found a deep pile of fragrant hay that made Sir Marmaduke yawn to behold.

"Are your feet—clothes—dry, Eve-Ann?" he inquired.

"Yes, John, but——"

"Then lie down, burrow well in and let me cover you with your cloak." Mutely she obeyed, but as he stooped to fold the long garment about her, she caught him by the shoulders and drew him close:

"John," she whispered, "I don't like that man!"

"Which is not surprising, child."

"Where wilt thou sleep, John?" she questioned, in the same tense whisper.

"Somewhere near at hand, child."

"Let it be . . . very near, so near that I may touch thee . . . promise, John, promise!"

"I promise you, Eve-Ann. Now go to sleep, you are quite worn out—close your eyes—come!"

"Very well, John," she answered humbly, "only . . . mind thy promise."

"Give me your hand," said he, seating himself beside her, "I'll stay here until you fall asleep."

"God bless thee, John!" she whispered.

So there he sat until the warm, vital clasp of her fingers relaxed and her deep, regular breathing told him she was fast asleep; whereat he arose softly, yawned again prodigiously, and glancing where lay his overcoat drying beside the fire, crossed thither, and was in the act of taking it up when a loud knocking sounded at the door with a hoarse, inarticulate shout.

"Lord love me, here's Tom!" exclaimed Mr. Vamper scrambling hastily to his feet. "Sit down, Squire, and if Tom seems a bit raspish at first, don't distress yourself, for Tom's got a good heart—'specially where the lovely Sex is concerned." So saying Mr. Vamper

began to unfasten the door, while Sir Marmaduke
stood watchful and alert.

After a moment's awkward fumbling the door swung
open and, with a rush of blusterous wind, in strode
a tall, burly fellow, whose sodden garments clung
upon his powerful frame; a wild, fierce creature who,
dashing dripping hat to the floor, showed a thicket of
matted hair, and face hidden in a smother of black
beard and whisker, whence eyes glittered in the light
of the fire, a hairy giant who, closing the door with
savage kick, stood shaking the rain from himself and
growling like some great animal:

"A hellish night—ten thousand curses——!"

Sir Marmaduke stared, for this man spoke with
educated tongue.

"Nothing, Jimmy—curse the rain, nothing!   No,
not a demmed——" He paused suddenly as his
frowning glance encountered Sir Marmaduke, and,
scowling blacker than ever, he viewed him from head
to foot, a long and calculating scrutiny, then his bright
eyes darted to something that lay very plain in the fire-
light, and looking thither also Sir Marmaduke saw this
was Eve's bonnet.

"Aha, a woman—eh?" questioned the fellow, and
his black beard split asunder to show a thick, red-
lipped mouth, beholding which grimace Sir Marmaduke frowned slightly, and, stooping swiftly, he picked
up the bonnet.

"A woman here—eh, Jimmy?"

"Yes, Tom, a lady—came in along of our friend
here, as wet as Venus rising from the sea and as lovely,
as handsome as——"

"A lady and handsome, eh, Jimmy?   I'll judge o'
this later, but first I'll eat my supper."

"So you shall, Tom, there's plenty o' cheese
and——"

"Cheese?" exclaimed the other with an evil look,
"what about that stew—what?"

"The lady wanted it, Tom, and being a lady, and such a beauty, poor Jimmy couldn't refuse—now could I, Tom? You know Jimmy! And so——"

"I bought it!" said Sir Marmaduke, dryly.

"Eh—did ye so, be Gad! And for how much?"

"A fair price, Tom, a very fair——"

"Seven shillings!" said Sir Marmaduke.

"Seven—— Ha, demme, fork out, Jimmy!"

"Hold hard, Tom!" exclaimed Mr. Vamper, eluding the big man's fierce clutch. "Don't Jimmy always divvy up? Come over here, come on now and let me explain."

"Explain? Ha, damn ye, you're always explaining!" growled Tom, yet followed his companion into a shadowy corner. And seated beside the fire Sir Marmaduke watched them, the little man's quick gestures, the big man's slow responsive nods; also, at such times as the booming wind-gusts died away, he even caught snatches of their talk, but could make little of it.

"Yeamons, Tom, and plenty of it . . . he flashed his cole . . . and the delog, I tell ye . . . pretty dimber mort . . . and besides . . . reglar damber dell . . . and divvy's the word . . . you know Jimmy——"

Espying a stout length of wood within reach Sir Marmaduke took it up and began therewith to poke the fire thoughtfully, and thus he saw the thing he held had once been the spoke of a waggon-wheel.

And presently he was aware that the big man stood on the opposite side of the fire staring down at him across the leaping flame, but Sir Marmaduke continued to poke gently at the embers, serenely unheeding, until at length the big man spoke; and though word and speech were rough, yet in both Sir Marmaduke sensed again that same vague suggestion of breeding and refinement.

"What's the good word, pal?"

"Nothing!"

"Eh—you aint one of us, that's certain?"

"Most certain," answered Sir Marmaduke softly and without glancing up, "thank God!"

"Come, none o' your superior airs and graces unless you want trouble—do you?"

"That depends on circumstances."

"Circumstances be damned! Now what's your game? Tip us your lay?"

"Speak plainly."

"Well, who are ye and what?"

"A traveller."

"Where away?"

"Anywhere."

The man Tom laughed sneeringly:

"Ain't very sociable, are ye?"

"Very seldom."

"Well, it pays to be sociable with me—when I'm so disposed—I say, it pays and——"

Sir Marmaduke yawned behind three fingers.

"Ha—sleepy are ye, my lord?" snarled Tom.

"I am."

"Well now, see here. I'm socially inclined to-night and you've got a woman along, why not ask her to grace our fire-side?"

Then Sir Marmaduke looked at the speaker, at his thick brows and at that which cleft one asunder, the jagged white line of an ancient wound, a scar half hidden beneath dark locks of matted hair. So they stared upon each other eye to eye in a silence broken only by the mournful sobbing of the wind.

"Lord love us what a night!" exclaimed Mr. Vamper at length, glancing apprehensively from one grim face to the other; but still neither man stirred or spoke while the rioting wind smote and tore until the barn's ancient timbers creaked and groaned above the pitiless lashing of the rain. Then the man, Tom, questioned, sudden and loud, as if against his will:

"What the devil are you staring at?"

"The scar above your right eye-brow."

The heavy lidded eyes narrowed to shining slits, and the shaggy head jerked forward—peering.

"What of it?"

Sir Marmaduke's keen gaze shifted to the ragged, discoloured neckerchief that swathed the hairy throat.

"I am—wondering!" he answered. And for the third time the man, Tom, questioned in the same strange manner, as if the words were wrung from an unwilling tongue:

"Wondering what—what, I say?'

Sir Marmaduke yawned again and rose.

"Impossibilities," he answered, and nodding carelessly, sauntered over to the hay-pile in the distant corner, swinging the wheel-spoke lightly in his hand. There stood he a while looking down at Eve's dim form half-buried in the fragrant hay, but his slender brows were close-knit as in painful concentration of thought.

"Impossible!" he said within himself. "Impossible, it would be justice quite too poetic!"

Then mindful of his promise, he lay down within easy reach of Eve's hand; but his brow wore the same perplexed frown as he stared up at the warped roof-beams which, dim-seen in the vague firelight, seemed endued with stealthy movement and became things that writhed fantastic in the gloom.

"I must not sleep!" thought he, sighing in utter weariness. "I will not sleep!" But the hay was soft, its fragrance stole upon his drowsy senses a soothing anodyne; his eyes closed . . .

He awoke suddenly to a sense of desperate fear; a hand was upon his mouth, soft hair brushed his forehead, and in his ear a faint, faint whisper:

"John . . . oh, John, wake! Wake up! Hush . . . listen!"

Silence . . . for the wind it seemed had died away; a glimmering dusk, for the fire had sunk to a dull glow of rosy embers . . . and then, upon this silence, stole a soft, vague sound, heard only to be lost again, but which brought Sir Marmaduke to his elbow, every faculty painfully alert, for in this ominous, oft-repeated sound he sensed murder and a hateful evil that chilled him.

"Someone creeping . . . towards us . . . a hand . . . feeling along the wall!" said Eve, in the same dreadfully hushed whisper.

Sir Marmaduke loosed her tremulous hold and, groped about in the hay with desperate fingers until they clenched upon the wheel-spoke; then slowly, stealthily he got to his knees, to his feet; and crouching thus, wide eyes staring upon the dark, every tense nerve and sinew strung for merciless conflict, the high-bred, fine gentleman was quite lost in the elemental man, a fierce, savage creature desperately calm and therefore deadly.

The stealthy rustling drew nearer, nearer yet . . . Sir Marmaduke kept his wide gaze upon the faint glow of the fire . . . now he distinguished the soft sound of a creeping foot . . . suddenly the fire-glow was blotted out, before him loomed a moving shape . . . a head, shoulders, arms—Sir Marmaduke leapt and smote . . . tripped, recovered and struck again, heard a dreadful, neighing cry, saw long, shadowy arms wildly up-tossed and, using the wheel-spoke like deadly small sword, lunged with unerring aim . . . A groan, a heavy fall, and then a moment's deathly stillness, a silence split all at once by a high-pitched, quavering cry:

"Tom! Tom! Oh, Tom!"

Sir Marmaduke, glaring down at his handiwork, was conscious of a wild patter of feet, the rattle and creak of wide-flung door, and then of Eve's voice.

"John—ah, dear John, art safe?"

"Quite safe."

"What—oh, John, what was it?"

"Villainy!" So saying, Sir Marmaduke stooped above the sprawling thing at his feet and dragged it towards the smouldering fire upon which he piled a handful of brush which, bursting to crackling flame, showed him the man, Tom, with a trickle of blood oozing from an ugly contusion half-hidden in matted hair; but it was not at this Sir Marmaduke looked but rather at the old scar which marked his brow, he even drew back the shaggy locks to examine this the better; thence his quick, slim fingers went to the stained neckerchief, wrenched it loose and tearing open the shirt collar, laid bare the hairy throat whereon, plain in the fire-light, he saw that which he sought.

Sir Marmaduke recoiled, rose to his feet and stared down at the unconscious man, his breath whistling through sudden-distended nostrils, then he glanced towards that spot where lay the wheel-spoke.

"John, is he—dead?"

"Not he!" answered Sir Marmaduke between white teeth, and stooping he began to drag the man towards the open door.

"Ah, what now, John?"

"His place is outside in the mud, Eve-Ann. Yes, he will be safer—outside."

"But it still rains—he may die, John.'

"I don't think so," answered Sir Marmaduke grimly, "but if he does I prefer him to do his dying—outside." So saying, and while Eve stood watching with terrified gaze, Sir Marmaduke dragged his still unconscious antagonist out of the barn and, shutting the great door, barred and made it fast; then coming back to the fire, stood looking down into the flames, his handsome features serene no longer.

And presently Eve stole near and ventured to touch his nerveless hand, questioning him fearfully:

"John? Oh, John, what is it? What makes thee seem so fierce . . . so terrible?"

Sir Marmaduke bowed his head, and for a moment covered his face with his hands, when he looked up he was smiling.

"Here was an evil thing, Eve-Ann," said he, his voice and look serene as ever, "but it is gone, and you may sleep secure, child."

"Sleep? Ah, no, indeed I couldn't. 'Tis a hateful place, this, pray let us go."

"Why 'twill be cold and wet, child, let us rather sit here beside the fire and wait for the dawn." So he brought cloak and great-coat and made for her a nest; and here they sat, side by side, staring into the fire and listening to the desolate beating of the rain, and each of them very silent, until she dozed at last, and so fell asleep, her head pillowed upon his knee; and thus, his sombre gaze bent ever upon the fire, Sir Marmaduke waited the new day.

Very still he sat there through the long hours while the fire languished and died all unheeded, for in his mind he was back when the world was younger and knew again the agony of heart-break and disillusionment, and was tormented anew of those youthful sorrows he had striven so long and vainly to forget, and thus was darkness within him and without.

But, little by little came a vague glimmer, a grey dusk, an ever-growing brightness, and lifting heavy head, he saw the ancient barn, its every chink and crevice, a darting glory of sunshine, for it was day. But still he sat there, watching a sunbeam that stole across the floor until at last it reached the lovely face upon his knee and, sighing, Eve awoke, and opening drowsy eyes, blinked and shaded them from the glory the better to look up into the face above her.

"John!" sighed she, and smiled up at him. "I was dreaming o' thee."

"And what was your dream, child?"

But now she sat up to smooth her garments and order her ruffled hair, looking at him with eyes suddenly shy.

"So then I did sleep, John, and left thee to watch alone—and oh—upon thy knees, thy poor legs will be so cramped and stiff—oh shameless, thoughtless me! And thou'rt so pale and worn, my poor John! Soon thou shalt sleep and I watch over thee, but not in this hateful place! Come, let us go—out into the sunshine."

"First tell me your dream, Eve-Ann," said he, sitting to rub at his cramped limbs.

"Nay, 'twas merely one o' my vain and foolish dreams," she answered, shaking her head. "Pray let us go."

And so, when he had donned great-coat and knapsack, he opened the door, his brows knit above eyes that glanced expectant this way and that—to see only a world, all fresh and tender green, backed by a cloudless heaven, whence beamed the young and kindly sun, for the man, Tom, had vanished utterly.

"Oh, John," said she, looking upon the day gladeyed, "'joy cometh in the morning!' Behold this sweet, clean earth!" and she reached out shapely arms as if she would embrace it all. "Oh surely, surely God is very good and goeth ever beside us, so smile John—do now!"

Then Sir Marmaduke smiled, and Eve-Ann, slipping her hand within his arm, led him out from the gloom of the barn into the radiant glory of the new-born day.

CHAPTER XIV

WHICH INTRODUCES ONE, HORACE, A SOMEWHAT REMARKABLE ASS

SIR MARMADUKE, still somewhat bemused with sleep, sat up in the ditch and looked about him expectantly; it was a dry, grassy ditch where wild flowers bloomed, and honeysuckle breathed its sweetness upon him from the hedge above; birds twittered, butterflies hovered, larks soared carolling, a brook bubbled softly near by, the sunny air was full of a joyous stir, but Sir Marmaduke, little heeding, glanced about anxious-eyed, and thus caught sight of a scrap of paper pinned to his sleeve, whereon in bold, round caligraphy he read these pencilled words:

"Dearest friend John,

"I am gone to seek our dinner. Wait and do not worry for

"thy loving friend, Eve.

"P.S. Take care of this pin, I have so few."

Having read which, Sir Marmaduke leaned back, luxuriating in his ditch, and what with the lark's joyous carolling, the brook's glad ripple and the fragrance of earth and flower, felt uncommonly glad to be alive.

"Orris!" exclaimed a harsh voice at no great distance, "consarn y'r mangy 'ide, do that agin an' I'll gie ye a touch o' the tickler. You ain't got no respect for nothin' nor nobody and I 'ates ye! Anyone could 'ave ye for fi' bob as would be fool enough to gi'e s'much for a lop-eared limb o' Satan. . . . Take ye snufflin' nose out o' that saucepan or I'll 'eave my gully at ye! And leave them boots alone, ye warmint—a gent's toddlin'-cheats aint to be dewoured no more than 'is dicer! An' keep y'r willainous 'oof out o' the fryin'-pan will ye, ye wagabone!"

Now turning whence this admonishing voice proceeded, Sir Marmaduke found himself looking through the hedge, down into a deep, green hollow or dingle shaded by trees and screened about by blooming thickets; and here, perched upon a stool before a small tent, sat a little, plump man weaving a basket of rush, from which occupation he glanced ever and anon to reproach, thus fluently, a diminutive and very touzled donkey who cropped the herbage, above, below and around, at the end of a long rope.

"Orris," exclaimed the little man, pausing to shake his fist. "Orris, I 'ates ye—ah, from muzzle to rump, 'oof and 'air! I'd drownd ye in b'iling ile if ile was only cheaper."

Hereat the donkey raised shaggy head and, chewing busily, wagged first one ear and then the other.

"That's owdacious imperence, that is!" snarled the little man. "I've a good mind t' boot ye in the belly for a ill-conditioned wiper, that I 'ave!"

The donkey stamped a hoof and snorted.

"All right, Orris me lad, you wait! I knows a cove as'll gimme as much as two-pun-ten for ye, an' more fool 'im! A cove as'll treat ye crool 'ard, me lad, a cove as'll kick y'r inside out an' in again, and expect ye to work into the bargain—sure as me name's Samivel Spang."

The donkey tossed his head and, whirling about, lashed out with both hind legs, whereat his master started back so suddenly that he fell off the stool.

"Now jest for that," cried he, rising in a fury, "I'm a goin' to boot ye in the bowels!"

"Don't do that, Mr. Spang."

The little man started round and, espying Sir Marmaduke looking down from the hedge above, stared up with very round eyes set in a very round face.

"D'jer s'y?" he demanded. "'S that?"

"I desired you not to kick your ass."

"Why not? Ain't 'e allus up to 'is devil's tricks an' capers?"

"The ass, I believe, is generally regarded as a patient animal——"

"Patient? Look at Orris' Bit me in the breeches last Sunday, an' what d'ye say to that?"

"Surprising!"

"It were!" nodded Mr. Spang with reminiscent scowl, "and painful, too! An' not content wi' that, didn't 'e bite a lump out o' me dicer this very day?"

"Dicer?" inquired Sir Marmaduke, gravely.

"Ah, me castor, me 'at! Now ain't 'e a windictive toad?"

"Still, don't kick him, pray."

"Why not? Ain't 'e my property?"

"Until someone buys him," answered Sir Marmaduke, viewing the donkey with speculative eye.

"Oo?" demanded the little man scornfully. "Oo'll buy a four-legged piece o' willany like Orris?"

"I will."

"Wot—you?"

"I will give you—two pounds ten for him."

"Yes, you will!" exclaimed Mr. Spang in bitter irony. "Walker, young feller!"

"And here is your money," said Sir Marmaduke, taking out his purse. The little man became thoughtful.

"'Ow much?" he inquired.

"I will take him for the price I over-heard you name, two pounds ten."

Mr. Spang shook his head violently:

"Don't you never think no such thing. Two-pun-ten? I tell ye five golden guineas couldn't buy my Orris! there's a donkey as is all ass, every bit— a reg'lar proper moke is my Orris, fit as a fiddle an' nary a particle wrong with 'im but himperence, dang 'im! There's lots o' mokes in this wicked world, but there's only one Orris and fi' pun won't buy 'im—no!"

"I'll make it ten!"

"Lord!" gasped Mr. Spang, sitting down upon his stool very suddenly. "Ten pun for Orris—!"

"Guineas!" said Sir Marmaduke, jingling the coins. "Ten guineas for Horace, the tent yonder, pack-saddle and complete outfit."

"Blind me!" ejaculated Mr. Spang, "Governor, it's a go, strike me blue if it ain't! Tip us the blunt."

Forthwith Sir Marmaduke descended the steep bank and, having counted the money into the little man's eager hand, turned to survey his new possessions which Mr. Spang obligingly enumerated, thus:

"One donkey, a tent, two pots, a kittle, two mugs —one tin, t'other cracked, a pack-saddle, a fork, one ,orn spoon and—a tickler."

"A what?" inquired Sir Marmaduke, whereupon Mr. Spang showed him a stout crook-handled stick armed with a long, iron spike.

"This here!" he explained, "this tickler is about the only thing in this yer wicked world as Orris 'as got any respect for. The King? No! The Pope o' Rome? No! But this 'ere? Watch now! Orris, ye warmint—the tickler!" So saying, Mr. Spang, flourish-ing the stick approached the donkey, whereupon that astute animal dropped a vivid hued object he had been munching and backed away to the fullest stretch of his picket-rope.

"What was he eating?" enquired Sir Marmaduke.

"Why—b'ile an' blister 'im," exclaimed the little man, snatching up the mangled object, and shaking

mournful head over it, "t'is me noo neckerchief, me
Sunday wipe!" And, fired by indignation, he turned
upon the offending animal, but Sir Marmaduke interposed:

"Pray don't strike my donkey," said he gently.

"Eh—not? But jest look at me ruinated wipe!"

"What is it's value?"

"Cost me a tanner at Petworth fair las' week, it did."

"Accept this shilling."

"A bob!" ejaculated Mr. Spang. "Lord!"

"A donkey must eat," said Sir Marmaduke gravely,
"and since he is my property I must keep him in fodder.
So here is the shilling, pray return him your neckerchief."

"Well, blow my dickey!" exclaimed Mr. Spang,
pocketing the shilling, "I never heered tell o' feedin'
wipes to a moke afore, but if you says so why—there
y'are!" And he tossed the neckerchief to the donkey,
who snuffed at it, mouthed it superciliously, and finally
chewed at it blissfully, his eyes half shut and ears
a-dangle.

"He appears to relish it," said Sir Marmaduke thoughtfully.

"Ah!" growled Mr. Spang. "'Tis a shame and a
pity as we ain't got a flat-iron or so to foller my
wipe."

"Are there any oats included in the outfit?" inquired Sir Marmaduke, still watching his four-legged
purchase with profound interest.

"Oats?" exclaimed Mr. Spang, opening his round
eyes very wide, "If you was to feed that creeter oats
'e'd be climbin' trees like a perishing squirrel."

"Hay, then?"

"'Ay?" repeated Mr. Spang, shaking his head, "'Ay
'ud be champagne an' eysters to Orris. No, young
feller, grass is 'is feed, with a occasional thistle and
anything else 'e can steal—look at me dicer, will ye!"
And Mr. Spang took off his hat, a woefully shabby

I

object, and pointing to its mutilated brim, shook mournful head at it. "Good as noo—afore that warmint tried t'eat it!" he sighed. "Cost me seven bob and only——"

"And his name is Horace, is it?'

"No it ain't! Orris is 'is monnicker vith a Ho an, a Har, an' a Hi an' a Hess. And ye needn't stare, young feller, for Sam Spang can write an' cypher, ah and read print and some writin' if wrote plain. . . . And remember when Orris gits obstropolus a touch o' the tickler will work like a charm. . . . An' I won't say as you ain't treated me fair, except in regard to me dicer as your moke ruinated as you can see."

"But the animal was not my property then,' said Sir Marmaduke, smiling.

"No more 'e were!" sighed Mr. Spang. "I may as well toddle off, I s'pose. Well, good-day young feller, good luck t' ye an' 'appy days."

"The same to you, Mr. Spang."

The little man scowled balefully at the touzled donkey, nodded cheerily to Sir Marmaduke and, climbing the steep bank with surprising nimbleness, paused suddenly to glance back.

"Orris ate a piece out of the tent last Toosday," said he, as if moved by sudden impulse, "but 'ang the pot-lid agin it an twill keep out rain an' wind."

"I am grateful for the suggestion," answered Sir Marmaduke.

"Don't mention it!" said Mr. Spang, taking a step forward only to pause again. "The kettle leaks 'ere an' there if it ain't pegged proper!" he announced.

"Then properly pegged it shall be, Mr. Spang."

"Likewise one o' the pots ain't got no 'andle and wants treating cautious!"

"Caution shall be my watchword, Mr. Spang."

"Under these carcumstances p'raps I ought to give ye back that theer extry bob as you allowed for me wipe?"

"A bargain is a bargain, Mr. Spang, but I thank you for the thought. The pack-saddle is in fair condition, I trust?"

"Young feller, that pack-saddle is so good it can werry nigh pack itself!"

"I rejoice to hear it. . . . Is that all, Mr. Spang?"

"Only this, sir—I can see as you're a gent, ah—an' a true-blue sportsman as well, and as sich, sir, Samivel Spang saloots ye most 'umble an' 'earty!"

So saying the little man doffed his battered "dicer" to wave it in farewell, whereupon Sir Marmaduke very gravely flourished the "tickler" in response, until Mr. Spang's round visage and plump person had vanished from his sight.

Then, seating himself upon the stool, Sir Marmaduke fell again to absorbed contemplation of this, to him, hitherto unknown quadruped, the so-called patient ass.

CHAPTER XV

Eve-Ann was coming along the shady cart-track,
moving with that lithe and gracious ease which spoke
of youth and the long, smooth action of vigorous
young limbs. And, sitting in his ditch, Sir Marmaduke watched her as he might the graceful wheel and
poise of skimming swallow, the fleet bound of fallow
deer in his own park, the effortless motion of fish a-
glimmer in pellucid depths—or any other beautiful
thing, until, becoming aware of the large basket she
bore, he rose and went to meet her.

"Egad!" he exclaimed as he took this burden from
her, "'tis even heavier than it looks!"

"Take heed lest thou spill the gravy, John—pray
keep it steady!"

"Gravy, forsooth?" he inquired.

"Yea, indeed! I met a farmer's wife, such a dear,
kind soul, and bought of her a steak and kidney pie,
John!"

"Excellent, child! And I have bought an ass whose
name I strongly suspect to be Horace."

"Nay, but John," said she, looking at him a little
anxiously, "what dost mean?"

"Also a tent, two pots and a kettle!"

"Art dreaming, John?"

"Come and see!" Forthwith he led her down into
the leafy dingle where they found Horace devouring

a rush-mat with great apparent gusto and who, champing serenely, raised touzled head to cock one shaggy ear and roll an inquiring eye at them. Quoth Sir Marmaduke:

"Eve-Ann, permit me to bring to your notice one, Horace, the future companion of our wanderings."

"Oh," laughed Eve delightedly, "how wise he looks!"

"A noticeable fact, child, considering he is a donkey!"

"But the poor thing is hungry, John, famished!"

"Extraordinary!" said Sir Marmaduke, musingly. "Our Horace has already finished a fair-sized bandana neckerchief which, with a large rush mat, should satisfy the cravings of one small donkey. And yet who knows? The ass is as yet a profound mystery to me."

Thrusting her hand into the capacious basket, Eve drew thence a large carrot and proffered it to Horace, who raised his head to snuff at the delectable vegetable with quivering nostrils and, dropping the mat, reached forth velvet muzzle and very gently and delicately took the carrot from Eve's fingers.

"He's a dear!" she pronounced.

"I wonder?" murmured Sir Marmaduke.

"And needeth grooming—oh sadly, John!"

"True! On close inspection he looks deplorably moth-eaten, child. But come, let us examine our other possessions."

And truly delightful was it to behold the pleasure she took in everything, more especially a certain battered, three-legged pot:

"'Twill be so useful, John!" she exclaimed, viewing this grim object with kindling eyes.

"Two pots and a kettle!" said Sir Marmaduke, a little despondently. "I observe the kettle lacks a spout! One pot leaks, I am informed, and both are revoltingly dirty! We must throw them away."

"Oh—never, John! I can clean them, 'deed 'twill be a pleasure!"

"Amazing child!"

"And . . . the little tent," she exclaimed rapturously.

"The tent," said he, his gloom deepening, "now that I inspect it more nearly, is also extremely dirty."

"Nay, 'tis brown canvas, John."

"And has a large hole in it!" he sighed. "Though I am advised that a pot-lid, adequately secured——"

"I can mend it easily, John."

"Nevertheless, Eve-Ann, the tent is a grave disappointment."

"Then wherefore didst buy it?"

"Firstly because it was the sole tent available for instant purchase, and secondly because it looked remarkably well—at a distance."

"Didst pay much for it, John?"

"The vendor appeared satisfied."

"Well, 'tis a dear little tent, and I shall love it."

"God bless you, child—such gratitude for so little! The thing must serve you until we can acquire a better."

"But I want no better, and indeed thou'rt very good to me, very thoughtful—this tent means so much."

"Its late possessor," said Sir Marmaduke, eyeing it a little dubiously, "seemed reasonably clean, still I think I'll pitch it in a new place, say under the tree yonder—if you care to sleep in this dingle to-night."

"Yea verily, 'tis a beautiful spot, so very solitary, John, and with a little brook over there by the willows, so we will bide here to-night. Besides, there is the steak pie must be heated, so I'll make a fire."

"Then I will move your tent."

Taking off his coat Sir Marmaduke set to work forthwith, and after no little difficulty contrived to get the tent down, a tangled disorder of canvas, poles and guy-ropes, which he hauled to the place chosen, a sheltered spot adjacent to the murmurous rill, where shady tree and bush made a leafy bower.

The afternoon had been calm hitherto, with scarce a breath to fan the drowsy leaves, but no sooner did Sir Marmaduke begin to erect the tent than up sprang a sudden, elfish wind to hamper him, a wind that frolicked with flapping canvas, and turned what should have been a tent into a fluttering, flapping perversity, a thing seemingly endowed with fiendish life, that mocked his lack of skill and set his most determined efforts at defiance. With admirable patience he strove to order this chaos of rebellious canvas, but as time passed, and his every attempt wholly futile, he grew hot, flurried, angry, and the struggle between himself and this elusive thing became a combat bitter and grim. To and fro he reeled, battling fiercely with this Thing that was no longer a tent but a detested monster rather.

Thus at last when came Eve thither to fill the battered kettle, she beheld Sir Marmaduke completely involved in wildly-flapping canvas and flying guy-ropes.

And then, of course, the wind dropped, and, breathless and perspiring, he turned to see Eve leaning against a tree helpless with silent laughter:

"Oh, John," she gasped, "forgive me that I laugh at thee, but . . . oh, John!"

Sir Marmaduke frowned and threw back haughty head.

"Eve-Ann!" he exclaimed.

"Don't!" she cried. "Oh, pray don't be dignified, John!"

Sir Marmaduke laughed suddenly and mopped perspiring brow.

"By heaven," he exclaimed, staring ruefully at the tangled heap of canvas, "anyone who can set up a tent unaided has my profoundest respect."

"And now, pray let me aid thee."

And so between them they contrived to pitch the tent securely at last, which done, Eve surveyed it glad-eyed:

"Oh!" she exclaimed, "'twill be joyous to live out o' doors!"

"So long as the weather prove fair!" he added.

"Nay, what matter if one be happy, John?"

"Are you happy, Eve-Ann?"

"Yes," she answered, and then paused to stare down at the sparkling brook sombre-eyed. "Yes, I am very happy—until I remember."

"Then forget," he retorted, "forget the world and its worries, child."

"But will the world forget us, John."

"Assuredly, in time, as it forgets everyone and everything."

"Dost think I am as safe here as in London?"

"Quite!" he nodded.

"And—art thou happy also, John?"

"Astoundingly!"

"I wonder why?"

"Heaven knows—perhaps because of the novelty."

"Only that, John?"

"Or my amazing appetite."

"Is that all, John?"

"Child, this is the abiding wonder." Now here Eve-Ann suddenly glanced at him, and as suddenly turned away, so that, wondering, he questioned her:

"What is it?"

"Nothing."

"Have I angered you?"

"Oh no!" she answered with petulant gesture of rounded shoulder.

"Eve-Ann, what are you thinking?"

"That 'tis time I fed thee again." Then, having filled the battered kettle, she hurried away, leaving him to stare after her in amazed perplexity.

CHAPTER XVI

OF GABBING DICK, A PEDDLER, HIS NEWS

THE steak and kidney pie was no more, and Sir Marmaduke, lounging beside the cheery fire, knew that sense of placid and reposeful comfort which is the aftermath of a good supper (or should be); but all at once, becoming aware of a dismal wheezing, he sat up to peer into the adjacent shadows, for evening had fallen and the leafy dingle was full of a fragrant dusk.

"It sounds as though someone were choking," said he, rising.

"Horace!" exclaimed Eve. "'Tis Horace, he must have wound himself up again. He will go round and round trees until his rope chokes him, the poor thing!"

"The foolish ass!" quoth Sir Marmaduke, and going in among the thickets, presently found Horace sure enough with his long picket rope lapped and twisted about bush and tree, and himself a prisoner, his touzled head close against a tree-trunk, the very picture of patient dejection. Forthwith Sir Marmaduke proceeded to unwind him, an intricate business requiring both time and labour, meanwhile apostrophising the meek-seeming animal thus:

"Horace, thou art by nature a veritable ass, and yet, being an ass of experience, one would have thought——" he paused suddenly arrested by the wholly unexpected sound of a man's harsh voice, and hastening where he might glimpse the fire, beheld a squat, dark-visaged fellow with a great pack on his back who stood staring at Eve across the leaping flame.

"So there y'are, Eve?" he was saying, "But not by y'self, I'll lay odds!"

"How—how dost know my name?" she questioned breathlessly, yet facing the intruder steady-eyed.

"Because you're a ooman, ain't ye?'" growled the man. "And every ooman's a Eve and all Eves is bound to trouble some Adam, 'tis only nat'ral! Ah, by Goles, if 'twasn't for the first Eve I might ha' been driving my coach-an-four in the gardin o' Eden at this minute 'stead o' peddlin' truck as nobody don't want—dang 'em! Ah, an' wot's more——" The man paused to turn sharply as Sir Marmaduke stepped into the fire light.

"Aha, so 'ere's Adam—eh?" nodded the man. "I knowed there'd be a Adam for such a good-lookin' Eve, there allus is. 'Ow goes it, Adam?"

"What do you want?" demanded Sir Marmaduke, frowning.

"To sell ye a broom or a belt, a mop, a knife or a neckerchief—wot'll ye take?"

"Nothing, thank you."

"I thought not! Then wot about a pair o' garters for Eve?"

"No."

"Well, say a razor for y'r noble self."

"Nothing, I tell you."

"Very good, then seein' as England be a free country and me a free-born Briton I'll set down an' eat me bit o' supper an' warm me aching bones at this 'ere fire, an' no thanks to nobody for axing me!" And to Sir Marmaduke's indignant astonishment he loosed off his pack and sat down forthwith.

"Get up!" said Sir Marmaduke.

"Not me!" answered the Peddler, busy with his pack. "Oh, it ain't no good a s-cowling at me, Adam, no nor lookin' so 'igh an' 'aughty, not a bit. Y'see this ain't no private drorin-room, nor yet a perfumed boodwar, and you ain't got no more right 'ere than me——"

"Get up!" repeated Sir Marmaduke with threatening gesture.

"Nay, John," said Eve, gently interposing, "do not drive him away."

"And there y'are, Adam!" nodded the Peddler triumphantly. "Ark to Eve! And it ain't no good comin' any vi'lence, I'm used to vi'lence, I am. Besides Eve ain't agoin' to stand by an' see a innercent cove 'armed—not she. So sit down Adam an' put up wi' me for a bit, I ain't so bad as I look."

Sir Marmaduke laughed and, sitting beside Eve, surveyed the intruder curiously.

"Hast travelled far, friend?" inquired Eve, viewing the man with eager intensity as he champed and snorted over his food.

"Reigate!" he mumbled.

"Dost know the country well—hereabouts?"

"Ah, every road, cross-road, lane an' footpath."

"Then . . . dost hear much news?"

"Noos?" cried the Peddler so suddenly that he choked. "Noos—I should think so! Lord, I'm so full o' noos as a egg o' meat! And wot I 'ears I tells, so they calls me Gabbin' Dick. I ain't wot you may call a merry-soul p'raps, nor yet a ch'ice sperrit, but I'm choke-full o' information, an' can tell ye a powerful lot about the dark doin's o' this wicked world an' mankind in general, for all folks bein' born in sin, bred in sin an' consequently sinful, sins constant—which is only to be expected. Ah, folks have been sinning ever since Cain killed Abel, which was murder, wasn't it? Very well then, folks has been murderin' each other ever since, an' a good job too, for I 'ates mankind—dang 'em! I says. And talkin' o' murder—"

"We will not!" said Sir Marmaduke.

"And why not, Adam? There's nothin' like a good murder, I loves to tell of a fine murder wi' plenty o'——"

"Enough!" said Sir Marmaduke, sharply.

"Oh pray . . . pray let him speak!" said Eve leaning eagerly towards the Peddler, her eyes very wide and hands tight clasped.

"Well, there's a fine murder just been——"

"Hold your tongue and go!" said Sir Marmaduke, rising.

"No, no! I must hear him," cried Eve, rising also. "Speak, friend, speak!"

"Well, there's a gent—keep y'r eye on Adam, Eve—just been murdered most shocking and crool, found wallerin' in 'is gore with 'is 'ead blowed off—and sarve 'im right, I says! Set me in the stocks 'e did for a vagrant, and now 'orrible dead, glory be!"

"Do they know who . . . who killed him, friend?"

"Ah, for sure. And because why? Because floatin' about in the gory blood they found——"

"Off with you!" exclaimed Sir Marmaduke advancing upon the Peddler, who rose nimbly as Eve stepped between them.

"What," she cried, "what did they find?"

"Why part of a gen'leman's cane wi' a gold knob on to it.

"No!" cried Eve in gasping voice. "Ah—no!"

"Yes!" nodded the Peddler. "Oh yes! A cane belongin' to a fine gent an' consequently they're arter this gent and they'll 'ang this gent an' a good job too! An' wot d'ye say to that now!" But Eve stood dumb, staring down into the fire with horrified gaze, her hands clasped as if in prayer, then turning suddenly she vanished into the tent.

"Ecod!" exclaimed the Peddler, smacking his lips, "there ain't been a prettier murder since——"

"Get out!" said Sir Marmaduke, "Go this instant!"

"Eh—well, so I will when I'm ready, so don't——"

Sir Marmaduke kicked over him a shower of sparks from the fire whereupon the Peddler sprang back, and caught up his pack:

"Burn me would ye?" he snarled. "Well then, I opes you burns, brimstone and sulphur, the fiery lake, I 'opes you burns soon, world without end, Amen!" So saying, he spat venomously into the fire and trudged heavily away.

Then Sir Marmaduke began to make up the fire, for the night was upon them, in the midst of which occupation he glanced up and saw Eve watching him.

"Oh, John," said she in reproachful, weeping voice, "thou dost make life very hard, very difficult for me, for now—now must I confess to thee I did not kill Squire Brandish."

"Of course not," answered Sir Marmaduke busy with the fire, "I knew this from the first . . . at least, almost——"

"Then why—why didst go back and leave thy cane? Why didst seek to shield me?"

"Because you were trying to shield—someone else.'

"Oh, John," she murmured, clasping her hands in that reverent gesture he knew so well, "thou brave, noble, wicked John to place thy life in such peril! And yet . . . 'tis my fault, all mine . . . God forgive and pity me! Suppose thou'rt taken, how canst prove thine innocence?"

"Why 'tis for them to prove my guilt," he answered lightly. "And I am not taken yet. Moreover, to one who has been a hunter there is an engaging novelty in becoming the hunted——"

"That thou shouldst be hunted!" she exclaimed with sudden passion. "Oh miserable me . . . thou art in the very shadow of the gibbet! Forgive me, John, forgive me!" And falling on her knees before him she hid her face in her hands.

"Child, do not grieve," said he, touching her bowed head very tenderly, "Go to bed, Eve-Ann, these terrors

will quite vanish with the morning, so get you to bed."
And taking her two hands he raised her gently.

"Thou wonderful John!" she whispered, looking at
him through her tears. "Surely there is no man in
the world like thee! Good night, my brother!" Then
suddenly her warm lips were upon his cheek, his mouth.
"God bless and shield thee, brother!" she murmured,
and so left him. And presently Sir Marmaduke lay
down in sheltered corner hard beside the fire and,
rolled in his blankets, composed himself to sleep.

CHAPTER XVII

He awoke suddenly to see Eve-Ann leaning above him in a rosy dawn.

"Eh . . . ah, yes, child?" quoth he, stifling a yawn and glancing about, sleepy-eyed.

"Breakfast . . . 'tis—'tis nearly ready!" she answered, turning from him to the fire that burned cheerily.

"Breakfast!" he repeated. "But why so early, the sun is scarcely risen? Why, what troubles you, child?" he questioned, sitting up, for he saw her pale and anxious.

"Thyself, John!" she exclaimed, with strangely passionate gesture of her shapely hands. "O, 'tis thee and thy . . . gold-knobbed cane! Last night I dreamed horribly . . . that they had taken thee . . . were dragging thee away to shameful death! Then I woke . . . and every rustle of the leaves a terror! So I came and mended the fire and watched over thee, imploring the Lord to thy protection . . . and all about us the shadows—so menacing! And I full o' terror for thee . . . even whiles I prayed."

"Yet surely all heaven heard your prayers, Eve-Ann, for behold the night is gone! And yonder comes the sun in glory to promise another golden day. Also here are we, safe and sound, with none to trouble us but ourselves. . . . And the kettle, I observe, is on the boil, so if you will spare me some hot water and the mirror I will retire to some shady grove and, there sequestered, shave myself."

"Then art not angry I should ha' waked thee so early?" she inquired, smiling a little tremulously as she busied herself eagerly to serve him.

"Eve-Ann, I am profoundly grateful. Hark to the birds! List to the kettle! Behold the sun!—and, as I live, there in the pan ready for the fire—bacon!"

"No, John, a gammon rasher."

"Excellent! And yourself, Eve-Ann, as glorious as the morning—though a little heavy-eyed—a veritable dryad!"

"John, what is a dryad?"

"A goddess o' the woods."

"O!" she exclaimed softly. "A goddess? That sounds a little blasphemous, doesn't it?" And flushing beneath his look, she drooped her eyes with an unwonted shyness, and thus contrived to become lovelier than ever.

"It is very truth!" said he solemnly. "Indeed, what with your noble shape and gracious carriage, no dryad or goddess might compare . . . for child, I vow . . . you are strangely beautiful this morning."

"Nay," she murmured, "and my hair so wild . . . half-tumbling down! I did not trouble with it this morning, I were too unhappy."

"Your hair? Indeed yes, that's it, I think, it must be. Child, take off your little cap."

"Nay, 'twill all come down then, John."

"I would see it so, Eve-Ann."

"But . . . John. . . ."

"Please, Ann."

So, with swift, shy gesture, she took off the plain, close-fitting small cap she always wore and, shaking her head, down fell her hair in rippling glory to her shapely hips.

"Why, Ann!" said he softly, "Eve-Ann . . . God-bless-my-soul!"

"What?" she whispered. "O what is it?"

"Yourself!" he answered, in the same hushed voice. "Your beautiful hair!"

"Nay, 'tis vanity . . . ah, 'tis wicked vanity!" she cried, and hid her face between sudden hands, "to stand before thee so . . . making wanton show o' myself. . . . O, I shall blush for this! Am I shameless, John? . . . No man ever saw me so, before, no not even my two dears, 'twould ha' shocked them, for they are truly Godly men! . . . And now . . . thou'rt a man, John, yet here stand I . . . O, I feel so wicked and worldly!"

"Yet look like an angel o' light! For, child, as I look at you——"

"Your shaving-water grows cold!" she cried, and, turning suddenly, fled from him into the little tent. Then, having collected the needful tools therefor, Sir Marmaduke went down beside the brook and, fixing the small looking-glass conveniently, proceeded to shave, in the midst of which operation he paused, for Eve-Ann was singing as she prepared breakfast; to be sure she sang very softly, and the air was somewhat lugubrious, but Sir Marmaduke smiled, recognising it for one of the penitential psalms.

And presently, wafted upon the sunny air stole odours delectable, fragrant coffee and the mouth-watering aroma of frizzling ham. So, having laved hands and face in the sparkling brook, he dried himself briskly, combed his hair hastily and hurried foodwards; to behold breakfast neatly set forth on snowy napkin, waiting to be discussed.

And when Eve-Ann had murmured grace, they sat down together and began to eat. Nor did he speak for some while then, setting down his half-emptied cup:

"O Ann—alas, Eve child," sighed he, "to think I have lived five and forty years and missed so much!"

"Dost mean the coffee and ham, John?"

K

"These among other things. I begin to discover joys in life quite new in my experience."

"Pray, John—what?"

"Our comradeship . . . for we are true friends and comrades, I venture to think. Agreed, Eve-Ann?"

"O, yea, verily, John!"

"So here sit two comrades, delightfully solitary and supremely content with such solitude and—each other. Agreed, Eve-Ann?"

"Verily, John."

"To be sure we are still a long way from London, comrade."

"How far, dost think?" she inquired, viewing him a little anxiously.

"Sixty miles, more or less. And to be sure you are anxious to get there——"

"Nay, anywhere," she exclaimed, "anywhere so long as we be together and thyself safe."

"Anywhere?" he repeated. "You mean?"

"Just anywhere!" she nodded. "'Tis no matter whither or what direction."

"Egad!" he exclaimed. "And once or twice I suspected you were a highly common-sense young woman!"

"Alas, I fear not!" she sighed, regretfully.

"Thank heaven!" he answered fervently.

"O, art glad, John?"

"Heartily, child, for there are few things I find more exasperating than Common-sense."

"But surely," said she, opening her grey eyes at him, "'tis a virtue folk do pride themselves upon?"

"I believe some misguided egoists do," he nodded, "but such unhappy wretches, so cursed, may never enter the golden joys of Arcady."

"And thy coffee will be cold, John!"

"Coffee?" he exclaimed. "Child, I am talking of Arcadia."

"Yes, I heard. But please drink thy coffee, 'tis so much better taken hot."

"And there spoke Common-sense! But the coffee is delicious so——!" here he emptied his cup with gusto and held it out to be refilled.

"Then I suppose," said she, busy with the coffee-pot, "I am common-sense, after all?"

"Only occasionally," he answered, watching the play of her sensitive lips, "for who ever heard of a common-sense goddess or dryad? The thing is impossible and absurd. Hence I entertain a strong and growing hope that you possess no more common-sense than myself."

"But, pray tell me, John, is not Common-sense Wisdom?"

"To my thinking it is often Wisdom's opposite. And its other names are: Low-cunning, Prudence, Policy, Calculation . . . indeed, it is a very matter-of-fact, uncomfortably chilly thing to clip the soaring pinions of Imagination and clog the foot of Adventurous Enterprise. For Common-sense loves the beaten track, the well-worn road, the safe way."

"Yet surely 'tis a safe-guard, John?"

"And as surely a fetter, Eve-Ann!"

"And what is Arcady, where is it?"

"The French, being a singularly daring people, say it is in Paris and call it the Elysian Fields, the Saxons named it Valhalla, the Buddhists Nirvana, the Greeks Elysium, the Jews, Eden. But all true Arcadians know it for the world of great, simple things where Contentment meets and takes us by the hand."

"Art thou so content, John?"

"I am."

"Because o' the coffee and ham?" she enquired, with sudden smile.

"And . . . other things."

"Pray what other?"

"Well, firstly, yourself, child."

"O! And how do I content thee?"

"Because you are so exactly what I think you."

"And mam—no wonder!" said the game-keeper, touching bushy eye-brow.

"Now supposing," said Sir Marmaduke, his keen gaze still upon the man's battered features, "supposing we invited Twister's master to drink a cup of very excellent coffee?"

"Why then, young cove, I 'spose I might say thankee.'"

"Then you are heartily welcome—so sit down, Bob o' Battle."

"Eh?" exclaimed the man with a kind of pounce, and became at once a creature transfigured; his sombre eyes brightened, his cheeks flushed, his grim mouth curved to sudden smile, and he beamed upon Sir Marmaduke as he had been a long-lost brother.

"Lord love ye, comrade," said he in shaken voice, "you warms my very 'eart—ah, that ye do. Nobody ain't so called me this ten—ah, fifteen year—shake, brother, shake!"

So up rose Sir Marmaduke and grasped the extended hand, while Eve looked from one to the other, great-eyed.

"Fancy you a-reckernising o' me, young covey! Fancy you aknowing Bob arter arl these years! Lord love both on us!"

"Eve-Ann," said Sir Marmaduke, "I present to you Battling Bob o' Battle, one of the gamest, one of the cleanest men that ever tossed hat into ring, a singular adornment to the Fancy."

"Indeed, John?" she answered, acknowledging the introduction with smiling nod, "but pray what kind o' fancy?"

"Mam," explained the old fighting-man, "your 'usband means the P Har . . . the Game, mam, the Ring . . . fightin'."

"Ah, you were a soldier?"

"Lord love your pretty eyes, mam, no! I were a pug, a prize-fighter—a pugglist, mam."

"O!" exclaimed Eve with a little gasp.

"Six an' forty battles I fit, mam, and was only beat four times—which were Jem Belcher, Bob Gregson, Jack Barty and Natty Bell." So saying, the Battler set by his gun, seated himself upon the grass and, leaning broad back to convenient tree, beamed from Eve's glowing loveliness to Sir Marmaduke's aquiline features and smote mighty hand on brawny thigh:

"Lord love arl of us!" he exclaimed. "this be a rare treat for me, ye see it aren't often as folks remember me now-a-days, and if by chance some do, I dassent let 'em talk . . . ye see, I'm married! And though my Martha be still a fine figure of a woman—spite o' six children and arl doing well—Martha's Methody, oncommonly so, and is nat-rally set agin the Game and arl mention o' the Game . . . pore Martha's so Methody she can't see no good in the Game even now than she could the first time she see me—just arter I beat the Snob . . . to be sure I were a bit bloody-like. . . ."

"So this was why you gave up the ring, Bob?"

"Ay, 'twere arl along o' my Martha. Ye see she were a oncommon fine young creeter, though Methody, and I were in love wi' her then, like I am now. But when a cove's in love all the fight's took out o' that cove, and so to please Martha, I (here a profound sigh) quit the Game and (here another sigh) got married, and now wot wi' marriage and Martha so Methody I've growd that mild and meek 'twould as-tonish you, comrade. . . . An' now—fancy you a-knowing me! When did you see me fight, eh, my covey?"

"Very many times, Bob."

"Well, name a time, friend."

"I was at the ring-side when you beat Scroggins."

"So long ago, my lad! You must ha' been pretty young then, comrade?"

"I was, Bob. But then I'm a little older than I seem," answered Sir Marmaduke, glancing across at

Eve-Ann. "I also saw you beat Donelly, the Irish Champion."

"Did ye though. . . . Lord love ye there was a pot o' money changed 'ands that day! Them were the days I were fightin' for Sir Marmyjook Vane-Temperly and a mighty good patron 'e were . . . ah, a reglar, true-blue sportsman and bang-up Corinthian . . . 'twere 'im as thrashed and well-nigh killed Buck Mowbray in the Prince's Pavilion at Brighthelmston. I were there along o' the Prince an' sees it! 'By God', says the Prince, 'Marmyjook'll murder the Buck—part 'em, Bob, part 'em!' Which I dooly done, and the Prince tips me ten pound. . . . But there's me wi' a lump on me nob like a apple, and Buck Mowbray a smother o' blood and his eyebrow gashed open. . . . O' course they was to fight a dool wi' pistols——"

"His . . . eye-brow?" cried Eve-Ann, breathlessly.

"Ay, mam, my Governor, Sir Marmyjook, 'ad marked the Buck for life. . . . Ecod, there was wildish doings at Brighthelmston in them days! They was a wild hell-fire lot—saving your presence, mam—reckless and free they was, and sportsmen all, leastways—most on 'em. I mind how Sir Mar——"

"Suppose you tell us of your own doings, Bob?" suggested Sir Marmaduke glancing at Eve's intent face a little askance.

"Nay, friend," said she. "I pray thee tell us more about thy master, this Sir . . . Marmaduke."

"Why so I will, mam, and j'yfully, seeing 'twere him as took me out of his own stables and 'ad me trained for the Ring, God bless 'im! Though 'e were only Mr. Marmyjook then, for this were twenty odd years ago, and a tippy young blood 'e were too, so merry and affable with a laugh for everyone and everything, though a sight too wild an' reckless wi' his money . . . cards, d'ye see, mam, 'osses . . . anything."

"Ah, a . . . gambler, friend?"

"Gambler, mam? Lord love you, I should think so! Thousands at a sitting! O 'e were a proper young genelman, I promise you, and ekally ready to drink and fight wi' any man, being pretty tidy wi' the mauleys, d'ye see——"

"In fine, a young fool!" sighed Sir Marmaduke, gazing up into the cloudless sky, "so no more of him, Bob."

"Comrade," quoth the Battler ponderously, "I likes yer looks. I'm took wi' y'r talk and I'm drawed by y'r ways, but . . . I don't like that 'ere last remark, not by no manner o' means! 'Fool' I think it were?"

"'Fool,' Bob, yes."

"Well, my cove, I've worked for that genelman, I've ate that genelman's salt, I've fit for that genelman, ah, an wot's more, I've drank wi' that genelman! Consequently I must now ax you, very meek and 'umble yet determined-like, to take back that 'ere 'fool'."

"Very well, Bob. But now tell us about the time you fought John Barty——"

"Not so, friend," said Eve, refilling the Battler's cup. "I beg thou'lt tell us more concerning thy wild gentleman. . . . Did he fight the duel?"

"Why no, mam, 'e did not! Ye see, my genelman 'ad fit dooels afore—ah, many's the time."

"Ah, a duellist was he, friend?"

"Dooelist, mam—Lord love your pretty featers 'e was always at it . . . used to go over to France and shoot genelmen reg'lar, same as other sportsmen shoots game—ah, that 'e did! So this 'ere Buck Mowbray cuts 'is stick, as you might say, mam . . . 'ops out o' London, ah, and England too."

"And did . . . did thy gentleman . . . follow him?"

"'E sure-ly did, mam—went a-seeking and a-searching for the Buck arl the world over . . . this was

'ow I come to leave 'is service. . . . Sir Marmyjook
leaves 'ome, fame, friends an' fortin' to go a-lookin'
for the Buck . . . leaves 'is grand 'ouses be'ind,
not to mention the la——"

"Bob," exclaimed Sir Marmaduke, "you are letting
your coffee grow cold."

"Why, comrade, so I am, but when I talks of the
old times——"

"Friend," said Eve, gently persistent, "wert going
to say 'ladies', I think?"

"I were, mam. Ye see, being so young, rich and
dashing . . . sich a reglar Tippy and down-right
'eavy Toddler, the ladies was all very determined and
set on marrying' 'im, poor, young genelman!"

"Indeed, poor young man!" sighed Eve.

"The Duchess o' Camberhurst was allus trying to
marry 'im off to one or t'other on 'em and come precious
near a-doin' of it once! For the Duchess, though
small, were very determined for her size—a reglar
rasper!"

"Then this poor young man escaped being married,
did he, friend?"

"Well, I dunno, mam. I never 'eerd as any lady
got 'im . . . but then I never 'ear nothing now-a-
days."

"And where is he . . . to-day, I wonder?"

"Last time I 'eered tell 'e were back in London—
but that were years ago. Bless you, mam, 'e may be
dead."

"I . . . wonder?" said Eve, pulling the dog
Twister's nearest ear.

"Ah, them was the days!" sighed the Battler,
mournfully. "Him an' me, mam; across two bits o'
blood trying their paces—'cross country . . . 'edge
detch, fence and wall, straight as arrers! And me
never sure but I wouldn't 'ave to bring him 'ome a
corpse on a 'urdle! Lord love us, them was the days!
Look at me now . . . buried alive, nobody to talk

to about old times, Church twice o' Sundays, and
Methody at that! O love my eyes!"

"Yet you look hearty enough, Bob, ay—and confoundedly happy!"

The Battler lifted his round head sharply to glance
at Sir Marmaduke with sudden keenness:

"Eh, my cove," said he thoughtfully, "you aren't
always been padding it on the roads, no nor very long,
that's sure. . . . There's summat about you as
brings back old times oncommon——"

"The mention of 'time'," smiled Sir Marmaduke,
"warns me it is time I began to 'pack off'!"

"Suit y'rself, comrade, suit y'rself. There ain't no
call for you to 'aste nor yet 'urry . . . ecod you can
stay if ye will, my chap, and as long as ye will. Hows'-
ever 'tis time I went sure-ly . . . my Martha'll be
expectin' me so I'd better be off." Saying which,
Battling Bob o' Battle arose, albeit unwillingly, and
taking his gun, turned to Sir Marmaduke with hand
outstretched:

"Comrade," said he, "you've done me a power o'
good, wi' your talk, this day, and wot's more, young
feller, I'd like to meet ye again, for there's summat
about you as draws me amazin' . . . I rackon 'tis
y'r voice."

"But I haven't spoken much, Bob," laughed Sir
Marmaduke.

"Well then, mebbe it's the cock o' your eye, but
you brings back the old times remarkable strong. . . .
Ah, them was the days! Good-bye and good fortin'.
. . . And to you, mam, 'ealth and 'appiness, and
if your first's a boy may 'e tak' arter 'is father here!"

Then the Battler whistled to his dog and strode
away, gun on shoulder, leaving Eve-Ann with burning
cheeks and bowed head. As for Sir Marmaduke he
turned rather hastily and went in quest of Horace.

CHAPTER XVIII

WHICH IS, MORE OR LESS, ASININE

"I FEAR 'twill tumble off!" said Eve, surveying Horace's well-laden pack dubiously.

"Child," quoth Sir Marmaduke, wiping perspiring brow, "I venture to think not. The surcingle is reasonably light (here he scowled at broken finger-nail) and so is the strap."

"Yea, John, but that strap should go round his chest, I'm sure."

"That strap, Eve-Ann, is adjusted to a nicety, and in the precise place Nature intended! Were our Horace endowed with speech which, thank Heaven, he is not, he would himself admit the fact." At this precise moment Horace turned patient head and, chewing placidly, having surveyed the strap in question, wagged one ear derisively.

"Egad!" exclaimed Sir Marmaduke, "we seem to possess a somewhat extraordinary animal!" Even as the words were uttered, Horace shook himself, reared gently, and down slipped packsaddle and panniers, and freed thus, began to crop the grass serenely.

"Well . . . upon my soul!" exclaimed Sir Marmaduke, frowning in angry bewilderment until, hearing Eve's laughter he laughed also, though somewhat ruefully.

And when with Eve's ready assistance he had re-harnessed the patient animal, Sir Marmaduke took up that spike-shod staff hight Tickler and turned to

be gone and then stood, his gaze bent earthwards,
lost in sudden gloomy reflection.

"What is it, John? What troubles thee?"

"Yourself, Eve-Ann."

"How—pray how?" she questioned in swift anxiety.

"My dear child," he answered very solemnly, "I
fear I am no true friend to you."

"Nay, dear John."

"I mean that being so very much your elder it is
my duty to protect you and, more particularly, advise
you to the best of my judgment. Agreed, Eve-Ann?"

"Yea, John, but——"

"Then as your friend I do most earnestly beg you
to return home. There is nothing now may prevent
you, and to tramp all these weary miles to London
needlessly or upon the vague chance of finding a sister
who may not be there, is merest folly."

"Perhaps!" sighed she softly.

"Indeed it is most certain!" said he. "For you
are now quite aware that happily all danger . . .
all suspicions have been diverted from——"

"From me to thee . . . thy gold-mounted cane,
John!"

"Hence your troublesome journey becomes quite
unnecessary and, being a rational creature, you will
take my advice and instantly abandon it."

"Shall I, John?"

"Why, of course you will. . . . It is now," said
he, consulting his watch, "about thirty-three minutes
past eight and in four or five hours of reasonably sharp
walking——"

"Dost not desire my company any longer? O,
John, have I wearied thee already?"

"This has nothing to do with the matter," he
answered, a little peevishly.

"Nay, forgive me, but I think so," said she, gentle
but persistent. "So tell me, have I indeed worn out
thy patience so soon?"

"Nothing whatever of the kind," he answered, more peevishly. "Such suggestion is as preposterous and unwarranted as unjust!"

"O!" said she, meekly.

"I trample down my own desires in the matter that I may serve you the more faithfully, child. I mortify my own feelings——"

"O!" said she again, her meekness growing.

"And because I am indeed your friend, beg you to return at once to the comfort and safety of your home. . . . Child, I am advising you to your own good!"

"But, John," she murmured, gazing away into the sunny distance, "all you say is so very—common-sense!"

Sir Marmaduke blinked and eyed her somewhat askance.

"Also we are in Arcadia, aren't we, John?"

"Eve-Ann," said he, a little ponderously, "pray remark that I am profoundly serious!"

"Ay, but so am I!" she breathed.

"To lose yourself in London . . . friendless and without money—it would be madness."

"But thou'rt going there too," said she in the same meek and gentle fashion and with gaze still on the distance, "so I shall not be friendless, John."

Again Sir Marmaduke was stricken momentarily dumb:

"But think, Ann, think of the long, rough road——"

"'Deed I am!" said she, and smiled.

"Consider the innumerable annoyances and discomforts you must endure, the fatigue, the . . . weariness no delicate creature should have to encounter. Imagine all this——"

"I am, John—I have. And so 'tis I am truly grateful unto the good Lord for making me none delicate but strong and able. . . . So now, come—pray let us go on."

"Now . . . God bless me!" exclaimed Sir Marma-duke.

"Amen!" she answered softly. "I pray he may bless us both and bring us safely to . . . our journey's end! And . . . O, John, thou art not . . . not sorry to have me with thee? Say thou art not sorry."

"O child," said he in altered tones, "Eve-Ann, can you not guess . . .?" Then, beholding the look in her eyes, he leaned towards her impulsively, but checked himself, and turning away, grasped Horace's leading-rope.

"Heaven make me worthy of your trust, child," said he. And so they set forth together.

CHAPTER XIX

CONCERNS A WITCH AND VARIOUS OTHER EVILS

THEY went by shady woodland ways and field-paths pleasantly sequestered until the track they followed, having climbed a grassy slope, lost itself in an open heath where a soft wind met them, a fragrant air warm with the spicy odours of gorse and bramble; and here they paused to consult the compass and look about them.

Before them stretched the heath, a wide expanse, thick with bush and briar and dotted, here and there, with trees strangely gnarled and stunted; beholding which desolation, Eve shivered despite the kindly sun:

"Here is an evil place!" said she, glancing about apprehensively.

"To be sure these briars will make it awkward going."

"Then let us take another way, John."

"But our course lies north-westerly and——"

"O John," she whispered, "there is a man watching us, peeping . . . among the bushes yonder!"

Glancing up swiftly, Sir Marmaduke glimpsed a weather-beaten hat which, in that moment, vanished behind an adjacent thicket.

"You saw him, John?"

"Merely a wanderer like ourselves, child."

"But why should he watch us—so slyly?"

"Pray hold our Horace and I will inquire." So saying Sir Marmaduke advanced swiftly and peered round thicket only to see the elusive hat flit from view behind a bush farther away. Sir Marmaduke frowned, and hurrying forward, had a fleeting vision of a man's bowed figure, a man who, despite his awkward, crouching posture, ran very fast. Therefore Sir Marmaduke halted and beckoned to Eve whereat she hurried towards him a graceful, light-footed creature who, despite haste, contrived somehow to keep her petticoats free of the thorny tangles.

"Did'st see what like he was, John?"

"Yes, a small, mean fellow."

"He was not a . . . Bow Street officer? Art sure, John, art sure?"

"Quite sure, so do not worry, child." But reading dread in her eyes and in the quiver of her sensitive mouth, he began to talk of the "wonderful city" which had proved a never-failing source of interest ere now . . . "and London, Eve-Ann, has stood from time immemorial. Beneath her pavements lie the ruins of many another London—British, Danish, Saxon, Norman, age upon age and——"

"Dost think he may be a Bow Street officer in disguise?" she questioned suddenly.

"Good heavens——" he began, but checked suddenly for a voice, very harsh and discordant, was hailing from no great distance. They had entered a grove and here, pitched in the shade of one of these unlovely stunted trees, they espied a small and very dirty tent, and seated hard by this, an aged, wrinkled hag, herself as ragged, as grimy and unkempt as the tent; and now as they stood she cried out to them again in harsh croak and beckoned with skinny finger.

"Oho," she chuckled, peering up at them beneath a tangled mass of matted white hair, "aha, wot a fine genelman, to be sure, an' sich a bonny lady—O lor! Old Sal's peepers is precious sharp, me dearies, an' sees as far through a brick wall as most, so ye'd best be kind t'old Sal an' treat 'er generous, dearies, generous." Having said which, she chuckled, nodded, and sucked noisily at a short, black clay pipe.

Leaning upon Tickler, Sir Marmaduke surveyed this ancient being with profound interest.

"What do you want?" he inquired.

"A penny," she croaked, "spare a penny to poor, old Sal! Spare tuppence, spare a groat, spare a tanner —oho spare a shillin' to old Sal, my proper, 'andsome genelman!"

"And why do you name me 'gentleman'?" inquired Sir Marmaduke, thrusting hand into a pocket of his rough garments.

"Becos old Sal can see beyond 'er nose—aha, a sight beyond. Sich a noble genelman to be a-paddin' it in the dust . . . and the pretty lady too! Goin' fur, dearie, goin' fur, me pretty bird . . . London is it?"

But Eve was dumb, staring down at the leering old creature beneath wrinkling brows.

"London, oho! Mak' it five bob, me noble genelman, mak' it ten—say a guinea.—Say five!"

"Why should I give you five guineas?"

"Becos me eyes is so precious sharp! And your 'andsome face so noo shaved! And your fine, curly 'air noo cropped! And your delicate 'ands so white. And you sich a grand genelman! And me sich a old wise one as sees so much more than others can."

"What do you see?"

"Wot others is a-lookin' for, p'raps—oho! Wot others is a-seekin', eh—me fine genelman? So give old Sal six guineas an' she'll well-wish ye . . . ah, and wot's more she'll keep 'er trap shut and 'er clapper still, and 'er son's, and 'er grandson's—nary a tongue shall wag. And wot be seven guineas to such a grand genelman? Lor!"

Sir Marmaduke's delicate brows twitched slightly, and his eyes grew keenly alert.

"Seven guineas is a lot of money!" said he in gentle musing tones.

"Seven? O Lorramitey!" croaked the aged creature with cackle of laughter. "Us 'll mak' it eight
. . . an' wot be eight guineas to one o' the Quality—
lor!"

"Hum!" quoth Sir Marmaduke staring down into
the evil old eyes that leered up at him. "But tell
me, why should I pay you eight guineas?"

"For valley received!" she chuckled. "Aha, an'
cheap at the price! Oho, a valleyble as 'ud be cheap
at any price! So us'll mak' it ten guineas an' call it a
bargain—hey? Ten guineas for summat as is beyond
all price, dearie! Only ten guineas!" And she leered
up at him again, sucking wetly at her short, black pipe.

"Pray let us go!" said Eve, and slipped her hand
into his; but, sensing danger, he merely smiled at her
re-assuringly, and turned again to meet the cunning
eyes of the aged hag.

"Ten guineas, you said, I think?"

"Twelve, dearie! Twelve guineas for old Sal's
blessin', and summat as you couldn't buy from nobody
else so cheap. Fifteen guineas for summat as others
prices at fifty and I be only axin' you twenty
for——"

"So it is twenty guineas now?" smiled Sir Marmaduke. "And—for what?"

"Y'r life, dearie!" screamed the old woman, stabbing up at him with her pipe-stem. Eve's fingers
tightened suddenly on his and she gasped, whereat the
old woman nodded and chuckled in evil triumph.
"'Is life, my pretty!" she cried. "Only 'is life! And
all I ax is twenty-five guineas for poor, old Sal as
can see so much further——"

She paused suddenly in scowling bewilderment for
Sir Marmaduke was laughing:

"Poor ancient soul" said he, and tossed her a shilling. The old woman clutched up the coin with scrab-
bling claw-like fingers, raving the while and cursing
until she choked. Then Sir Marmaduke, turning to

be gone, beheld Horace (that omnivorous creature) chewing the tent-flap with much apparent relish, and thus for a moment Sir Marmaduke stared into the tent's dingy interior; then Eve seized the head-rope and drew the predatory animal away. Bur Sir Marmaduke yet stared in the one direction for within the tent he had glimpsed a face he instantly recognised; therefore, hearing the old woman calling him, back he went and watched while, gasping and grimacing, she drew a folded paper from beneath her ragged apron and thrust it at him. Then, turning his back to Eve, he unfolded this paper and saw it was a hand-bill, headed thus:

MURDER

FIFTY POUNDS REWARD
DEAD OR ALIVE

WHEREAS: upon the 11th inst. of June, Charles Brandish, Esq., of Radley Place, Harting, Sussex, was barbarously murdered by one believed to be A PERSON OF CONDITION, this gives notice that anyone laying such information as may lead to the apprehension of the BLOODTHIRSTY VILLAIN shall . . .

He had read thus far when the old woman clawed the paper from him and, hiding it beneath her apron, peered up at him with eager cupidity.

"Fifty pound!" she croaked. "And old Sal's price is only twenty-five guineas . . . only twenty-five, my noble genelman, an' I keeps me trap shut and me son's and me grandson's—nary a tongue shall wag, an' all for twenty-five guineas, dearie! Come, wot d'ye say now?"

Sir Marmaduke laughed again, and taking Horace's rope from Eve, on they went together while the old hag shrieked and raved and cursed herself breathless again.

And after they had gone some distance, Eve questioned him in troubled voice, casting a fearful glance behind.

"O, John, that terrible old woman was verily a witch."

"Perfectly!" he answered, a little absently.

"What was it she showed thee?"

"Showed me?"

"Yes, John, I mean the paper. What was written there?"

"Written, child? Why—ah—a kind of incantation to be sure, a mere thing of words."

"Tell me, John, did'st see within the tent?"

"A brief glimpse, yes."

"There was a man hiding there!"

"So I thought."

"But—O, John, did'st not see who he was?"

"He seemed very like the man, Jemmy Vamper, who sold us his companion's supper in the barn."

"Indeed, 'twas himself, and he surely recognised us."

"And what then, Eve-Ann?"

"I fear he means thee harm."

"Nay how should he trouble us? He knows nothing except that we are travellers who sheltered in a barn."

"But that dreadful old witch," said Eve shivering, "she suspected us I am sure."

"A singularly unlovely creature, a grisly harridan . . . and yet even she was innocent once, and perhaps reasonably clean and comely," said Sir Marmaduke, his keen eyes roving.

"Dost believe in spells and witchcraft, John?"

"Well, I believe in witchery, Eve-Ann, which is much the same but with a difference."

"But why should she suspect thee?"

"Heaven knoweth!" he answered lightly. "If she be truly a witch it was undoubtedly witchcraft, black magic, spells or enchantment——"

"Nay, John, 'tis no matter for idle laughter . . . yonder was evil. I feel it—I know it." Here Eve shivered and glanced back over her shoulder again . . . "And the Scriptures tell us there are witches."

"To be sure!" he nodded, "there was the Witch of Endor. . . . And yonder is a peculiarly attractive wood!" and directing her gaze thither with Tickler, he cast a swift, backward glance in his turn.

"Let us go that way, John, for I do love the woods."

"Which is but natural, being a dryad, Eve-Ann, besides which I——"

"O!" she exclaimed suddenly, clasping his arm, "there is a man following us!"

"Two men, my child."

"What . . . what will they do to us? Ah, have they come to . . . to take thee? O let us run . . . pray let us run, John."

"Not a step!" he answered grimly. "Bear yourself boldly as if you had not seen them."

"But why do they creep after us? John, they mean thee harm. . . . O, I'm afraid. . . . I—I shall swoon!"

"Never dare to!" said he, between clenched teeth.

"But . . . I . . . must!" she gasped. "O John . . . hold me!"

"Eve," said he fiercely, "Eve-Ann Ash. I despise a coward . . . command yourself! Walk on and don't look behind."

"Ah . . . wilt not run?" she pleaded.

"Not until necessary."

"But these men?"

"Shall not dog us very far if you will obey me."

"Then pray walk faster, John."

"No, they must not suspect we are aware of them, so talk to me."

"What . . . what shall I say?"

"Anything you will."

"Am I a coward, John?"

"Are you going to swoon, or run?"

"Nay, I dare not, and thou so fierce with me."

"Then I retract the expression and pronounce you no coward, Eve-Ann."

"And yet verily I must be, John, for I fear these men so greatly that I should now be running my hardest if I didn't fear thee more."

"Child, am I so terrible?"

"Thou mightest be, wert thou not so inhumanly placid and . . . dignified, John."

"Inhumanly, Eve-Ann?"

"Whoever saw thy like, John?"

"As to that," said Sir Marmaduke, swinging Tickler in an airy flourish, "it is as well to be original . . . exempt from the herd."

"But I would rather have thee a more ordinary person . . . just an everyday sort of man, John."

They had reached the woods at last and now, screened within this leafy shelter, Sir Marmaduke stood to view their pursuers, two ill-looking fellows who hastened after them.

"What now, John?"

"Take our Horace farther into the wood and tie him securely and pray be still and silent."

"And what o' thee?"

"I shall accost these fellows." So saying Sir Marmaduke stationed himself behind a thicket on the edge of the wood whence he might watch the approach of these two men: rough, ill-clad fellows they were, the one a tall man conspicuous by reason of moth-eaten fur cap, the other a squat man, plump and evil. Close upon the edge of the wood they halted to peer and listen.

"I don't 'ear 'em!" said the tall man.

"Gone to earth!" quoth the other. "But they

can't shake we. . . . Jimmy swears it's 'im, and fifty pound ain't come by so easy."

"Then stow y'r whids . . . come on!"

"Is y'r barker ready?"

"Ar."

Then the two men stepped into the leafy shade and were immediately confronted by a grim-faced, determined-looking countryman who bore a formidable staff shod with an iron spike.

"Well?" demanded Sir Marmaduke, "what do you want?"

"Nothink!" answered the squat man, recoiling.

"Then off with you, or——"

"Drop that stick!" growled the tall man and whipped forth a small yet very serviceable pistol. "Drop that stick . . . d'ye 'ear!"

"Shoot 'im, Sol, shoot 'im!" cried the squat fellow. "It says 'dead or alive', so shoot!"

"So I will, but I'll count three first. . . . One . . . T——"

Swift and lithe as a panther Eve sprang and, seizing the man's pistol arm, clung there; and then as they strove together, down upon moth-eaten fur cap thudded Tickler and, dropping his pistol, the smitten man fell to his knees and rolled over, whereat his companion turned and fled, but with the long-legged countryman hard on his heels. . . . Again the heavy staff rose and fell.

And presently back came Sir Marmaduke, a little scant of breath, to find a white-faced girl, pistol in hand, crouched on her knees above an evil-looking man who lay snoring stertorously.

"John," she whispered, "hast thou killed them?"

"No!" he answered, stirring the unconscious man with Tickler, "such evil things as this, like other vermin, are unreasonably difficult to slay. This rascal has merely lost interest in us for the time being, meanwhile let us depart."

"Nay, he breathes strangely loud!" said she, viewing the fallen man with growing apprehension, "and thou did'st smite him very hard, John."

"In the hurry of the moment, I did, child. But the human skull, owing to its convexity, is peculiarly adapted to withstand the rapping of stick, bludgeon, and other weapons of percussion, so do not—ah, calm your anxiety, our slumberer waketh!" Even as he spoke, the man groaned, sat up, clapped hand to head and swore vehemently, but meeting Sir Marmaduke's eye, immediately betook him to whining lamentation and, quick to remark Eve's terrified distress, addressed himself to her, rocking back and forth like one in direst agony.

"O mam. . . . O lady, 'urted bad, I be . . . dyin' I think, mam! And if I takes an' dies, wot's to become o' me poor old dam . . . and oo's to pay for me buryin'?"

"Ah, John," said Eve staring at the man's contorted features: "What—what can we do for him?"

"Do child? Pray stand aside and I will rap him to a comfortable unconsciousness again," and Sir Marmaduke swung Tickler lightly aloft, whereat the fellow sprang to his feet and, throwing up an arm to ward the expected blow, backed away, scowling murder. Then Sir Marmaduke lowered the staff and bowed to Eve-Ann; quoth he:

"Behold the virtues of an English quarter-staff which can abase a man and raise a man with equal celerity! Rascal," he continued, advancing upon the man who retreated precipitately, "begone, take your unlovely head away, it is a temptation—do not let me see it again or I shall instantly smite it soundly. Now go!"

"Well, but wot o' me barker?" whined the man.

"Ah, you mean the pistol? I will accept it as a gift. No, I will purchase it for—one shilling, there it is!" And Sir Marmaduke tossed the coin at the man's feet. "And no recriminations, rogue!" For the man was

scowling at the shilling and muttering fierce impre-
cations.

"Well, but wot o' me cap?" he demanded, "you'll
gi' me me cap?"

"To be sure, you may take your cap.'

"O can I!" cried the man in sudden passionate
anger, "'ow can I? Look at it, will ye!"

"O John!" exclaimed Eve, "see yonder!"

Sir Marmaduke glanced round and beheld Horace,
ears drooping and eyes blissfully half-shut, munching
at a shapeless object that had once been a fur cap.

"Ha," sighed Sir Marmaduke, turning to the indignant owner, "it appears that your cap has become
fodder for our Horace, and as such I must purchase
this also . . . a florin. Take your money. . . .
And remember, you follow us at your peril! Should
I catch sight of your tempting head I shall immediately rap it with my good quarter-staff until you sink
to harmless oblivion."

Having said which, Sir Marmaduke uncocked the
pistol Eve had thrust into his hand, glanced at flint
and priming, and dropping it into capacious pocket,
shouldered Tickler, grasped Horace's lead, and, with Eve
close beside him, went on into the wood, leaving roguery
to snarl and scowl after him in murderous futility.

CHAPTER XX

"Think'st thou they'll follow us, John?"

"Eve-Ann, I do not."

"And yet they may . . . they may. And they will surely guess we are for London."

"Egad and that's true enough!" said he, glancing at her in quick approval. "Most fugitives make for London."

"Then don't go to London, John."

"Where then, child?"

"Anywhere."

"Tempting and truly Arcadian!" he nodded. "But it were as well to have some objective, I think . . . London lies north-westerly from here."

"Then go south-east, John."

"North-west or due north awhile should be sufficiently safe course for us." And taking out the compass he set their direction accordingly.

Yet still Eve seemed fear-haunted, often glancing behind; and more than once she halted him, insistent that someone was following them, yet though they stood to listen no sound disturbed the pervading quiet save the vague stir and rustle of the myriad leaves around them.

By thicket and hedgerow they tramped, following no path, by lonely copse and sleepy stream amid greeny shadows, by rolling meadow, hill and dale, while the sun climbed high above them, his ardent beams tempered by a gentle wind fragrant with herb and flower; birds twittered to them, larks soaring on fluttering wings carolled to them and Sir Marmaduke, hugely glad of it all, talked blithely of the present, drew pictures of a happy future until she, growing glad also, plied him with eager questions most of which he answered; thus:

SHE.   And art thou indeed happy?

HE.   What poor wretch would not be? Listen to yonder lark!

SHE.   Why truly 'tis pretty sound, and yet 'tis such small reason for thy happiness. . . . Canst think of none . . . other cause, John?

HE.   A hundred! Look around you.

SHE.   I see only trees and hedges and grass.

HE.   Yet all good things, Eve-Ann.

SHE.   Ay, but when we reach London, how then?

HE.   Plague me not with thought of teeming, roaring Babylon. We are in Arcady, God's free gift to man. We walk with angels about us, spirits o' the wilderness, spirits o' the trees and rippling brooks. The birds are our choristers. Thus we, content with these solitudes and each other, should be happy.

SHE.   (tenderly) Art quite . . . quite content with poor me, John?

HE.   Yes, most certainly. You are so perfectly suited to our surroundings.

SHE.   (frowning a little) These . . . trees and things?

HE.   I mean Arcadia, child—this Eden without a serpent, this—this world where sin and sorrow may not be . . . our Arcady, Eve-Ann——"

Turning at this moment he saw that she was staring back over her shoulder with that wide-eyed look of dreadful expectancy, whereupon he stopped and questioned her, a little wearily:

"Child, what is it now?"

"John, I . . . I'm afraid."

"Of what?"

"Forgive me," she pleaded, for he was frowning at her, "forgive me, but . . . I don't know . . . 'tis a sense of coming danger. . . . I feel something evil is following us . . . creeping after us, always out o' sight, yet . . . always following."

"Preposterous!" he exclaimed.

"Now thou'rt despising me for my cowardice. . . . I can see it in thine eyes."

"And yet you leapt upon an armed man, child!"

"Only because I was so greatly afraid, John."

"And probably saved my life."

"I am here but to serve thee!" she murmured.

"And so I am grateful beyond mere words, Eve-Ann. I grow eager to prove my gratitude by any means."

"Tell me how, John?"

"Well, by living ever more worthy of your friendship."

"Nay, how could'st thou be more worthy?"

"By regarding you always as a charge most sacred to be shielded from every danger . . . even . . . myself, perhaps."

"Thou'rt no danger . . . nor ever can be . . . to me."

"No, thank Heaven!" he began, but beholding the look in her eyes, the glowing cheek, the quiver of ruddy lip, he hesitated and laughed a little oddly. "And yet," he continued, "even I am . . . merely human and ridiculously young at present! . . . It is well I should remember this, yes, a little caution may be necessary."

"Even in Arcady, John?" she murmured. To which question finding no answer, he turned and they went on again, nor did they speak for some while.

"Bread, cheese—and onions!" said he suddenly at last. "Art hungry, Eve-Ann?"

"Nay, John."

"Then you should be, for it is high noon. With your leave we will stop at the first likely hedge-tavern we meet with. Agreed, Eve-Ann?"

"Agreed, John."

"Bread, cheese, onions, and a pint of nappy ale! Lusty fare, child, clean and wholesome, which I should have shuddered at a week ago—O marvellous! How vastly changed am I! And with every day the marvel grows. . . . Sober Middle-Age shrinks from me appalled! The wheel of time spins backward. Joy like an elf sits perched upon my shoulder. Yes, as I said before, I am ridiculously happy."

"Because of so many trees, so much grass, John? O, can these bring such happiness or make an old man, young?"

"An . . . old man?" he repeated in rueful surprise. "Great heavens, I am only forty-five, and——"

"O," she cried, turning on him in sudden passion, "dost think thy miracle is wrought by a lot o' dusty roads and ragged hedges, and hateful lumpy fields? 'Tis vain and foolish thought, for hedges be only hedges, and fields mud with grass on it, and roads mud without grass."

"Why, Eve, what——"

"Thou'rt blind . . . blind, so blind thou canst see nought but . . . silly trees! That any man so old may be so blind is well nigh past belief!"

"Is forty-five so old?" he sighed.

"So old he should know better! . . . Trees and hedges and fields indeed! Hadst lived and laboured among them so long as I, thou wouldst know a tree is only a tree, and a field a field, and never made any old man young and never will—never! And what's more, I don't believe there is any John Hobbs!" So saying, she flashed scornful eyes at him and before he could make reply, hurried on, leaving him to follow as he would.

"Horace," said he, looking after Eve with thoughtful eyes, "Horace, she does not credit there is a John Hobbs! Did you mark that? . . . Moreover, my fellow, forty-five is not an age of dotage or decrepitude . . . how think you?"

Horace merely blinked and switched flies with inadequate tail. "A very singular exhibition of temper, Horace, and quite incomprehensible unless hunger be the reason . . . she may indeed be hungry, heaven knows I am, and you are, of course, my fellow?"

Horace snorted loudly.

"So be it!" answered Sir Marmaduke, "let us seek a tavern forthwith." At this moment Eve turned swiftly and came hasting back.

"John," she cried distressfully. "O, John, we must go back."

"Indeed? Pray why?"

"Because I have lost my purse . . . all my money."

"Was it very much?"

"O, a great deal, all I had in the world! There was a guinea, a shilling, two sixpences and a groat!"

"Highly regrettable, but do not grieve——"

"Ah, verily I am a great, careless wretch!"

"No, you probably lost it saving my life, and a guinea or so is not an extravagant price for the life of a man—even one so stricken in years—egad such an ancient ruin as myself. Come, let us food-wards."

"But so much money—and lost! I am penniless!"

"What matter since we are not. Money is the one thing we need never lack."

"Art so vastly rich? Is John Hobbs a——"

She gasped suddenly and started about, hands clenched against resurgent bosom, wide eyes staring into the depths of the coppice hardby, whence came a sudden stir of leaves and snapping of twigs that grew ever louder.

"O . . . God——" she whispered. "Almighty Father——"

Sir Marmaduke dropped Horace's lead, and clasping an arm about her rigid form, gripped tickler in ready hand, staring also in the direction of this ominous rustling. . . .

And presently from behind tangled thicket bobbed a little, old man; an aged though cheery soul he seemed as, leaning upon crutch-stick, he peered and nodded and beamed at them in friendly manner:

"That's right, lad!" he piped in shrill yet hearty voice, "cuddle 'er, squeeze 'er and don't mind me, I be only a old chap. But Lord it du mak' me young again t' see ye! Warms me old 'eart, it du, so if ye could manage a kiss I'd tak' it kind-like. I be a bit beyond kissin' a lass these days, but I likes to see them as can. Love's a flower and a thorn, pain an' j'y. . . . Love leads to weddins an' children, an' care, an' trouble, an' sorrer an arl manner o' botherations, but it 'as its sweets, for Love as be true love's a blessin' an' a comfort an' a crown o' glory! So kiss 'er, lad, an' never mind a old man like I be—besides I'll turn me back—ay, I'll go an' leave ye to it. . . . Goin' to me dinner, I be. But kissin' is better than feedin'—unless you 'appen to be 'ungry, I rackon— and good luck!"

Then the old man flourished his stick and hobbled away. Eve's rigid form relaxed and sighing tremulously she bowed her head between clasping hands.

"My poor child," said Sir Marmaduke, loosing his hold, "so long as I have life none shall harm you."

"Me?" she exclaimed, glancing up at him in wonderment. "'Tis thyself, John, thy peril—ah, 'tis this that dreads me so! To think they may come on thee at any moment . . . may drag thee to prison! This was why I came . . . to watch over thee, serve and comfort thee . . . share thy prison with thee an I may. For . . . O, John!" A great sob choked her, and, turning swiftly, she clung to him, hiding her face against his rough jacket and instinctively his arms crept about her. She was wearing hood and cloak, for her new finery was packed carefully away in Horace's panniers; and her hood had fallen back; he could see her glossy hair, the tip of a little ear, the smooth, soft curve of her neck.

"Ann, child!" he whispered.

"Ah no!" said she, her voice muffled in his coat, "alas, alas I am no child. And thou . . . thou'rt so wonderful, John, so brave and gentle! Surely there is none the like o' thee!"

The throb of her heart on his woke in him a new delight with a sense of all her vivid youth and loveliness, and there woke in him a sudden yearning hunger all undreamed; in place of his serene and placid self was another self, long shackled by an iron will—but now these fetters were riven asunder. . . . Within reach of his eager lips was her hair, her mouth, her creamy throat; his clasp tightened, and he bowed his head.

"And thou'rt a man so sure o' thyself . . . even here in the wilderness, so truly good and noble that I am the better, having known thee!"

Sir Marmaduke raised his head:

"God bless you, Eve-Ann" said he, a little huskily, and, keeping his yearning gaze averted, he put her gently from him. Then they went on again and each so rapt, so lost in thought, and thus they had gone some distance when Eve stopped suddenly, whereupon he did the like, and, staring upon her beauty, beheld her more lovely than he had imagined, and she, meeting this look, flushed hotly, drooping her eyes in a sweet shyness wholly new in her; so stood they awhile, neither speaking; at last:

"Eve-Ann," said he, and even his voice seemed subtly changed, "why do you stop?"

"Stop?" she repeated, stealing a glance at him, "why, to be sure, 'twas for Horace—what hast done with him, John? where is he?"

"Where indeed? I . . . forgot him, it seems."

M

So back they went and presently found the errant animal half buried in a bed of thistles.

"This way, John, there is a lane runs yonder.'

"Well, what do we want with a lane?"

"It shall bring us to the road, and on the road are taverns, John, and thou'rt so hungry and yearning for onions."

"Why yes . . . of course'" he nodded, "so I am'"

CHAPTER XXI

OF SUNLIGHT AND SHADOWS

LONG sunny days, blithe with the song of bird and rippling brook; fragrant nights jewelled with stars or glorified by the white magic of the moon; a life carefree and uneventful; a very Elysium wherein they walked in the sweet communion of an ever-deepening friendship, remote from the work-a-day world, wasting no thought on the morrow.

And each day Eve-Ann seemed but to grow in beauty; every hour served only to teach him something more of the strange creature she was, with her thousand contradictions and bewildering changes of mood that went to the making of her loveliness. Her sincerity and sweet frankness of soul, her sudden angers and swift repentance, her gentleness and ready sympathy, her shy coquetry, grave demureness and the hidden passion of her young womanhood that peeped at him beneath drooping lashes, whispered to him in her voice, thrilled in her merest touch.

And Sir Marmaduke, very aware of all this, seemed ever his most placid self, supremely assured and serene . . . But there were nights when, seated alone, looking up at the stars or staring into the fire, Eve might hardly have known him . . . a haggard-faced man haunted by the mad folly and sordid misery of twenty years ago . . .

Thus sped stealthy Time on swift, winged feet, and to-night their camp-fire filled the leafy nook with rosy glow, it danced on rugged tree-bole, upon the little tent, pitched hard-by, and upon Eve-Ann's loveliness where she sat perched upon the stool, dimpled elbow on knee and smooth, round chin in hand, staring dreamily into the leaping flame. And Sir Marmaduke, being very conscious of all the lure and witchery of her, became at once profoundly sententious:

"Time," said he, stirring the fire lazily, "is a wheel for ever turning and spins fast or slow according to giant Circumstance: care and sorrow, anguish of mind or body, these are grinding brakes and check it—how slowly drag the weary hours! Then comes joy and that strange, rare mental attitude we term happiness —and, alas, how speeds the wheel, the flight of time, how fast! . . . Eve-Ann, a week is gone . . . fled . . . vanished so soon, a whole week and we still so very far from London!"

"Very far!" she answered softly and looked at him radiant-eyed. "Would'st be there, John? Art weary o' the road?"

"Not I."

"Nor I, John. And thou'rt sunburned, brown as a gipsy . . . and it becomes thee. Also I mark other changes in thee?"

"And how—what are these changes you remark?" he inquired placidly, though eyeing her a little askance.

"Well," she answered, pondering on him, lovely head aslant and eyeing him as a mother might, "one while thou'lt laugh and be merry, and other while thou'lt sigh—very deeply, John?"

"Perhaps because, like Horace, I am grieved with a continual hunger."

"Verily 'tis joy to cook for thee," said she with sudden smile. "But what beside hunger should make thee sigh, John—so profoundly? And then," she continued, finding him silent, "I have caught thee looking at me, sometimes, as if—O, as if I made thee sad. Pray why, John?"

"Do I, child?   'Twould seem I am becoming a somewhat moody person."

"Thou art . . . at times.   And why?"

"Heaven knows!"

"So shall I if you tell me."

At this, he dropped his gaze to the fire again and
was silent so long that she questioned him anew:

"What art thinking now?"

"That our finances are low.   To-morrow I must
to the nearest town and write for more."

"Thou art a very rich man?"

"So far as money goes, yes."

"Also I find thee a very secret man."

"Yes, perhaps I am."

"Even to me!   'Tis strange how little I know of
thee . . . thy past life.   Am I not worthy thy confidence?   Wilt not tell me of thyself?"

"It is mostly a tale of wasted years, child."

"Alas, dear John!   And yet thou hast worldly goods
. . . and thou'rt very learned . . . clever . . .
John, who art thou and what?"

"One who dreamed mightily and achieved very little
—who lost faith in all things and lastly—in himself."

"My poor John!" she sighed.

"And so, enough of myself, for I am a wearisome
subject."

"Nay, tell me . . . was it this made thee a wanderer?"

"Yes, child."   Now seeing how she hung upon his
words, he attempted a lighter vein.   "So forth set I,
in my uncomfortable boots, to find the very—treasure
of life."

"Yes, John, yes?"

"The best and sweetest gift the gods have to offer."

"Oh," she murmured, "dost mean . . . love?"

Here, though he had expected the question, he averted
his gaze and stirred a little uneasily; then contrived
to laugh:

"Heavens—no! Nothing so—trivial!"

"Trivial?" she repeated faintly.

"Eve-Ann, the treasure I sought is that which is never justly valued until lost, and then never found but by a miracle."

"Dost mean only fame, glory and the like vanities?"

"No, I seek that which is mankind's most glorious possession, that thoughtless, unreasoning joy in life which——'

Eve-Ann yawned audibly, whereat Sir Marmaduke glanced up, startled and not a little shocked.

"I fear I weary you," said he in lofty reproof.

"Yea, John, a little. Thy speech is so . . . so ponderous, and I know what thou would'st say."

"Indeed?"

"Indeed and verily! This marvellous treasure that is so much greater than love or aught else in the world is thy youth, and thou hast found it because . . . trees are shady and grass green. And to-morrow is washing day!"

"Now what under Heaven——"

"Thy clothes and mine and the tent—all must be washed, and I would be up early therefore. So good night, John. Sweet dreams attend thee!"

Being alone, Sir Marmaduke presently lay down and composed himself to slumber; but it seemed some evil memory haunted him, banishing gentle sleep, for at last, tossing aside his blanket in feverish impatience he sprang up and began to pace restlessly up and down beyond the fire, head bowed and hands tight-clenched behind him. And having tramped thus some while and no respite, he sank down upon the stool, staring into the fire, hot brow between fierce-clasping palms.

Presently as he crouched thus, there broke from him a sudden, groaning sigh—and then Eve was beside him, had sunk to her knees, her gentle hands upon his drooping shoulders.

"John," she murmured, "what is thy grief? Why are thy dear eyes troubled? Let me share thy sorrow!" Her arms crept about him, strong, compelling arms that drew him. And yielding to that tender embrace, conscious of all her yearning tenderness, cold reason fled, the icy barriers of Restraint were swept away, the serenely-calculating fine gentleman was whelmed and merged in the elemental man whose fierce arms clasped and crushed their helpless prey in merciless gripe.

And thus he held her, fast prisoned against his breast, his head bowed over her as she lay trembling and with eyes shut, quick-breathing yet utterly docile.

Suddenly she opened her eyes and looking up into the eyes above her, shivered violently.

"John. . . . O John!" she whispered, and covered her face with her one free hand.

"Eve-Ann . . . are you afraid?"

"Not if thou'rt—my John Hobbs."

"I am not."

"No, I . . . guessed this."

"Well, do you fear me?"

Again he felt her whole soft body shudder violently, but his clasp only tightened, his head bent lower— a whistling breath close by, a heavy touch upon his shoulder and starting round he beheld Horace snuffing at him with quivering nostrils. Sir Marmaduke laughed harshly, and next moment Eve was upon her feet. Then he rose, and taking up the trailing picket rope led the errant animal back among the adjacent thickets whence rose the sudden sound of snapping twigs, a floundering among the thorny tangles; and guessing what this meant, Sir Marmaduke sprang thither.

It was very dark among the trees for the moon was not up as yet, but the underbush still rustled before him, guiding him in his headlong pursuit. Twigs lashed him, unseen obstacles tripped him, briars plucked and tore at him, but on he sped fiercely determined and relentless.

Suddenly from the gloom ahead rose a cry, the sound of a heavy fall, and, leaping thither, he descried a dim shape above which he stooped with fierce, groping hands . . . touched a shock of hair, a throat, a neckerchief which he seized and twisted savagely.

"Don't . . . don't kill me, sir. O, Sir Marmaduke . . . don't kill me!"

"Who are you?"

"Only poor Jimmy, sir . . . only poor Jimmy Vamper as never meant no 'arm. O Lord, never choke me, never choke Jimmy, ye won't, ye mustn't! Listen to me, sir—O listen to Jimmy! I know where she is, I do. Jimmy's oath! Tom let it out. . . . Tom used to talk sometimes when drunk, so I know where she is."

"Who, damn you?"

"Y'r poor wife, sir . . . y'r wedded wife as run off with him twenty years—O, mercy, for the love o' God!"

CHAPTER XXII

MR. VAMPER IS INFORMATIVE

THE rising moon made a patch of silvery brightness amid the surrounding gloom, and thither Sir Marmaduke dragged his captive who, crouched there upon his knees, a miserable, abject wretch, mired and ragged, pinched and haggard with want, now began to plead his hunger and supplicate for money.

"A shilling, sir, to buy food, a few pence——" but, meeting his captor's fierce and stony glare he fell silent and shrank away.

"So you followed us?"

"Only in friendship, sir, Jimmy's oath! Only to tell ye what you didn't know and wanted to know. Tom used to say you'd give your eyes to find her. And so, seeing he left me to starve arter all I done for him, and me happening so fortunate to chance across you, I followed to tell you."

"Where is she?"

"O, I'll tell you, Sir Marmaduke, but I'm starving, sir, so you'll give poor Jimmy a shilling or two?"

"Where is she?"

"In London, sir. And you'll give——"

Sir Marmaduke spurned him with vicious foot.

"Where in London?"

"Southwark, sir, a place called Giles's Rents—ye see she's lost her good looks so times is bad." Sir Marmaduke blenched and stared blindly at the rising moon; then spoke in the same toneless voice;

"And where is—he?"

"Not five mile away—Godalming. He's come into money, a fortin', and left me to starve, damn him!"

"Godalming."

"Ay, a mansion, blast him! Next to Lord Wyvel-stoke's place. . . . But you'll gimme a shilling or so sir—a few pence——"

"Who told you my name?"

"He did, that night you nigh killed him in the barn."

"And your gipsy friends, are they with you?"

"No, no, I told 'em you was for London, and they took that road."

"Why do they follow?"

"Because th' old woman's got some crack-brained notion you're the murderer as is looked for."

"And why did you follow?"

"To tell you where you could come at Tom . . . give 'im another beatin'—break his arms and his legs— kill him. He's after your woman . . . he is, he is! Mad for 'er, he was— called 'er Venus, Jimmy's oath, raved about her face, her shape. . . . if you'd heard you'd ha' killed him for foul dog."

"I probably shall."   -

"Yes, yes—kill him!" cried Vamper with a dreadful glee, "blind him first, smash him, make him die nice and slow . . . ah, give him time to suffer. . . . "

"Enough!" said Sir Marmaduke fiercely. "Here is money——"

"Yes, sir, yes!" said Vamper, scrambling to his feet. "I'll go, and think on ye kindly, for Jimmy's grateful, Jimmy's y'r friend, and if only you'll smash him, Jimmy's your slave, world without end, Amen!" So saying Vamper turned and stole away into the shadows like the furtive thing he was.

Then Sir Marmaduke went back to find an anxious-eyed young goddess standing rigid beyond the fire, a pistol in her hand.

"Ah, 'tis thou—thank God!" she exclaimed and, hurrying to him, thrust the weapon into his grasp. "Who was it?"

"Our acquaintance, Mr. Vamper. You were right, someone was following, it seems."

"What did he want with thee?"

"Money."

"Did'st give him any?"

"I did."

"And we so poor."

"Eve-Ann, I fear I startled you a while ago. . . . I would beg you to forgive and—forget."

"Forget?" she whispered, clasping her hands in strange, nervous fashion. "You . . . would have me . . . forget?"

"It would be kind in you," he said, viewing her shrinking loveliness gloomy-eyed, "yes, very kind . . . for when one yields to folly to forget it is the act of a friend."

"Folly? Was this indeed . . . only . . . folly?" she questioned in dazed manner.

"What else?" he answered, lightly.

"O cruel! O wicked!" cried she, in sudden passion. "Thou hast then shamed me in my soul . . . but hast shamed thyself more! Thou hast defiled a holy thing, and so art thou an evil man, thou . . . thou that I dreamed so good!" And, shrinking from him, she covered her face with trembling hands.

"And yet," said he, his voice a little harsh, "God knows I am a man would not hurt you for the world, child!" And he leaned yearningly towards her desolate figure, but with hands tight-clenched beside him. "Go to bed, Eve-Ann, get you to bed, child, and, if you can, remember me in your prayers . . . none need them more than I."

"Yea, I will indeed pray for thee," said she, looking at him through her tears, "but O, I would thou hadst proved the true man I esteemed thee." Then she left him, moving with lagging foot and head bowed, but reaching the tent, paused and spoke, with face averted from him:

"To-morrow I will go back. . . . I will go back home."

"Very well, Eve-Ann. . . . Good night!"

"O good night!" said she and, sobbing, vanished.

Long after she was gone to bed he sat, staring into the fire, yet not alone, for all about him were the ghosts, those evil phantoms of past days, jibing at and mocking him in cruel triumph.

CHAPTER XXIII

GIVES SOME DESCRIPTION OF SIR MARMADUKE BY EVE-ANN

Frying-pan clutched firmly between his knees, Sir Marmaduke had just poised an egg above rim when Eve stepped forth into the early sun's level beams and looked about her, heavy-eyed.

"Am I so late?" she inquired, glancing at the frying-pan.

"No, I am early."

"And wherefore?"

"Well, for one thing, I am escorting you home to-day, and——"

"But thou'rt not."

"You certainly shall not trudge back alone."

"But I am not!" said she, gently possessing herself of the frying-pan, "I have changed my mind."

"But you assured me, and very solemnly, last night, that——"

"Never put eggs in before the bacon or they'll burn."

"But last night you solemnly pronounced your intention——"

"Ay, but that was last night."

"Well?"

"Well, last night is past and done with, and this morning I am content to go along with thee."

"O!" he exclaimed, and then: "Indeed!" And sat watching her as she moved lightly to and fro preparing their breakfast.

"Thine eyes look weary!" said she at last.

"You have not so much as glanced at them!" he retorted. "But why will you not return?"

"Because my mind is changed! Thou didst not sleep very well, I think."

"Well enough, I thank you. Pray what is your reason for going on with me?"

"Because in the night I . . . had a vision from the Lord! . . . Moreover thou'rt such a helpless sort of man."

"Helpless? I?"

"Ay—thou! To put eggs into a dry pan! And with no ideas to thine own comfort, poor soul—'twould be cruel in me to leave thee! Also cowardly, and I yearn to be brave. . . . Pray reach me the coffee . . . in the canister, yonder."

He did her bidding like one in a dream; and thus she kept him fetching and carrying until, their meal being ready, down they sat together.

Sir Marmaduke ate in silence, conscious of and musing upon some subtle change in his companion; and presently glancing up, found her watching him.

"Pray, how much money is left?" she inquired.

He drew forth his purse and found therein three guineas and some odd silver.

"Verily here is enough to take us to London—ay, and back again."

"I doubt it!" said he, eyeing the money dubiously.

"I am sure."

"However, I will write and procure more."

"How long should this take?"

"Eve-Ann, why so careful avoidance of my name?"

"Because 'tis a mystery. What is thy name?"

"You know it very well."

"Nay, 'twas 'John' I called thee."

"And 'John' am I."

"So I thought—so I believed because thou didst

tell me, but——" She shook her head and the doubt in her eyes hurt him.

"And so it is! Upon my honour!" said he very earnestly. "Why will you doubt me?"

"Because I have great reason, sir."

"Child," he began, even more earnestly. "O child!"

"O man!" she retorted. "O man, canst not see the child is a woman? Dost not know—even yet? Canst not see, hear, understand, thou poor, blind soul?"

Sir Marmaduke started, and stared at the piece of bacon on his fork much as if it had snapped at him.

"And all women are wiser than most men," she continued, "especially such a very dignified, gentlemanly, ponderous person who knows so much about the great world that he knoweth himself none at all! Let me refill thy cup."

"Thank you!" said he, a little dazed. "I never suspected myself of being . . . ponderous."

"Thou knowest thyself so little. Thou'rt as ponderous as some great castle with its battlements and towers and turrets . . . as stately, as cold, as hard. . . . Here is thy coffee!"

He sat awhile staring into the cup and stirring the fragrant contents round and round while Eve watched him askance.

"It appears," said he at last, "that I am only just beginning to know you."

"Because I am a woman."

"However, one short week has wrought marvellous change in you."

"Two weeks and three days!" said she.

"I thought you a sweet country girl, very young, very artless, very shy——"

"Because thou'rt only a man!"

"And one who has evidently judged you amiss hitherto—unless you have consistently acted a part."

"Acted?" cried she, fronting him with flashing eyes, "acted? Sir, I am as God made me!"

"An exceedingly beautiful creature!" said he, bowing as he might have done in Mayfair.

"O!" she exclaimed furiously, "I'm no languishing, great lady for thy empty flatteries, but only Eve-Ann, with a day's washing to do!"

Sir Marmaduke arose, superb with the dignity of a thousand ancestors:

"Madam——" he began, but her sudden gesture checked him.

"NO!" she cried, throwing up her hands. "Thou'rt going to be ponderous. Pray, O pray take the axe and cut me some fire-wood, instead." For a moment he stood motionless, his black brows knit in haughty frown, then, all at once, he laughed and turned to do her bidding.

Thus obediently he cut and hacked and chopped, yet doing it with the nicety that characterised him in most things, cutting each faggot to precise length and stacking the whole neatly to hand; from which engrossing business he was aroused at length by Eve calling in startled tones:

"John, O pray come and look at Horace."

Laying by the axe, down he went to the brook where Eve, round arms bared for her labour, stood regarding a blissfully munching Horace with eyes of anxiety.

"Dost think he seems quite well?"

"He seems positively sleek!" answered Sir Marmaduke, stroking the animal's fluffy coat.

"Because I comb him every day. . . . But see how uneasily he rolls his eye!"

"Well?"

"Well, he hath just eaten my largest dish-clout!"

"Precisely, and now glances about for other succulent morsels, the scrubbing-brush, or soap. Our Horace is an ass of catholic taste. . . . And now, if you'll make a list of what we require, I——"

"Ah, thou'rt going into Godalming, John? 'Tis a large place and may hold danger for thee! I will go."

"No," said he, smiling reassuringly. "I must go, and after all, what is to be, must be, and——" At this moment Horace, stealing nearer, touched Eve's bare arm with velvety muzzle, whereat Sir Marmaduke interposed: "Not so, Horace," said he, his fingers closing, instinctively, upon this smooth, firm flesh. "Devour my hat, my overcoat, the tent, but spare me Eve-Ann."

"But O, why run needless risk?" she inquired, very conscious of that clasp upon her arm. "Hast no fear, no dread o' the future?"

"None—except desolate old age."

"Need it . . . be desolate . . . John?"

"Old age is always solitary, my dear."

"Surely not if . . . love be there."

"Eve-Ann, do you still think me an evil man?"

For a moment she was silent, her face averted, nor did she look at him when she answered:

"Thou biddest me to . . . forget! Thou didst name it . . . folly! And for this I did hate thee . . . at the time, for this was wicked blasphemy. . . ."

"And now, Eve-Ann?"

"And now, John, God only knoweth thy soul . . . what manner of man thou truly art . . . and thou didst hurt me very sore, and hast wounded my faith in thee . . . and yet . . . do but ask me and I will follow thee . . . to the end o' the world, John."

He loosed her arm, turning from her very hastily, and there broke from his lips a sound, half-smothered, yet very dreadful to hear from one of such fierce self-repression.

And in a while, having buckled Horace into pack-saddle and panniers, he waved Eve-Ann good-bye and fared town-wards, little dreaming that their days of solitary companionship were ended.

N

CHAPTER XXIV

ALARUMS AND EXCURSIONS

It was a brilliant morning with a fresh wind abroad that set leaves a-quiver with joyous fluttering, and creaking boughs a-swing to cast their shadows on the white road beneath, a jubilant day in every sense: yet Sir Marmaduke's feet lagged in the dust as, with head bowed in troubled thought, he followed whither Horace led, an erratic course that ended, finally, in a bed of thistles.

"Life grows very difficult!" sighed he, staring at Horace with haggard eyes. "Hitherto I have reckoned myself an honourable man . . ."

Horace, finding the thistles beyond his reach, rolled baleful eye at the speaker and curled mobile lips as in sardonic contempt.

"Life, my Horace, is a drama somewhat crudely constructed . . . climax and anti-climax, yet replete with surprises. . . . And remembering one—Jimmy Vamper, I think it highly probable your master—*me mihi*—will soon be in durance vile . . . the Grip o' the Law; this would, at least, resolve a certain riddle for me. . . . And so—come on!"

A lane brought them to a road, and the road to a finger-post where four ways met, and against this finger post Sir Marmaduke's expectant gaze beheld a large bill imprinted in fair black and white, thus:

MURDER
FIFTY POUNDS REWARD
DEAD OR ALIVE

WHEREAS: upon the 11th of June, Charles Brandish, Esqre., of Radley Place, Harting, Sussex, was BARBAROUSLY MURDERED by one believed to be a PERSON OF CONDITION, this gives notice that anyone laying such information as may lead to the apprehension of the BLOODTHIRSTY VILLAIN, shall receive the above REWARD.
The description of the wanted man as follows, viz:

About 5-ft. 11-in. in height, of slender yet powerful build.
His eyes dark. Hair and whiskers black.
Last seen clad in bottle-green coat with gold or gilt buttons, flowered waistcoat, black kerseymere pantaloons, Hessian boots with tassels and no spurs.
His age about 36 or under.

GOD SAVE THE KING

The "Person of Condition" stroked smooth-shaven chin and smiled.
"Thirty-six, Horace, my good animal, there it is in black and white! In the eyes of an intelligent community I am no more than thirty-six. Incredible, but true, though to-day I feel forty-five or over! . . . Ah, well, Horace, we must each face our several destinies with what philosophy we may. . . . Forward!"
Towards mid-day they reached the ancient town of Godalming, and following the High Street, turned aside into the fragrant yard of a cosy-looking inn;

Horace comfortably stabled, Sir Marmaduke stepped into the tap to assuage a noble thirst.

And here, prominently displayed, he beheld another bill with the awful heading:

MURDER

Sir Marmaduke glanced from the bill to the heavy-faced man who served him, and nodded.

"Have they caught anyone yet?" he inquired with a jerk of the head towards the placard.

"Lord love ye, yes—I should say so! They're allus a-catchin' 'em—ah, dozens they caught an' let 'em go again, on account o' all bein' the wrong man. And, wot's more they ain't a-going to catch the right un."

"You think not?"

"Course I think not! Here's weeks gone and they ain't got the villin' yet! And they won't, not they, the villin's got clean away—London or the coast, I'll lay."

"Think o' that!" said Sir Marmaduke, giving the ale in his half-emptied tankard a swirl. "And no news of him, either, eh?"

"Oceans!" snorted the heavy-faced man, indignantly. "There ain't a soul comes in at that door as ain't heard summat. The villin's been seen and recognised on every road and in every village twixt here and London—this here murderer ain't a murderer, e's fifty—ah, an 'undred."

"And not even a trace of him then?"

"All over the place! Joe Miggs, as be ostler at the Angel over to Petworth, come in tother day wi' some tale o' some chap buyin' a lot o' noo clothes an' such."

"Sounds suspicious!" nodded Sir Marmaduke encouragingly.

"Well, I dunno . . . but Joe says as this chap likewise goes an' gets shaved."

"He would, of course."

"Well and so might anyone—I might, you might."

"True!" sighed Sir Marmaduke.

"Though Joe says as this chap walks out o' the town and vanishes—cool as any cowcumber!"

"The rascal!" quoth Sir Marmaduke.

"O and why?"

"How dare he disappear?"

"And wot's more, he says this chap buys a lot o' women's clothes, which sounds ridic'lous as I told 'un."

"Women's clothes?" repeated Sir Marmaduke, "did he, by Jove—the cunning scoundrel!"

"Wot you mean for disguisen' hisself. That's wot I thought, dressed up like a woman d'ye see. Well, I'd like to glimp' my eye on 'im, woman's duds and all, jest one glimp', that's all!"

"You think you'd know him?"

"Know 'im? Ar! Fi' foot 'leven, black 'air and whiskers—as ain't, same bein' shaved off, eyes dark——"

"And aged," murmured Sir Marmaduke, "aged thirty-six or under. A sensible, vigorous, happy age, that!"

"O, I'd know the villin' on the spot and only wish I 'ad the chance—an' fifty pound be a mort o' money!"

"Which reminds me that I have a letter to write," quoth Sir Marmaduke, and finished his ale. "Can you furnish pen and ink?"

"In the snuggery yonder."

Thus presently seated in remote corner beside a lattice that opened upon a pleasant garden behind the inn, Sir Marmaduke indited the following letter:

"My faithful Hobbs and devoted John,

"The letter of instruction I left for your guidance will have informed you that I am upon a pedestrian expedition which, so far, has proved remarkably fateful, and promises to become even more so. I dispatch this from the Angel Inn, Godalming, whither you will immediately bring me the sum of fifty, or say a hundred, pounds. I shall expect you here without fail, my trusty John, upon this coming Thursday at approximately two of the clock. You will inquire for John Hobbs, whereby you see that I have borrowed your name, though somewhat inadvertently, my dear John, for what name has been oftener upon my lips, more especially these last years, than your own? An honoured name, John, which you may trust to the keeping of

"VANE-TEMPERLEY."

Sir Marmaduke was in the act of sanding this letter when he paused suddenly, sand-box suspended in air, as from the tap issued a clear, tenor voice which sounded vaguely familiar:

"Is there a Mr. Denton here, m' good fellow?"

"Ar! 'E says you was to go out to him—in the summer-'ouse at the end o' the gardin . . . though I don't like your sort about."

"Egad—what's that?"

"Well . . . look at your 'at. Look at your coat, you don't——"

"How, fellow?"

"No offence, sir! . . . In the gardin, sir . . . summer-'ouse, sir!"

"Brave boy, much thanks!" answered Tenor-voice, and thereafter was the sound of a light, firm tread, a cheery whistling, and, peering from the window Sir Marmaduke beheld Tenor-voice for a young man whose tall, athletic figure was topped by a defiantly-worn hat which, despite divers bruises and dents in crown and brim and general air of decrepitude, yet preserved some haggard semblance of its one-time smartness, and perched upon it's owner's curly locks at a devil-may-care angle; indeed a remarkably down-at-heel, out-at-elbows young gentleman this, whose garments, though jaded by much long and hard usage, sat upon their wearer's powerful form with an easy jauntiness

quite unsubdued by Fortune's buffets. With a certain swaggering air, this young gentleman strode to
the summer-house, bowed and entered.

"Extraordinary!" murmured Sir Marmaduke, and
proceeded to fold, seal and wafer his letter, then, having addressed it, set by his pen and, glancing towards
the summer-house which chanced to be in view, murmured again. "Yes, extraordinary!" After this, he
sat as it were in profound reverie and, having mused
thus awhile, was about to ejaculate "extraordinary"
for the third time when, hearing a hoarse cry, he glanced
towards the summer-house and there beheld a con-
vulsed face, which contorted visage he instantly recognised as that of Mr. Denton. And behold, as he watched,
forth of the summer-house shot Mr. Denton in a high
state of arms and legs, propelled by some energy behind,
which resistless force presently revealed itself as Tenor-
voice, who, urging his cursing and desperately-reluctant
victim to a small water-butt up-ended him therein
with surprising ease and dexterity, held him there kicking and withdrew him gasping.

"That, sir," said Tenor-voice in dulcet tones, "is
because you mistook me for a scoundrel like yourself!" Here he shook the gasping Denton and rapped
his dripping head, once—twice—thrice, against the
water-butt:

"And that, sir, to teach you that I am a gentleman!"

Which done, the gentleman in question picked up
his ill-used hat, which had fallen by the way, dusted
it with needless care, and clapping it on at haughty
angle, strode to the adjacent wall, vaulted lightly
over, and went his way, whistling cheerily.

CHAPTER XXV

INTRODUCES AN OLD FRIEND

IT was in the full heat of the afternoon that Sir Marmaduke reached the finger-post before which stood an aged person, who, hands crossed on crutch-like stick, was busied in reading the police-bill; he was a small, slim old gentleman in somewhat shabby attire, but his worn garments seemed dignified by their wearer and, despite age, his white head was proudly up-borne. He glanced round as Sir Marmaduke approached, beckoning him with imperious gesture; and beholding this aged person's features, Sir Marmaduke murmured, once again, the word:

"Extraordinary!"

"Murder," said the old gentleman, motioning towards the bill, "murder is a terrible thing, my friend, but if ever crime so dreadful could be any way justified, this was."

"You talk strangely, sir."

"And yet naturally, I venture to think, for I had some small knowledge of the murdered scoundrel."

"Ha!" exclaimed Sir Marmaduke, "killing no murder? A dangerous philosophy, sir!"

The aged person turned to scan the speaker with eyes remarkably keen and bright in one so old.

"Sir," said he, shaking his head, "your speech does not accord with—your boots! And your eyes, your voice, your air strike a note that makes memory. Pray approach sir—hum! Though an aged person most of

my faculties still function . . . and I never forget
faces. And yours now . . . yours—ha! Pray do
me the favour of smiling . . . why surely, by all
that's wonderful—Vane-Temperley."

"I confess it, sir. But your lordship amazes me!
Am I indeed so little changed?"

Lord Wyvelstoke laughed.

"Changed indeed, Marmaduke—John, in all but
your voice, your eyes—and those ears. Gad, sir, I've
pulled 'em many's the time—so, give me your hand.
You were a strange child, John, a remarkable youth,
an amazing young man, and to-day! . . . Egad, the
once particular bright ornament of a—hum—somewhat
graceless court . . . leading a donkey! Were I
younger I ought to be surprised, as 'tis I laud your
originality. You were always engagingly-exceptional.
But a donkey—hum!"

"He answers, sir, more or less, to the name of
Horace."

"And now, my dear Marmaduke, how is His Royal
Highness and the—ha—rest of 'em?"

"Blooming, sir, as usual, I believe."

"To be sure I heard you had fled the splendid follies
of London, shut yourself in your country place, turned
cynic—philosopher girding at the frailties o' mankind."

"But principally my own, sir."

"And to-day I meet you sans whiskers, flowing
locks and all those gauds that went to the making of
that erstwhile so notable dandy and buck!"

"Alas, sir, to-day I am older, and yet a little wiser
let us hope."

"And—lead an ass, Marmaduke-John! The natural,
and I hope excusable, question is—why?"

"For one reason, sir, because I happen to be the
'bloodthirsty villain' of the bill yonder."

Lord Wyvelstoke glanced from the speaker's serene
face to the grim placard and back again, his strong,
black brows knit in sudden perplexity.

"Gad's my life!" he murmured. "John, you do, indeed, actually surprise me, a remarkable feat in itself! It was a duel, then?"

"Sir, it was murder."

"Then, of course, there is some ridiculous mistake?"

"I am grateful, sir!" said Sir Marmaduke, bowing. "It is indeed a mistake, but one deliberately occasioned by myself——"

"Your arm, John! Marmaduke, your arm! There is a small inn, down the by-lane yonder, kept by an old retainer of mine—come and tell me your story, for the old, like the young, love stories, and consequently are good listeners."

So, arm in arm went these two fine gentlemen, the younger moderating his pace to the elder's limp, and with Horace, that sedate beast of burden, ambling dutifully behind.

CHAPTER XXVI

WHICH DESCRIBES THE HEROICAL ADVENT OF A DEMI-GOD

"My superbly arrogant and ridiculously quixotic John," quoth his lordship when he had heard the story, its every detail faithfully recounted, "here is amazing tangle infernally confounded!"

"And becoming more so!" nodded Sir Marmaduke. "I am wondering if it were wiser to take chaise to London."

"And carry your rustic nymph with you, John?"

Sir Marmaduke stared thoughtfully out of the window.

"You believe she is sheltering someone, John?"

"I am positively sure of it, sir."

"Whom do you suppose?"

"An uncle. One of them, very recently, threatened to kill the fellow, I understand."

"So your lips are sealed."

"Of course, sir."

"Hum! And suppose you are apprehended and clapped in prison?"

"It will, at least, be a new experience!"

"Which will require all your philosophy. Can you prove an allibi?"

"None, sir. I was alone, and within a few hundred yards when the fatal shot was fired."

"And to be hunted remorselessly, John, to know the hue and cry is up, hard on your heels! A devilish trying situation."

"Yet, sir, the quarry, I fancy, knows a certain joy up to a point. And should I be taken they must prove my guilt."

"Ay, and by heaven they probably will! There your cane, John, your confounded and confounding cane, damnit!"

Here Sir Marmaduke stared silently out of the window again.

"And is she truly worth such risk—is she, Marmaduke?"

"Who, sir?" he inquired, absently.

"Why, the girl, John—this girl, Eve-Ann Ash, to be sure."

"Yes, sir. Yes—she is!"

"To be sure I like the sound of her, Marmaduke, and you paint her beauties, both mental and physical, in glowing terms."

"Egad, sir, I don't think I even mentioned the colour of her hair."

"Twice, John." Ensued a moment's pregnant silence, then: "Do you propose to marry your lovely quakeress?" inquired his lordship. Sir Marmaduke started and glanced aside, twice he essayed to speak and yet was silent, all of which the keen, old eyes opposite were very quick to heed.

"'Tis very evident, friend John, that she powerfully attracts you, and marriage with any good, womanly creature is precisely what I should prescribe for your somewhat unique temperament. So, as your oldest friend, I ask—do you propose to marry her?"

Still Sir Marmaduke was silent, and Lord Wyvelstoke, watching his furrowed brow with kindly eyes continued:

"To transform a rustic nymph into a lady o' quality and fashion may present certain drawbacks—especially for the nymph. From dairy to drawing-room . . . poor child! And yet, knowing you as I do—or did, John, I think you might do worse, always supposing she possesses half the perfections you describe."

"But, 'pon my soul, sir, I protest I hardly mentioned——"

"So much, Marmaduke, that she would seem to have pleased your well-tutored and somewhat finical judgment. So, if you intend marriage, I would give away the bride. Why not at once?"

"Sir . . . I cannot!"

"Eh? You mean——"

"O, I have been married these twenty years!"

"Astonishing!" exclaimed his lordship. "Yes, by heaven, you have amazed me again—astounded even me at last! Married . . . so long . . . you?"

"I was a fool!" said Sir Marmaduke, softly, "a young confiding fool, and she . . . well, I married her and then . . . discovered the blasting truth too late. . . . In the end she eloped with him. . . . I tried to kill him and failed. I was the fool, the poor, futile fool of the comedy. . . . And now . . . now, when I might——" Sir Marmaduke sat back in his chair and was silent, then Lord Wyvelstoke leaned to lay slim, veinous hand upon his knee:

"Marmaduke-John," said he, "I suggest the time has come to cast off the incubus. Let present joy blot out past pain. Forget, man, and learn to live, at last!"

"How, sir?"

"Well, there is such law as divorce."

Sir Marmaduke blenched.

"Impossible!" he exclaimed. "To parade to a gaping world the sordid horror of it—and worse, it seems, than ever I had dreamed . . . never!"

"Others have so endured, John, with names as old, as proud and honourable as your own!"

"So will not I, sir!" answered Sir Marmaduke, between shut teeth. "It is too detestably squalid, and I am——"

"You are Marmaduke, John de la Pole, Vane-Temperley! Forget your damnable pride and take your only course to freedom and happiness."

Sir Marmaduke rose, and crossing to the window again stood there, silent for so long that his lordship stirred, sighed and spoke:

"And the man, John, was Thomas Mowbray, I think?"

"Yes, sir . . . my one-time friend! Scarcely a fortnight since I saw the scoundrel in a barn, a ragged, miserable wretch. . . . To-day he is your neighbour, I hear. He inherits from his cousin, I presume?"

"True!" sighed Lord Wyvelstoke. "A good man is dead and buried and a bad one reigns in his stead— in so short a while."

"Yet, sir, I venture to prophecy he will not reign long."

"John, what d'ye mean?"

"I intend to shoot him, sir, as soon as a meeting can be arranged." His lordship rose and, limping forward, laid his hands upon Sir Marmaduke's shoulders.

"To what end?" he demanded. "The wrong done so long ago cannot be mended by bloodshed."

"Sir, this scoundrel in his misery and rags was merely vile, but as a man of position he becomes a menace also, and I propose to—remove him."

"Precisely but—what of your gentle Eve-Ann?"

Sir Marmaduke took up his hat and stood fumbling with it.

"Kill the fellow if you will, John, your pistol-hand is deadly as my own, I know, but—after? What?"

Sir Marmaduke still fumbled with his hat.

"However," continued his lordship, "I confess a wish to see and talk with your handsome quakeress and, referring to your present awkward plight, why not become my guests awhile, you and she? The law will hardly seek a murderer beneath my roof!"

"Sir, you are infinitely good, but——"

"Which means that you refuse? Well, so be it, but at the least take reasonable precautions and remove your present place of encampment—where is it, by the by?"

And when Sir Marmaduke had described the place as fully as he might, its situation and bearings, Lord Wyvelstoke stood a moment lost in smiling thought:

"So young, my John, so beautiful—in spite o' which she cooks and washes for thee . . . a dryad domestic! O happy man, thine altruism brings its own reward, I think. Now harkee, John, I shall institute inquiries far and wide, I shall pull strings, set divers wheels agoing and, should danger of arrest threaten, you shall be warned by one, a trusted agent—you remember Atkinson, I think?"

"Very well, sir."

"He shall bring you to a haven where you may lie secure. And now, John-Marmaduke, you have honoured me with your confidence so will I plague you with my advice, for I am an old man and you are——"

"Forty-five, sir."

"Ha!" nodded the earl, "too old for impulse, yet young enough to blast your happiness for sake of an idea!"

"Happiness, sir?'

"Home, John! A wife, Marmaduke! Children, Vane-Temperley! Responsibility for the coming generation and world in general, sir! Ah, my John, surely man is born for greater things than mere happiness and, these achieved, who knows but happiness shall crown him, after all, here or—in the hereafter."

And thus, talking together like the old friends they were, these two fine gentlemen walked back through the afternoon sunshine, the patient ass plodding in their rear. Thus evening had begun to fall when Sir Marmaduke, turning from the dusty road, began to traverse a certain leafy path, then halted in sudden, dreadful dismay as from the shady thickets before him rose a noise of desperate strife, gasping oaths, a fierce laugh, the thudding smack of heavy blows. Guided by these appalling sounds he hastened forward and reaching the little glade, that sequestered nook, beheld three men who staggered to and fro in close affray; but as Sir Marmaduke stepped forward, one of these combatants broke free and, using his fists with remarkable precision and address, drove his assailants reeling backwards, and leaping in before they might recover, knocked them sprawling with powerful left and right in the most approved heroic manner.

A tall, athletic, very down-at-heel, extremely cheerful young man who, smiling triumphantly above his fallen antagonists, addressed them in accents of a dulcet tenor, albeit somewhat breathlessly:

"Stand up again, my rose-buds . . . never say die! Up and fib, my tulips . . . or shall I wipe . . . my boots on you?" But the battered foe, muttering darkly, scrambled up and made off at speed, leaving their debonair conqueror to stand master of the field like the veriest hero of romance.

And it was now that Sir Marmaduke turned to find Eve-Ann at his elbow.

"O, John!" she exclaimed in awed tones, clasping her hands and viewing the Conquering Hero in an ecstasy, "O, John . . . what a glorious young man!"

CHAPTER XXVII

THE Conquering Hero, seeing the enemy in full
retreat, picked up his sorry hat and began to smooth
its weather-beaten nap very tenderly with ragged
elbow, whistling soft but cheerily the while; him Sir
Marmaduke now approached with his stateliest air:

"Pray, sir," he inquired, "to whom are our thanks
due?"

The Conquering Hero bowed with a flourish of shabby
hat; quoth he:

"To no one in particular, sir, who, being on his way
to anywhere you please, heard this lady cry out and,
espying the da—— I mean desperate villains, fell
upon 'em forthwith and . . . er . . . very happy,
I'm sure."

"And O, 'twas very brave of thee!" exclaimed Eve-
Ann with look and tone exactly suited. "I am deeply
grateful to thee, friend."

The Conquering Hero flushed youthfully, and bowed
to her in turn and so profoundly that he dropped
his hat and picked it up again redder in the face than
ever.

"Madam," said he, "a . . . ah . . . 'pon my
soul it was nothing . . . I mean, of course, very
happy to serve you and . . . get in a brace of levellers
. . . er . . . that is to say I am always glad of
a little fibbing and . . . d'ye see the pleasure and

gratitude are entirely mine, I assure you and . . .
Good evening!"

"Nay, young man, I beg thee to tell me thy name
that I may remember it in my prayers."

The Conquering Hero seemed to start slightly, and
staring hard at his weatherbeaten hat, turned it aim-
lessly this way and that.

"My name, madam, is Rupert Bellamy and I . . .
I'm much obliged, I'm sure!"

"'Tis a pretty name and suits thee, friend Rupert
Bellamy, for thou hast a good face, though thy hair
needs the comb——" Mr. Bellamy dropped his hat
again.

"And art thou indeed a wanderer, young man?"

"Exactly, madam, I rove . . . here and there
and . . . ah . . . in short, I wander."

"Then mayhap thou'rt hungry?"

"Candour, madam, obliges me to . . . admit that
you are right, I have been hungry for weeks."

"Then tarry and sup with us. John will be glad
of thy company. Thou wilt, John, I think?"

"Certainly!" answered Sir Marmaduke, and turned
away to loose off Horace's burdens.

"So then, thou wilt sup with us, friend Rupert."

"You are vastly kind," he answered, "but"—and,
hesitating, he glanced from his lovely would-be hostess
to Sir Marmaduke's uncompromising figure, and shook
his curly head:—"under the circumstances I had
best be going, madam."

"What circumstances?"

"Such, madam, as are quite beyond our control,"
and once again his fine eyes turned, a little wistfully,
towards Sir Marmaduke, so that Eve glanced thither
also and, beholding all the rigid aloofness of that most
eloquent back, her red lips curved to the ghost of a
smile.

"And so, madam, farewell!"

Sir Marmaduke turned to glance where they stood

surveying each other; a glorious pair and splendidly young, vivid with life and the sheer joy of it, she all womanly loveliness from head to foot, he a gallant, devil-may-care fellow, nay—a young demi-god superbly confident in his strength.

"But," said she softly, "John would have thee sup with us."

"Infinitely kind in him," answered Mr. Bellamy, contriving to look handsomer than ever, "but—ah— all things considered, I——"

"Will accept our hospitality, of course!" said Sir Marmaduke a little dryly.

"On the contrary," retorted Mr. Bellamy with dignified gesture, "I beg to make my——"

"A beef-steak, grilled," continued Sir Marmaduke smiling, though somewhat wryly, to be sure, "should appeal to heroes and even—demi-gods."

"Beef . . . steak!" sighed the demi-god, looking surprisingly human.

"So, Mr. Bellamy, if you will bring an arm-full of kindling from the wood-pile yonder while I collect the embers of the fire, which it seems was trampled in the affray, supper will be ready the sooner."

The demi-god thrust fingers through touzled, golden hair and glanced from Sir Marmaduke to the wood-pile and back again then, smiling radiantly, reached out and grasped Sir Marmaduke's hand, shaking it like the warm-hearted, ingenuous youth he was.

"Sir, 'pon my soul 'tis uncommon good and kind in you!" he exclaimed. "Makes a lonely fellow feel at home, y'know—friends and so forth. . . . Grilled steak! O Lord, 'tis a—a . . . in short, a rare luxury these days, and I, b'gab, I'm very confoundedly grateful, and the dooce of it is I can only say thankee!"

"However," answered Sir Marmaduke, smiling, and more naturally now, "you may help me with the fire."

"Ah—b'George! Wood, of course!" And off strode Mr. Bellamy, whistling cheerily.

Now, turning suddenly, Sir Marmaduke found Eve-Ann watching himself very intently where she sat busily preparing supper.

"Yes, my dear," he nodded. "I agree with you—he is a glorious young man."

"And—so brave, John!"

"Of course, Eve-Ann."

"And very strong, John!"

"Very."

"And so—young!"

"And consequently, child, I have decided to take him with us on our wanderings."

"O!" she exclaimed, in sudden, breathless fashion, and dropped the potato she was peeling. "But why, John, why?"

"Because," he answered, picking up the errant vegetable, "he is indeed so gloriously young."

"But . . . will he come?"

"O yes, child, my mind is quite made up."

In due season the steak was grilled and eaten with such wholesome enjoyment as cometh only of healthy appetite, of good company and of the clean, fresh open air, which last is of itself ten thousand times more stimulating than any of your cunning aperatifs, sauces, seasonings or relishes whatever.

And now, the platters duly washed and set away, and the fire made up, they sat, all three, in friendly communion while a young moon shyly peeped down at them through faint-whispering leaves, filling the little glade with its soft, mysterious light.

Sir Marmaduke gazed thoughtfully into the fire, Eve-Ann, seated upon the stool, elbow on knee and chin in hand, watched his lean high-bred face beneath puckered brows, while Mr. Bellamy, broad back against convenient tree, glanced at Eve, at Sir Marmaduke, the fire, Eve, a grey form among the adjacent shadows that was Horace, at Eve, the moon, Sir Marmaduke and Eve, and sighed.

"Beautiful!" he exclaimed suddenly.

"Indeed?" inquired Sir Marmaduke, "to what or whom do you refer, pray?"

"To everything, my dear Hobbs! The moon, yonder, the world in general and this part of it in particular, this cosy fire, the jovial spirit of good-fellowship and— ah—in short, to life. Life seems an excellent thing after all, full o' promise, possibilities and—so forth."

"You are still thinking of the steak, I imagine."

"Mr. Hobbs, I'll not deny it. Gad, I've tasted nothing like it since I became a homeless wanderer and confounded outcast."

"Poor youth!" sighed Eve. "Art indeed homeless and friendless?"

"Absolutely!" answered the outcast with a cheery smile. "You behold in me the victim of Circumstance and a Soulless Relative, for I am afflicted with an uncle!" Here Mr. Bellamy scowled, sighed, shook his handsome head and, picking up a stick that chanced near, he poked the fire viciously.

"Ah, an uncle?" repeated Sir Marmaduke.

"Egad, yes, Hobbs, and no less a person than that once famous Buck and friend o' the Prince Regent— Vane-Temperley."

"O!" exclaimed Eve, and glanced furtively at Sir Marmaduke. "And what was thine uncle's other name, friend?"

"Marmaduke, John, Anthony, Ashley, de la Pole, madam."

"But is all this only one uncle, friend Rupert?"

"Merely one!" nodded Mr. Bellamy. "Indeed the merest one, although he sounds like a half-a-dozen, and with pride enough for a thousand ordinary uncles; an over-powering uncle with the haughtiest air, enormous influence, vast possessions, and the soul of a rabbit, my dear Hobbs."

"A remarkable person, Mr. Bellamy! Pray continue."

"Ha, this reminds me, Hobbs! If we are to be companions, fellow travellers and so forth as you were good enough to suggest, let us sink all social distinctions, my name is Rupert, so do not 'mister' me, I beg."

"I am grateful for such condescension, Mr. Bellamy. So, Rupert, pray continue. Your description of this most unworthy uncle has a peculiar interest for John Hobbs. . . . He neglects you, I apprehend?"

"Consistently, m'good John. Nature made him my uncle in the confident expectation that he would fulfil his destiny and—ah—do the right thing by his orphaned and dutiful nephew. . . . I ask you, John, as man of sensibility, what are uncles created for? You answer : To fulfil their sacred obligations to their nephews! Precisely, John! But my uncle Marmaduke, Fortune's pampered minion, rolling in Luxury's lap, utterly regardless of his avuncular duties, has spared no thought for the lonely, orphaned child, the solitary boy, the struggling youth or the embittered man, but left him to—ah—in short, to struggle."

"Unhappy young man!" murmured Sir Marmaduke.

"With the natural result," added Mr. Bellamy, folding his arms and nodding at the fire, "that I sit here to-night Pride's disconsolate victim. And yet upon the whole, my dear John, I—though perfectly destitute, was never so content as now and so, although my pockets are empty and my garments not all they might be, you shall find me, I hope, a worthy companion and, in short——"

"A gentleman!" said Sir Marmaduke, whereupon Mr. Bellamy looked at him with eyes eager-questioning and wistful, glanced down at his own dilapidated exterior and shook his head ruefully.

"The fact is somewhat apt to escape notice, I fear," sighed he.

"You made it sufficiently obvious this afternoon," smiled Sir Marmaduke. "I allude to a certain water-butt."

"Eh—you saw? Fellow deserved it, John! Fellow's a most complete scoundrel!"

"Beyond question!" nodded Sir Marmaduke.

"Who?" inquired Eve, stifling a yawn.

"Let me tell you!" quoth Mr. Bellamy joyously. "In my dismal ramblings of late I've met some queer characters, miserable, homeless dogs like myself and most of 'em rogues. Among 'em I fell in with a pitiful sort o' rascal called Vamper——"

"Yes—yes?" said Eve-Ann in sudden awakened interest.

"Well, he told me of a gentleman—gentleman, mark you, who had a job to offer would pay me well. So, directed by Vamper, I went to the fellow's inn, met the fellow, talked with the fellow, and naturally soused the fellow in the water-butt."

"O!" exclaimed Eve. "But why?"

"Well . . . ah . . . for one thing the water-butt stood conveniently to hand you see, and besides the fellow needs drowning."

"And his name," said Sir Marmaduke, "is Robert Denton."

"Ah!" exclaimed Eve-Ann, frowning at the fire. "What, d'ye know of the scoundrel, John?" inquired Mr. Bellamy.

"We do. And he offered you money perhaps to help in abducting Eve-Ann?"

"By heaven, he did! The fellow described this place very particularly, so when I'd soused the fellow I rambled this way in hopes of a little fibbing."

"Ah, now I understand!" sighed Eve, "O hateful! . . . I had almost done the washing, John, when two men crept out of the bushes yonder. At first I was only surprised, then I grew afraid and tried to run to the tent for the pistol, but one of them caught me and then——"

"I grassed him!" smiled Mr. Bellamy. "And a very pretty turn-up we had while it lasted. Did me a power o' good!"

"If Denton described this place so accurately," said Sir Marmaduke, "it is evident Vamper must have told him. To-morrow we will remove."

"My dear Hobbs, why?" Rupert demurred, "where's your hurry? The situation's ideal for camping and so forth, grass, trees, water. And we are more than a match for this Denton fellow and his rascals any time, you and I and miss, I mean 'madam.'"

"Thou may'st call me Eve-Ann, friend Rupert," said Eve, rising, whereat he sprang lightly afoot, "for verily thou hast proved my friend to-day and I am grateful, and so, before I sleep I shall pray God's blessing on thee, Rupert Bellamy," and she reached him her hand; and taking that slim yet capable hand, he looked at it as if he would have kissed it had he dared, shook it instead —let it go much as it had been some holy relic.

Then Eve turned to Sir Marmaduke, looking at him with slow, strange smile:

"See now, John, how strange are the Lord's ways to send this Rupert to thee here in the wilderness to be thy friend henceforth, I pray to his good and thine own."

For some while after she had left them they sat in a thoughtful silence, though more than once Mr. Bellamy glanced at his companion as if about to speak, but checked himself as often; at last, after hemming once or twice, quoth he:

"Hobbs, old fellow, will you be good enough—ah— that is . . . may I ask you a question?"

"Rupert, you may."

"Well . . . and pray don't think me impertinently curious, m' dear John, but if we are to be friends indeed . . . as she said . . . comrades and so forth, . . . well . . . d'ye see? Eh?"

"You are, perhaps, a little vague," suggested Sir Marmaduke.

"Er—yes, confoundedly, John. But what I would put to you . . . that is, the question I would ask is—ah—is . . ."

"Well?"

"Is she . . . Miss Eve-Ann . . . madam . . . is she your—wife?"

"She is not."

"Ah—pardon me! Your daughter?"

"No!"

"I . . . I beg ten thousand pardons, my dear fellow! Your niece?"

"We are not related."

"Ah, to be sure! Certainly! Quite so! Not related —no!"

"Nor are we lovers."

Here Mr. Bellamy, being a little agitated, took off his hat, glanced at it and put it on again.

"And now," said Sir Marmaduke, smiling a little grimly, "I would beg you to answer me a question."

"'With joy, m' dear John."

"Then pray, what is the immediate cause of your so evident destitution?"

Mr. Bellamy sighed and shook his curly head.

"Fate, my dear fellow, Destiny, John—in shape o' the elusive quadruped, the pasteboards, the nimble bones, in short, gambling. Tis in my blood for, in this one particular I take after my confounded uncle Marmaduke, like him I am, or was, a gambler—though never, no—never so reckless. And now, Johnny, I'm infernally sleepy, so I'll bid ye good night and pleasant dreams."

CHAPTER XXVIII

DESCRIBES TWO BOW-STREET RUNNERS AND A CONFABULATION

Sir Marmaduke was chopping wood for the fire when he started in surprise as, borne to his ears, came a burst of rippling laughter, a trill so joyous and light-hearted such as he had never heard from Eve's lips before, and he turned to glance where she and Rupert were busied side by side down by the brook: and now, listening to their merry voices, he set by the axe and, sighing, sank upon the stool, staring down at the square toes of his clumsy shoes, rueful and a little dismayed.

"Youth!" he murmured at last. "Youth will to youth, and poor, sober Middle Age may go hang for tragic fool! Surely there is no fool like your fool of middle age." Here he bowed head on hand dejectedly and fell to deep and bitter reverie until, roused by a sound nearby, he turned and saw Horace, who ceased munching to cock a shaggy ear at him.

"Horace," sighed Sir Marmaduke, shaking gloomy head, "if thou'rt a donkey I am the greater ass, and grieve because yonder two children laugh together. Hark to them—the world is their playground, while the sun shines, and thou and I are out o' mind. . . . I am elderly and . . . ponderous, and may not, even if I would . . . by reason of a spiteful fate. And he is gallant with joyous youth, and free as the winds of heaven to woo and—win. Well, this should resolve me this difficult situation . . . this would mean happiness for her (I think) . . . redemption and an assured future for him (perhaps). . . . And yet, being human, I grieve and hanker for—the Might-Have-Been! So, my pipe is out o' tune, Horace, my cake is dough, life stale and the world an unprofitable, dreary waste! Thus here I sit extremely middle-aged yet, grieving like any callow youth. Shame on me, Horace, forty-five should be of sterner stuff! Let us then, like true philosophers, say that what is to be, the best must be, so all's well with the world—and the like sophistries. And thus, forgetting the Might-Have-Been, laugh at Melancholy and make a mock of broken dreams. . . . And to-day is Wednesday, the day appointed to our faithful John, so will we incontinent steal hence to meet him . . . leaving them together. Youth with youth, to prattle in the sunshine."

So saying, he arose, albeit somewhat heavily, and proceeded to gird Horace with pack-saddle and panniers, which done, he clapped on his wide-eaved hat, donned his coat of homespun, and reaching the Tickler, that formidable, iron-shod weapon, took Horace by the halter and set forth. But he was not to steal away thus, for he had gone scarcely a dozen yards when Rupert intercepted him:

"Old fellow," he began cheerily.

"Young man!" retorted Sir Marmaduke sombrely; Mr. Bellamy beamed and clapped him on the shoulder:

"Whither away, my tulip?" quoth he cheerily.

Sir Marmaduke blenched, and before he could find an adequate rejoinder, Eve was beside him, her cheeks flushed, lovely eyes adance, herself more radiantly alluring than usual—or, at least, so it seemed to Sir Marmaduke.

"Why, John!" she exclaimed. "Where art going? What is it?"

"Business," he answered, smiling.

"Ah, thou'rt going to Godalming. . . . Shall I— shall we go with thee?"

"No, no, bide you here, child. You will be safe with Bellamy."

"Trust me for that, John, old fellow!"

"But," said Eve rebelliously, "'tis my desire to go with thee, John."

"And it is my will to go alone," said he gently. . . . "You are better here."

"Am I, John?" said she looking at him very wistfully. "I wonder why?"

"It will be hot and dusty on the road, Eve-Ann."

"Dusty!" she repeated, flashing her eyes at him. "Did I mind the dust, before?"

"I shall return about tea-time, I hope."

Eve merely nodded, and went back to her cooking; therefore when he had gone some little distance he must needs glance back, and saw Eve and Rupert bending above the great stew-pot, their comely heads very close together; Sir Marmaduke frowned and thrust the Tickler sharply into Horace's plump ribs whereupon that patient animal turned to view him with eyes of such reproach that Sir Marmaduke, becoming apologetic, pulled his nearest ear caressingly.

"Petulance, Horace," said he, "merest petulance which I will thank you to overlook. Also thy ruffled feelings will I cherish later with a plenitude of oats."

Heedless of dust and sun-glare he had trudged on some distance when, becoming conscious of heavy footsteps behind, he glanced over his shoulder and beheld two men who walked close together conversing fitfully in muttered undertones and, beholding a vague furtiveness in their air and their portentous red waistcoats, his gloom gave place to a sudden exhilaration. Were these men dogging him? With a certain joyousness he proceeded to test this, and, increasing his pace, strode along with such hearty goodwill that Horace's plodding amble became a shuffling trot; and yet, when after some half-mile he reached the crossroads and glanced back, he saw the two men were as near as ever; therefore he paused opposite the finger-post with its placard, and, seating himself on the grass beside the way, watched these men as they approached. Burly fellows they were, yet each the opposite of the other in that one smiled and one frowned.

"Goo' morning, chum!" quoth the smiling man, halting to beam down upon Sir Marmaduke, while his comrade, halting also, scowled blacker than usual.

"And good morning to you, both of you," answered Sir Marmaduke cheerily. "A fine day for walking, though dusty?"

"And precious 'ot!" said the smiling man.

"Are you going far?"

"Why that depends, chum—don't it, Toby?"

"Ar!" growled the gloomy man.

"Depends on what?"

"Well, on yourself p'raps, chum—eh, Toby?"

"Ar!"

SIR M.: (leaning back the better to stretch his legs) How on me?

FIRST MAN: (mysteriously) We'm a-coming to that.

SIR M.: (pointing to police bill with contemptuous gesture) Meanwhile what do you think of that? Fifty pounds!

FIRST MAN: Why, that's the question, chum—wot do you think of it?

SIR M.: That any murderer would be cheap at the price, especially if he be a Person of Condition.

FIRST MAN: (mopping perspiring brow) Fifty pound be a lot o' money.

SIR M.: Not for a Person of Condition.

SECOND MAN: (surveying Sir Marmaduke in gloomy speculation) Five foot, eleven!

SIR M.: (nodding lazily) That is about my height.

SECOND MAN: (scowling and intent) Ar!

FIRST MAN: (also intent) But . . . black whiskers, Toby!

SECOND MAN: Razors, Bob!

SIR M.: (smoothing new-shaven chin) And aged thirty-six or under.

SECOND MAN: (scowling imperious) O? And 'ow hold might you be?

SIR M.: (smiling) About as old as I seem, my lad! And looks are often deceiving.

FIRST MAN: (seating himself beneath the finger-post and removing dingy white hat to use his dingy handkerchief) Fifty pound is a sight o' money for jest arf a dozen words, chum! And the money's yourn if you can say them words.

SECOND MAN: (scowling and suspicious) Not 'im!

SIR M.: (serenely) Try me. I'd say a good many words for fifty pounds.

FIRST MAN: Well then, 'ave y'ever seen any cove anywheres, like this cove in the bill yonder—hey?

SIR M.: (conning the bill over) "About five feet eleven . . . hair and whiskers black . . . bottle-green coat with gold buttons . . . flowered waist-coat . . . Hessian boots . . . age about thirty-six or under . . . ?" To be sure, I have.

FIRST MAN: (starting eagerly) Eh? You 'ave?

SIR M.: Many a time.

FIRST MAN: Where, chum, where? Spit it out, say where and the money's yourn.

SIR M.: In London at St. James' or Mayfair you may see scores, hundreds o' the quality dressed exactly so.

SECOND MAN: (fiercely) Yah! The cove's flamming us, Bob. Lookee here you—don't come none o' your games wi' we——

SIR M.: (smiling) Emphatically no! I should never choose you for a playmate, your face forbids, Toby.

SECOND MAN: (threateningly) Wot's my face to you?

SIR M.: Nothing, thank heaven!

SECOND MAN: Well then, cut your gab—and lively

d'ye hear. You got too much to say—ah, and you says it wrong. You ain't wot you seems to be, you ain't.

SIR M.: True enough. For instance, I have not always led an ass.

SECOND MAN: No, I thought not——

SIR M.: No, I have sometimes, when younger, suffered asses to lead me——

SECOND MAN: (loudly) Yah! Speak up an' no gammon! Gimme an account o' yourself—who are ye, where d'ye live?

SIR M.: I am a solitary soul and I live here and there—but who are you, pray?

FIRST MAN: Bow Street, chum, officers both and——

SECOND MAN: (roaring ragefully) Are you agoin' to gimme a straight answer?

SIR M.: Pray don't bark.

SECOND MAN: (clenching fists in menacing fashion) Eh—bark? Bark d'ye say?

SIR M.: And do not attempt to strike me or I shall instantly give you in charge of yourself and comrade for an assault.

SECOND MAN: (murderous, yet calm) Wot's your name, my flash cove, where d'ye live, where d'ye come from? Give us an account o' yourself or——

FIRST MAN: (distressfully) Lord, I'm that 'ot! 'Old 'ard, Toby—Lord I'm that dry I couldn't spit a sixpence! 'Old 'ard, Toby lad, and lemme 'ave a word.

SIR M.: (cheerily) No, no, Bob—and there's an alehouse down the road yonder—no, no, I like Toby! Toby's bark is worse than his bite, his heart kinder than his face—continue, Toby.

The saturnine Toby glared at the tranquil speaker, clenched his fists, spluttered a vehement oath and turning about kicked savagely at the finger-post.

FIRST MAN: (sighfully) And did you say "ale-'ouse," chum?

SIR M.: I did, friend Bob. And an ale-house naturally suggests ale—in barrels, in beakers, foaming in tankards.

FIRST MAN: (rising suddenly) And we that dry! . . . Ale! . . . Come on, Toby.

SECOND MAN: (scowling on Sir Marmaduke) But wot about this cove? I'm arf-minded to take 'im along for a suspicious character.

SIR M.: (rising cheerily) Toby, I'm coming along, and while we walk together I will talk to you——

"Not me!" snarled Toby and, turning his back, trudged off after his thirsty comrade.

CHAPTER XXIX

IN WHICH EVENTS MOVE APACE

OPENING the door Sir Marmaduke paused a moment to watch the man who stood, hands behind him, gazing so thoughtfully out of the window; a very neat, grey-headed man with the demure look and dignified gravity of an archdeacon, the jaw of a fighting man, the upright carriage and trim legs of a light dragoon; at the opening of the door he wheeled sharply and surveyed the intruder with the keen eyes of the man of action but, though his chin appeared slightly aggressive, he spoke with the gentle urbanity of the church dignitary:

"My good man permit me to inform you that this room is engaged, is private."

"Precisely, my faithful John," said Sir Marmaduke and closed the door. John Hobbs, the veritable, stared, drew a sharp breath, made two quick strides forward and bowed:

"Sir Marmaduke!" he exclaimed. "Excuse me, sir, but—— Good heavens! Those . . . extraordinary garments! And you yourself are——"

"Thirty-six or under, John!"

"Sir, you seem as I remember you—three and twenty years ago—a care-free youth of vast ideas, eager for a tilt at any and every windmill——"

"Ay, a young fool, John, chasing rainbows. E'gad, 'tis a weakness with me yet, it seems!"

"I trust you are well as you look, sir?"

"Indeed, I was never better—physically. You ordered dinner, I hope?"

"They should be ready to serve it, sir. Shall I ring?"

"Ay, do, John, for I am preposterously hungry."

"Hungry, sir? God bless me!"

"Ravenous, John! My escapade has at least taught me to appreciate food again—yes, this at least."

"Pray forgive my staring, Sir Marmaduke, but the change in you is past belief! Your eyes so bright, your voice so resonant, your air so brisk, so vigorous! Time rolls back and leaves you as I mind you—twenty-three years ago!"

At this repetition Sir Marmaduke glanced keenly at the speaker, but just then John Hobbs was reaching for the bell-rope.

And presently appeared waiters heavy-laden, who set forth the table with speedy deftness, whisked napkins, bowed and vanished, leaving behind them cates savoury and delectable . . .

"And now," said Sir Marmaduke, after some while, as he watched the bubbles rising in his glass, "you will naturally be wondering, my dear John, at this my latest—well, let us say, freak o' fancy. The explanation is that, acting on Doctor Wotherspoon's prescription, I went forth on the quest of—Youth! . . . An absurd, a most ridiculous quest, John . . . and yet——"

"Prodigious!" exclaimed John Hobbs, his eyes wonderfully bright and glad. "Surely you have found it, this marvellous and so happy change in you tells me as much."

"Alas," sighed Sir Marmaduke, shaking head and with rueful smile, "as well seek to grasp a sunbeam, John, or gather last year's roses. . . . Though, mark you, I began to think I had actually achieved the impossible! But who shall find that which is but a memory? No, John, my Youth lies hid beyond the sunset, and so in place of this I have found—a nephew."

"Nephew, sir? You mean——?"

"I mean Rupert, Ashley, Bellamy, my dead sister's orphaned son whom, it seems, I have consistently and shamefully neglected! . . . I repeat, John—neglected!"

John Hobbs lifted his gaze to the ceiling and was mute.

"So, John, you agree with him, then?"

"Agree? With him, sir? Can you mean that Mr. Bellamy actually dared tell you so—to your face?"

"He did, John. He also informed me that I had the soul of a rabbit! You see, he knows me as—John Hobbs."

The habitual gravity of John Hobbs proper was visibly shaken, and meeting Sir Marmaduke's whimsical look, he laughed suddenly.

"But you yourself think I have neglected him—eh, John?"

"Sir, since you ask, I would beg you to remember that you have deigned to see him but three times since he was born!"

"Ha—yes, very true. I made you my intermediary . . . and why?"

"Sir, you were always a man of many affairs."

"Ay, to be sure—my own affairs came first always. . . . Regarding myself from proper perspective my habitual yet little-dreamed-of selfishness astounds me. . . . And now as to screening myself behind your name—first, accept my apology."

"Sir, you honoured me."

"Being in want of an alias, John, your name sprang first to my lip. . . . And now, my faithful John, fill your glass and list to the tale of my adventures."

As his relation proceeded, Sir Marmaduke's eyes twinkled to see the square, honest face of John Hobbs widen to sudden smile, become drawn with anxiety and grow longer and longer until, the narrative concluded, he sat back in his chair staring at Sir Marmaduke in horrified dismay:

"But—you, sir, you to be in actual danger of arrest! It is preposterous! It is unthinkable!"

"Yet positive fact, my John, and upon my soul," said Sir Marmaduke, smiling a little wistfully, "just now I hail the possibility with joy."

"But, sir, what do you propose to do——?"

"Marry them, John."

"Sir?"

"They are both so suited to matrimony and each other," continued Sir Marmaduke staring at the table-cloth a little absently, "a perfect pair, John; young handsome and unspoiled, children o' the sun in an Eden without snakes or the like vermin. She is . . . her wonderful self and he, a likeable young scamp deplorably out at elbows and detestably youthful and self-assured, utterly destitute yet profoundly cheerful—indeed I already entertain hopes of him. . . . On the whole a very excellent match, John—with myself to play the *deus ex machina*, of course. He is up to his ears in love already—yes, they should be . . . ridiculously happy!"

"But pray, sir, how do you propose to right your own somewhat desperate case—what of yourself?"

"Sufficient unto the day, John. I have scarce given it a thought as yet."

"Lord, sir, but you worry me!" sighed John Hobbs, shaking his grey head in reprobation. "Indeed you are as joyously reckless as you were twenty-three years ago."

"Ha—again, my John!" exclaimed Sir Marmaduke, pausing with wine-glass at lip. "Three times you have mentioned that span of years and you are one of the very few who know that twenty-three years ago I married a . . . one who blasted my faith and happiness then—and forbids it now! Three times, John! What do you mean?"

Then John Hobbs leaned across the table and spoke in harsh whisper:

"Sir, she is—here! I saw, I carried her into this inn!"

Sir Marmaduke set down his brimming wine-glass very carefully and sat a moment staring at it:

"Here, my John? You are—sure?"

"Sir, I had scarcely dismounted before the door when the London mail drew up and began to discharge its passengers. One of them, a lady, seemed stricken with sudden illness. I ran and caught her as she swooned and bore her into the house. As she lay in my arms her bonnet and veil slipped back so I looked at her . . . she is greatly altered but there was no mistaking that face. . . . Sir, she was Lady Vane-Temperley."

"Why then I . . . must see her," said Sir Marmaduke, passing hand wearily across wrinkling brow. "Yes, I must speak with her, at once—now!"

"Ah, sir, to what end? Why so distress yourself?"

"Man, I've heard she is ailing, ill and in want. So, John, go you and inquire for her . . . make known my presence here, ask her to be good enough to see me—go!"

Meeting Sir Marmaduke's eye, John Hobbs rose and departed without another word, closing the door softly behind him.

Rigid in his chair sat Sir Marmaduke, staring blindly before him, fists tight-clenched upon his knees, while Disgust and Pity strove and grappled within him. And presently from his grim lips breathed a hushed whisper:

"Eve-Ann . . . sweet soul . . . thou fragrant memory—thus am I the better, having known thee! O Eve—Eve-Ann!"

Anon came back sturdy John to find Sir Marmaduke, wine-glass in hand, watching the bubbles rise:

"Well, my John?" he inquired serenely.

"She is gone, sir. She left more than an hour ago, so soon as she recovered of her faint . . . but——"

Glancing up Sir Marmaduke saw that the demure
and gentle archdeacon was transfigured into the fighting-man.

"Well, John?" he questioned.

"Sir," answered John, his square jaw fiercely out-
thrust, his thick brows close-knit. "Sir . . . he is
here!"

"You mean?"

"Mr. Tom Mowbray, sir."

"No, no—Sir Thomas Mowbray, he has but recently
inherited his cousin's title and—fortune, touching which
I will speak a word with him.   Where is he?"

John Hobbs hesitated:

"Sir," he began.   "Sir, I do beg——"

Sir Marmaduke gestured slightly with one finger and
rose, whereupon his companion shook grey head, sighed
and led the way out of the room, along a passage, to a
door from behind which issued voices and a chuckling
laugh.

"He has company, John?"

"Only Mr. Denton, sir."

Nodding grimly, Sir Marmaduke threw open the door
and stepped into the room. . . .

They were seated at their midday meal, but both
started round in angry surprise at this sudden intru-
sion.   Mr. Denton stared speechless while Sir Thomas,
huge and menacing, rose from his chair lifting a large,
be-ringed hand imperiously.

"Why . . . what the devil!" he exclaimed for Sir
Marmaduke entirely unheeding threatening look and
commanding gesture, advanced to the table and leaned
there. . . .   And so, for a tense moment they stared
into each other's eyes.

The past few weeks had wrought a miracle of change
in the erstwhile vagrant desperado for, to the eye, Sir
Thomas was a very grand, a very imposing gentleman indeed; his clean-shaven face was bold of feature
and handsome, despite scarred eyebrow, his herculean

proportions were off-set by modish and splendid attire
—all this Sir Marmaduke saw at a glance; but Sir
Thomas Mowbray looking into the unwinking glare of
the eyes that confronted him, beheld nothing else, for
in these eyes he read scorn, hate and a purpose cold,
deadly and infinitely assured.   As for Mr. Denton, he
surveyed the intruder from head to foot, through
narrowing lids, noting every article of his homely and
rustic apparel from coarse and vivid neckerchief to
clumsy, square-toed boots.

"Mowbray," said Sir Marmaduke at last in pas-
sionless voice, "after our last meeting I cherished
the hope that it would indeed be our last and you
dead——"

"Ha—did ye so?" exclaimed Sir Thomas loudly.
"Did ye so, by God!"

"Learning recently that you still lived, however,
and had inherited a fortune, I decided that no time could
be more proper to call you to account and, incidentally,
blot you out of existence——"

"What," cried Sir Thomas, clenching hairy fists,
"d'ye dare threaten me, you . . . you——"

"Tush—do not rant!" said Sir Marmaduke, leaning
nearer. "Remember you are no longer a gutter-
crawling bravo. Listen, sir! I have, upon further
consideration, resolved to suffer you to live and plague
the world still——"

"Aha, have ye so? Vastly kind, I swear. But
damme, I'll fight you at any time and anywhere, Vane-
Temperley and no!"

Mr. Denton's narrowed eyes opened suddenly, and
he stole furtive hand into his bosom, perceiving which
stealthy movement, John Hobbs began to edge towards
him all unperceived, while Sir Thomas, flourishing
mighty fists, grew louder and more defiant:

"I say I'll fight you whenever you will, despite your
reputation! Ha, damme, I'll fight you here and
now."

"And I should certainly kill you!" nodded Sir Marmaduke. "As indeed you know—and always have known! However I shall permit you to live—but on one condition only, that you may provide, in your present affluence, for the miserable creature whom you betrayed to infamy, and heaven knows what suffering, three and twenty years ago. Fail in this and I swear by the God who sees and hears us that I will hunt you out, force you to fight and shoot you dead for the detestable animal you are."

Sir Thomas drew up his magnificent person with a fierce, swaggering air, but his eyes quailed before the speaker's unswerving gaze, therefore he swore ferociously whereat Sir Marmaduke turned contemptuous back——And then Mr. Denton was on his feet grasping a small yet very serviceable pistol:

"Ha—Vane-Temperley!" he cried. "Stand, I say! Stand where you are! He's wanted, Mowbray, wanted —for murder, I tell you! And there are Bow Street Officers in the town! Raise the house while I hold the villain!" And he levelled his pistol at Sir Marmaduke but, in that moment a powerful fist smote him beneath the chin and he sank to the floor and lay inert.

"In the stables, sir," said John Hobbs standing above the unconscious man and levelling the pistol at the shrinking Sir Thomas, "you will find my horse—or rather, your own, the sorrel with the silver blaze. I will keep these gentlemen quiet meanwhile."

"And what of you, John?"

"I shall contrive handsomely, sir—only be gone, I beg. Go sir, or you will compel me to use violence to Sir Thomas also for sir, you must not be taken."

Sir Marmaduke smiled:

"My faithful John!" said he, "neither shall you!" And he picked up a table napkin.

And after some while they came forth of the chamber together and, having locked the door and pocketed the key, descended the stair, paid their reckoning and so to the stable-yard whence, so soon as their horses were saddled, off they cantered together out and away through the busy High Street, leaving two gentlemen, very securely gagged and bound, staring at each other in raging futility.

CHAPTER XXX

TELLS HOW THEY SET OUT FOR LONDON

WITHIN some half-mile of a certain familiar finger-post Sir Marmaduke checked the horse he rode and, leaping to earth, tossed the reins to his companion.

"The moon rises late to-night, John," said he, glancing up at the sky, "so be here at half-past nine or as nearly as possible. Drive the light closed carriage with the bays. And send a man ahead to order post horses for we must travel fast. Three changes should be enough and—ha, confound it!"

"What now, sir?"

"John, I have forgotten Horace, the poor patient soul!"

"Pray, who is Horace?"

"A donkey, a veritable ass, John, yet the sharer of my secret meditations. Alas that we should part! And yet Fate should be kinder to him here in the country than amid the roaring traffic of London. . . Well, John, until to-night then," said Sir Marmaduke grasping his companion's ready hand; then John Hobbs spurred his horse and galloped away in a cloud of dust.

Evening had fallen wherefore Sir Marmaduke stepped out briskly until a plaintive voice arrested him; he had reached a place where trees grew on either side of the way casting much shadow and, peering in the direction of this voice, he beheld a vague shape crouching against a mile-stone and out towards him came a slim, suppli-cating hand:

226

"O please . . . spare something to a poor——"
The words ended in a fit of coughing, a fierce convulsion
that shook the wretched creature so violently that
she clutched the mile-stone and leaned there helpless
until the paroxysm was over: "I . . . I must get
back . . . back to London!" she gasped. "And I
have lost my purse . . . all my money. Please give
me enough to take me there. I am not strong enough
to . . . walk so far." The gasping voice spoke in
cultured accents, the pleading hand was small and
shapely.

Sir Marmaduke drew certain coins from his pocket
and laid them in the beggar's cupped palm.

"Is this enough?" he inquired gently. "If not, you
shall have more——" But, as he spoke, she started
and shrank away so suddenly that the money fell into
the dust; so he stooped and picking up the coins re-
placed them in her nerveless hold and went his way,
the desolate sound of her coughing in his ears.

He had almost reached the finger-post when to his
surprise he saw Eve and she, beholding him, came running and caught his hand, clasping it to her heart; and
thus he felt the surge and tumult of that rounded bosom
and the tremors that shook her from head to foot.

"O, John!" cried she in agonized voice.

"Why, Eve-Ann—my dear, what is it?"

"The bill yonder!" she whispered. "They have
printed a description of thee!"

"No, no, child, only of my late clothes," he laughed,
drawing her tremulous hand within his arm. "But
why are you here—and alone?"

"I began to fear for thee, thou wert so late! So we
came to meet thee, Rupert and I . . . and still thou
didst not come, so I sent him on to the town to find
thee. . . . But—O, John, the bill. Fifty pounds
for thee . . . dead or alive."

"Ridiculously inadequate, of course!" he nodded,
smiling down into her anxious eyes reassuringly. "But

then, you will pray remark that I am further described as—thirty-six or under, and this is inspiring."

"But wherefore so late, John?"

"Dear child, I have passed a somewhat busy afternoon."

"And O—where is Horace?"

"Horace, my dear, will be eating something or other. somewhere or other, you may be sure. Yes, he will certainly be eating wherever he is, for . . . Eve-Ann, Horace's path and ours lie far apart henceforth, he remains in the country, happy ass, but we must be on the road in an hour or so."

"The road, John? You mean?"

"The road to London, child, at least—I shall!"

"And what of me, John?"

"This, Eve-Ann, is the question, and one I find difficult to answer, for Inclination says one thing and Common-sense another."

"And thou didst warn me against Common-sense, so will I answer thy question, 'tis very simple: Thou art for London because . . . danger threatens thee—nay, I know, I feel it! And since danger threatens thee needs must I share thy danger, 'tis my right! So if thou go to London, I go to London—yea, John, even though I tramp every step! So the matter is settled!"

"Eve-Ann, my dear," said he, very tenderly, "you are a wilful, a most determined young woman—and for once, I am heartily glad of it."

"And Rupert? Shalt take him, also?"

"Ha, Rupert! Of course! Never fear, child, he shall come."

"O? Why?"

"Because . . . well, it is my whim."

"Art sure he will obey thy whim?"

"Quite sure."

"What dost think of him, John?"

"That he is a fine fellow, a handsome youth!"

"What more, John?"

"That he is confoundedly cheerful—I mean, a merry companion for you."

"And what else, John?"

"That he is magnificently, gloriously young!"

"Yes, he is—very young! So young that I—hark! what is that? O John . . . someone is coming . . . creeping yonder!" And she glanced fearfully where something moved in the ever-deepening shadows. "O pray, let us go . . . nay, why, John . . . 'tis a woman! 'Tis a poor creature, see how feebly she goes!" Even as she spoke, the woman stumbled and falling to her knees, sank into the dust and lay moaning. And then Eve was beside her, had lifted her in strong, young arms and laid her upon the grass beside the road.

"O John, pray come, she has fainted, I think——"

But as Sir Marmaduke approached, a little reluctantly, the woman sat up and, muttering that she was better, struggled to her feet, took a few steps and would have fallen but for Eve's ready arm.

"John, we cannot leave her, she is ill."

"But, my dear child?"

"In the eyes of God she is our sister! So pray, John, come and aid me with this thy poor sister . . . take her other arm!"

Sir Marmaduke stood hesitatingly, full of a strange reluctance, and in that moment was the tread of quick feet, a cheery whistle, and Rupert hurried to them.

"Why, Johnny!" he exclaimed, "are you there, my buck? And I've been searching the town for you, every inn, tavern and ale-house in the place and by Gad, Johnny—why, hallo, who's here?"

"A woman," answered Eve, "a poor woman, Rupert, and cannot walk! So take her up, I pray thee, and bear her along with us."

"Eh? O! B'gad! A woman? And carry her? Why certainly, but—ah—what does the lady say?"

"She is sick, fainting, I think. So Rupert, carry her!"

"O certainly, Eve-Ann! Your word is my law and —ah—so forth, of course." Saying which, Mr. Bellamy raised the swooning woman in his powerful arms and bore her lightly along, with Eve beside him, while Sir Marmaduke followed in frowning perplexity.

Reaching the encampment at last, Sir Marmaduke sat down beside the dying fire where, presently, he was joined by Mr. Bellamy who stood looking back with eyes of ecstasy towards that shady grove where Eve's little tent was pitched.

"She's an absolute angel!" he murmured, "an angel o' mercy, John, a positive——"

"What does she propose doing with this woman?"

"Eh? Woman? Lord knows! I was saying that she is——"

"An angel, precisely, Rupert. But this woman will complicate matters."

"John, old fellow," quoth Mr. Bellamy, casting himself down and speaking in tones of the utmost dejection, "she's too good for any ordinary human fellow, confound me if she isn't!" Here Mr. Bellamy shook his head and sighed profoundly. "And she looks, John, and b'gad she sounds so . . . so holy, old fellow! When she 'thees' and 'thous' me and opens her great, beautiful eyes at me, I . . . I feel the unworthiest of dogs and . . . and so forth, John. She has glorious . . . wonderful eyes, y'know —eh?"

"I have noticed them, Rupert. But what is she doing with that woman, I wonder?"

"Ministering to her like the spotless angel she is, old fellow . . . And then, her form, John! Her shape! Let me tell you it is the very absolute of per- fection, makes me think of goddesses and so forth . . . Greece and Rome, John, Aphrodite, Helen o' Troy, Cally—what's-her-name . . . Callipyge—"

"Helen of Troy was not a goddess, Rupert."

"Neither is Eve, thank heaven! But she's handsomer, John, lovelier, more confoundedly beau——"

Here Sir Marmaduke stretched his arms and yawned; Mr. Bellamy stared in pitying disgust.

"Lord, man!" he exclaimed, "I speak of a glorious creature, a regular blooming Venus, I endeavour to open your eyes to her perfections, and e'gad—you stretch and gape like a perishing fish! However, let me tell you, 'spite of her shy-sweet demureness, when she loves 'twill be the real thing, the positive, absolute, genuine article . . . passion, John, fire——"

"Which reminds me it requires mending," said Sir Marmaduke, "pray throw on another faggot or two."

Mr. Bellamy stared, sighed and shook his head; quoth he:

"You're a rum customer, Hobbs, a queer, cold-blooded card! I suppose it's your age . . . the tempered flame, and so forth, yet you've the look of a regular dasher at times."

"Now as to yourself," said Sir Marmaduke, stirring the new-made fire very gently, "being so conspicuously young, Rupert, and such profound amateur of beauty, you have no wish to part company with me and—Eve-Ann?"

"Heavens and earth—no!" cried Mr. Bellamy in accents of horror. "Though, of course," sighed he with rueful look, "seeing I am a beggar dependant on your bounty, John, you have only to drop the merest hint and I'll instantly take myself——"

"However, Rupert, you are quite willing to accompany us to London?"

Mr. Bellamy jumped at the word.

"London?" he repeated in joyful tone, "to London? God bless you, John old fellow, when do we start?"

"In something less than an hour."

"Ye Gods! But why such haste?"

"Because it so happens I am being pursued for murder."

"For mur——" Mr. Bellamy sat down again, very suddenly, and gasped.

"For the recent murder at Harting, Rupert."

"Eh? O Lord! You, John, you? Fifty pounds reward . . . dead or alive—you? The fellow who trussed up the two fellows at the inn, dodged the Bow-Street runners and left Goldaming in such uproar this afternoon—you, John?"

"Need I tell you that I am innocent of the crime?"

"No, no, devil take me, no! Some cursed mistake somewhere or other, of course. I'm with you, old fellow, thick and thin, hand and glove, fire and water and—so forth! But, Lord love you, John, they'll be after you, y'know!"

"They probably are!" nodded Sir Marmaduke, taking out his watch and consulting it by light of the fire.

"O egad, they may find their way—here!"

"I expect they will, Rupert. But in half-an-hour or so a carriage will be waiting in the shade of that clump of trees half a mile beyond the finger-post, you know the place, I think?"

"To be sure I do."

"Well, you will escort Eve-Ann there . . . and I fancy you had better start now."

"Yes, yes—but what of the sick woman?"

"Leave her . . . get Eve to the carriage."

"Trust me, old fellow. But what of you?"

"I shall join you later. Should I be detained you will wait fifteen minutes, no longer, then away for London. The driver is a friend of mine whom you can trust implicitly. But now—remember I place Eve-Ann in your care."

"I take it as an honour, John. But . . . suppose she refuses to leave the woman behind—eh?"

"Then take her also, if you must. But get Eve-Ann into the carriage at all hazards. Now go, and keep away from the high-road as much as possible."

Up sprang Mr. Bellamy, settled his weather-beaten hat with rap on the crown and, glancing down at Sir Marmaduke, hesitated.

"But you, John?" he inquired, a little anxiously. "Why stay behind?"

"For very sufficient reason, my dear Rupert."

"Well, good luck to you, old fellow!" said Mr. Bellamy and reaching down, very suddenly, grasped Sir Marmaduke's hand, wrung it hard, and hurried away.

Then Sir Marmaduke rose and, stepping out of the fire-light, vanished amid the leafy boskages beyond; and presently, hidden in this gloom, he heard Eve and Rupert in disputation which, ending suddenly, Eve appeared in the fire-light, peering round about, anxious-eyed, in a kind of desperate eagerness.

" John!" she called, " John, where art thou ? "

A moment's silence, then again: "O John, why hast left us? I will not go without thee, John!" And now Rupert's voice in answer.

"He will meet us at the carriage. So come, Eve-Ann, hurry now or we may miss him altogether." Here-upon, slow-footed and unwilling, she turned and was hidden among the deeper shadows.

Then Sir Marmaduke, leaning against a tree, folded his arms and waited . . . Thus, after some while, his sharp ears caught the sound he had expected, a rhythmic drumming that resolved itself, little by little, into the wild beat of on-coming, galloping horse-hoofs, yet he never stirred: the gallop became a trot, slowed to a walk, halted, and in the ensuing silence was menace; yet still he waited. . . . And now was a stealthy rustling that drew ever nearer until out into the fire-light stepped the tall figure of Sir Thomas Mowbray, and behind him three other men in two of whom he recognised the Bow-Street runners.

Q

"The birds is flowd," quoth the saturnine Toby, in growling dejection.

"Well, they ain't got far, Toby, I'll lay!" answered the optimistic Bob. "Look at the fire, so bright and noo-made."

"True enough!" answered Sir Thomas, with savage oath. "The damned villain can't ha' got very far. Scatter and beat the coverts and—shoot on sight!"

Then Sir Marmaduke turned and began to run, forcing his way through the under-brush like one who fled in panic, whereupon was a fierce, exultant shout and the gloom behind was full of the wild stir of pursuit. On ran Sir Marmaduke over familiar ground, making all the noise possible, until, being come beneath a certain tree, he leapt with arms up-flung, gripped a bough and drawing himself up, crouched there until his pursuers were gone by. Then, dropping lightly to earth, he doubled back and speeding silently by open ways, ran fast until he heard the sounds he hearkened for—the jingle of champed bit, the snort of horses. And presently he espied them, the four animals tethered to a tree; deftly he loosed them and, mounting one, off he rode, leading the other three. And thus, after some while, he saw a twinkle of lights and easing to a trot, drew rein beside the carriage.

"Art safe, John, art safe?"

"Quite safe, Eve-Ann!"

"What, only you, old fellow?" cried Mr. Bellamy cheerily. "B'gad, you sound like a troop of cavalry! Are they after us?"

"They were," answered Sir Marmaduke, glancing up at John Hobbs who sat upon the box, reins in hand, "but if they follow us now they must do so on foot."

"What ha' you stolen their mounts? O prime!"

"And thou'rt not hurt, John?"

"Not even a scratch, my dear! However," he continued, eyeing the noble carriage-horses that pawed the dust eager for swift action, "there will be some hard spurring after us to-night, I imagine, so if you are ready, my faithful John, whip and away!"

"Wait!" cried Mr. Bellamy, leaping from the moving carriage and slamming the door, "if you are riding, John, and will spare me one o' your herd of steeds, I'll ride with you."

And thus they presently set off Londonwards.

CHAPTER XXXI

OFF and away with the sharp crack of whip plied
by practised hand, a clatter of hoofs, a rumble and grind
of wheels; faster and faster until the thudding hoofs
and rumbling wheels merged into a ceaseless hum
waking echoes far and wide. Away through a summer
night, cool and sweet with a thousand odours from
dewy hedgerows, from hidden flower and herb, and with
a rising moon whose level beams made of the broad,
dusty road a white track narrowing upon the vision,
up hill and down, until it glimmered and was lost in
distance. Away past motionless trees that loom up,
grow gigantic and are gone, past lonely farms where
dogs bark fitfully, rattling through sleeping hamlets,
thundering over bridges that span unseen streams, up
the long curving ascent of a hill and to an inn where
presently is a gleam of lanterns, a scurrying of heavy
boots and men come running to unbuckle harness,
loose traces and trot off with foam-spattered horses;
whereafter come other men with horses that rear and
caper, snort and dance, eager for the road. So harness
is rebuckled, traces made fast, the men jump aside,
John cracks whip and away they go again, fast and
furious as ever, the open road before, a rolling, billow-
ing cloud of dust behind. . . . Jingling bits and curb-
chains, rumble of wheels and beat of hoofs, now
muffled in dusty bottoms, now roaring loud over cobbled ways, past cottages beneath whose steep, thatched

roofs Innocence slumbers, past desolate woods in whose black solitudes Murder may lurk, past babbling streams that dimple to the moon, plodding up hill, thundering down and thus, at last to a second inn. More twinkling lanterns and hoarse-throated ostlers who cry: "Whoa there!" and "Stand over!" And now it is discovered that one of the wheels is running hot. Down clambers John Hobbs, feels it for himself, shakes grave head and commands:

"Grease!"

The chief ostler, also shaking grave head, suggests removal of wheel, and fining down of axle.

"No!" says John.

"Yes!" nods Sir Marmaduke, dismounting. "We have made excellent time." Then he sees Eve leaning from the carriage window to speak to Mr. Bellamy who bends to her from the saddle, a dusty figure; therefore Sir Marmaduke turns to the matter of the wheel but Eve calls him softly.

"Thou . . . thou'rt dreadfully dusty, John!" says she, looking at him with troubled eyes: yet surely, her trouble is not because of this.

"We shall be dustier yet, child," he answers, lightly.

"When . . . when do we reach London?" she asks him in the same timid, hesitating manner, and he wonders to see how her hands clasp and wring each other.

"Before dawn, at this rate," he assures her. "Meanwhile, my dear, are you comfortable . . . hungry—thirsty?"

"Nay, John, nay . . . I thank thee."

"And how is your invalid?"

"She has fallen asleep. . . ." And here, Eve draws a shuddering breath, looks down on him wide-eyed, then leans nearer as if she would whisper, but then John Hobbs comes up:

"We must wait here ten minutes or so," says he.

"Excellent!" murmurs Sir Marmaduke. "I suggest ale and a sandwich."

"Prime!" exclaims Mr. Bellamy and dismounts instantly. And so they enter the inn, all three and there refresh themselves; but very soon John goes out to the wheel, Mr. Bellamy wanders forth to gaze on the moon, perhaps, and thus Sir Marmaduke is left alone.

Suddenly the door opens and he glances round, expecting John Hobbs, but instead sees a veiled woman who, entering swiftly, closes the door and leans there; then, with quick, febrile gesture, she throws back her veil disclosing a face still rarely beautiful despite the tell-tale lines at delicate nostril and quivering lip.

Sir Marmaduke rose and stood with sunburnt right hand fast clenched upon his chair-back, staring on this woman in speechless amazement. And so, for a moment was deadly silence.

"Marmaduke," said she at last, in voice strangely rich and soft, "you look younger than I had expected. Time has been kind to you, Marmaduke! Yet neither am I altered beyond your recognition, I see."

Sir Marmaduke bowed.

"So you have been tramping the country with your handsome young Quakeress? O, marvellous! The supercilious fine gentleman is become human at last, it seems. A miracle indeed! And yet I confess she is a decidedly handsome creature, though a simpleton. But coy simplicity, a demure innocence is an irresistible lure for the man of middle-age, to be sure, and yet—this rustic——"

"Shall we converse of—ourselves?" he suggested.

"Then, Marmaduke, 'twas you drove me to it, 'twas you made me the castaway I am . . . 'twas you, before God it was! You were so cold, so aloof . . . so inhuman!"

"Madam," he answered bowing, "I accept your reproof and with it the responsibility. And now, pray how may I serve you?"

"Three times, Marmaduke, I wrote imploring your pardon . . . supplicating your forgiveness . . ."

"And I sent you money!"

"O . . . money?" she exclaimed, so passionately that she choked and fell to a dismal coughing, a spasm so fierce and prolonged that he went to her at last and placed her in a chair; then, the door having no key, he in turn, set his back against it.

"You know," said she, so soon as she could speak, "you know he wearied me in a week!"

"And he, madam, the very opposite of myself!"

"You know, if you had only forgiven, you might have saved me, Marmaduke . . . saved me . . ."

"From everything except—yourself?" Sir Marmaduke retorted serenely unmoved.

"You know how cruelly, how bitterly I regretted——"

"But repented—never, madam!"

"Marmaduke. I am ill . . . death has touched me. . . . I cannot live very long."

"Meanwhile, how may I serve you?"

"O implacable!" she exclaimed, with hopeless gesture. "Have you no mercy? No pity for a dying woman and she . . . your wife, Marmaduke?"

"Beyond expression!" he answered gently. "But——"

"But," she repeated, leaning towards him in sudden, fierce petulance, "the sooner I die the better for you! O, I see it all . . . you love at last! Your cold heart is touched, your haughty magnificance all forgotten to tramp the country like a gipsy—you of all men! You are in your second youth and sick with doting passion for this piece of rustic, coy virginity——"

"Madam, I beg——"

"Bah! Your high and mighty stateliness counts for nothing with me, sir! You are become no more than a love-sick swain . . . though somewhat superannuated, poor man!" And she laughed in shrill derision, a pitiful laugh soon ended in choking cough. . . . "Your virginal quakeress—so immaculate! Your lofty self, so virtuous, so correct and entirely impeccable, would shudder at a lawless kiss ! . . and so, most honourable husband, my cruel death means your delight, the sanctification of your bliss . . . this creeping death I shudder at . . . that fills me with such dreadful horror, means freedom for you and your quakeress, my grave will be your bridal——"

"Enough—enough!" exclaimed Sir Marmaduke, and taking out his purse he laid it gently upon the table before her. "Here, madam, in notes and gold are some fifty pounds, pray take them and——"

"Ah—money!" said she, her vivid lips drawn in bitter smile, her handsome eyes very bright, "keep it, Marmaduke, I have the money you bestowed on a beggar to-night, and besides I am not so destitute as I seem."

"However," said he with an air of serene finality, "you will remain here for to-night. A room shall be prepared for your reception at once, and——"

"Whimsical man!" she murmured, glancing up at him, handsome head aslant. "Order what rooms you will, I go on with all of you to London."

Sir Marmaduke merely looked at her and shook his head.

"Foolish creature!" said she, in the same soft, cooing voice, "attempt to stay me and I will scream and raise the house on you."

"Regrettable!" he sighed. "But I fear you must scream."

"O donkey!" she exclaimed with a little laugh, "leave me and you leave your beautiful Eve also! I have told her my story—O, indeed, quite truthfully and your tender-hearted, soft-sided, virgin-innocent will never desert a dying woman friendless and desolate . . . how little you know her, Marmaduke! But you never truly understood women and never will, for all your worldly wisdom and——"

A rap on the door and the voice of John Hobbs announces the carriage ready and waiting.

"Come in!" cried my lady imperiously. So John Hobbs opened the door but, beholding my lady, stood upon the threshold, his square face bleak and grim.

"Why, John," said she, nodding gaily at his stern, silent figure, "my good John Hobbs, you know me, it seems, after all these years . . . so pray, if you remember my names also, speak them—all of them!"

John Hobbs bowed and spoke as might an archdeacon in gentle reprobation:

"Marian, Eleanor, Lady Vane-Temperley."

"That being so, John," said she, rising with a certain majesty, "pray conduct me to the carriage."

Thus, laying frail hand on John's dusty, stalwart arm, she went forth of the inn.

Then Sir Marmaduke took up his purse, stared at it with vacant eyes and thrusting it into his pocket, sighed wearily and stepped out into the moonlight.

Mr. Bellamy, laughing cheerily, closes the carriage door leaps lightly to saddle and calls to Sir Marmaduke who, mounting also, nods grimly to John and they are off again.

Grinding wheels, thudding hoofs, the creak and jingle of harness. . . . Away across heaths stretching desolate beneath the sinking moon, through narrow ways and leafy glooms shot athwart by silver moonbeams, on and on until the moon is down and the world about them a place of brooding darkness. Jingle and rumble and tramp until stars pale to the dawn, until trees and hedgerows give place to houses growing ever more dense, to cobbled streets, to the echoing thoroughfares of the mighty city . . . to the Horns Inn, hard beside Kennington Cross.

John swings his foam-spattered horses aside, beneath a lowering arch into dim-lit stable yard a-throng with carts and great waggons, a place of noise and bustle where people hurry to and fro, horses stamping, ostlers shouting, post-boys swearing while anxious passengers peer and gape and ask questions innumerable, and all despite this so early hour. Some half mile behind the dusty carriage Sir Marmaduke and Mr. Bellamy urge on their jaded animals, but at the entrance to the yard are checked by a great, country wain that lumbers heavily before them.

"Egad, old fellow," yawns Mr. Bellamy, surveying his own and companion's rough and dusty attire so ill-sorted to the saddle, "we look like beggars a-horse-back, more especially your humble servant. Lord, Johnny-man, think of it—a bath! Aha, breakfast! A bed! Come on!"

Amid the ceaseless bustle of the inn-yard Sir Marmaduke dismounts, stiff and heavily and is leading his exhausted animal stable-wards when he is startled by a wild shout and Mr. Bellamy comes running to grasp him by the arm:

"John," he gasps, "the carriage is empty! They . . . the woman . . . Eve—she's gone! Come, come and see!" Sure enough they find a very puzzled and distressed John Hobbs standing beside the open carriage door that gapes on emptiness. . . . So, together, they search the crowded yard from end to end, but without success.

"Now the inn—try the inn!" cries Mr. Bellamy. "Perhaps they're ordering breakfast——"

"We will see!" says Sir Marmaduke, grim-lipped. So the great inn is ransacked, yawning waiters, sleepy chamber-maids, boots, ostlers and grooms are questioned but no one seems to know anything of the fugitives, Eve and my lady have vanished utterly. Mr. Bellamy, nevertheless, pursues his search with passionate zeal and determination, he dashes to and fro in yard and stables, he pervades the inn itself vociferous with breathless inquiry.

"Sir," says John Hobbs, glancing somewhat anxiously at Sir Marmaduke's grim face that shows so pale and haggard in the dawn, "Sir, what now?"

"Why now," answers Sir Marmaduke, laying dusty hand on John's broad, dusty shoulder, "it is fare-thee-well my John, for a while at least; I go to find Eve-Ann."

"You suspect where she is, sir?"

"I do so."

"You think my lady has taken her to——"

"I think, John, that there is nothing so merciless as the hate of an erring woman. . . . Now as to nephew Rupert, you will supply him with money and all necessaries, establish him in suitable lodging and say that his unworthy uncle proposes to . . . settle him once and for all if he can comport himself with a reasonable sanity. . . . And now, good-bye, my faithful John, you shall hear from me later." So saying, Sir Marmaduke shook hands and turning, hastened from the bustling yard into the growing bustle of the street.

CHAPTER XXXII

SOME DESCRIPTION OF GILES'S RENTS, MR. SHRIG AND AN ACTOR

THE men were behind him still, three vague shapes flitting amid the shadows for, among these noisome lanes and narrow alleys, night gloomed already; and within this thickening dusk sinister figures moved, furtive, slip-shod men and slatternly women, who peered at him with eyes that scowled or leered with nameless evil. A bad place by day, an unsavoury place at any time but at such hour as this, surely a place of danger for the unwary or too-confiding stranger.

Thus Sir Marmaduke went his way, alert of foot and eye, his deadly right hand in that capacious pocket of his countryman's coat where lay a certain short-barrelled pistol; for whenever he glanced behind, he espied these same three men, the one burly and tall with a great shag of hair, the second a small, mean creature, the third a thin, cadaverous fellow who walked with a strange, dancing step.

Turning a sharp corner he found himself in a narrow gut or passage running between very high brick walls and thus darker than any he had traversed, wherefore he paused a moment and then went on again with lengthened stride. . . . Footfalls behind him . . . quickening . . . creeping rapidly nearer . . . Sir Marmaduke halted suddenly and swung about, his finger on the trigger of the weapon in his

pocket for the men were so near he could see the whites
of their eyes.

"Well, my lads?" said he in country accents, "are
ye wantin' aught?"

"Why yes, chum," answered the little man, promptly,
in shrill, small, whistling pipe, "us wants a friendly
word wi' ye, us wants to ask ye if ever——" With
sudden gesture, right and left, he dug small, sharp
elbows into his companions, whereat they turned tail,
all three, and, running very fleetly, were suddenly
gone.

Sir Marmaduke was staring after them in astonishment when he heard the leisured tread of heavy feet
and, glancing round, beheld a man approaching; a
short, broad-shouldered, sedate-looking person from
neatly-brushed top-boots to broad-brimmed hat and
bearing under one arm a remarkably nobbly stick,
otherwise he seemed a very ordinary man indeed though,
to be sure, he possessed a bright and roving eye.

The man stopped and viewed Sir Marmaduke with
his bright eyes, that is to say, he glanced at his boots,
his neckerchief and the top of his hat, and smiled in
friendly greeting.

"Bunty Fagan, Dancing James and Vistling Dick!"
he nodded. "Werry desprit coves, 'specially Vistling
Dick, the littlest un as a-costed of you."

"You know them then?"

"Friend, I do—like a feyther! Two buzmen and a
prig. Ah, and they knows me and acts according. Was
they mo-lesting of you, friend?"

"No."

"But they follered you, p'raps? Ay, I thought so.
Rum customers, queer coves with a wengeance—rob-
bery wi' wiolence, thievery or murder, that's them!
Knife, pistol or bludgeon, bless you, all's vun to 'em!
Werry promising coves all three, true Capitals, but
the littlest un's the prime tulip, Vistlin' Dick—slit more
nor vun innercent throat 'e 'as, to my knowing."

"Then why not arrest the miscreant?"

"The oo?"

"The guilty villain," said Sir Marmaduke as they walked on together, "if indeed you know him guilty."

"Ah!" sighed the man, "I knows a lot, but all as I know ain't no good without proof, friend. 'Tis proof as sp'iles so many beeootiful cases! Lord, if it weren't for proof I could top plenty o' murderers as is a-walkin' about 'appy as birds at this i-dentical minute—and there y'are!"

"Are you then a law officer?"

"Friend, I won't go for to deny same. Law's my trade and murders is my line, werry much so. Murder is meat and drink to me. . . . Name o' Shrig, baptismal Jarsper. And I can't say no fairer. . . . You're a stranger in these parts p'raps?"

"Yes."

"Up from the country, p'raps?"

"Yes. And I'm looking for a respectable lodging hereabouts, can you advise me of any such, Mr. Shrig?"

"To be sure, friend, I knows of a inn, small but werry cosy and kept by a one-armed soldier, Gray's Inn Lane way."

"That would be too far off."

"Too fur!" nodded Mr. Shrig, staring at his nobbly stick. "To be sure! And a stranger—hum!"

"I desire to reside in the vicinity of Giles's Rents."

"You desires . . . wicinity . . . and werry nat'ral too!"

"On the contrary, life here will be quite detestable but I am looking for a young lady, who has lately come to live in this neighbourhood with an older lady —an invalid."

"Friend, there's plenty o' invalids in Giles's Rents, ah, shoals, but you wouldn't 'ardly call 'em ladies— leastways, I shouldn't, bein' a nat'rally truthful cove."

"However, if you can direct me to some likely lodging, I shall esteem it a favour, Mr. Shrig."

"Friend, I'll do better, I'll take ye there—a attic werry nice an' clean as is to let off by a pal o' mine name o' Ponsingby—baptismal Augustus, vich same is a actor. This vay, friend, and keep close, if you vas follered vunce you may be again and strangers is apt to get 'urt hereabouts now and then, but you'll be right along o' me. And vot did you say your name was?"

"I didn't mention it," said Sir Marmaduke, glancing keenly at his companion's face.

"Didn't you, friend? Why think o' that now! My y'ears must be deceivin' o' me."

"My name is Hobbs and I think you may speak for me as a respectable character."

"'Obbs!" repeated Mr. Shrig, beaming. "And a werry good name too! And you're from the country, eh? And vich part, friend 'Obbs?"

"Sussex."

"Sussex—to be sure!" nodded Mr. Shrig, staring hard at his nobbly stick again. "Think o' that now! A werry pretty county is Sussex and they've lately 'ad a werry bee-ootiful murder down there! You've 'eard of it, friend, o' course?"

"I've heard of it!" nodded Sir Marmaduke, glancing at his companion's placid features again.

"Done in a vood . . . at sunset . . . and birds a-chirping so peaceful! Might call it a werry poetical murder, eh, friend? A vood, d'ye see, vith a corp in same, and his napper blowed off! Vot more could 'uman 'eart desire? A pretty case, friend 'Obbs, this pore gent shot at close quarters and no gun, nor pistol, nor nothing!"

"But there was something!"

"O?" murmured Mr. Shrig, his roving glance upon a murky chimney-pot.

"Beside the body they found a gold-mounted cane, I hear."

"Ah?" murmured Mr. Shrig.

"I am surprised that you, a police officer, should not be aware of this."

"Hum!" murmured Mr. Shrig, beaming up at the sky pink with the last beams of sunset; then, taking a small notebook from breast pocket and turning its pages with questing finger, he halted suddenly and held it towards Sir Marmaduke:

"Friend," said he, "the light's a bit bad, but vot d'ye make o' these?"

Now looking where Mr. Shrig's blunt finger pointed Sir Marmaduke saw this:

Beholding thus his own monogram so accurately drawn, Sir Marmaduke stood a moment staring at the familiar letters.

"It looks like the letters M.T.V.," he answered and glancing at his companion, saw his placid smile vanish.

"Eh?" exclaimed Mr. Shrig, in changed voice, "A Wee, says you? Why, Lord love us . . . so it is A Tee, a Em, and a Wee! By goles, friend, you've got good eyes, as'tounding and the light so bad! . . . A Wee, says you, quick as a flash, and a Wee it is!"

After this Mr. Shrig walked some little distance in profound but placid thought.

"Pray where are we going?" inquired Sir Marmaduke at last.

"To number six Apple-tree Court, friend—though there ain't no trees there, apple or otherwise."

"And your friend is an actor, you say?"

"Werry much so!" nodded Mr. Shrig. "Hows'ever he's 'ighly respectable and quite a gent though, being a actor 'e's generally be'ind wi' the rent and sich . . .

and 'ere we are!" So saying, Mr. Shrig halted before a small, sulky-looking door that glowered from the very darkest corner of a dismal little court full of small dejected-looking habitations, a stagnant back-water, as it were, yet seeming in the half-light, some-what less squalid than its neighbours.

Having twice rapped loudly upon this sulky, little door without producing the least effect, Mr. Shrig reached forth and tapped softly upon small and grimy window, at the same time emitting a peculiarly sweet and melodious whistle; and lo, in that same instant of time the door swung open with startling suddenness and a gentleman appeared swathed picturesquely in a table-cloth and bearing in one hand a be-floured rolling-pin; a commanding gentleman portentous as to nose, hair and eye-brows; as for the table-cloth, though time-worn and besprent with coffee and other stains, seen thus in conjunction with the eye-brows it became at once the *toga virilis* clothing the stately form of a Senator of Imperial Rome.

"Shrig!" exclaimed the gentleman saluting with the rolling-pin as it had been a two-edged sword, "Hail and thrice welcome, good my friend! For any delay untoward accept our heart-swelling regrets but—in point of fact we apprehended you were the King's Taxes. Enter, good friend, be good enough to set to our gates and follow me!" Saying which, he led them into a small and somewhat stuffy apartment where a blonde lady of somewhat languishing cast of feature was couched upon shabby sofa in jaded bed-gown and a Roman attitude.

"Eudoxia, my soul," said the Senator, calling the lady's attention with magnificent gesture, "our friend Jasper Shrig with a stranger."

The lady rose with superb grace, and reaching forth both hands in greeting, smiled upon Mr. Shrig with large and soulful eyes which, if a trifle haggard, held the light of very sincere welcome, none the less.

R

"O Mr. Shrig!" she sighed, "dear Mr. Shrig. . . . O my poor heart, I thought you were the water!"

"Vater, mam?"

"Indeed! The iron-souled monster threatened to cut us off yesterday or the day before . . . when was it Gussie dear?" The Senator's eyebrows showed a marked agitation but he merely groaned.

"But, dear Mr. Shrig, if they do cut off the water, I say—let them! There is a pump in the yard and there hangs my comfort, for while we have a devoted bucket remaining, my Augustus shall not lack while these two hands——"

"Cease, Eudoxia—noble woman, no more!" quoth the Senator, lifting rolling-pin as high as the low dingy ceiling would allow. "For ye gods, upon this oft-imbrued sword I swear the dogs of Circumstance may howl, but by this blade, this final and most pointed argument, I vow all hell shall roar and crash in ruin damned ere those fair hands the servile bucket grasp——"

"Dear noble Augustus, I live but to serve thee—and O pray mind the plaster, love! Dear Mr. Shrig and friend, you find us rehearsing, for Augustus has a part at last in Mr. D'Abernon's new play—to be sure he dies in the first act, yet surely better die then than not at all, as I tell him."

"Ponsingby, mam and sir," said Mr. Shrig, seizing opportunity for a word. "I've took the liberty to bring you a lodger for your attic—Mr. 'Obbs here, as desires to take a peep at same if convenient?"

"A . . . lodger?" exclaimed Eudoxia with a faint shriek, "O Mr. Shrig. . . . O husband . . . a lodger —alas!" And she covered her face.

"Why vot is it, mam?"

"Nay ask Augustus—Augustus, speak!"

The Senator groaned, a strong man in his agony, while his eyebrows——!!

"O cruel spite!" quoth he. "Damned Fate! O Fortune thrice accur-sed!" He clasped his brow, clutched at throat and scowled terrific upon the empty air. "A lodger! O detestable perversity!"

"Explain, my husband!" wailed Eudoxia, "poverty being no shame—confess."

"Nay, beloved creature, my withers are sufficiently wrung, my lofty crest is bowed, my faltering tongue its customary office abhors! Speak thou!"

Eudoxia wrung her shapely hands:

"O, Mr. Shrig," she wailed, "alas dear friend, our attic is no longer void . . . we . . . we have. . . . O me, a man in possession . . . a bailiff for rent . . . he sleeps there!"

The Senator folded arms within his toga and moved them gently up and down, quoth he:

"Admirably put, my soul! Terse, my Eudoxia, and to the point most apt. . . . There is, my friends . . . surge not proud heart! . . . for paltry sum, divers coins of values various, a being base on us impounded, a thing of affliction he on legs two upreared in form and semblance of humanity, yet, man or no, good my friends, a being unto us most hateful, insensible to reason as monster fell or the Hyrcanian——"

"For how much?" inquired Mr. Shrig.

"Friend this know I not, nor care—'tis sordid matter of pounds, shillings, pence, more or less, yet more than we can for the moment command, alas!"

"It is four pounds, ten shillings and three-pence farthing!" sighed Eudoxia.

"And why," demanded the Senator with sudden passion. "O ye stars—why the odd farthing? The rest I might endure with stoic fortitude, these pounds, these shillings and these pence—but . . . this farthing! By the unshakable firmament of heaven this mads me . . . mocks me with my poverty most dire—one farthing!"

"Madam," said Sir Marmaduke, bowing. "I will engage your attic, pray accept a month's rent in advance," and he placed notes and gold upon the table.

"Ten pounds!" exclaimed Eudoxia, gasping. "And for . . . one month! O, sir. . . . O no, no, we couldn't charge so much, it would be out of all reason!" And she pushed the money from her with trembling hands while Mr. Shrig, glancing from this to Sir Marmaduke's high-bred features and thence to the ceiling, pursed his lips in soundless whistle.

"Madam," said Sir Marmaduke with his air of serene finality. "I never pay less than . . . ah . . . two pounds ten shillings per week."

"Ye eternal stars!" exclaimed the Senator. "O lamps of heaven!"

"But, sir," reasoned the trembling Eudoxia, "it is too—too much! Augustus what must we do? Augustus—speak!"

"Nay my soul," cried the Senator, making a light pass with the rolling-pin, "settle it between you."

Eudoxia stared down at the money with shining eyes, and Sir Marmaduke, glancing from her pallid face to her husband's lank form and reading there privation, took up the money and putting it into her hand, gently closed her fingers upon it.

"O, Mr. Shrig," sighed she, "what shall we do?"

"Mam, I should pay off that cove in possession if I was you."

"I will . . . I will. . . . At once!" she cried, and sped from the room. . . . Thus presently was a sound of heavy feet on creaking stair, the mutter of harsh and sulky voice, the slam of front door and she was back again, radiant-eyed.

"Mr. Hobbs," said she, a little breathlessly, "our garret will be at your service this night, for which we ask you . . . a pound a week—and this is too much!"

"Madam," answered Sir Marmaduke, smiling, "I pay two pounds ten shillings or nothing! Indeed, you may find me a somewhat exacting lodger—for instance, to-night I should desire something . . . savoury for supper."

"Supper!" exclaimed Mr. Ponsonby, tossing off the table-cloth and ceasing to be Roman. "Supper. . . . O music sweeter than the throb of harps . . . supper, Eudoxia! Cates succulent—here shall be no Barmeicidal feast! Shrig, what d'ye suggest?"

"Pigs' trotters is tasty!" answered Mr. Shrig thoughtfully. "Then there's eyestars, à-la-mode beef, cheese, porter, stout or ale."

"All," cried Mr. Ponsonby, benevolence throned upon the eye-brows, "all these shall grace our board this night. Eudoxia, my love, the table furniture prepare. I will incontinent summon the small minion and with him the viands hither bring." And opening the window, Mr. Ponsonby thrust out his head and whistled shrilly, whereafter appeared a small and touzled boy with whom he departed, returning soon heavy laden to find the supper-table laid. So down they sat and ate with hearty good-will, Mr. Ponsonby proposing the toast of "My lady wife! Our princely lodger! Our good friend Jasper Shrig!" with stately, Tudor-like verbosity, and all was good-fellowship. But even so, there were times when Mr. Shrig, glancing askance at Sir Marmaduke's aristocratic features, would turn his roving eye to floor or dingy ceiling and purse his lips in their soundless whistle. And once Sir Marmaduke's sharp ear caught the murmur of these words:

"A Wee!"

CHAPTER XXXIII

DESCRIBES THE MAGIC OF A FIDDLE

A WEEK has dragged its weary length of days, and leaning forth of his eyrie beneath the tiles, so far as he might by reason of narrow and inadequate dormer-window, Sir Marmaduke looked down upon weather-beaten roofs, toppling gables and jagged chimney-stacks decrepit with years, blackened by the smoke of countless generations and in every stage of ruinous decay. Beyond these and below he gazed upon that sink where the stream of life ran, old life and young, but little of it sweet and pure; court and lane and alley whence rose an unceasing, inarticulate hum which yet was the voice of this human hive. A never-ending monotonous drone, the blend of many sounds. Laughter and weeping, vague cries, childish shrieks of joy or passion, footsteps, discordant singing, harsh voices in clamorous argument, shrill hoots, the wail of the new-born, the groaning of stricken age, the blare of drunken shouts—it was all there, blent into this never-ending hum that was the voice of this close-packed hive of teeming humanity.

And Sir Marmaduke, listening to this unceasing drone, looking upon those toppling, dilapidated roofs which hid so much of sordid misery and shame, beneath which, good languished and evil throve apace, felt a sudden, great pity for it all, a passionate desire to help, and therewith a mighty yearning for the fragrant countryside; shady lane, darkling copse, rolling heath and open down where cool, sweet winds stirred. . . . But oftenest and most bitterly he yearned for one who had seemed the very embodiment of it all—for Eve-Ann Ash.

It was Saturday evening, and all the week he had haunted Giles's Rents and the neighbourhood, had trod and re-trodden these evil courts and alleys and always in vain. Yet that she was hereabout he felt persuaded, therefore his hope never failed him quite, his determination never faltered. If not to-day then —to-morrow. Thus he had sought her and would so seek until he found her.

Much in this short week had he seen and much learned of suffering nobly borne or endured with dull and hopeless apathy; of sin and shame bred of want, of grinding hunger and brutish ignorance. . . . Also he had marvelled that in this human cess-pool should spring such flowers as Generosity, Sympathy and even Purity, for Innocence had no being hereabouts. But it was Saturday evening wherefore the hive hummed with louder and more sinister note for Drunkenness reeled abroad more flagrantly even than usual. . . . From somewhere rose the dreadful scream of a woman in pain or terror, drowned in hoarse clamour of voices —shouts, wild laughter, the chorus of a song howled fitfully. . . .

And somewhere amid these loathly horrors, these thousand nameless evils, was—Eve-Ann! For all he knew to the contrary that agonized scream might have been hers! This thought sickened him, and he wiped sweat from wrinkling brow with clenched hand, breathing sudden passionate prayer for her safety . . . and then, rising above all these hateful sounds, high and clear and purely sweet as the voice of singing angel, rose the sound of a fiddle.

Sir Marmaduke held his breath to listen; and gradually, little by little the hive ceased its dreadful hum —its laughing, screaming, savage voices were hushed, spell-bound and enthralled, as it seemed, by the sweet, soothing magic of that fiddle. Hurrying downstairs he dound Eudoxia at the open front-door, hands clasped and eyes uplifted in an ecstasy:

"O, Mr. Hobbs, listen to it!" she whispered. "It is the little fiddler. . . . He came last week. . . . He plays to the children, the sick, even the drunkards. They call him mad, though what a master . . ."

But with word of brief apology, Sir Marmaduke hurried on until he was among the crowd that pressed about the silver-haired musician, men and women and children, an unlovely and ragged concourse, off-scourings of humanity for the most part; and yet, as he scanned each face with quick and eager glance, he beheld a very marvel for, inspired by these noble strains, familiar, homely airs played by the hand of Genius, these same faces, bloated, vicious, care-worn brutalized by Hardship and Want, were all wonderously transfigured—the habitual Brute was exorcised awhile and through eyes a-swim in tears of memory, peeped the original Angel of younger, better and happier days.

Presently the Fiddler turned and began to move off, playing as he walked; children, bare-footed, pattered after him in their rags, drunken men and women reeled along beside him, the aged crept to door and window the better to hear or wave sorrowful farewell. . . .

Now surely, O surely if Eve-Ann should chance to hear the wonder of this playing she must come forth for word with the white-haired master, her own so familiar friend!

Sir Marmaduke pushed and strove amid the press following where the music led from court to court, through alley and lane, peering about him before and behind, up at crowded windows and thronged doorways and then . . . he saw her. She was fast hemmed in among the surging crowd and yet his eyes saw only her. . . . And she more radiantly lovely even than her memory because, perhaps, of her sordid environment. . . . And the sweet familiarity of her face,

her form, her every look and feature wrought in him
an emotion so fiercely keen that her vivid image grew,
all sudden, blurred upon his sight. . . . Shoulders
jostled him, sharp elbows staggered him, but he never
heeded . . . and thus, he came beside her.

"My dear!" said he, and that was all.

"John!" she exclaimed, and the word was a sob;
then her hand was within his arm . . . their fingers
clung. "Thou art safe," she murmured. "O I have
prayed for this!"

The Fiddler had entered a narrow alley and the
throng, eager to follow, strove about them and pushed
so hard that instinctively he set his arm about her
loveliness, drawing her close, and in this moment there
occurred to his memory Lady Vane-Temperley's words:
"This soft-sided, tender-hearted virginity."

"So child, I have found you!" said he lightly.

"Thank God!" she murmured, nestling closer within
his arm.

"Rupert," said Sir Marmaduke, tightening his clasp,
"Rupert will be glad!"

"Ah yes!" she sighed, "poor Rupert!"

"Good heaven—why pity the youth?" demanded Sir
Marmaduke, peevishly. "Is he not—confoundedly
young, good-looking and with the world and happiness
all before him?"

"Yes, he is very young—and handsome," sighed
she, "and I think thou'rt a little pale, John, and thine
eyes look weary!"

"You ran away, Eve-Ann, you upset my plans, you
worried me!"

"Yet thou hast found me, John!"

"Thanks to our Fiddling Jack, heaven bless his
white head!"

"O—Jackie!" she cried, "I would speak with him."

"Certainly!" said Sir Marmaduke. So they looked
away from each other at last, and stood amazed to find
themselves alone and the narrow alley all deserted.

"We are too late, I fear," said he, and becoming, all at once, very conscious of his enfolding arm, he loosed her, whereupon she glanced up and meeting his look, flushed rosily and stood abashed, insomuch that he questioned her with a fatherly aloofness:

"My child, pray am I to learn your present hiding-place?"

"Yea verily, John. Though indeed 'tis no hiding-place—everybody seems to know it and . . . her . . . I mean . . . thy lady wife, John. She hath been expecting thee, every day."

"Ah?" said he gravely. "Indeed?"

"So pray come with me now, John."

"You mean . . . to her?"

"Thy wife, John, yea verily. Come now!"

"To what end, child?"

"Because she is sick and desires word with thee."

For awhile he stood frowning at the cobbles under-foot, but at last, feeling Eve-Ann's hand within his arm, he turned and followed whither she led.

CHAPTER XXXIV

OF GATHERING SHADOWS

A GREAT house that soared above the huddle of its meaner neighbours disdainful in decay; a very ancient house spacious as the times wherein it was built, but age and neglect had worked its ruin long since, and yet, as if dreaming of its vanished splendour, it frowned upon court and alley in gloomy stateliness.

Up broad uncarpeted, grimy stair to wide and desolate landing panelled in oak, its deep-graven moulding brutally defaced and marred and so to a lofty door, battered and age-worn that opened to Eve's hand upon thick carpet—a noble chamber nobly furnished. . . . Now glancing from this unexpected splendour to Eve-Ann's fresh loveliness, his eyes grew all at once fiercely alert. And now, drawing aside silken curtain, Eve opened another door:

"He is here, Marian!" said she gently.

"Dearest angel!" sighed a voice, "pray him to come in."

So Sir Marmaduke went in and found himself alone with my Lady Vane-Temperley. She lay upon a broad divan with a book in her hand but now she laid this by.

"Ah, Marmaduke," said she, smiling, "so you have found us at last. I mean of course, your Eve-Ann. I guessed you would sooner or later. And now you are here, I think, to take her from me?"

259

"What, madam, what is your purpose with her?" he demanded so sharply that my lady opened her very beautiful eyes even wider than their wont.

"Why, Marmaduke," she murmured in her soft, cooing voice, "I behold you actually . . . positively a little agitated.

"Be good enough to answer me!"

"Shall I?" she murmured. "Yes, I think I will, lest you ravish the sweet creature from me in a huff. Well then, Marmaduke, I want her for three reasons: First, because I am lonely and dying. Second, because I would remove temptation from you—O, I shall soon be dead! And thirdly, because I know while she is here—you will remain close by, and I would have you look upon my dead face before they—bury me. A silly whim, of course, and yet natural in a wife—even one who has transgressed so unforgiveably as I. . . . As for your Eve, do not fear, she is utterly and completely safe with me. Yet, if you doubt—then take her! Heaven forbid that such as I should keep her from—such as you, in such a place as this!"

"Why live here, Marian?"

"Because my place is among the outcasts. I am a fallen woman, Marmaduke, an abandoned creature like my poorer, wretched sisters out yonder. . . . Nay, do not look so unutterably shocked! I only desire to play my part of faithless wife with the same art as you enact the rôle of injured husband. What an actor you are, Marmaduke—even to yourself! But pray endeavour to be natural for a moment, less statuesque, forget your grand-seigneur airs and sit down like an ordinary man —do! By the way, I am known here as Mrs. Baddeley."

Emotionless as ever, he obeyed her while she, throned among her pillows, viewed him with a singular interest, his face serenely grave, his rough frieze overcoat and clumsy shoes.

"Do you always wear that heavy coat—even in June?" she enquired suddenly.

"Only in Giles's Rents" he answered, wondering.

"Ah, you mean it saves you from too close contact with the vulgar herd!" she nodded. "Marmaduke, has it ever occurred to you that because I deceived your young adoring innocence years ago, destroyed your boyish ideal of me and knew it shattered beyond repair, that I—hate—despise—abhor you?" She spoke in the same soft, cooing accents, but her slim, delicate fingers clenched themselves upon the quilt that covered her; and beholding the passionate quiver of this clutching hand, he spoke with an unwonted gentleness:

"Poor tortured soul!"

"How sir," she flamed, in sudden petulance, "will you dare to pity me?"

"Infinitely, Marian!" he answered, "I never dreamed in you such depth of feeling."

"Not feel—I?" she murmured. "Silly man! I feel so deeply that I should know a very positive joy to hear you were dead, my husband—a stately corpse in the ancient tomb of your so stately ancestors!"

"Marian," said he in pitying wonder, "you are not yourself——"

"Then think me mad and—pity me the more!"

"And now, I will take my leave, madam," said he and rose; but she stayed him with gesture half imperious, half imploring:

"Wait!" said she, breathlessly. "We have yet to talk of your Eve-Ann. But first . . . do you fear death, Marmaduke?"

"Not unreasonably," he answered.

"And you are always so hatefully reasonable, yes—even in your relations with your spotless ewe-lamb, your virginal quakeress! Well, do you not yearn to live—for her sake? To make her your own so soon as I am buried out of the way? A young, adoring wife, Marmaduke! An apt mother to give you children—sons to become stately Vane-Temperleys . . . ah!"

His serene brow showed trouble at last, his steady gaze wavered and, because of her merciless eyes, he bowed his head.

"Aha!" she exclaimed in lilting tones, "so I touch you at last! A chink in your armour! Children!" And she uttered a soft trill of mocking laughter, then frowned as suddenly, for Sir Marmaduke had raised his head and was smiling at her, serene as ever.

"Not so, madam," he answered, "this dream is past! As an amorous swain I find myself quite too . . . superannuated as you prophesied. Also . . . she is half in love with one much younger and altogether better suited than I."

"Liar!" whispered my lady. "Liar!"

Sir Marmaduke rose to his stately height and looked down at her in dignified yet pitying reprobation:

"Madam," said he bowing, "I will bid you good-bye——"

"O!" she whispered, staring up at him great-eyed, "I hate you—more than I thought."

"And now," said he, taking up his hat, "if there be anything needful to your comfort, pray remember a line scribbled to John Hobbs——"

"Hobbs!" she exclaimed with vehement gesture; then she laughed: "O most bountiful husband!" said she in cooing mockery, "generous man, confess you would snatch from me the only comfort I have left—confess you are here to take from me Eve-Ann!"

Sir Marmaduke bowed.

"Then take her!" cried my lady passionately. "Take her from me—if you can!" And raising her voice she called: "O Ann, dearest Eve-Ann——" A violent coughing choked and shook her; and then Eve-Ann opened the door and ran to clasp that pitiful shaken body in strong, cherishing arms until the awful spasm had passed, then pillowing that flushed face upon her tender bosom she wiped the moist brow, murmuring words of comfort.

"Dear . . . dear angel . . . of light!" gasped my lady and, opening tear-dimmed eyes, looked up at Eve with a very real passionate gratitude and lifted unsteady hand to touch her cheek, caress her bright hair, clasp her hand with gesture that had in it something wild and pitiful in its intensity.

"Ann—beloved child," she murmured, pressing sudden lips to the hand she fondled. "Sir Marmaduke is here to take you away and I . . . would have you go . . . for he is right, this is no place for you."

"Nay," answered Eve, smoothing my lady's still beautiful hair, "God brought thee to me, Marian, and so long as thou art lonely and dost need me, here will I abide with thee."

"But Sir Marmaduke desires you to go, dearest Ann, and . . . this neighbourhood is . . . so vile, so wicked!"

"Yea verily!" sighed Ann, "yet God is here, indeed He seems closer to me in this place than in the country. And thou wouldst not that I leave thee, Marian?"

"No!" she cried eagerly. "Ah—no. And yet——"

"So then," said Eve in her smooth placid tones, "here will I stay with thee."

"You hear her, Marmaduke, you hear her?" But he had crossed to the door, had let himself out upon the wide landing and turned to descend the stair, then hesitated, for a man was coming up, a slim, stooping man who moved with strange, dancing step. He was watching the approach of this man when Eve came beside him.

"Art greatly angry with me, John?" she questioned wistfully. Bur Sir Marmaduke was gazing at this man who, as he passed them with his quick, jerking walk, touched battered hat and leered at Eve, muttering hoarse salutation, and went on up the next flight of stairs.

"That man," inquired Sir Marmaduke, sharply, "he knows you . . . who is he?"

"One who talks sometimes with Marian. She names him Jim." Sir Marmaduke frowned.

"Are you ever frightened, Eve-Ann, molested in any way?"

"Never, John! The men here are all very respectful to us, indeed they seem to . . . fear Marian, almost, which is strange, I think——"

"Very strange!" he nodded, thoughtfully, and turned to gaze up the wide and gloomy stair.

"John, she is very sick!"

"And, I think, dangerous!" he muttered, then, moved by strange impulse, he caught Eve's hands, holding them tight. "She is a dark, inscrutable, creature," said he, "and no fit companion for you child!"

"O, I am no child, John! No one may be a child here in Giles's Rents, even the children are not childish. . . . And Marian needeth me, she is so solitary, so wildly despairing at times and . . . I do think . . . in spite of all . . . loves thee, still."

"Enough!" said he, sternly. "Such love would be a curse, a hateful calamity! She is what she is by reason of her own acts—reaping as she has sown."

"Art not a little hard and . . . something merciless, John?"

"Then God forgive me!"

"Amen!" murmured Eve. "She is thy wife, John, and so . . . I cannot, I will not leave her."

"Then," quoth he turning away, "there is no more to be said." And he made to descend the stair, but her hand upon his arm arrested him.

"Be not angry with thy poor friend," she pleaded. "For . . . O John, I do yearn for my . . . dear little tent . . . to hear the birds sing of a morning and awake to know thou art near me!"

"I am still near, and shall be!" he answered gently.

"And thou wilt forgive me my disobedience?"

Here again he acted upon impulse which was surely

very strange in him, for, in answer, he stooped and kissed that pleading hand upon his arm.

"'Tis great comfort . . . to know thee . . . near me, John!" said she, a little unevenly.

"I stay with an actor and his wife, named Ponsonby, at Number six, Apple-Tree Court," he answered. "And this reminds me, have you found your sister, Tabitha, who married an actor?"

"Nay, John, I have been too busy to seek her."

"How so?"

"O, the children!" sighed she, shaking lovely head in quick distress. "There is so much sickness! 'Tis cruel place, this London . . . especially for the babies."

"Werry true, mam!" said a cheery voice, and glancing up they beheld Mr. Shrig beaming down at them over the banisters. "Babies ain't wanted in Giles's Rents, and they generally don't last long 'specially in the 'ot veather, they comes an' they goes, 'ere to-day, gone t'morrer, as you might say!" With which, Mr. Shrig descended to the landing to be greeted by Eve-Ann with eager welcome.

"O, friend," said she, "how is Mrs. Casper's little girl?"

"Better, mam!"

"She took the medicine?"

"She surely did, mam! I give it to her."

"You?" exclaimed Sir Marmaduke.

"Ar—me, friend—v'y not? I ain't always topping murderers, more's the pity. And now, if you're a-going my way, friend, I'm a-going yours."

Sir Marmaduke glanced at the speaker a little haughtily, whereupon Mr. Shrig beamed and slowly closed one eye. And then Eve opened the door:

"I think Marian called me," said she, "I must go, John, but——"

"Must?" he repeated frowning. "Heavens, child, do not make a slave of yourself."

s

At this she only smiled a little sadly and shook her head:

"Friend Jasper Shrig, if thou chance to see old Mrs. Stot, she lives in the cellar opposite, pray tell her I will bring her the lotion for her rheumatics to-morrow . . . and God be with thee."

Mr. Shrig touched his hat and nodded.

"John," she murmured, "thou'lt come again—soon, very soon?"

"Every day!" he answered and stood watching until the great, oaken door, closing slowly, hid her from his sight.

CHAPTER XXXV

CONCERNING MR. SHRIG'S DEDUCTIONS

MR. SHRIG awaited him at the foot of the stair; so Sir Marmaduke descended and stepped forth into the evening glow, then paused to frown up at the great house that in its ruin and grime seemed to scowl down on him bodeful and menacing.

"Shrig," said he suddenly, "do you think she is safe there?"

"Ah, safe as the Bank of England, sir—safe as a nangel!"

"But the house has a . . . strangely evil look!"

"Vich I don't deny, sir. It is a rum place, and there's been rum doings there, ah and vill be again . . . but your young lady's safe enough. The folk hereabout know her a'ready, ye see she's got a trick o' mothering all the children. . . . And talkin' o' children, babies or infants, I takes a interest in same per-fessionally—on account o' their parents."

"Surely you would not use a child to convict its own mother?"

"Friend, I'd use a dozen, a thousand children to conwict a murderer. Vot's a murderer for? To be conwicted and hung—and conwict and hang 'em I do and will by 'ook, sir, or by crook. If by 'olding a babby I can find out where its feyther 'appened to be on a certain day or night, I 'olds said infant j'yful. I has my own methods, sir—f'r instance I'm 'ard at work on this 'ere Sussex Murder at this i-dentical minute

though you'd 'ardly think so, p'raps. . . . But run-
away Murder generally comes creepin' to 'ide itself
in London, and vot place better for same than Giles's
Rents?"

"And . . . you think she is in no danger, Shrig?"
inquired Sir Marmaduke for the second time, and
stopped suddenly to turn and glance back at that
great house which, as he looked, seemed somehow
more threatening and ominous than ever; since Sir
Marmaduke had stopped Mr. Shrig had also stopped
and stood with his keen, bright eyes on his questioner's
anxious face, viewing it askance in furtive, watchful
fashion.

"You apprehend no danger for her, Shrig?"

"Not a natom, sir?"

"You winked at me on the stairs yonder, why?"

"Did I, sir?"

"Unmistakably!"

"Then, p'raps I did."

"Which reminds me, that fellow Dancing James
passed me on the stair."

"And, sir, he was a'watching of you on the stair
and a-harking! P'raps that was why I took the liberty
to wink at you."

"Ah, that damned house!" exclaimed Sir Marmaduke, fiercely.

"Amen, sir!" nodded Mr. Shrig, his eyes still intent
and seeming keener than ever. "And you own that
same, said house, I think, sir?"

Slowly Sir Marmaduke turned and met his questioner's gaze with one as keen and steadfast.

"I do!" he answered.

"Ah!" sighed Mr. Shrig gently and beamed up at a
certain decrepit chimney-stack.

"Then of course you know who I am?'

"Sir, according to the conclusions I've drawed you
are (here he spoke in hoarse whisper) Sir Marmadook
Vane-Temperley."

"Precisely!" answered Sir Marmaduke and walked on again. "I wonder," said he after they had gone some way, "if you will tell me how you discovered this?"

"Sir, werry simply, by lookin' and harkin' and addin' two and two. . . . Your clothes and your face! 'A Wee,' says you, 'a Em, Tee, Wee,' says you, quick as a flash and the light so bad. Now 'ow was you to know there was a Wee hidden in that monneygram unless you'd seed same afore—precious often? Then there's me on the stairs above harkin', and you and young quaker mam on the landing below. 'She's your wife!' says young mam. And I've knowed oo her ladyship was, for years, though folks calls her 'the Countess' hereabouts."

"Yes, it all sounds simple enough," nodded Sir Marmaduke, "yet I perceive you have sharp wits. My congratulations, Mr. Shrig."

They had reached Apple-tree Court and here Sir Marmaduke paused.

"You are now, of course, aware that the cane, found beside the dead man, was mine?"

"Ay, sir, I am so."

"Well?" inquired Sir Marmaduke, glancing into Mr. Shrig's placid face.

"Werry well, indeed!" nodded Mr. Shrig.

"Are you going to arrest me?"

"Vell—no sir. Ye see it's the murderer as I'm arter."

"But good Heavens man! My description is posted up all over the country!"

"No matter, sir! Fax and common-sense is my meat! Now a murderer don't carry a gun and a walking-cane both at once—leastways it ain't nat'ral. And you ain't got a Capital-face, and you're a precious sight too ready to be took-up. But I vish you'd tell me jest why you left said cane so nice and 'andy for ijjits to find. I vish as you'd tell me oo you're trying to shield —ah, that I do!"

"You can hardly expect me to tell you that, Shrig!'

"No, sir, I don't. That's the reason I shall ha' to examine Miss Eve, pore young mam! P'raps she'll tell me——"

"Shrig," said Sir Marmaduke imperiously and laying compelling hand on his arm, "she has a morbid horror of Bow Street Officers . . . the law. . . ."

"And werry proper, too, sir. Glad to know same, 'twill be easier to make 'er speak."

"Damn you—no!" exclaimed Sir Marmaduke, fiercely, and Mr. Shrig winced beneath his gripe. "Rather than suffer her to be tormented I shall tell you myself."

"I thought you vould! All the fax as you can swear to—Bible oath, sir?"

"All that I know, upon my honour!"

"Werry good, sir! Shall us step up to your attic?"

So thither they went, and there Sir Marmaduke faithfully recounted all that chanced since he set forth on his quest.

"Lord!" exclaimed Mr. Shrig when all was told. "Sir, it sounds like a book, one o' these here ro-mances, plenty o' blood in it and plenty o' love a-coming, but never no sign of any murderer vich comes a bit 'ard-like on Jarsper! You ain't got no suspicions o' nobody, I s'pose? You can't give me no 'int—eh! sir?"

"Not one, Shrig—unless it be the scoundrel Denton. But he is a poor, mean rogue, to be sure."

"And werry active agin' you, sir, my lads report, him and this Sir Thomas Mowbray. No, sir, nat'ral suspicion p'ints mostly to vun o' these uncles, Jeremiah or Ebenezer Bybrook—their werry names sounds promising. I'll question 'em again this werry night."

"To-night, but they are in Sussex—"

"No, sir—at Bow Street. I had same took a week ago, Toosday."

"Egad!" exclaimed Sir Marmaduke, shaking his head, "so all our scheming was utterly futile!"

"I dunno about that, sir, but 'twas all labour in wain! And now a vord to yourself, sir—are you armed, do you carry a vepping?"

"Yes."

"Werry good. Now, talkin' o' that old house o yourn?"

"I'd almost forgotten it is mine."

"I vonder as you dont' 'ave same pulled down."

"I probably shall."

"Full o' secret rooms, it be, passages and sich. I've heered—ah, they do say there's vun leads as far as the river. A proper murderous place, Sir Marmadook, and reminds me of vun as I lost, a partic'lar, bright specimen, vanted 'im bad, I did and nigh got my daddles on 'im—but he cut 'is stick, sir, wanished and left me a disapp'inted man. But, sir, I've a feeling e's a-coming back someday, they most generally do—and this time I shall get him, for this time he'll be coming for—murder."

"Whom d'ye mean, Shrig?"

"Sir, I means a cove as they used to call 'Black Tom,' werry tall, werry fierce, black 'air and viskers . . . and a scar acrost vun eyebrow. Do you 'appen to lock your door a-nights, sir? I should if I vas you—ah, and bolt it, too!"

"For what reason?"

"For a reason as is neither here or there but precious solid vherever it is—ah, werry much so! And now, I'll be toddling!"

"You think I am in some danger?"

"Sir, I won't go so far as that but—since your advent my birds has been all of a flutter, so—if you goes out at night don't go alone and keep your peepers, or, as you might say, your ogles werry wide open!"

"I will!" answered Sir Marmaduke and grasping Mr. Shrig's hand he shook it in hearty grip, and thereafter stood, grave-eyed and thoughtful, to watch him descend the stair; slowly and thoughtfully he closed the attic door and, seated at the rickety table, took pen and paper and wrote as follows:

"My faithful John,

"Tell Rupert I have found Eve-Ann in Giles's Rents. Let him bring plenty of money with him.

"It is possible that I may return soon the better and wiser, I hope, for my adventures. Meanwhile do you continue to act for me in all things.

"VANE-TEMPERLEY."

"P.S. Let Rupert also bring my duelling pistols— the Mantons."

And in this same hour my lady, smiling at Eve-Ann, nibbled the feather of her pen and added this postscript to letter already written:

"He is here in Giles's Rents ready to your so cherished purpose. So Tom, heroic brute, come and end your feud once for all."

CHAPTER XXXVI

IN WHICH MAY BE FOUND MENTION OF DEVILLED KIDNEYS

THE kindly sun which, with God-like impartiality, shines on rich and poor, the virtuous and vicious, the highly blessed and utterly damned, poured his genial beams upon this crowded rookery called Giles's Rents with such hearty and generous good-will that some of his glory contrived to find a way even through the small, grim window that lighted Sir Marmaduke's attic; an inquisitive beam which shot athwart narrow truckle bed, faded carpet and diminutive wash-stand, to play upon the frieze over-coat whose ample folds draped the solitary arm-chair, and upon Sir Marmaduke's glossy head where he stood brushing his hair before the small mirror grown dim and sad with over-much reflection, and which showed him a face so distorted and of such bilious hue as might have shocked one unused to its vagaries. None the less Sir Marmaduke paused more than once to study his features, to scrutinize the short, crisp curls at his temples amid whose black, here and there, peeped a glint of silver.

"Thirty-six or under? Ha—ridiculous!" he sighed, and tossing away the hair-brush, pulled on his jacket and went down to breakfast.

The Eye-brows, posted majestically before the mantel-piece, inclined themselves in stately welcome, and Mr. Ponsonby stretched out a hand whose grip was unexpectedly firm and hearty.

"Good my friend, all hail!" quoth he. "Though early the hour my soul ecstatic soars for, what with radiant Phœbus, his beamy brightness, and—I fancy it is devilled kidneys—all's well with the world! In point of fact, my dear Hobbs, as saith the Bard of Avon, 'the play's the thing!' Our tragedy is now a proven success—though in some sort it flags after the first Act! But my death scene shook the house, ay—smote dumb and awed the very groundlings!"

"I rejoice to know it!" smiled Sir Marmaduke.

"Sir, women wailed and strong men silent wept. But then I am one in death most experienced and deeply versed! I never play but I die in some sort or other. I have perished of poisons, succumbed to shot, been smit by sword. I have died in dungeons, upon beds, chairs, on the scaffold, and, once across a table! Dying, sir, is become with me a curious art and—ha, but here . . . soft! I think our kidneys approach!" So saying he opened the door and indeed the kidneys and Eudoxia entered. . . . So down they sat and with pleasant rattle of coffee-cups—somewhat ponderous—they began breakfast.

"The world," said Eudoxia, peeping into Sir Marmaduke's half-empty cup, "let who say what they will, is a small place!"

"My soul," quoth Mr. Ponsonby, fork graciously flourished, "other philosophers, at divers times and places, have remarked the same curious fact! But you, dearest creature, to what extraordinary march of circumstance do you allude?"

"Well, my love and Mr. Hobbs, last night by the merest of accidents, and quite fortuitously, here in the wilds of this vast metropolis, our dear Tabitha D'Abernon met—her sister! You, Mr. Hobbs, know her, I hear, I mean dear Tabby's sister Eve—— Miss Ash, the handsome quakeress. So charmingly rustic and companion to that mysterious Mrs. Baddeley—who has been such an angel to the children—especially babies, since she came—I mean Miss Ash!"

"We are acquainted," answered Sir Marmaduke.

"So I am informed. Indeed Mrs. Mowlem thinks you make the handsomest pair—next door but three and most genteel! I mean Mrs. Mowlem. And Mrs. Meecher, across the way, highly superior and extremely romantic, begged to know if you two were affianced. I said this was on the lap of the gods——"

"We are not," answered Sir Marmaduke.

"La, dear Mr. Hobbs, say not so!" sighed Eudoxia. "Yourself—pardon me!—so dark, so dignified and stately, so distinguished, and she so demurely delicious, such cream and roses! Could Giles's Rents but dream you each other's own, ah me, how many hearts would in tender sympathy—flutter!"

Here the eye-brows attempted a playful archness:

"Aha!" quoth Mr. Ponsonby. "Eros! Eros! O Cupid sweet, stealthy archer! Pray, Eudoxia, am I acquainted with the Ladye Fayre?"

"You must have seen her, Augustus, she pervades the Rents—so statuesque and with tresses like Aurora— I mean the poorer quarters—babies, you know!"

"Your description, my love, though excellent, leaves me groping. However, I——"

Shrill hoots and shrieks, a hoarse clamour, a hubbub wild and sudden.

Up sprang Mr. Ponsonby, and in a single stride was at the window, where he was joined by Eudoxia and Sir Marmaduke.

Ragged urchins who shrieked and danced in savage glee; ragged men two who sprawled blasphemous; ragged men three who scowled and crouched fierce for strife, and fronting this rabblement a slim young, exquisite, indeed a very magnificent young gentleman from gleaming, be-tasselled Hessians to jaunty hat the which perched on his curly pate at a defiant, devil-may-care angle.

"Ha!" exclaimed Mr. Ponsonby, knitting Olympian eyebrows. "One gentlesome gallant 'gainst the *hoi polloi* shall never be!" And catching up the poker, he opened the window and stepped out with remarkable quickness and agility.

"Base scullion rogues avaunt!" cried he in terrible voice. "Ha—a rescue! England and Saint George!" And he advanced to the conflict, poker gleaming high in air; whereupon, either by reason of voice, poker, or Eye-brows, the crouching assailants gave back—the howling urchins scattered, the men, vociferating blood-curdling threats, sullenly retired until, save for divers heads out-thrust from door and window, Apple-tree Court was itself again. Then, tossing aside broken cane, the young gentleman turned to his deliverer with radiant smile:

"Sir," he began, "you're a trump, a brick—confound me if you aren't a true blue.—"But here, beholding the Eye-brows, he took off his hat and bowed profoundly. "Pray sir," he began, "accept my humblest, grateful —why, John! Why, Johnny, old tulip!" and leaping forward Mr. Bellamy caught and wrung Sir Marma-duke's hand, beaming joyously.

"Happy fortune!" quoth Mr. Ponsonby, poising the poker as if about to perform the ceremony of knight-hood. "Blest fate that thus on stricken field friend with friend should meet! Eudoxia, my soul, another cover lay for the friend of our friend Hobbs!"

Then beneath the eyes of Apple-tree Court, Sir Marmaduke performed the introductions, and they clambered back to breakfast through the window.

Mr. Bellamy, having bowed to Eudoxia and kissed her hand whereat she instantly curtseyed in the "grande" manner, sat down to table with as ready a grace and easy an air as if he had sat there from infancy.

Quoth Mr. Ponsonby, helping Rupert to the last of the kidneys:

"Mr. Bellamy, sir, in your friend, our honoured—hum—lodger, you behold our good angel! Since his adventition hither, the cruel fist o' Fortune hath become a hand caressing, instead of buffets benefits bestowing. Thanks to friend Hobbs our fortunes soar!"

"I believe you!" cried Mr. Bellamy heartily, "there's nobody like old John!"

"True!" sighed Eudoxia. "O, indeed, most true!"

"Sir," continued Mr. Ponsonby, "you behold in me an Act-or, a child of Thespis, Melpomene or Thalia, The Sock and Buskin, sir!"

"O!" murmured Mr. Bellamy. "B'gad—really?"

"In very truth, sir. Humble slave of the Tragic Muse, I. Yet whatsoever part I play henceforth, from reeking corse to scurvy, slippered pantaloon, deep, deep within my unchanging soul I bear undying sentiments of grateful friendship for—John Hobbs!"

Having delivered himself of which, Mr. Ponsonby raised cup to lip while his eyebrows quivered with an emotion beyond mere words.

"How nobly expressed, my husband!" sighed Eudoxia in awed tones. "Suffer that I add—amen!"

Breakfast done, Sir Marmaduke led the way to his attic, but no sooner had he closed the door than Mr. Bellamy hugged him in mighty arms, released him to execute a jig, tossed up his hat, caught it, settled it on his curls with resounding slap, and taking it off again, pitched it joyously on the bed.

"John!" he exclaimed, "my dear old tulip—behold me!"

"Extremely à la mode!" smiled Sir Marmaduke.

"I believe you!" said he, glancing down complacently at his resplendent person. "But, old fellow, a miracle has happened! The lion's a lamb, the Ogre's turned human, the Gorgon's become a—ah—in short, my unnatural uncle is eager to peck out of my hand, John!"

"You surprise me!" said Sir Marmaduke.

"And no wonder! I'm surprised myself! For my uncle, Sir Marmaduke, old flinty-souled Gruff and Glum, has done the right thing at last, John! Good old party, stout old trump, after all—so, blessings on his old bald knob, say I!"

"Hum! Bald, Rupert?"

"Well, if he ain't he should be—at his age. However, here I am, old fellow, my pockets bulging with rhino, to place my purse and person at your service, give you a general leg-up and—er—so forth."

"You are . . . very good!" said Sir Marmduke looking into the speaker's eager face. "I am grateful, Rupert——"

"Good? Grateful?" exclaimed Mr. Bellamy seizing his hand to grip it very hard. "No, no! John—boot's on t'other leg, old fellow! I . . . I owe you so much I can never do—never tell you all my gratitude and—and so forth! For John you . . . trusted me, honoured me, gave me back my . . . self-respect—and named me 'gentleman' spite o' my pitiful rags. . . . And so, old fellow . . . and so, John . . . I . . . O damme I can never——" Sincerity choked him, and he bowed his head, then, throwing up his chin, looked at Sir Marmaduke through gleaming tears. "Frightful ass I am . . . of course!" said he unsteadily, "but O Johnny man I . . . I'm so devilish grateful! It is an honour to call you friend, and—I hope"—the quavering accents stopped suddenly; and Sir Marmaduke, looking with the keen gaze of experience into the eyes that met his so steadfastly, and reading in their tear-wet depths all the quivering lips left unsaid, smiled and in his face a radiance not altogether of the sun.

"Rupert," said he, "old fellow, friends we are, and shall be, to the end, I prophesy. And as for trusting you—well, Eve-Ann will be glad to see you. Go to her, now, you will find her in the great, old house fronting on Crowsfoot lane yonder."

"But you, John? Why not come too?"

"I have affairs, Rupert—letters to write. So off with you to Eve-Ann. Tell her your good fortune. Take her walking. Buy her things. Talk to her, I mean persuade her to leave this neighbourhood. . . . She has a married sister in London, a Mrs. D'Abernon, get her to introduce you to this sister and urge her to quit Giles's Rents—at once!"

"Begad, I will, John! It is a frightful hole, this, the men are bad enough, demmem, but the women— shocking! And so dooced hideous!"

"However, get her away as soon as possible—do your utmost."

"Trust me, old fellow." And so, with fervent hand-clasp off turned Mr. Bellamy, out and away buoyant with youth and the joy of it, leaving a grave-faced man to stare very forlornly at smoking chimneys and dilapidated roofs, to sigh wearily and sit down to write to John Hobbs a screed anent the making of a new will; the letter finished he arose, got into the frieze overcoat whose capacious pocket held that weapon so sure and deadly in his hands and putting on his hat, forth went he into the sunny air.

CHAPTER XXXVII

TELLS OF THE NOBBLY STICK OF MR. SHRIG

RAGGED children pattered about him at their play filling the place with their shrill clamour; touzled women lounging in grimy doorways ceased their strident chatter to watch him as he passed; hoary age and puling infancy mopped and mowed from dingy casements. But Sir Marmaduke went his solitary way, hands in deep pockets, blind and deaf to it all and thus quite unaware of the man who, detaching himself from shady corner, began to dog his footsteps, a burly man with great shag of hair whose furtive eyes never left that slow-pacing figure in frieze overcoat, shapeless hat and clumsy shoes. Thus from court to passage and passage to alley paced Sir Marmaduke all unconscious of the danger that crept upon his heels, for just now, his mind was full of unhappy speculation concerning his future. . . . A lonely man he must be, as he had ever been. . . . Well, he would have his books . . . music . . . John Hobbs. . . .

Lost thus to his immediate surroundings he trudged on, his head bent—and yet he saw her the moment she crossed the alley and followed instinctively. . . . Small children trotted beside her, chattering and joyous, they held her hands, they grasped her petticoats while she smiled down on them and talked with the aged crone who hobbled beside her—and yet, glancing round all at once, as if she sensed his nearness, she saw him, and her smile, the light in her eyes, drew him.

"John," said she, "there is a poor woman hurt and needeth help—come with me."

"My Nancy, master!" croaked the old woman, "scalded 'er poor legs crool bad along o' Mowles frowin' the kittle at 'er, and the childer starvin', an' Nan on 'er back and me wi' the 'matics, an' nobody dassent come a-nigh us 'count o' Mowles bein' mad-like!"

"Mad?" inquired Sir Marmaduke.

"Ah—it be gin, sir!   Gallons on it an' not a drop for me or Nancy o' course—O no!"

"Who is Mowles?"

"Nancy's man, sir.   Got the 'orrors bad.'

"Eve, you can never go——"

"But, John, these poor souls need me——"

"And 'ere y'are !" said the old woman, halting sudden at a flight of steps, slimy and very narrow that led steeply down to a noisome cellar. "Down the dancers, lady, they're a bit slippy-like so foller me and go cautious—you little uns leave go the lady, run off now!" So saying, the old creature, having driven off the clinging children, led the way down these steps unspeakably foul into a fetid dimness wherein, little by little, they descried two children who wailed, a woman, upon ragged pallet, who groaned fitfully and in a remote corner a writhing heap of misery whence issued sudden howls and gasping objurgations.

"This," exclaimed Sir Marmaduke recoiling in horror, "this is frightful!"

"Yea verily!" whispered Eve, "I have seen few places worse."

"'Ave ye got 'er, mother?' moaned the woman on the bed.   "O 'ave ye brought the Good Lady?"

"Ay, 'ere she be, Nan—ah an' a kind gen'leman to look at yer bad legs——"

"O mam!" cried the sufferer, raising herself amid the rags that covered her. "They says as you're good t' the children—be good t' mine."

T

"Nay, friend Shrig," said she, laying tremulous hand on his well-brushed coat-sleeve, "thou didst save John's life. O dear friend, I pray now the Lord's blessing on thee. . . ."

"And vot might you be a-doing here, mam? 'Tis a werry bad place 'ereabouts and no error!"

"This poor Nancy! She is sore hurt."

'O!" quoth Mr. Shrig and turned to examine the sufferer's injuries. "Ay, pretty bad, mam, though I've see vorse."

"I need a sponge, clean water, oil——"

"Or say—lard! Lard's vot she needs, mam, but most of all—a doctor!"

"O, if 'twere only possible, friend! If we could but find one!"

"Ay, a surgeon's the vord, mam!" nodded Mr. Shrig. "Also I've got to cage this 'ere bird o' mine!" Having said which, he set two fingers between his lips and emitted an ear-splitting whistle which seemed, almost immediately, to find an echo afar, whereafter ensued a sound of heavy feet upon the cobbles above, upon the slimy stair and into the cellar came two powerful fellows who trod with an air of authority:

"On the job, chief!" quoth Number One, touching an eye-brow to Mr. Shrig.

"Ever and allus!" quoth Number Two. "You got 'im, eh?"

"Ah," sighed Mr. Shrig, "I got 'im, George, but—not for murder, no! I could ha' took and topped 'im for murder, yes, but—the corp vould ha' been this 'ere young lady's friend, so I 'ad to drop Bunty about thirty seconds—say fifteen, too soon—and there y'are!" Here Mr. Shrig sighed again, shook his head and tapped the yet unconscious Bunty with his stick, gently and regretfully. "Hows'ever, cage him, lads, though 'twill only be 'Murderous Assault!' more's the pity! And George, send the surgeon, say as I vants him."

"Werry good, Jarsper!" answered Number Two: then hoisting the unconscious Bunty Fagan between them, the burly officers hove and dragged him up the narrow stairs out of sight.

"And there goes vun on 'em!" nodded Mr. Shrig, "vich leaves Dancin' Jimmy and Vistlin' Dick."

"It seems you prophesied truly, Shrig!" said Sir Marmaduke, leading him aside while Eve busied herself with the sufferer.

"Meaning, sir?"

"My being in danger.'

"Danger, sir? Well, I dunno as you're ardly in any particular danger—and because vy? Because I'm lookin' arter you like a feyther and a mother—ah, like a brother an' a sister all rolled into vun."

"I am heartily grateful, Shrig!"

"Grateful, sir? Well, so am I. And because vy? Because you are a-droring my birds into my net—you are the lime on the twig, in a manner o' speakin' and——" But at this moment, from regions above was the sound of a clear, tenor voice:

"Pray, are there any of you ladies can tell me if a Mrs. Mowles lives hereabout?"

A shrill chorus of assent, with voluble directions and Mr. Bellamy's elegant boots and shapely legs appeared descending the stair, somewhat gingerly, and finally Mr. Bellamy himself entered the cellar, peering, and (marvellous to see) laden with very many parcels and packages.

"Ha, Johnny!" he exclaimed, in glad surprise, "bear a hand like a good fellow! Butter and bread, meat, sugar, tea and the Lord knows what."

"O yes, he is quite an old acquaintance. He brings me medicines for my cough which I throw away and sometimes talks over his cases with me."

"Damme, but you're the sly one, Nell! Shrig your friend! O but you're clever, devilish, superlatively clever!"

My lady yawned delicately.

"The man may be useful . . . someday."

"How? How useful, Nell?"

"I prefer you to call me 'Eleanor', as you know."

"Shrig . . . a visitor here, eh? And . . . no word o' this to me! No, by heaven, you never breathed a word! Why?"

"And I only breathe it now as a —warning."

"A warning?" he repeated staring about him in fierce and sudden apprehension. "A warning d'ye say! Ha—damnation, ye vixen, what d'ye mean?"

"Do not bluster with me!" she retorted contemptuously.

"Speak woman! Tell me what ye mean—speak" cried he, savagely and seizing her in mighty hands, he whirled her back among the pillows and glared down at her with terrible eyes; but she, meeting that look, mocked him with trilling laughter.

"What sheer terror!" she murmured. "But you were always a coward at heart, weren't you, Tom?"

"Damned witch suppose I choke ye!"

"You will hang the sooner, fool Tom! I have written a letter . . . explaining everything. . . . Stop, you are bruising me!"

"Ha, a letter—a letter?" he raved, his cruel grip tightening, "where is it? Give it to me! Where is it, I say? Speak, will ye!" And he shook her so violently that she began to cough dismally, but even while the dreadful spasm racked her, she lifted fumbling hand to her throat and next moment he sprang back clutching at bloody wrist.

"I . . . don't permit . . . such as you . . . to hurt me!" she gasped, thrusting the jewelled pin back into the bosom of her dress. "Now . . . sit down and . . . listen to me, Tom fool."

"Forgive me, Nell!" cried he, dabbing at his wrist with dainty handkerchief. "Ah, forgive ne, lass. Eleanor, I'm a brute! But you're so devilish tantalizing, you drive a man frantic. Come now, Nell, what's all this of a letter, where is it, my dear? And what d'ye mean by a warning?"

"I mean . . . Eve . . . Ann . . . Ash!" said my lady, viewing him from her pillows with contemptuous eyes. "You are a satyr Tom! Well, attempt any one of your old tricks with her and I will see that you are taken and hanged, for——"

A murmur of voices from the outer room and Sir Thomas crouched with one hand within his breast and wide eyes upon the door:

"Shrig!" said he in fierce and threatening whisper. "So then, damned Jezebel, ye've betrayed me——"

"Not yet, Tom!" she whispered. "The door is locked and you may go as you came—the panel! And take your hat and coat with you, poor, craven fool!"

Speaking, she arose, crept lightly to the door and, turning key soundlessly in well-oiled lock, returned slow and feebly, to her couch; sinking down gracefully she composed herself among the pillows and, sighing, closed her eyes as came a gentle tap.

"Come in!" she called, wearily and then as Eve appeared, reached out her two hands in eager welcome.

"Dearest, but you've been a weary time!" sighed she in gentle reproach.

"Forgive me, Marian, a sick woman had need o' me . . . But friend Shrig is here."

"Then bid him enter."

Mr. Shrig appeared forthwith, as placid and beaming as usual.

"Mam," said he, regarding my lady with his cheery smile, "a werry good day to you! And how is the cough?"

one must needs think of death frequently, it is only natural. . . . Good-bye, Shrig, you are a strange, kind soul and have helped me pass many a weary hour —Good-bye!" So saying, she threw herself back upon her pillows and closed her eyes wearily.

Mr. Shrig looked down at her and his usually placid features seemed a little troubled.

"Mam," said he gently, "my lady, is there ever anything as I can do for ye?"

"Oh—no!" she answered, shaking her head in swift petulance but with eyes still closed. "No one can! Good-bye, Shrig. Good-bye and—thank you!"

Slowly Mr. Shrig crossed to the door, but there paused to glance at Eve who sat busied with her sewing, but meeting this look she followed him softly from the room; but, being come to the outer door Mr. Shrig paused to shake his head and glance back over his shoulder, yet all he said was:

"Werry rum!" and so departed. Then back went Eve to find my lady lying with eyes still shut and very still, apparently fast asleep, but scarcely had Eve poised her needle than my lady spoke sharply:

"What d'you sew there, Eve-Ann?"

"I am making a wrap for Mrs. Trimber's new baby, but indeed——" Eve paused aghast, for burying her face in the pillow, my lady burst into a wild and passionate weeping; up started Eve and setting by her work, caught that grief-stricken figure to her heart.

"Marian," she pleaded, "Oh my dear, what is it?"

"A . . . little baby!" gasped my lady. "Eve . . . Oh Eve-Ann . . . if only I had been a mother! . . . A little baby of my own . . . I might have been . . . so different . . . so much better, instead of the evil creature I am——"

"Nay, hush thee, my dear!" murmured Eve, folding her closer. "Thou'rt none evil, 'tis only that thou hast lost thy way awhile. But someday, my dear, someday God shall take thy hand . . . the Good Shepherd shall bring thee safe to His fold——"

"No—not my hand . . . not mine—ah no!" cried my lady wildly, raising her slim hand to stare at it with eyes of sudden horror. "God will never touch—my hand!"

"Hush, thou dear, frightened soul!" said Eve, cradling the sobbing creature as a mother might. "God hears thee, sees thee and is all-merciful. . . . And verily there is in thee, Marian, so much of God that He can never leave thee forlorn. Thou art His child, the very child of His love. So hush thee, my dear, and trust thyself to the Lord's forgiving and everlasting mercy."

Thus my lady—the lonely, passionate, fearful child—clung to Eve—the gentle, strong woman—and presently found some solace in her murmured words, the tender clasp of her protecting arms.

"Eve—O my dearest," she questioned wildly, "do you believe God will be waiting for me beyond the dreadful shadows—do you?"

"I am sure of it, Marian."

"And will—take my hand? This wicked hand of mine?"

"Yea verily, dear soul, and lift thee up into His abiding glory.'

"Kiss me, Eve—O kiss me, thou angel of comfort."

So Eve kissed her and they clung together awhile; and now my lady questioned Eve in quick, passionate whisper. . . . "Tell me, Eve-Ann, do you—do you?'

But now was a sudden, inconsequent rapping on the outer door and when Eve would have risen, my lady held her fast. "No, tell me first, dearest! You shall not go until I am answered!"

Then Eve, flushing beneath her questioner's fever-bright eyes bowed her head and answered:

"Yea indeed, indeed, Marian—with all my heart."

imperious hand . . . whispers three words, whereat he, staying for not so much as his hat, speeds from the place, and out and away.

The Fiddler has reached Apple-tree Court and smiles happily as he plies his bow for his inspired gaze is up-turned to the glorious heaven, some radiance of which finds its way into Sir Marmaduke's attic; it shows his narrow bed and beyond this, the easy-chair and worn, frieze overcoat which falls in such revealing folds about the studious figure seated there whose quill pen squeaks so busily. . . . Stealthy feet that creep behind the door! But the pen squeaks on. . . . A stealthy hand upon the latch! . . . The busy pen never falters . . . a slow and furtive opening of the door and the pen is still at last, the studious figure straightens its shoulders, sits rigid and motionless . . . then Murder levels its deadly hand. . . .

The Fiddler is smiling down at the dancing children for now he is playing a joyous, lilting measure but—suddenly the music breaks and he stands, his bow arrested, staring up at a certain window with eyes of horror. . . . The dancing children are mute and still, the men and women have forgotten their dreams for where the Fiddler stares, all eyes are turned. And then from that little open casement crawls a slow-wreathing eddy of blue smoke, beholding which, the Fiddler utters a strangled scream and, tossing wild arms to heaven, staggers a pace and falls to lie inert in the dust as if smitten down by some unseen hand.

Then, the echo of that dreadful sound still ringing upon the air, pandemonium breaks forth: "Who is it? What is it? A shot! Someone is killed! Murder!"

And so is stir and tumult—a wild confusion and desperate trampling to and fro. And through the crowd, unheeded amid the uproar, comes a lank, stooping man with strange, dancing step who, pushing fiercely through the press, nudges the tall, cloaked figure beside him.

"All's bowmon, guvnor! The Vistler's done it!" he whispers. "Foller me!" He pushes his way to a small, sullen-looking door and, nodding to his companion, they hurry up dark and creaking stair, their hasty tread drowning the sound of other feet that mount after them. So they reach a half-open door, breathe an air acrid with burnt powder and behold the small, weazen-face of Whistling Dick who nods at them, a smoking pistol in his fist.

"Gorrim, governor!" he says and whistling nervously between his teeth, points to somethmg that sits sprawled across the rickety table. Slowly, almost fearfully, the tall man steps across the threshold, hears a gasping oath behind him, is set aside by a powerful arm, and he, in turn, gasps and cowers back and back to the wall, staring in speechless, wondering horror at Sir Marmaduke who, crossing to the still and awful shape, stoops and with reverent hand lifts off the hat and puts back the folds of that enveloping, frieze over-coat :

"Mowbray," says he, standing aside, "behold your handiwork!"

Sir Thomas looks and utters an inarticulate, broken cry, for the radiant sunset shows him the face of my lady Vane-Temperley, serene and glorified in death.

"Murderer!" he cries and turning, leaps at Whistling Dick, but the little man stoops, there is a glitter of quick-driven steel and Sir Thomas staggers back and stands swaying, tears at his breast with clutching fingers then, groaning, sinks to his knees, to his face.

"Eleanor!" he gasps. "Nell . . . beloved . . . at last——"

Slowly painfully, he drags himself, crawling until his fumbling hand may touch the hem of her gown, her slender foot and, clasping this little foot he pillows his great head upon it . . . sighs and is still.

The heavenly radiance is fading fast, yet enough light remains to show a sheet of paper beneath slim,

U

white hand, with these words boldly penned, the ink scarcely dry:

> "This is my way and I take it gladly for the sake of my so loved Eve-Ann, a dark way yet I go unfearing since there is a light beyond, and perhaps happiness for even such as I who missed my——"

A rush and clatter of heavy feet upon the stair and men are in the room, first and foremost Mr. Shrig, short-breathing, bloody and dishevelled:

"Too late!" he cries, and dropping to his knees turns up the man's face to the light.

"Black Tom!" he gasps in breathless, peevish complaint. "Black Tom and . . . by Goles . . . you've diddled me again . . . for good and all!"

CHAPTER XL

"Six days and there it lies," sighed Eudoxia, shaking tragic head, "there it lies, Mr. Shrig, his poor fiddle, so silent, so useless, so pitiful—never to sound again, alas—nevermore!"

"Meaning as you think he's a-going to hop the twig—mam—die, eh?"

"Shrig, we gravely fear so!" nodded Mr. Ponsonby. "The Dark Angel yet hovers above this our habitation. Our invalid, thanks to the boundless magnanimity of friend Hobbs, lacks for nought, my Eudoxia and Miss Ash, angels in women's guise, bend o'er him all unremitting, yet, in fostering care's despite, he sinks, Shrig, strength ebbs with the fleeting hours away, he hovers on death's grimly marge."

"Mm!" mused Mr. Shrig. "And all because 'e chanced to hear that there fatal shot! Screamed, so they tell me, throwed up his arms and fell, eh, Mrs. Ponsingby, mam, you vitnessed same, I think? Fell werry suddent-like, eh?"

"O very suddenly, Mr. Shrig, as if indeed he had been shot instead of that poor, poor Mrs. ——"

"And he's never been conscious since, eh, mam?"

"Not once, poor soul! And, oh, Mr. Shrig, yonder on the chiffonier lies his poor fiddle, so silent—so useless! I weep each time I look at it."

"Then, mam," said Mr. Shrig, rising, "don't look at it."

299

gesture; the elfin fiddler had become a haggard, care worn man yet dignified, forceful, compelling.

"Nay," said Eve, stroking his white hair with caressing hand, "I am here——"

"Yes, madam, yes!" he answered peevishly. "But my daughter, my Rosamond, where is she?"

"Thy . . . daughter?" whispered Eve, shrinking a little before his fierce, bright eyes. "O dear Jackie, dost not know thy Eve-Ann?"

"No," said he impatiently. "No, indeed. Pray have the goodness to send for my daughter . . . Rosamond should be with me. . . . I fear I am not well. I seem to have . . . dreamed . . . very strangely."

"Comfort thee," murmured Eve in her soothing accents, "thou'rt my dear friend Jack o' the Fiddle."

"Never—never!" he exclaimed. "True I am a violinist, yes—but my name is . . . I am . . . ah, God! Who am I? There is a mist on my brain. . . . I cannot remember—ha, my violin! Bring it and I will play, you shall know me then . . . all the world knows me—especially when I play. Give me the violin. Rosamond will come when she hears it calling her." So he took the instrument, drew bow across strings with a master's touch, tightened a string and, with eager gaze upon the door, began to play. . . .

. . . A golden, singing note that swelled to die away upon a minor trill, a sweet poignant summons thrice repeated—then came sudden silence and into those eager, watching eyes a growing horror:

"Dead!" he whispered. "I dreamed her dead! My Beautiful . . . my Rose . . . withered—blasted . . . trampled and mired! . . . Rosamond!" he cried and shivering violently, covered his face, while from beneath those wasted fingers slow tears crept. And then while Eve watched him through gathering tears and Eudoxia sobbed aloud, Mr. Shrig crossed

silently to the bed and stooping swiftly breathed a
word in the Fiddler's ear:

"Ha . . . Brandish!" he repeated staring wildly
around. "That murderer of Innocence! O Villainy
gloating on corruption! . . . That he should plague
the earth and she lie dead! That he should eat and
drink and laugh yet! No wonder the pallid, dead-
faced moon should seem to mock me! . . . O God
of Justice, since murder is sin, do Thou smite him! O
Death consume him ere he bring shame and ruin on
others. . . . Thy lambs, O God, protect them from
this slavering wolf. . . . The blood of Thine innocent
cries to Thee for vengeance! Strike him from life,
O God of Justice! Let him die!" The words ended
in a gasp, and once again the speaker hid his face in
clutching hands.

Eudoxia had hushed her sobbing, Eve-Ann knelt
motionless beside the bed, and in this awed silence
Jasper Shrig spoke, his voice strangely gentle, each
word very distinct and deliberately uttered:

"In . . . Down . . . along . . . Spinney!"

A moment of deadly stillness and then—from behind
those clutching, veiling hands came a soft, chuckling
laugh, the clasping hands fell away to reveal the dancing
elfin eyes of Fiddling Jack.

"Yes—yes," he nodded, smiling joyously. "Down-
along—Spinney, it was there I shot him."

"Ay, to be sure!" said Mr. Shrig, nodding also, "shot
'im in Down-along-Spinney vith a two-barrelled gun, eh?"

"Yes, yes—Ebenezer's gun. I'd seen it many
times hanging above the mantel, but it never occurred
to me what it was for until I heard my sweet Eve-Ann
cry out in the wood . . . saw her struggle in his wicked
arms, then I knew it hung there on the wall waiting
to do the Lord's work—to avenge, to protect, to remove
evil from the earth."

"Ay, to be sure!" said Mr. Shrig nodding again.
"So you fetched the gun and give him both barrels?"

"Well, John, you saw Rupert yesterday, how is he—I mean is the . . . the matter arranged?"

"I believe not, sir, though he seemed in the very best of spirits."

"Ah, then you may be sure . . . she has accepted him. I suppose we shall have them . . . married shortly—eh, John?"

"Possibly, sir. Mr. Ballemy is very anxious to meet his Uncle Marmaduke—to express his gratitude for your last generous offer."

"They should be very happy—eh, John?" inquired Sir Marmaduke, frowning thoughtfully at his reflection in the cheval-glass. "They are so admirably matched . . . both so young!"

"Yes, they are both young!" answered John Hobbs, glancing at Sir Marmaduke's gloomy brow.

"I shall in addition to the settlement give them this place, John, it is much too large for an old—bachelor, besides I am going abroad for an indefinite time as soon as the . . . business is over."

"Business, sir?"

"The wedding, man, the wedding. I'm off on my travels again . . . and this brings me to—yourself, John. I have, as you know, left you the property in Kent at my decease, but why not take possession at once? Say the word and I will—what in the world?"

A sound of approaching hoofs coming at break-neck gallop and a horseman flashed beneath the window.

"It looked like Mr. Bellamy, sir."

"It is Mr. Bellamy, John. I will see him in the library."

Thus when Sir Marmaduke opened the door of that stately apartment he beheld Mr. Bellamy, somewhat dusty and dishevelled, striding impatiently up and down; perceiving Sir Marmaduke he hurried forward, hand eagerly outstretched:

"Why, John!" he exclaimed. "Why, Johnny man, what do you here in the ogre's lair?"

"Exist, Rupert."

"Exist? Eh, d'ye mean you live . . . here?" he demanded and then, becoming aware of Sir Marmaduke's so altered appearance, he fell back a step, gasping: "O . . . b'Geroge, d'you mean . . . ye Gods, will you tell me . . . Lord love me, John . . . who . . . what are you?"

"Make a guess, nephew."

"Neph——!" Mr. Bellamy gaped and appeared to totter. "No . . . John, you can't be . . . Uncle Marmaduke?"

"Wrong, dear lad! I am indeed that unworthy relative who now begs to shake hands with you, Rupert."

"Lord love me!" ejaculated Mr. Bellamy feebly, and sank into a chair, only to spring up again to bow, drop his hat and stand utterly confounded.

"Have I to . . . congratulate you, Rupert?"

"So you . . . you, sir, are . . . John Hobbs, Uncle?"

"I was! And this should make us the better friends. But here stands the real John Hobbs—don't go, John! Let us sit down all three and talk over the details of——"

"Johnny—I mean, Uncle," said Mr. Bellamy, a little wildly, "I'm here to . . . to thank you for all your goodness . . . your generosity . . . faith in me . . . schemes for my future welfare but . . . the dream's shivered to atoms. . . . I mean the bubble's burst . . . everything's eternally smashed . . . upside down . . . in short, my dear old tulip—sir . . . it's no go!"

"No go?" repeated Sir Marmaduke puzzled.

"Instead o' settling me as a county squire and . . . ah— . . . so forth, John—Uncle, I'll go for a soldier or sailor—anything wi' plenty o' change and movement in it, my dear old fellow."

"What under Heaven do you mean, Rupert?"

"John," sighed Mr. Bellamy, shaking doleful head. "Uncle, old fellow, the whole affair . . . romantic dream, hopes of marital bliss and—so forth, is a . . . a . . . in short, a flam! She . . . Eve-Ann don't want a husband—at least, not me. So . . . game's up and—I'm off!"

Sir Marmaduke drew a deep breath and leaned back in his chair:

"Rupert," said he, his usual serenity a little ruffled. "Do you . . . are you suggesting that . . . she . . . has actually . . . refused you?"

"Actually and finally, sir! And Johnny, old tulip —confound it no, I mean, sir—I believe there's— another!"

"Good heavens!" murmured Sir Marmaduke. "God bless my soul!" To be sure he frowned, also he averted his head, yet not before Mr. Bellamy had seen the sudden light in his eyes and opened his own eyes very wide.

"Sir," said he, "my dear old—Uncle, I'm positively sure she loves . . . but not your very unfortunate, obedient humble!"

"But, Rupert, I was so sure that she . . . that you . . . my mind was quite set upon it!"

"But then, Uncle, her mind is set on—ah—in short —elsewhere!"

"Rupert, I was quite persuaded, quite confident that she—loved you——"

"O she does, sir, she does!"

"Eh?" exclaimed Sir Marmaduke, starting.

"In a . . . sisterly fashion, Johnny!" answered Mr. Bellamy with reassuring nod but smiling a little ruefully. "As a friend, old fellow, but not—no, not as a lover, spouse, husband and . . . ah . . . so forth!"

"Are you sure of this, Rupert?"

"Sir, she told me so!"

"Astounding!" murmured Sir Marmaduke.

"You see, old—uncle, she adores another!"

"Did she tell you this also, Rupert?"

"Well, not in so many words, sir, but it was suffi-
ciently evident—even to me, and I'm as blind as a
confounded mole—or have been! D'you remember,
John, sitting beside our camp-fire, says I to you:
'She's a goddess. . . . Greece and Rome! . . .?
Pointing out her lovely points to you—you of all men!
Johnny—I mean Uncle, what a precious ass was I!
And now, John—sir, I would humbly, but with all
my heart, wish success to . . . the better man,
whoever he be, and every happiness, old tu——.
Uncle Marmaduke. . . . You'll find her at Monk's
Warren, and . . . God bless you!" Saying which,
Mr. Bellamy suddenly grasped his uncle's hand, wrung
it hard and dashed out of the room.

Sir Marmaduke stood awhile staring out of the
window, and his eyes were bright as the morning and
youthfully eager.

"Ten miles, John!" said he at last. "Twelve at
most. Pray order our horses, for you will ride with
me, my faithful John, this I hope is the end of my
quest."

And very soon the horses were stamping and snorting
at the door.

So together they mount and ride off through the
sunny morning, side by side, and in silence for the
most part, since Sir Marmaduke forces the pace, also he is
thoughtful, and John Hobbs is never a talkative man.
At last, says Sir Marmaduke, glancing up and around:

"Truly a glorious morning, John!"

"And warmish, sir!" agrees John Hobbs.

Silence again save for the thud of speeding hoofs,
the creak and jingle of saddles and bridle-chains; then
says Sir Marmaduke, his bright eyes uplifted:

"John, how wonderfully the larks are singing this
morning!"

"Yes, sir," nods John, "but so they did yesterday."

The dusty road spins away beneath them, mile after mile, until Sir Marmaduke checks his speed somewhat and speaks his thought aloud.

"Of course it may be—someone else, John!"

"Possibly, sir."

"Though I . . . don't think so, John."

"Neither do I, sir."

"However, we shall soon know, for there is Monk's Warren," and he pointed to the gables of a goodly house rising above the green of trees.

Avoiding this house, Sir Marmaduke turned down a narrow, shady lane and so came into the wide farm-yard and, drawing rein, sat looking round upon neat ricks and the prim orderliness of time-mellowed barns and stabling. From the home meadow came the pleasant sound of whetted scythe and cheery voices, from thatched out-house adjacent, the clank of a pail. And then Eve-Ann stepped into the sunshine—aproned to the throat, round arms bare, face shaded by deep sun-bonnet, and upon her supple shoulders a yoke whence depended two pails abrim with foaming milk. Three steps she took ere, glancing up, she saw the horse-man watching her and, beholding the light in his eyes, stood still and caught her breath in a little sob.

"Dear!" said he, baring his head. "O Eve-Ann!"

Yet she stood there motionless, but seeing all the yearning eagerness of him, hearing it in his voice, the light grew in her eyes also. Then swiftly he dismounted and came towards her, and his step was quick, and eager as his look.

"So it was—not Rupert?"

"Nay, 'twas never Rupert!" she answered.

"Eve," said he reaching out his hands, "my Eve-Ann!"

"O . . . nay . . . bide a moment, John!" With sweet gracious movement she bent her knees, bowed her shoulders and, setting down pails and yoke, stood viewing him beneath the deep brim of her sun-bonnet, a little wistfully.

"John," said she softly. "Sir . . . . Marma-duke——"

"Call me 'John', my dear."

"Hast come . . . at last?"

"To the end of my quest, I hope!" he answered.

"Hast then found . . . thy youth, John?"

"I wonder!" sighed he. "But I have found an infinitely better thing—Eve-Ann Ash. . . . Can you love me, child?"

"But, John dear," she answered, a little breathlessly, "thou art . . . Sir Marmaduke . . . a great gentle-man, and I . . . I am only Eve-Ann!"

"Indeed you are the only Eve-Ann!" said he, taking her two hands. "So, child, will you come to me . . . give yourself to my keeping? Will you?"

"First—O first," she whispered with swift passion, "dost love me, John, not—ah not as a child but as a wom——·" She was in his arms, swung aloft, slim feet helpless in air.

"Love you?" said he. "Heaven knows I do—Eve-Ann . . . kiss me!"

When he set her down at last, the deep-brimmed sun-bonnet lay on the ground between them and lay awhile all unheeded.

"John," she whispered, "to be so loved . . . by such as thou, awes me for very wonder of it. . . . And, O my dear, let us mind how 'twas she gave us to each other, she that lost her life for thee, she that knew I could love but thee—and now looks down from heaven, happy in our happiness——"

A stifled giggle behind them and, glancing round, they espied the flutter of a print gown ere it vanished into an adjacent doorway.

"O, John!" exclaimed Eve-Ann flushing. "Yon was Nancy, one o' my dairy-maids! Verily I forgot all else in the world save thee and me."

Sir Marmaduke laughed gaily and picked up the rumpled sun-bonnet.

"And yet," said he, becoming grave, "I am . . . forty-five!"

"But thine eyes to-day are a boy's eyes, my John. Love hath indeed given thee back thy youth at last."

"And my hair is turning grey!"

"Where, pray thee?"

"Here at my temples."

"Stoop thy dear head, John!"

"And now," said Eve, lovely face tied demurely into sun-bonnet, "come, let us tell my two dears!"

As they went there met them John Hobbs who, baring his grey head to Eve-Ann, seemed so very like an archdeacon about to pronounce a blessing.

"My John," said Sir Marmaduke, cheerily, "pray now, exactly how old do I look?"

"Sir," answered John Hobbs, glancing from one happy face to the other, "I should say—about thirty-six or considerably under, indeed as I——"

Forth of nearby cow-shed stepped a shortish, broad-shouldered man, broad-brimmed hat in one hand, a remarkably nobbly stick in the other.

"Shrig!" exclaimed Sir Marmaduke.

"That werry i-dentical, sir!" answered Mr. Shrig grasping Sir Marmaduke's extended hand. "'Appening to be in the wicinity, sir and mam, I took the liberty to drop in, and now, seeing 'ow matters are betwixt you or—as you might say—the vind a'blowing matrimonially, I begs to offer you my werry best respex in the words o' the old song for

Sir and mam, I vish you j'y
First a gell and then a b'y——

and, Sir Marmydook and lady, no man can say fairer than that!"

THE END

For a Complete List of

Mr. Jeffery Farnol's Novels

see last page of this book

❧

Other notable

Current Fiction

will be found on the
intervening pages

THE CAP OF YOUTH

JOHN A. STEUART

Author of " Robert Louis Stevenson; Man and Writer "
" Minister of State," " Wine on the Lees," etc.

7/6 *net.*

¶ The private life of Robert Louis Stevenson has had a good deal of new light cast upon it during recent years, not always to the satisfaction of his admirers. They are now hearing whispers concerning a love affair in his early manhood in Scotland which moved him deeply, and remained for ever fresh in his memory. The heroine is said to have been a beautiful girl worthy to stand alongside Burn's Highland Mary. Years afterwards, in the maturity of his powers, Stevenson wrote the story of this experience, but for reasons which are easy to understand it was withheld from publication. Mr. John A. Steuart, whose biography of " R.L.S. " caused much discussion a few years ago, came across this unpublished work during his researches, but he found it inadvisable to deal with it at the time. He regarded it, however, as too vitally interesting and significant to be passed by, and he has therefore retold the story in the form of a novel.

John A. Steuart's critical biography of

ROBERT LOUIS STEVENSON

MAN AND WRITER

Library Edition, 2 vols., 32/- net. Popular Edition, 12/6 net.

¶ " I repeat, this is the best book that has yet been written about Stevenson."—CLEMENT SHORTER in the *Sphere.*

" His book may offend some Stevensonians, but I confess I read it with the deepest of interest from beginning to end. Few readers are likely to dip into it without going on to the last page."—ROBERT LYND in the *Daily News.*

MORNING GLORY

H. ST. JOHN COOPER

Author of " Sunny Ducrow," etc.

7/6 net.

¶ Mr. Cooper is no realist of the sordid and unhappy school. He has seen more than one side of life, and knows that the summer is as real as the winter. Many of us are still old-fashioned enough to love our heroes to be manly and clean, our heroines sweet and simple, and we are grateful to Mr. Cooper that he gives us such books, and helps us to realise that there is still romance and truth and purity for all who love them.

Other Novels by

HENRY ST. JOHN COOPER

THE GALLANT LOVER. 7s. 6d. net.

¶ " The author has been whole-hearted in his treatment of this Queen Anne story."—*Daily Telegraph*.

THE GOLCONDA NECKLACE. 7s. 6d.

¶ " Alive and interesting throughout. A story it is a pleasure to recommend."—*Universe*.

THE FORTUNES OF SALLY LUCK. 2s. 6d.

¶ " Sally is a unique product."—*Daily Mail*.

SUNNY DUCROW. 2s. 6d.

¶ " Sunny Ducrow has that devastating ' everlasting smile.' "—*The Times*.

THE IMAGINARY MARRIAGE. 2s. 6d.

¶ " One of the best tales that could be found on the bookstalls."—*Scots Pictorial*.

THE GARDEN OF MEMORIES. 2s. 6d.

¶ " Mr. Cooper has written a story of compelling interest and joy."— *Sussex Daily News*.

JAMES BEVANWOOD, BART. 2s. 6d.

¶ " A striking and original tale of social life."—*British Weekly*.

CARNISS & CO. 2s. 6d.

¶ " The best book of its kind since Vachells successful ' Quinneys' "— *Yorkshire Observer*.

ALIEN CORN

PHYLLIS HAMBLEDON

Author of " Autumn Fires "

7/6 *net.*

¶ In Mme. Helvier and her preposterous husband Miss Hambledon has found an opportunity to use her considerable gift of humour to great advantage; in Jeanne and in Paul she has created figures which again demonstrate her gift of creating life-like characters; in the descriptions of the cottage on the moors, where Jeanne spends some weeks with a little niece recovering from illness she again shows her power of drawing landscape; in the entire work she demonstrates a humanity and wholesome philosophy that are very refreshing.

❧

AUTUMN FIRES. 7/6 *net.*

This was Miss Hambledon's novel of last year and was one of the best reviewed books of that season and quickly ran into a second edition.

The Morning Post says—
   " Her presentation is marked by distinction. Altogether an excellent novel."

Aberdeen Press & Journal says—
   " The characterisation in this study is admirable, and the plot credible, clear-cut, and satisfying."

THE LAST OF THE SAWLEYS

M. C. T. SAWBRIDGE
Author of " Shadowed Waters "

7/6 *net.*

¶ The cardinal idea on which the actual story in this novel turns is the possibility of the repetition or actual reproduction of an incident in the history of a family. In this instance the incident is the love of two brothers for the same woman, resulting in her betrayal by one and the killing of the seducer by the other, followed by his marriage to the woman to save her honour and to give her happiness.

☙

SHADOWED WATERS. 7/6 *net.*

A domestic story of great power and skill. *The Times* in an extended review praised the work highly and spoke of the solid merit and ingenuity of plot.

The Bookman wrote—

" Abjuring all sensational incident, the author contrives to interest us with no other background than the everyday life of a country house."

This is one of those quiet stories which it is a real pleasure to read.

Remarkable Novels by

FAITH BALDWIN

❧

THREE WOMEN. 7/6 *net*.

¶ " An uncommonly powerful and dramatic novel, subtle in analysis, yet simple in style."—*Spectator*.

❧

THRESHOLDS. 7/6 *net*.

¶ " It is a rare and grateful quality one meets in this book—a sincerity and fidelity of emotion. Well written. There is a sense of beauty that makes it worth reading."—*The Times*.

❧

THOSE DIFFICULT YEARS. 7/6 *net*.

¶ " Like a breath of sweet, pure air in a stuffy room is this tender, idyllic story that sweeps from the mind the sordidness of divorce cases and their attending evils and renews one's faith in the beautiful and noble things of life."—*Aberdeen Press*.

❧

THE MAID OF STONYSTREAM. 2/6 *net*.

¶ " A good tale: altogether a novel of distinction."—*S. Wales Daily News*.

Novels by

MR. DONN BYRNE

✧

" His books have been haunting me for the last year or two."—
RT. HON. T. P. O'CONNOR, M.P.

MESSER MARCO POLO. 5s. net.
The Romance of the Great Venetian Adventurer.
¶ " Delicious magic mingled with just a little poetic tragedy."—*T.P.* & *Cassell's Weekly.*

THE WIND BLOWETH. 7s. 6d. net.
The Story of a man's quest for happiness.
¶ " The author has a magic touch of his own, a strange power to bring music from words."—*The Bookman.*

THE FOOLISH MATRONS. 7s. 6d. net.
A novel of feminine psychology.
¶ " The book is well and gracefully written, and the climax one of the best we have read for some time."—*Birmingham Post.*

CHANGELING. 7s. 6d. net.
Stories of many things.
¶ " It is emphatically a distinguished book."—*The Observer.*

BLIND RAFTERY and his wife Hilaria. 5s. net.
A beautiful legend of the Gaelic itinerant poet.
¶ " It is something greater than a novel."—*The Glasgow Herald.*

AN UNTITLED STORY. 5s. net.
The tragedy of De Bourke O'Malley.
¶ " It has a beauty all its own, and stands out among realistic fiction."—*The Observer.*

HANGMAN'S HOUSE. 7s. 6d. net.
Redolent of the soil and wind of Ireland.
¶ " People will return to the pages of ' Hangman's House ' as they return to the masterpieces of Blackmore and Hardy."—*Sunday Times.*

BROTHER SAUL. 7s. 6d. net.
Dramatic epic of the Great Apostle.
¶ " Excels in gem-like passages."—*Daily Telegraph.*

Romances *by*

MR. JEFFERY FARNOL

❧

THE BROAD HIGHWAY. 4*s. net.*
 A romance of Kent

THE AMATEUR GENTLEMAN. 4*s. net.*
 A romance of the Regency

THE MONEY MOON. 4*s. net.*
 A romance of to-day

CHRONICLES OF THE IMP. 4*s. net.*
 My Lady Caprice

BELTANE THE SMITH. 4*s. net.*
 A mediæval romance

THE HONOURABLE MR. TAWNISH. 4*s. net.*
 The rollicking days of the eighteenth century

THE GESTE OF DUKE JOCELYN. 4*s. net.*
 A romance in verse and prose

THE DEFINITE OBJECT. 4*s. net.*
 A romance of New York

OUR ADMIRABLE BETTY. 4*s. net.*
 An early Georgian story

BLACK BARTLEMY'S TREASURE. 4*s. net.*
 A stirring pirate story

MARTIN CONISBY'S VENGEANCE. 4*s. net.*
 Continues Black Bartlemy's adventures

PEREGRINE'S PROGRESS. 4*s. net.*
 In the author's original vein

SIR JOHN DERING. 4*s. net.*
 A romantic comedy

THE LORING MYSTERY. 4*s. net.*
 A mystery story of " Merrie England "

THE HIGH ADVENTURE. 7*s.* 6*d. net.*
 Another intriguing mystery story